Charlotte Mary Yonge

A Book of Worthies

Charlotte Mary Yonge

A Book of Worthies

ISBN/EAN: 9783337376390

Printed in Europe, USA, Canada, Australia, Japan

Cover: Foto ©Andreas Hilbeck / pixelio.de

More available books at **www.hansebooks.com**

A

BOOK OF WORTHIES

GATHERED

From the Old Histories

AND NOW WRITTEN ANEW

BY

THE AUTHOR OF "THE HEIR OF REDCLYFFE."

London:

MACMILLAN AND CO.

1869.

PREFACE.

THE NINE WORTHIES.

IN old times, when brave men had little time to read, and fewer books, they still kept clusters of glorious examples gathered from all times, to light them on the way to deeds of virtue.

Such were the Seven Champions of Christendom ; the Dozipairs, or Twelve Peers of France ; the Seven Wise Masters ; and, above all, the Nine Worthies. These nine were, three from *Israel*—namely, Joshua, David,. and Judas Maccabæus ; three from *Heathenesse*—to wit, Hector, Alexander, and Julius Cæsar; and three from *Christendom*—Arthur, Charlemagne, and Godfrey de Bouillon. This last was quite a recent personage when he was reckoned among the Worthies ; and whereas we live full eight hundred years after him, and have rather more knowledge of ancient history than the original inventor of the Nine Worthies, whosoever he may be, it would be hard if we could not bring together nine times nine of those noble characters, who in all times and ages have reflected back upon their brethren that Divine Image in which their first father was made.

Perhaps, too, our judgment of what constitutes "Worthies" differs a little from that of him who collected the first nine. Cæsar hardly seems to us as *worthy* as he was great, and Hector and Arthur were no doubt images far clearer in the imaginations of our chivalrous ancestors than we dare to make them. Even Karl der Grösse, though great and worthy enough in his true self, is a widely different personage from the Charlemagne of their fancy. But where our means of judging are much the same as those of the old admirer of the great Nine, our conclusions are much the same. He has selected the noblest instances he knew of great, good, and true men and " happy warriors," and, so far as we may, we follow his guidance in our choice.

In fact, ever since sin came into the world, this earth has been a battle-field. Sometimes the fight is altogether between the evil and the good warring for the will, but often the bodily powers must take their part in the conflict, as well as the mental ones. And whereas these are outward and visible, the courage, the strokes, and the sufferings of the combatants displayed before our eyes, they have become as it were the symbols of the unseen inner conflict common to every one, whether living in times of external peace or war. The characteristics of the Hero, or the Worthy, are the characteristics of every true and rightminded man, woman, and child ; but there is room in them for infinite variety, and the special form of heroism has had again and again to vary with the period and circumstances that called it into visible action.

What those qualities are that make up the Worthy or Hero we will not here say ; we will instead trace them out in the life of the first of the Nine, the type and pattern of all Heroes, and in some respects the most honoured of all.

CONTENTS.

JOSHUA.

B.C. 1536—1426.

WHAT are the qualities that make a Hero? Let us study our first hero, and we shall see them manifested in the clearest light. Courage is, as all would say, the first essential; but it must not be the mere courage of a lion or a bull—the consciousness of strength passionately exerted; it must be courage based on faith, exercised in resolute obedience and, tried by patience, as well as bold to dare. It must likewise be tender to the weak, and stedfast in its promises.

And the first hero who became a leader of the wars of the LORD was surely an example of these things.

Hoshea, the son of Nun, was born of the tribe of Ephraim, in Egypt, in the time of the severest bondage; but the name chosen for him by his parents expressed their hope, for it signified " Salvation," or, " He will save." The tribe of Ephraim seems to have been settled in a part of Egypt exposed to much danger. Indeed, the whole land of Goshen, lying between the Nile and the Wilderness, seems to have been given to the sons of Israel that they might be ready to defend Egypt from the attacks of the wild nations of the desert. Ephraim, the more favoured son of Joseph, suffered greatly in a battle between his sons and the men of Gath, who had come down to take their cattle. His three sons all perished in the fight, and the bereaved man " mourned many days," even when a son of

B

his old age was born to him, whom in the sadness of his heart he named " Beriah," because it went evil with his house.

This Beriah was the ancestor of Hoshea, and it may be supposed, from the Ephraimites being exposed to the attacks of the Gittites, that they were settled near the borders, and thus, though in more danger from the enemies outside, would be less oppressed and forced to servile work than their brethren in the interior. At any rate their numbers were large, and their spirit does not seem to have been broken. Through all their two hundred years of suffering they had still that prime blessing that the dying Jacob had called down upon the head of Joseph, and on the crown of the head of him who was separate from his brethren ; and as their choicest treasure they guarded the remains of Joseph, which they hoped yet to place in the inheritance bequeathed to him and them at Shechem.

Such was the far-away hope in which the young Hoshea grew up, and when he had arrived at the prime of manhood the long hoped-for day began at length to dawn.

There stood among the broken and bowed down Israelites one who long before had descended from the Royal court to share their afflictions and revive their forgotten hopes. *Then* Hoshea had not been born, or had been an infant, and had had no share in their rejection of the leader who offered himself. *Now* he was of full age, able and ready to accept the promise of deliverance which Moses had brought from the desert, from the mouth of GOD himself. "The people bowed the head and worshipped." But there was a heavy trial of patience and faith ere the time of freedom came. The first consequence of the request that the people might go out into the Wilderness only led to greater severity from their oppressors, in which the superiors, or foremen, among the heavily-laden slaves were the greatest sufferers. The trust and hope of some failed. Others were upheld by the wonderful tokens of Divine power, bringing ruin and destruction on the Egyptians after every refusal to let the people go, and keeping the Israelites exempt from the peril always in such a manner as to show that the plagues were no chance visitations falling indiscriminately, but were guided to strike alone those destined for them.

Then came that night to be much remembered, when every believing Israelitish family were awake, in travelling garb, eating their meal of the roasted lamb beneath the bloodmarked threshold, till at midnight rose the great cry, echoed from stone-built palace to reedy hut, from wanderer's tent to gloomy dungeon, as the first-born in every house devoid of that bloody mark lay dead at one fearful moment.

Up rose the Israelites. Then, while terror and dismay still were on the bereaved land, they were ready to march and win their freedom before the reaction of revenge should have set in. When that time came, and the King of Egypt and his horses and chariots were pursuing after them, they were on the sea-shore, with the dark, ruddy, purple waves before them ; and beyond, the wild, terrific, white, black, and crimson peaks and gloomy ravines of the waste howling wilderness.

Through the parted waves of that sea they marched, and from the opposite shore they saw their enemies overwhelmed by the waters and lie dead on the shore. These were the scenes that were the training of Hoshea, the son of Nun, in common with all his fellow-countrymen ; but that it was a rare spirit is shown by the fact, that of all the six hundred thousand who witnessed the marvels, but one single heart was found that gathered strength and faith like Hoshea's. Here it is that Hoshea first appears in his individual character as the warrior hero. The manna had begun to fall, the water had sprung from the rock at the touch of Moses' rod, and the multitude thus sustained were threading their way through the Wadys, walled in with lofty marble rocks, when one of the robber tribes of the desert came on them. The Amalekites, savage marauders, fierce, wild, reckless, and lawless, such as are the Bedouins now, swarmed round the multitude, and cut off the stragglers, the faint and weary, or feeble, with a remorseless cruelty, hateful to God and man alike. And in Rephidim—apparently the fair oasis of Wady Feiran, a wider valley, with springs of water and palm-trees —these deadly foes were mustered to destroy that host of newly-escaped unwarlike slaves, encumbered with women and children. and with herds and cattle and loads of jewels, that made them a tempting prey.

It was to Hoshea that Moses committed the choice and the leadership of the men who were to fight with Amalek. The great Lawgiver himself had a more mysterious and typical part to fulfil when he went apart to the top of the hill with his brother and his sister's husband, and stretched out his hands all day in intercession for this people. In the strength of that intercession Hoshea fought that whole day. It is in the strength and faith of a like but unfailing intercession that every subsequent hero has fought and won. We may picture to ourselves the hills around, in shape and colour like flames, the green vale, the tents of the anxious Israelites, the savage hordes on their swift steeds, with long lances and floating striped garments, with hoods drawn low over their fierce eyes, the hosts of Israel scantily armed with the spear, the arrow, the straight sword, the tall-pointed cap, the leathern breastplate of Egypt, the bullock emblem of the standard of Joseph firmly upheld, wavering for a time as the mortal intercessor's arms grew weary; but again recovering ground, and by set of sun beginning the first of its many victories.

Hoshea was the victorious General, the hero of the host, who had cleared the path of Israel from the tormenting robbers. Nevertheless, he remained as Moses' minister or personal attendant. When Israel was encamped at the foot of the awful mountain covered with the cloud, whence proceeded lightnings, thunders, trumpet-blasts, and that most mighty of all voices proclaiming the Eternal Law, the voice that the people entreated not to hear again, it was Hoshea alone who with Moses ascended the mountain, even to the cloud that veiled the summit. Moses entered within the cloud. There he received the Tables of stone written with the finger of GOD. There he talked with the Almighty, face to face ; there he saw the eternal courts of Heaven, and was instructed how, feebly and faintly, to trace their model in the curtains and the gold of the Tabernacle. To him, among these things unutterable, the forty days and nights might well seem as one. To the fickle, impatient, turbulent crowd below, it appeared as though he had been lost in the thick darkness that covered the red crags among which he had disappeared. "As for this Moses, we wot not what is become of him." But there was one who neither was admitted among the unspeakable glories within the cloud, nor had the support of numbers in the vale beneath—one who had followed Moses as far as was allowed, and was left to hold his patient watch alone upon the bare mountain-side, in the dread solitude, awful in its silent grandeur even when left to nature, awful beyond measure when overhung by the cloud that hid the Divine presence. Out of sight, out of hearing of his fellows beneath—out of sight, out of hearing of the Master for whom he waited, but firm as the rocks around him, he tarried where he had been set to watch, through all those forty days and nights of awe, with unshaken heart, firm in the confidence learnt when he had " stood still to see the salvation of GOD."

Surely no patient, resolute watch ever equalled that of Hoshea on the Mount of Horeb; and that it was with an unwearied spirit, prompt to dare as well as resolute to wait, we see when Moses had at length come forth, with the precious Tables in his arms, and, as they descended, up came the wild tumultuous cries of the camp below, and the warrior listening cried : " There is a sound of war in the camp !"

Alas! the sword of the avenging Levites had to be drawn, not against the Amalekite robber, but against the idolatrous Israelite, reviving Egyptian superstition in the very face of their insulted God. The second condition of the terms proclaimed by God's own voice had been openly violated, and Moses had destroyed the pledge of those promises to which there was no further claim. But still, hoping for his people against hope, he placed a tent for worship afar outside the camp, and there the presence of God again manifested itself. Moses entered to commune with God, and Hoshea, the only other man entirely un-implicated in the calf idolatry, departed not out of the Tabernacle.

Intercession again obtained the renewal of the covenant once transgressed, and after nearly a year spent in the framing of the Tabernacle, the making of the priestly gar-ments, and the establishment, under Divine direction, of the great system of typical worship, the great multitude again moved on its way. There had now been time to marshal and array it as an army on the march, each tribe in its own place, with all its men numbered as warriors, and with their own standard, taken from the blessing of Jacob. at their head ; but as guide and leader to them all the cloudy pillar resting on the sacred Tabernacle. Around that holy tent camped the Priests and Levites, by hereditary temper the fiercest of the Israelites, but restrained by their sacred office. Eastward lay the goodly tents marshalled under the Lion of the tribe of Judah. Westward was the bull standard of Ephraim, beneath which Hoshea was ranked; to the south was the ensign of the water-bearer, whose burthen typified the instability of Reuben; and to the north the Serpent, or, as some say, the Eagle, of Dan. Beyond lay stretched the other tents of Israel, according to their tribes. When the cloud arose, the Ark was lifted by the Priests, the sacred vessels borne by the Levites, the trumpets were blown, and the chant uplifted by thousands of voices—

" Let God arise, and let His enemies be scattered ;
Let them also that hate Him flee before Him."

Thus, in princely, regular march, the armies of Israel proceeded on their way from the jagged rocks of the southern wilderness to the more dreary and monotonous, though less wild, undulating desert of Paran. Here Moses halted and chose out twelve chiefs, one from every tribe, to go on in advance and reconnoitre the promised home of their inheritance. Of these thus sent on so perilous an adventure the bravest, most faithful, most patient must surely be one ; and Moses therefore sent Hoshea as the representative of Ephraim, and at the same time apparently added to his name of " Salvation," or "He will Save," the Divine syllable, JAH, so as to make it "The Lord will save." Did Moses mean to predict safe protection for his true minister? Or was he guided by the spirit of prophecy to confer that name which in after times should belong to the true Captain of our Salvation, the Name above every name, at which every knee should bow?

As each of the twelve is called a Ruler of his tribe, it is probable that this was not a stealthy expedition of a few

spies, lurking on foot, but that they took with them a
small compact party of their swiftest warriors, able to
thread their way through the valleys and waste places, to
defend themselves if attacked by a small force, and to
depart before a large one could be got together.   They
went with the watchword of Joshua, " Be strong and of a
good courage," and they made good speed.   They viewed
the land of hills and vales, "their father's hope, their
childhood's dream," so utterly unlike the place of their
birth.   They saw its deep valleys, watered by mountain
streams, and full of fair pastures; the fields of waving
corn, the mountain slopes covered with vines and olives ;
the mighty shade of the cork-trees, and the broad foliage
of the figs.   They wandered up the deep-cleft Jordan
valley, even in sight of the forests of Lebanon and Hermon's snowy crown, and they made their way back by
the sacred Vale of Hebron, the home of Abraham, where
his oak-tree still spread its huge limbs, and the cave of
Machpelah near at hand held the tombs of their fathers.
And there they gathered those magnificent grapes that
they brought back with them, to prove the splendour of
the fruits of the land—a land, indeed, of promise.

But there had been failing hearts among them.   They
had not looked only at the corn and the vineyards : they
had looked to the summit of the hills, each one crowned
with a fortress built up of enormous stones, whose unbroken size after nearly four thousand years attest what
the builders must have been in strength.   And those first
inhabitants were seen by the startled Israelites walking
through their vineyards or gathering to make war.   The
last survivors of that giant race were ten or eleven feet
in stature, and at the spectacle of such foes the hearts
of the reconnoitring party sank within them, and when
they came back to the camp they could scarcely speak of
the loveliness of the country for describing the terrific

appearance of the inhabitants. The two, Joshua and Caleb, the stout-hearted deputy of the Lion tribe of Judah, did indeed speak undauntedly and full of hope and trust ; but their voices were lost among the doleful lamentations of their ten colleagues ; and throughout the whole night there was wailing and despair throughout the camp of Israel, till in early morning the populace had worked themselves up to such a pitch of senseless terror, that they proposed to choose a captain to lead them back to their bondage in Egypt. Joshua and Caleb, braver here than even when they searched the land, rushed forward to describe the beautiful land and remind them of the certainty that He who had wrested them out of the hand of Pharaoh could bring them into it ; but the enraged people would not listen, and only strove to stone them.

The wild and tumultuous scene was only arrested by a sudden manifestation of the Glory of the Lord on the Tabernacle, overawing for a time the factious despair of the people. Moses entered within the Tabernacle to hear the Divine will. It was an awful answer. Those who *would* not enter the land *should* not. For forty years longer should the tribes remain as wanderers in the desert, till there had been time for the younger generation to grow up to a nobler, truer manhood, and for all their elders, all the obstinate murmurers who were for ever pining for Egypt, to perish in the wilderness. Two men alone of those above twenty were exempted by name from the sentence ; those two were Joshua and Caleb, who alone had shown that trust which is true courage. Already, in earnest of this sentence, a sudden plague swept away the ten faint-hearted spies who had brought the ill report, but came not near the two brave friends. But, with fickle perverseness, the multitude refused to obey the command to turn back into the wilderness. They *would* go on into Palestine. They marshalled their armies and marched, without the Ark, without Moses, without Joshua, without the Blessing. Those who tarried beside the Ark on the top of the hill soon saw the wilful host return, diminished, broken, chased by the enemy in swarms like angry bees, and glad to hide their heads in the camp, under their wonted Guide, even though it were only to suffer their slow but certain doom.

Those forty years are well-nigh a blank. At their close there was not a man in the whole congregation under sixty years of age, save Moses himself, Joshua, and Caleb; and the younger race, trained up in the wondrous life of the Wilderness, beneath the discipline of Moses, were of very different mould from the slavish beings born and bred on the enervating banks of the Nile.

Victories had already been won over the mighty tribes who dwelt in the great cities of the fat pasture-lands of Gilead and Bashan, and over the corrupt and luxurious Midianites; the hills had been gained whence the narrow strip so longed for—the land flowing with milk and honey—could be viewed in its length and breadth. But there was one sentence first to be fulfilled—

> " Know ye not our glorious leader
> Salem must but see and die?
> Israel's guide, and nurse, and feeder,
> Israel's hope afar must eye."

" Show thy servants Thy work, and their children Thy glory," had been Moses' own words of submission; and now his work was ended, and he was about to enter into a fuller rest than that of Canaan, and it was to Joshua that his work was left—to the most faithful, the most courageous of all the men of Israel that the glory of conquest was to be given, on whom the charge of that mighty multitude was to be laid.

The subdued and awe-struck people waited day after

day in their encampment on the slopes above the Dead Sea, while their chiefs gathered up those last discourses in which Moses reminded them of all their wonderful course of training in faith and holiness that they had undergone under the very eye, so to speak, of their Maker. Speaking not for them alone, but for all generations to come, he ardently exhorted them to the keeping of the Law, and warned them of the dire effects of breaking it ; and, in the spirit of mournful prophecy, he was carried on to predict all the miseries that too surely the degenerate race would call down upon themselves.

Then came the Divine call, when Moses led the faithful Joshua into the Tabernacle, laid his consecrating hands upon him, and gave him the charge in which his office was summed up, " Be strong and of a good courage." And therewith the load and burthen of Israel were passed on to the warrior chief, whose strength lay in his simple obedience and fearless trust.

One prophetic song, one prophetic blessing, each rising higher in grandeur and beauty than aught which had yet passed the lips of the wonderful old man, whose eye was not dim, nor his natural force abated, and Moses climbed Mount Nebo to gaze on the promised land, and die in the majestic solitude, alone with the God who had ever been to him the nearest.

In the freshness of the loss came the voice of God promising that the new leader should never miss the aid that had borne Moses through the wilderness. To Joshua was thus vouchsafed the external assurance, faith in which braces every right spirit to face new responsibilities. " I will not fail thee, nor forsake thee. Be strong and of a good courage." That is the certainty that still makes Heroes, though they do not with their eyes behold, as did Joshua, the Captain of the LORD's Host, with His sword drawn in His hand, to maintain their cause.

The obedience of the great Captain of Israel was first tried. When the rushing torrent of the river Jordan barred the way, he had to send the Priests bearing the Ark straight down into the still dashing stream ; nor did the miracle that checked the current begin till their feet had touched the water, and they had thus proved their faith in the promise that they should be safe. Phinehas, the son of Eleazar, the High Priest, was a bold and fierce man, undaunted in his zeal : but was not the courage and faith very great that could dare to walk into the midst of a rapid stream in confidence that protection would be given ?

Obedience, not fierce attacks, was again imposed on the armies of Israel, when for six long days all these ardent fighting-men had to stand still and see nothing done to besiege the city of Jericho, except that the sacred Ark was carried round the walls by the Levites, while the seven Priests went in front and blew their trumpets. " What was the use ? " the faithless might have asked. There was at least this use. It is the maxim of armies now. Obedience is the soldier's first lesson : to stand still is the soldier's first exercise. The Divine Captain of the Lord's Host was teaching His army this first lesson.

The seventh day came ; the Army, the Priests, the Ark, marched round in obedient stillness, till at Joshua's signal the trumpets pealed, the warriors shouted, and the mighty walls fell—fell all at once, and flat to the ground, so that the army marched in without climbing or struggling. A sentence had been spoken on Jericho. The Canaanites had become horribly corrupt, and to exterminate them from the face of the earth was the only means of saving Israel from the infection of their vices and idolatry. Strict commands had been given that none should escape the doom, save one household, and Joshua's care for that house and the faithful compassionate Rahab shows how merciful his heart was, though he was compelled to act as the minister of God's judgment.

The first success had been gained for the Israelites without their own efforts. They were next to fight for themselves, and attack the city of Ai, without supernatural assistance. They thought it so small that only a few of their number would .be sufficient, leaving the whole multitude in the camp at Gilgal, beside the Jordan; but, behold, they were driven back by the men of Ai, and lost many of their number. Then, in grief and dismay, Joshua and the chiefs lay prostrate in the dust before the Tabernacle till eventide, when there breathed forth from the Divine Oracle a rebuke for their discouragement, and a revelation that a sin within the camp was the true cause of their disaster.

The sinner was traced out through lots by the Divine Disposer of events. And here it should be observed, that in spite of the crime, its consequences, and his own anxiety, Joshua spoke to the offender in the tenderest, most pitying tones : " My son, give, I pray thee, glory to the LORD God of Israel, and make confession unto Him ; and tell me now what thou hast done ; hide it not from me." The one grace of free confession yet remained for the unhappy Achan, and Joshua encouraged him by gentleness, even though to purify the camp the dreadful penalty of the sin had to be paid.

Ai was then taken, by means of an ambush which burst into the city when all the warriors had been decoyed away by a simulated flight of Joshua and the main body. This conquest enabled Joshua to fulfil the command of Moses, by placing half the representatives of the tribes on Mount Ebal, the other half on Mount Gerizim, with the Levites and the Ark in the narrow gorge between. The Ten Commandments were written on the face of the precipice of Ebal, and the blessings of God on those who kept the

Law, His curses on those who kept it not, were rehearsed by the Levites, and each followed up by a response of "Amen" from the multitude on either side : the mountain echoes blending with the thunder of voices, as thus were given out the terms on which Israel was to hold the land now partly won.

The pure, high, awful Law, and the victories of the men who proclaimed it, did not fall on entirely unheeding ears. The people, struck with terror, determined on winning the favour of these dread conquerors ; but, instead of dealing openly, they feigned to ask Joshua's friendship as distant allies, and their messengers showed themselves in the camp as travel-worn men. Promises were hastily made to them, and oaths sworn, and when, immediately after, the deception was discovered, the oath was still respected. The Gibeonites had not deserved to be free, but they became the servants of the Priests, an honourable office, in which they continued even after the Babylonish captivity.

Indeed, the greatest of all the battles of the Israelites was fought in their defence. Five neighbouring Kings of the hill fortresses around undertook to avenge the desertion of the Gibeonites, and no sooner had Joshua and his warriors returned to the camp at Gilgal than they began to close in on Gibeon to punish their recreancy. Terrified messengers sped to Joshua's camp, crying, " Slack not thine hand from thy servants ; make haste to come to us." And, instead of leaving these cowardly allies to their fate, Joshua and his brave men set out instantly, and by marching all night were enabled to surprise the five united armies in early morning before Gibeon.

There, on the slope of Beth-horon, was the great battle gained. Down, down the rugged ravine stumbled the terrified enemy ; while the LORD sent a furious hailstorm to increase their discomfiture—and the heavy jagged pieces of ice slew even more than the sword of the Israelites.

All day were the Israelites pursuing; and as evening drew on, Joshua, perceiving that darkness would prevent the advantage from being complete, was empowered to make that wondrous call, "Sun, stand thou still upon Gibeon ; and thou, Moon, in the valley of Ajalon," and thereupon daylight was continued even till the victory was full and absolute, and the conquerors returned to their great camp at Gilgal, their temporary home.

The five Kings, deserted and terrified, had sought shelter in one of the great caves on the hill-side. There they were found, and detained till Joshua and his warriors could come and execute them. For this was not only the sentence due to their guilt, but it was also true mercy where an honourable captivity was impossible. "Surely the bitterness of death is past," said the Amalekite chief, who had seen his whole family and horde destroyed ; and the ten Kings who gathered their food under the table of Adoni-zedec, the Jebusite King of Jerusalem, with their thumbs and great toes cut off, should have said the same ; and no doubt had many a cruel wrong to be visited on Adoni-zedec when he was hanged with the other four on the trees beside the cave of Makkedah.

Their cities were then taken, one by one ; but Josephus explains that only the lower city of Jerusalem was at this time seized, the fortress or upper city being still held by the Jebusites. These conquests gave the Israelite army the mastery of all the south part of Palestine ; but just as they had returned to Gilgal, probably to move the whole multitude into the land to take possession, came tidings of another confederation of the Kings of the north, who dwelt round Lake Merom, near the sources of the Jordan. Thither they marched, and had a great battle and victory by the lake side, and took the cities.

After this, as far as we can understand, the Tabernacle
was moved from Gilgal, and set up on the flat tableland
of Shiloh, while the people began to settle in the newly-
conquered lands.   The lot of the tribe of Joseph was clear
by the dying command of Jacob, who had left his favoured
son his own peculiar spot of the promised land—the Well
of Shechem and the country round.   There then, and in
Mount Ephraim, did the two tribes of Joseph find their
home, except those descendants of Manasseh's son, Machir,
who had left their families in the great walled cities of
Gilead and Bashan.   Some of the Ephraimites were discontented, and came to Joshua to complain that they had
nothing but forest.   To which he replied, that "they were
a great people and a strong ; they could cut down the
wood ; or they could drive out the Perizzite giants or the
Canaanites.   If the Canaanites *had* chariots of iron, was
not the LORD with the Ephraimites ?"   Well would it have
been for these his brethren could Joshua have inspired
into them such a spirit as filled his old companion Caleb,
who came to entreat of him the post of danger.

It was forty-five years since they two together had beheld the giants of Hebron, and brought away the grapes.
Now Caleb came to remind Joshua of that time, and to
request that his portion might be that very spot now held
by a notable giant named Arba, who had changed the
name of sacred Hebron to Kirjath Arba—the city of Arba.
He recalled to Joshua the Lord's promise that they should
survive to possess their inheritance, and showed himself
not only alive, but at eighty-five years old as strong for
war as he had been when he went forth as a spy.   The
grant was made, Hebron was won, the giants were slain,
all but a remnant driven into Gath, and Caleb offered his
daughter Achsah as the prize of the brave man who
should be the conqueror of Kirjath Sepher, the last city
in his portion.   Othniel, his nephew, was the winner of

the city and the maiden, and kept up the old heroic spirit through the next generation. Judah, the tribe to which Caleb belonged, was flowing into the valleys between Hebron, Jericho, and the Wilderness.

A great meeting was convened by Joshua at Shiloh, where he took leave of the two tribes and a half who were to dwell on the other side of Jordan, and divided the remainder of the land to the other seven tribes, settling the boundaries of each, and specifying the cities which they were to conquer for themselves. It was an evident appointment of Providence that the country of Palestine was not in possession of a single great nation, with a united government, but that almost every fortress was a separate kingdom, so that when it was taken and newly peopled there were no claims on it from a former master; and thus it was possible to follow out the command to take only the places that could at once be inhabited by the new comers, and by no means to live intermixed with the heathen natives. Thus was the task of Joshua fulfilled; and, an aged man, he took up his abode in his own portion at Timnath-serah, —there, however, to mark with grief the slackness of the people in carrying out the commands of the LORD, the number of secret and open enemies they left themselves, and the way that Manasseh was leaving open for the Canaanite chariots of iron from the north.

He convoked all the chiefs together at Shechem, near those engraven Laws on Mount Ebal's side, where the echoes of the blessings and the cursings might yet linger in their ears. There he sat beneath a mighty oak, and lifted up his voice of warning. They beheld for themselves that all God had promised had come to pass. Might they not thence conclude that on their disobedience all that He had threatened would equally come to pass? "I am going the way of all the earth," said the aged hero, in this which he probably thought would be the farewell meeting with

C

his people. He lived, however, to meet them a second time at Shechem, and once more to receive their oath that they would keep the promises which were their tenure of Palestine.

"As for me and my house, we will serve the Lord," said Joshua, speaking for himself with the grand singleness of heart that had marked him through life. The one simple duty in hand he had done to the best of his powers, from the hour when he had heard the call of Moses on the banks of the Nile, till that in which "Joshua, the son of Nun, the servant of the LORD, died, being an hundred and ten years old."

Where shall we find his like in faith, in patience, in obedience, in trust, in honour, in mercifulness, and in resolute courage?

DAVID.

B.C. 1085—1015.

MORE than four hundred years had passed since Joshua's death—years of chequered prosperity and adversity to the Israelites. Idolatry and alliance with the remaining Canaanites were sure to lead to an invasion by the enemy on the offending tribe, and then came severe suffering, repentance, and deliverance through some mighty warrior raised up by Divine appointment.

These vicissitudes chiefly affected the northern and eastern tribes. In the south, under brave old Caleb and Othniel, the tribe of Judah had made its home in the mountains more secure ; and though the hill-fortress of Salem still looked down on them as a Jebusite hold, yet, on the whole, it would seem that stern Judah and their near neighbours, the fierce mountaineers of Benjamin, had kept themselves free from the foul idolatries into which their neighbours were tempted, and still continued a free, brave, high-spirited people. They, however, had a very dangerous neighbour on the sea-coast. The Philistines were a race of far bolder temper, and with more power of combination, than the Canaanite nations, and the two tribes of Simeon and Dan—always somewhat inferior to the others—had left them in possession of five principal cities, which in process of time formed a league for the entire subdual of the rest of Palestine, and was further strengthened by having

C 2

amalgamated the remnant of the old giants whose fore-fathers had escaped from Caleb. Samson, though endowed with supernatural strength for the very purpose of acting as the champion of his tribe of Dan, was led away by temptation, and did nothing effectual or worthy of his powers ; and when he had been betrayed, and had perished in his last vengeful exertion of strength, and in one fatal battle the Ark had been taken and the Priests slain, the Sanctuary at Shiloh was broken up, and the whole of the open country seems to have become a prey to the Philistines, on the one hand, and the savage marauding Bedouin nations on the other.

True, the power of God had been shown in the rescue of the Ark from idolatrous hands, but it remained in concealment in the forests ; there was no public ritual, and such of the Israelites as still remained unsubdued in the mountain fastnesses of Judah and Benjamin were only maintained in their faith by the visits and sacrifices of the first of the prophets, Samuel, who had been bred up in the Sanctuary at Shiloh, and there had, in earliest childhood, received the Divine call.

Samuel was the first to revive the brave old godly spirit that made Israel invincible. Collecting the Israelites at Mizpeh, the great gathering-place of the southern tribes, he offered sacrifice and made public confession of the sin of the people. The Philistine host attempted to fall on them during their devotions ; but lightnings and thunderings from Heaven proclaimed, as it were, that God was again warring for his people : the enemy were discomfited, and with so great a slaughter that they ceased to molest Israel for many years.

Still the want of a central point of union was felt by the tribes, and all the more because the Sanctuary at Shiloh, where they used to meet, had been destroyed, and no fresh place chosen. As Samuel grew old, they demanded a king to collect and lead them out to battle, and the king who was chosen by the Divine appointment was, in many respects, fitted to be the leader of the host. He was born of one of the two tribes that had kept themselves most pure from idolatry, and had never been subdued by the enemy, even in the worst times. No taint of idolatry attached to the brave mountaineer of Gibeah ; he was courageous and fierce, as became the Wolf of Benjamin ; he was a man of magnificent stature, a dauntless leader, full of activity, and expert in the use of his weapons— above all, of his mighty spear, the favourite sceptre of the warrior chief. He had all the qualities of a truly worthy hero save one, and the lack of that one was his ruin.

It was in the midst of the reign of Saul, while the valour of the king and his noble son Jonathan was constantly called forth to defend their country from the perpetual inroads of the Philistines to the west, and the desert tribes to the east, that on the fair slope of Bethlehem, the border-land of Benjamin and Judah, close by the tomb of Rachel, was born the eighth son of Jesse, the head prince of the tribe of Judah in the direct line. No chieftainship seems, however, to have been held by the old man ; he pastured his flock on the hill-sides, tilled the fields that had gained for the place the name of the City of Bread—the same fields where his grandmother Ruth had gleaned; and it is said that he and his family were hereditary weavers of the hangings for the Sanctuary.

Even the personal appearance of this eighth son of Jesse has been distinctly described ; and we know that he was one of the fair-complexioned Jews, such as are still some-times seen, with auburn hair and beautiful blue eyes, small and slight of form, but active, expert, and light of foot as a gazelle. Even while very young he had proved his courage in the defence of his father's flocks against wild beasts and robbers, and he had likewise the fair gift of song and music:

> " With heart as free as mountain air
> He carolled to his fleecy care;
> With motion free as mountain cloud
> He trod where mists the moorland shroud."

This bright boy was watching his sheep on the hill-side when to his father's house in the village came the great and holy seer to hold a solemn sacrifice. David alone was not to share the feast. His seven brethren were surely enough to do honour to the prophet, and the youngest might be left in charge of the flock, without competing with those who already chafed against his unacknowledged superiority. But while he remained alone, left out from the festival, a message came to hasten him to come home. The seer would not sit down to the banquet until all his host's sons were before him. David hurried in, and found himself in the presence of the holy Nazarite, with the priestly garb, girt with the ephod or scarf, and with the long flowing grey hair unshorn since his birth. Father and brethren stood waiting round, and as the stripling entered the prophet met him, raised a horn filled with ointment, exhaling a rich odour as of holy incense, and poured it on the fair and golden head that bent before him.

Thenceforth there was a new spirit in David's song that deepened and sweetened it. When he sang of leading his flock to green fields and clear streams, he rejoiced in the great Shepherd who led him to the waters of comfort ; when he tuned his harp to rejoice in the stars that shone like lamps through his night-watch, it was because they spoke to his inward ear with the sound that is gone forth into all lands ; when his very soul bounded with exulting awe at the thunders rebounding from the mountains of Hermon to the wilderness of Kadesh, it was because in them he heard the Voice of the Lord, and the sweet undertone, promising the blessing of peace.

His minstrelsy became so well known, that, when by the Divine judgment a dark moody frenzy fell upon Saul, he was sent for, that his sweet songs might dispel the gloom ; but he returned home immediately after, and resumed his shepherd-charge for the last time.

Again the Philistines had collected, taking advantage of the king's old age and fits of insanity, and their mighty army marched over the border-land. Judah and Benjamin rallied around Saul, and among them went the three elder sons of Jesse. The two armies lay encamped, each on a hill-side, a valley about five miles wide, scattered with blocks of grey-stone, lying between them. Day after day passed without a battle ; and Jesse, at length, anxious for tidings, sent his youngest son over the hills from Bethlehem to carry provisions to his brothers and a present to the captain of their company.

Then it was that, as David sought out his brothers, he beheld, stalking along the valley, and threatening the host of Israel, a being fully twice the height of any ordinary man, and large in proportion, armed with brazen armour, with an enormous spear in his hand, and a shield-bearer before him. It was one of the descendants of the old giants who had escaped from Caleb and found a home among the Philistines, and his loud voice was shouting a defiance to the men of Israel to decide the entire war by a single combat.

David made inquiries from the bystanders, and heard that the defiance had now been made for full forty days, but that no Israelite, in spite of the king's promises of the hand of his daughter, had dared to offer himself as a champion against such an enemy. Eliab, David's eldest brother, came on him in the midst of his inquiries, and with the old jealousy chid him harshly as a truant and a boaster ; but something in the dauntless look and tone of the youth so impressed the officers that they brought him to the king's presence.   He was seventeen years of age ; still fair and slender-limbed, and very youthful-looking : but no one knew him as the same boy who had harped to Saul at Gibeah ; nor that the same Divine Spirit that breathed in his song now shone forth in his blue eyes as he stood in his shepherd garb, and bade the king fear not : he would go forth and fight with the Philistine.

Saul—almost a giant himself—spoke to the fair boy, as to an eager child, of the mere impossibility he was undertaking ; but David simply answered, that by God's help he had slain a lion and a bear in defence of his father's flock, and, by the same help, he trusted to slay the Philistine, *because* he had defied the armies of the living God.

No miracle had been wrought for Israel since the days of Samson ; but the trust that looked out of David's face inspired Saul, and he would have armed him for the encounter : but the slight stripling could not move under the great old king's ponderous arms, and preferred trusting to the weapons he understood.   His shepherd's sling hung at his shoulder, and he chose him five smooth stones out of the brook—the missiles with which he had often driven away wolves and jackals from the flock, and with which he was as expert as the great slingers of Benjamin.

Fierce was the scorn of Goliath at the sight of the only champion Israel could produce ; a shepherd boy coming out with a staff and a sling, as if against a wild dog ; but no sooner was the defiance spoken on either side than an unerring stone, sent forth from the sling; struck the Philistine on the forehead, and stretched him on the ground.   Then the young shepherd ran up, stood on the huge body, drew the mighty sword, despatched him with it, and cut off his head.

The utter discomfiture of the Philistines ensued; and the shepherd lad was honoured by the king, and received with due regard by the brave old general Abner, and fervent generous admiration by Jonathan, the king's son, who, though much older than David, loved him henceforth with ardent, noble, equal friendship.   In eastern fashion, he arrayed him in his own robe, and girt him with his own sword, and David became the chief hero of the army.   When the triumphant host returned home, and the women came forth with garlands, dancing and beating their timbrels as they sang—

> " Saul hath slain his thousands,
>   But David his ten thousands,"

the bitter suspicion crept into the king's heart that here was the person of whom Samuel had spoken to him—the man who was to be raised up to wear the crown in his stead; and he hated the youth accordingly.   It was impossible to act openly against David, who was beloved and honoured by all, and behaved with such prudence that no fault could be found with him; but twice, when he was trying by his music to sooth away Saul's frenzy, the wretched old king lost all sense of restraint, and aimed a javelin at him, hoping to slay him under the excuse of madness.

A command in the army was then given to him, to remove him from Saul's presence; but the promise of a marriage with Saul's daughter was first unfulfilled, and then was held forth as an incentive to further deeds of daring against the Philistines, in which the king hoped that the hated youth would meet his death.   The first daughter, who had been promised him, was bestowed upon another.   The second daughter, Michal, loved the noble and beautiful young warrior, and Saul offered her to David as the prize for the slaughter of a hundred Philistines.

David slew double the number, and returned unhurt ; so that, for very shame, Saul could not withhold his bride.

The near connexion, however, only rendered Saul's hatred stronger, though the influence of Jonathan and the universal admiration of David forced him to keep it in check, so that it seems only to have broken forth, under cover of frenzy, when some fresh exploit of David had aroused his jealousy. Thus, after another Philistine war, he again tried to nail David to the wall with the spear he always carried in his hand as a sceptre ; and then sent murderous slaves to follow up the pursuit.

David was only saved by the strategem of his wife, Michal, who let him down from the window, while she deceived his enemies by showing them a figure in bed veiled with a goat's-hair mosquito curtain, and declaring him to be sick. She then loved him ; but her affection was not enduring, and after a time she allowed herself to be given to another husband. David meantime had repaired to the sacred home where the aged Samuel dwelt, surrounded by young men who were being trained up amid prayer and psalmody to be the lights of the coming generation. Warrior and captain though he were, here was a congenial resting-place for the minstrel. He resumed his shepherd's harp, and poured out his heart in songs of prayer and thanksgiving, until Saul traced him out, and pursued him thither in person. David fled ; but when Saul found himself in the presence of the inspired guide of his youth, and heard the songs of the choir of young disciples, once again the Spirit of holiness breathed over him, he stripped off his robe, and sang once more the songs of the Lord.

It seems as if David was anxious to know whether this gleam of brighter days was to lead to permanent change on Saul's part, for he went to Jonathan and desired to know the grounds of this continued persecution. Jonathan, loving both his father and David and perfectly aware of the blamelessness of the latter, could not believe that there was any serious design against his friend, and it was resolved to put Saul's intentions to the proof. A family banquet was to be held on the feast of the new moon, and David's presence as the king's son-in-law would be naturally expected ; but he was to absent himself, under pretext of being required at the feast of his own family at Bethlehem. Jonathan was to observe how his father accepted this plea, and to communicate the result by the words he should say to the boy who attended him when he went out to practise with the bow, near a rock where David was hidden.

The absence of David, and Jonathan's excuse, produced a burst of ungovernable fury, in which Saul insulted his son, cast a javelin at him, and drove him from the feast in anger. The meeting took place as determined. David, concealed behind the rock, watched Jonathan shoot his arrows, and give directions to the attendant in the words that were to be a note of warning. Still it was possible to have one farewell meeting ; the boy was dismissed, and the two generous friends met, and wept in one another's arms, "till David exceeded." All was hope before David, in spite of the present distress : all was sorrow before Jonathan, who saw his father ever falling lower in crime and in frenzy, and knew that for these very crimes the crown had been forfeited ; and though he was treated as the heir, yet the future king should be this youth, whom his generous, noble-hearted affection forbade him to regard with jealousy. All he asked was, that when David's time of glory should be come, their love should be borne in mind, and that kindness might for his sake be shown to his children.

Then this true friend and son returned to his father and David went lonely on his way ; on his way visiting the High Priest, and obtaining from him the sword of Goliath, which he was now fully able to wield, and the sacred shew-bread, the provision of the priests. This transaction was reported to Saul by an Edomite herdsman in his service, and the cruel vengeance that in his frenzy he inflicted on the priests seems to have extinguished the last ray of hope that was left him.

David at first took refuge in the Philistine country; but he found himself there regarded with so much distrust and hatred, that he only escaped by feigning himself a madman, and taking advantage of the awe with which insanity is regarded in the East.

Under this cover he contrived to escape to his native hills, the wild ruddy rocks that lay between Bethlehem and the Dead Sea. His shepherd life had made every pass familiar to him, and he well knew the mighty caverns that ran far beneath the mountains. There he met many a brave comrade. All whom Saul's violent and uncertain dealing had offended came to the famed warrior in his outlawed state, and among them his own kindred, some of his brothers and his nephews; his sister Zeruiah's sons, who seem to have been about his own age. His parents, probably finding Bethlehem no longer safe, joined him also; but as they were unequal to the fatigues of his wandering life, he escorted them to Moab, where they were hospitably received and sheltered for the sake of Jesse's grandmother, Ruth.

Thus began David's outlaw life. With his little band he hovered about the mountains of Judah—now attacking the Philistines, now protecting the farms and cattle of the men of Judah from the attacks of the robber tribes of the wilderness, now making swift marches to elude the pursuit of Saul. Some of his followers, and specially his nephews, were fierce, lawless men, to whom their wild life was only too congenial; but all seem to have been attached

to David with the passionate devotion that is inspired by
the true hero nature. And, in constant restraint to the
dangerous tendencies of this adventurous life, David kept
God ever before his eyes. The only survivor of the priestly
city was with him, ready to minister to God, and he himself
was constantly pouring forth Psalms of entreaty, of thanksgiving, or of instruction to his warriors. Mighty men were
they, the bravest of the brave, with lion-like faces, feet
swift on the mountains as those of the gazelle, coping, like
David himself, with the giants of Gath, slaying the lions
whom they met in the hills and woodlands, and only three
together broke through the whole Philistine army to procure for their captain a draught from his beloved fountain
of Bethlehem.

Yet though the strongest and most courageous rallied
round him, David was content to fly before his foe, and
be hunted as a partridge on the mountains. And why?
Because his loyalty would not let him lift a hand against
the anointed of the Lord.

"O tarry thou the LORD's leisure.
Be strong ; and He shall comfort thine heart :
And put thou thy trust in the LORD."

Such was the spirit of his song and of his resolution. Thrice
he and his pursuers were brought very near together.
Once the men of Ziph betrayed his whereabouts to Saul,
who came in haste to pursue him through the forest. Here
the loving Jonathan stole out at night, and for the last time
took sweet counsel with his friend,—"Thou shalt be king
in Israel," he said, "and I shall be next unto thee ;" and
once more they parted in the strength of their unshaken
brotherhood of love.

On this occasion David and his mountaineers climbed
down the cliff on one side of the hill, while Saul was surrounding it on the other side, and the king was immediately after called off by a foray of the Philistines. Soon

however he was in full pursuit of David again : and on this occasion he incautiously entered alone the great cave of En-gedi, or of the wild goats, on the borders of the Dead Sea, little supposing that David and all his men were lurking in its dark recesses. David would not hear of injuring or capturing him, but, unseen, crept up and cut off the skirt of his robe ; then, when he had gone forth again into open day, followed him, and showed him this proof of his peril and his own forbearance. Saul was touched for a moment, wept as he acknowledged David's generosity, and even owned that he would be the future king, and entreated his mercy on his family.

But his persistent hatred again mastered the king, and he pursued David into the extreme south of Judah, where again he had his life given to him by this most loyal of outlaws. The whole army lay asleep within their drawn-up line of waggons, Saul in the midst, with his mighty spear planted beside him, and a jar of water—after the custom of the thirsty Easterns—close to his head, when David and his nephew Abishai, one of his three mightiest men, both of them light of foot as wild roes, stole into the camp and stood beside the sleeping king. Abishai would have slain him as he lay, but David forbade the treacherous and disloyal blow. He only bore away the spear and the water-jar, as tokens of what he could have done. And when he had gained the top of a crag, he shouted with something of gay triumph to his old captain Abner, showing him what careless watch he had kept, since one of the people "had entered the camp, and borne off the king's spear and cruse of water."

Saul knew the voice, and, in his fitful mood, once more relented, and spoke affectionately to his son-in-law ; but David durst not venture himself in his hands : and indeed by this time Saul had given away David's wife, Michal, in marriage to another, and David had taken to himself other wives, after the Eastern fashion—specially Abigail, the wise widow of the ungrateful churl, Nabal.

Finding that his wandering life could no longer be kept up, he again sought refuge among the Philistines; but instead of coming as before as a lonely fugitive, he brought 600 of the bravest men of Israel with him, and obtained from Achish, king of Gath, the grant of the city of Ziklag, where he dwelt for a year and four months, and there received reinforcements from his own country— mighty, lion-faced men of Gad, who swam the Jordan in time of flood to come to him, and even the boldest of Saul's own tribe of Benjamin, archers who could draw the bow and launch the stone with the left hand as well as with the right.

With these forces, David made attacks on the old foes of Israel, the Bedouin hordes of the desert, and, returning with their spoil, gave evasive answers that led Achish to suppose it was the spoil of his native country. When there was a great muster of all the Philistine troops for a mighty invasion of Israel, David was forced to bring his band to join them. What he would have done had a battle taken place is not known; the predicament was spared him by the distrust of the Philistine lords, who insisted that he and his warriors should be expelled from the camp.

On their return to Ziklag they found a woful sight. The Amalekites—the worst of all the Bedouin tribes—had fallen on the place, in the absence of all its men, and carried off all the women and children and cattle, so that nothing but silent, smoking ruins met the eyes of the troop. Their spirits gave way—they wept till they could weep no longer; and some in their rage were ready to turn against their chief, and stone him, for having brought this disaster on them, though he was an equal sufferer with themselves; for his own wives were among the lost.

His courage, however, first revived. He obtained Divine direction through the priest Abiathar, and set forth at once in pursuit, so swiftly, that 200 of his men had to be left behind on the way, from sheer exhaustion. Presently the pursuers came upon a miserable Egyptian slave, who had been left behind, dying of hunger and thirst, by the marauders. When he had been revived by food, he gave an account of the onslaught on Ziklag, and guided David and his men to where the Amalekites were eating, drinking, dancing, or sleeping in perfect security, rejoicing in the huge plunder they had gathered from many a ruined city besides that of Ziklag.

They fell an easy prey to the Israelite company. Only 400 young men succeeded in escaping upon their camels, and David's men not only recovered their wives and children and their other property, but there was an immense spoil to divide. A fit of selfishness made them wish merely to restore to the comrades who had tarried behind their own original property; but this their open-hearted leader forbade, and made a rule that the spoil of the enemy should be shared as well by the guards of the camp as by those who went forth to the battle—a wise as well as a just law, much conducing to safety and discipline. The booty of the Amalekites proved so large that there was enough for David to send rich gifts to all the friends who had befriended him in his wanderings in Judah.

But more stirring news was on the wing. That inroad of the Philistines had reduced Saul to extremity. He had worked his own desolation. The flower of his warriors were with David; he had slain the priests; driven away the Good Spirit; Samuel was no more: none stood by him save his true and faithful son. Otherwise he was deserted alike of God and man. In his misery he even crept round the camp of the Philistines, over broken, stony ground, and sought counsel in the cave of one of the witches whom in his better days he had striven to root out. Then, to complete his doom, and pronounce his sentence, the spirit of Samuel arose, even like a god from the earth, and summed up his whole life in one awful rebuke, which left the wretched king lying senseless on the ground.

Revived in part by food, the doomed man stole back to his army to defend to the last his own native mountains of Benjamin. There, amid these hills of Gilboa, died as a good soldier the noble Jonathan, amid his brothers; and there by the end of the day remained Saul, unable to escape, and dreading the scorn and torture that would meet a captive king. He tried to die by his own hand, but only wounded himself sorely, and was still alive when an Amalekite robber came up to strip the slain, and complied with the unhappy man's entreaty to end his life. Then, bearing the royal crown and bracelet as tokens of the truth, the robber sought Ziklag, and, falling at David's feet, presented him with them, and told his tale. David at once caused him to be put to death, as the murderer of an anointed king. And then, with no exultation, but only sorrow, he remembered no more that Saul had been his bitter foe, but only that he had been a mighty king, and Jonathan a dear, faithful friend, and he sung in their honour his most lovely and tender lament—

" The beauty of Israel is slain upon thy high places:
How are the mighty fallen !"

And, in honourable memory of the bow of the mighty archer Jonathan, he bade that his own tribe of Judah should be taught to become as expert in archery as the Benjamites.

Saul had left at least three young sons, and Jonathan a child of five years old; but when the king and princes had fallen on Mount Gilboa, upon their own highlands, the enemy seem to have overrun the land, and the

D

royal family fled in terror beyond the Jordan. Mephibosheth, Jonathan's poor little son, fell from his nurse's
arms in the flight, and was lamed for life. Abner, Saul's
uncle and general, as true a fierce Wolf of Benjamin as
himself, and apparently of the same self-willed untameable nature, collected the few adherents of the house of
Kish together on the utmost border of the land, at Mahanaim, the place consecrated by Jacob on account of his
meeting with the angels, and there set up Ishbosheth, the
eldest surviving son of Saul, to reign over the two tribes
and a half beyond Jordan, amid the rich pastures, oak
forests, and gigantic ruins of Gilead and Bashan, as well
as over many of the more central tribes.

David, however, had received the Divine sanction to
assume the crown royal at Hebron, the oldest sacred city
in the world, full of the memories of Abraham and of the
brave deeds of Caleb. Here he ruled over Judah, and defended the country from the Philistines, without attempting
to expel his rival, content to wait the LORD'S pleasure, and
too patriotic to waste the strength of Israel by a civil war.
Abner, however, came out to Gibeah, and there meeting
Joab, David's nephew, in the olive-clothed valley, by the
great reservoir called the pool of Gibeon, the two
generals proposed to decide their quarrel by a combat,
like that of the Horatii and Curiatii, of twelve young men
on either side, while they themselves sat to judge of their
prowess. The whole twenty-four were so equally matched
that all lay dead on the plain, stabbed by the side-thrust
of the deadly short-sword of Israel. The battle became
general; Abner was totally defeated and forced to fly, but
he was closely followed by the swift-footed young Asahel,
Joab's youngest brother. The gallant old warrior, unwilling to slay the fair agile lad, entreated him to turn
back, or at least put on the armour of one of the slain who
strewed the way; but Asahel rashly persisted in harassing

him, till he was forced to turn and give him a death-stroke. There is something very grand in Abner, who, though defeated, was still, in David's absence, the true prince among men, and even now, when he had gained a hill-top, put a stop to the pursuit by his commanding shout and remonstrance, which even the vindictive Joab durst not disobey, though in his first rage at his brother's death.

He kept his wrath, however; and when Abner became displeased with Ishbosheth, and came to Hebron to offer his adherence to David, Joab treacherously caused him to be followed on his departure, invited back to Hebron, and at the very gate slew him with his own hand. Hebron was a sanctuary city, and a few steps placed the murderer within its precincts, where he could not receive the reward of his crime unless there claimed by the revenger of blood, and tried by the Levites and elders. David was therefore forced to leave Joab unpunished ; but he marked his abhorrence of the crime by pronouncing a solemn curse on the blood-stained family, and causing a great lamentation to be held when Abner was buried at Hebron. He himself led the wailing chant over his ancient captain, the prince and mighty man fallen this day in Israel.

Deprived of his protector, Ishbosheth soon perished by the hand of two assassins, who sought to obtain favour from David, but met instead justice for their crime. If he had slain the murderer of Saul, he said, " How much more wicked men who had slain a righteous person on his bed?"

All opposition was now ended ; David was the chosen king of all Israel, and every tribe sent deputations to do him honour and bring presents of their fruits. He was crowned king in his thirty-seventh year, amid the enthusiastic greetings of the whole nation. And while they were thus gathered round him, it seemed to him that he might well use their zeal by winning the natural capital of

Palestine, which stood high amid her vassal hills, towering above Hebron, the Salem of Melchisedek, the Moriah of Isaac's sacrifice, the mountain-fortress that even when its king had fallen had resisted Joshua, the hostile Jebus, whose enmity must have been so often felt at Bethlehem. Let him win that city, and his kingdom would have an almost impregnable rallying-point, and his royalty would be that of a true king and lawgiver, not, like Saul's, that of a mere partisan chieftain, with a spear at his bolster.

The lower city was taken; but the upper fortress, the stronghold, defied him, as indeed it was again and again to defy any invader to whom it had not been destined by the LORD himself. The Jebusites seem to have thought their blind and cripples a sufficient defence for it, and the assault of the steep precipitous sides and giant ramparts was so desperate, that David offered the generalship of his army as the reward of the foremost chief who should win an entrance. Joab was the warrior who scaled the heights and won his way into the city, thus becoming captain of the host; and he was ever a brave upholder of David's power, though his rude lawless violence and cruelty made him a thorn in the side of the holy king. David's six hundred warriors had become the foundation of a mighty army, all on foot, in obedience to the inspired command against trusting to the horses and chariots that could never be really available in so hilly a land as Palestine. The men of the East believe David to have invented chain armour, and still call a particularly good hawberk after his name; and by the excellent order and great valour of his army, under the Divine blessing, he succeeded in completing the conquest begun by Joshua. The Israelites were no longer a people scattered among the remnants of old heathens; but the old land was uniformly under David's sway, and the ancient inhabitants—unless they belonged to the old proscribed races—had the privileges of the Jewish covenant opened to them, and we find the Hittite, the Jebusite, and the Philistine, Cherethite, and Pelethite reckoned among David's loyal subjects or soldiers. The Philistines were so reduced that, though they existed as a nation down to the time of Alexander, they never seriously molested the Israelites again. Syria, Edom, Moab, and Ammon were all conquered, and the Phœnicians were friendly allies, so that David's kingdom reached the old boundaries promised to Abraham, from the Mediterranean to the Euphrates, from Lebanon to the torrent of Egypt.

The victories were won, it would seem, in the summer campaigns, since winter fighting in the rainy seasons among the bleak mountains is nearly impossible in Palestine; and David was in the meantime freshly building the fortifications of Jerusalem, and raising a citadel palace on Mount Zion, with materials sent him by the King of Tyre. Moreover, he resolved to transport thither the Ark of the Covenant, and thus consecrate Jerusalem to be the religious as well as the civil and military capital of his kingdom. In this, no doubt, he had Divine direction; but his first attempt to remove the Ark from the forest house of the Levite, where it had been lodged for many years, was irregularly made. It was placed on a cart, in oblivion of the old command observed in the wilderness, that it should be borne on staves on the shoulders of Kohathite Levites; and this rashness and want of reverence were punished by the sudden death-stroke that fell upon the foremost of the Levites, who had thus disregarded the laws that hedged in the awful sanctity of this emblem of the connexion of the Israelites with their LORD.

After a year's delay, during which the Ark remained in the house of a Levite, it was again removed with all the honours enjoined by Moses, with a choir of Levites singing the old song of the wilderness journeys—

"Let God arise, let his enemies be scattered,"

with a beautiful triumphant addition composed by the minstrel king himself. All the chiefs of Israel formed a magnificent procession, and he himself, robed in white, led the solemn dance that welcomed the Ark to the Tabernacle that he had raised for it on Mount Zion, while his own glorious Psalm was sung from one rejoicing band to another—

> " Lift up your heads, O ye gates,
> And the King of Glory shall come in.
> And be ye lift up, ye everlasting doors.
> Who is the King of Glory?
> It is the LORD, strong and mighty,
> Even the Lord, mighty in battle."

David had caused his wife Michal, Saul's daughter, to be restored to him, partly, no doubt, to establish his right in the eyes of the friends of the house of Kish. With all her father's pride, she rebuked David contemptuously for lowering his kingly dignity by his share in the dance that welcomed the Ark, and for this ungodly scorn she was punished by being childless, thus losing the hope that would seem naturally to have belonged to his first and royal wife, of the Benjamite tribe, of being the ancestress of the unfailing line of kings that was to culminate in the Messiah.

David had already taken other wives, and had several sons, and he knew that his line and the city where he had fixed his home were under a peculiar blessing. His longing was to raise a magnificent Temple, instead of merely leaving the Ark in the curtained Tabernacle, where, however, he had taken care that the whole ritual taught to Moses should be daily observed, with the addition of a continual chanting of Psalms, mostly composed by himself. The prophet Nathan at first approved his design, but was afterwards instructed to tell him that his hands were too blood-stained, himself too much of a warrior, to be permitted to carry out this pious enterprise, but that it should be performed by a son whom the LORD would give him ; and at the same time blessings were promised to his lineage, and the throne confirmed to them for ever—in those words "for ever" a far more glorious future being included than merely a perpetual dominion over little rocky Palestine.

David was thankful, and, like Moses of old, was content to have the work, that his children might have the glory. He began to prepare materials for the future Temple. But it appears as if, even in the midst of his thankfulness, a certain slothfulness had come over David, perhaps that ease and presumption that are only too apt to follow upon any great honour or favour. For the first time, it would seem, at the season "when kings go forth to battle" he remained at home in his own house at Jerusalem, instead of leading his army in their campaign against Rabbah, the royal city of the Ammonites. While thus lingering he fell into temptation, through the beauty of Bathsheba, who, though apparently the grandchild of his cunning councillor, Ahithophel, was the wife of Uriah, one of the Hittite captains of his army. The sin and shame of David's life followed. He had learned to think a multitude of wives a mark of royalty, like that of the nations round, and he forgot that he was acting exactly as his old master Samuel had warned the Israelites that a tyrant would act towards them. Desiring to take Bathsheba to himself, he removed her husband by sending secret commands to Joab to place him in the forefront of the battle, where he could not fail to be slain.

Probably an ordinary Eastern monarch would have acted with more reckless violence and disregard of appearances, and for many months David seems to have been utterly unaware of the guilt he had incurred, until the prophet Nathan came to him with a brief tale that went straight to his shepherd heart, the touching story of a poor man who loved and cherished his one little live lamb, the darling of his house, and of a rich man who cruelly and wantonly snatched it from him to serve as a meal for his guest. David's spirit was again among the lambs of his flock at Bethlehem, and with all the fire with which he would in his bright boyhood have heard of injustice he broke forth with sentence of death against the cruel rich man, when the lamb should have been restored fourfold to his injured neighbour. Little did he expect to hear the stern words, " Thou art the man !" Bathsheba was the one little ewe lamb, Uriah was the injured owner, and he himself was the cruel tyrant. Nor could he fulfil his own sentence, and make restitution ; for he had done even worse than him whom he condemned. He had slain Uriah with the sword of the enemy !

Then it was that David's true greatness became most plainly seen. He saw the whole truth instantly, and his grief for it put out all false shame, all thought of kingly pride, all displeasure at the bold reproof.

" I have sinned against the LORD," he said.

Those simple words were full of the intense repentance in his heart, and the prophet at once assured him that the sin so repented of was forgiven. His life would not be taken instead of Uriah's life, his soul should be relieved from God's anger ; but chastisement must be sent on him in love, though not in anger, " because he had given great occasion to the enemies of the Lord to blaspheme." Most true are these last words. No sin recorded in Scripture has been so lightly or so improperly spoken of by the enemies of the Lord as this sin of David's, even to our own day.

And yet no sin, perhaps, has turned more to the good of the world, for it was in David's anguish and humiliation, when he was crushed to the ground by the thought of his sin, that he composed those mournful Psalms of repentance, which have ever since his day been the chief assistance to sinners in rightly deploring their sin and praying for pardon.

The first chastisement was the death of Bathsheba's child, for whom David wept and mourned, so long as he hoped that his own humiliation and prayer might avail to save its life ; but when it was dead he submitted, with the trust that " I shall go to him, but he shall not return to me." Yet, though the sin had been forgiven, the loving heart of David could not be as it was before ; the brightness of his life had passed away : and though Rabbah, the royal city of Ammon, was ready to fall after a weary siege, it was only by an urgent summons that Joab could bring him to the camp to enjoy the honour of the final taking of the inner stronghold. Though another son was born to him of Bathsheba, and marked out by God himself as the heir of the glorious promise, still David continued to humble himself as one who could not forget that he had offended and grieved the God of his love.

Man of war as he was, peace was the craving of his life :

" The LORD shall give his people the blessing of peace "

had been the sweet conclusion of his youthful song of the Seven Thunders. Absalom—(Father of Peace)—was the name he gave his son, born among the strifes and perils of his residence at Hebron : Jerusalem—(Vision of Peace)—was the name he restored to his royal city : and Solomon—(Peace)—was the name given to the infant destined to the work that he might not carry out.

But peace was not to be for David. The sons of the many wives he had taken when deprived of Michal were growing up in the pride and lawless habits too common in young princes ; and Absalom, whose mother was the daughter of a petty Philistine prince, and who stood pre-eminent in the glorious beauty that David had himself possessed, was the favourite alike of his father and the people.

He was not the eldest son, but Amnon, the first-born of David by a different mother, committed an unpardonable offence against him, which David passed weakly over, as if his sons were above the law. Absalom revenged himself by the murder of his elder brother, and then fled to his mother's kindred at Geshur, where he remained until his pardon was obtained by Joab. No doubt the conduct of his sons quickened David's grief, and his penitence, not being understood by the world, was thought by them unworthy of what no doubt they deemed a mere trifle. Idlers in the shady, arched gateways of the city made a joke of the king's self-abasement, and drunkards made songs upon him. Young Absalom, jealous of his little brother, and unforgiving of his banishment, took advantage of these discontents. He sat himself down in the gateway, intercepted all the persons who were going up to his father for justice, and, with soft and pitying words and caresses, told them that it was of no use to proceed, the king was too much occupied with his devotions, and with preparations for his new Temple, for which no doubt they would be heavily taxed, and there was no one to attend to them : " So Absalom stole the hearts of the men of Israel." At last, when his time was come, he obtained leave from his father to go to Hebron, to fulfil a vow that he pretended to have made in his banishment. There he blew a trumpet, caused himself to be proclaimed king, and obtained an immense following of all the persons whom he had inflamed with discontent. With them he advanced on Jerusalem ; and no doubt the city itself was disaffected, for, in spite of its exceeding strength, David durst not await his attack there, but quitted the place in haste, sending his wives and children away for protection.

Never was there a sadder scene than when that great warrior and prince went from the city his own sword had won, expelled in his old age by his ungrateful son, whom he still loved so earnestly. Barefoot he went, with ashes on his head, down the steep pathway of the rocky ravine of Kedron, and on the other side of the narrow valley ran, scoffing and triumphing, a kinsman of the family of Saul, railing at him, and crying, " Come out, thou bloody man : the LORD hath returned on thee all the blood of the house of Saul." David's heart was already very sore with respect to that family, for Mephibosheth, the lame son of his beloved Jonathan, whom he had placed at his own table, and recovered to all the private possessions of his grandfather, had, he was told by Ziba, the steward of this recovered property, remained behind at Jerusalem, ungratefully hoping to raise a party to confer on him the crown of Saul ; and when Abishai, that passionately affectionate nephew, who had once brought the water from the well of Bethlehem, would fain have darted across the valley to slay the reviler, the sorrow-stricken king withheld him, saying, " The LORD hath said to him, Curse David."

The king was by no means wholly deserted in his distress. Joab seems to have gone to raise the loyal in his favour. His faithful Philistine guards followed him, though he generously tried to persuade them that they were not bound by duty to his service ; and the Priests themselves would have carried the Ark with him, but that he would not expose it to danger in his wanderings. Ahithophel, the grandfather of Bathsheba, had gone over to Absalom ; but Hushai, another councillor famed for wisdom, came to his king's assistance, and was told by

David that he could most efficiently serve him by pretending to espouse Absalom's cause, and endeavouring to
defeat the counsel of Ahithophel.   Other loyal followers
were with the king, and, above all, such spiritual comforts
were poured into his soul, that in this the saddest time of
his life many of his most plaintive, yet most cheering,
songs were composed.   After that weary, sorrowful day,
when the wild wilderness leading towards Jordan had
been trodden by David and Abishai, with steps very unlike
the bounding tread of the undismayed cheery young outlaws they had once been on those same rocks and hills, and
when the mournful band of fugitives had rested for a long
night of watching and guard, lest they should be pursued
by Absalom's overwhelming force, there rose in the morning this song of thankfulness :—

> " LORD, how are they increased that trouble me !
>   Many are they that rise against me.
>   Many one there be that say of my soul,
>   ' There is no help for him in his God.'
>   But thou, LORD, art my defender ;
>   Thou art my worship, and the lifter up of my head.
>   I did call unto the LORD with my voice,
>   And he heard me out of his holy hill.
>   I laid me down, and slept ;
>   And rose up again ; for the Lord sustained me.
>   I will not be afraid for ten thousands of the people
>   That have set themselves against me round about.
>   Up, LORD, and help me, O my God : for thou smitest
>   mine enemies upon the cheek-bone ;
>   Thou hast broken the teeth of the ungodly.
>   Salvation belongeth unto the LORD ;
>   And thy blessing is upon thy people."

That safe awakening had not been owing to want of
foresight on Ahithophel's part.   He had advised Absalom
to follow and surprise his father while weary and weak-
handed, this familiar friend truly laying great wait for his
master ; but Hushai had represented that David was a

mighty man of war, and would be fierce as a bear robbed
of her whelps, and advised waiting to collect more forces
before attacking him. The overruling power that protected David had made Absalom incline to Hushai's
counsel, so much to the anger of Ahithophel that he actually went home and hanged himself, probably because he
saw his party must fail, and could not bear to face the
king he had deserted. Meantime Hushai, through the
priest's sons, despatched a warning to David, without loss
of time to put the river Jordan between him and his
enemies.

Here then he came to the outmost borders of his land,
to Mahanaim, the place consecrated by one of Jacob's
visions, and where Ishbosheth had so long reigned, near his
recent conquest of Rabbah. Grand, beautiful, and fertile
is that pasture-land, with lovely meadows, rich cornfields,
and magnificent oaks clothing every hill-side, among the
giant cities that were chosen by half the tribe of Manasseh.
There the princely old chieftain Barzillai showed himself
most loyal, and amply provided for the wants of the fugitive king and his troops out of his own mighty stores ;
and there, it may be, the sorrowful king and father
sang the saddest and most prophetic of all his Psalms.
When looking out at the fierce high-fed cattle closing in
with their horns on some helpless creature who had
crossed their field, he thought of his own foes besetting
him, and sighed that—

> " Many oxen are come about me ;
> Fat bulls of Bashan close me in on every side : "

and then went on—carried out of his own sufferings into
a foreboding of that mightier sorrow that is unlike all
other sorrows, and yet like them all.

Meantime the forces were gathered on either side : the
disloyal, who wanted an ordinary, fierce, godless prince,

who would lead them to battle, feed their pride, not trouble them with devotion, and be another Saul, had gathered round Absalom ; and the loyal, who loved the great name of David, the Chosen of the Lord, flocked to the Lion of the Tribe of Judah.

All was prepared for battle, and David would himself have acted as general, in the hope, it would seem, of being able to save the life of his guilty son ; for when Joab and his other captains insisted on his not exposing his life, but remaining with the reserve in the city, all his entreaty was, " Deal gently with the young man, even with Absalom." The battle took place in what was called the Wood of Ephraim, probably from the slaughter Jephthah had thereabouts once made of the perverse Ephraimites. It was part of the grand forest-land of Gilead, broken ground covered with terebinth trees and luxuriant vegetation ; and when Absalom's forces, ill generalled, and with hearts full of misgiving, broke their ranks under the assault of Joab and his well-practised mighty men of war, the wild depths of the tangled forest proved as fatal to the rebels as the sword itself. Absalom himself, riding away on a mule, became entangled in the branches of a terebinth tree. His head seems to have been jammed between two strong boughs, and his luxuriant hair added to the difficulty of disengaging himself ; the mule made its escape from under him, and he was seen thus hanging in the tree by one of the pursuers, who told Joab where to find him. The unscrupulous captain of the host, knowing that David would assuredly spare his son's life, resolved that he should have no choice ; and taking three javelins, thrust his unhappy cousin through with them, while yet suspended in the tree ; hoping, perhaps, that he could represent Absalom's fate to the king as having taken place in the ordinary chances of battle.

David's grief was intense. He sung no elegy over the

rebel, but his broken-hearted cry, "Would God I had died for thee, O Absalom, my son, my son!" has ever since resounded in every heart. And it was only by the rough and harsh words of Joab that he could be roused from his grief enough to thank his brave deliverers. He could not, however, forget that Joab was the murderer of his son, and so far punished him as to put him down from his generalship of the whole army, raising in his stead Amasa, the son of another daughter of Jesse, on the plea, as it would seem, that Amasa, who had taken part with Absalom, must be won over to his side.

The people of Israel had entirely changed their minds. They were now fervent in their passionate affection for the great old monarch against whom they had so lately rebelled. There was universal triumph when he was brought back to his own city, and the lurking jealousy of the ten tribes against that of Judah only showed itself in a dispute as to which should be foremost in bringing back the king. The reviler Shimei came with abject humility to entreat the pardon that David freely granted to him, and Mephibosheth came forth, with hair and beard untrimmed since the king had been driven away, to explain that he had called for his ass, in order to accompany his benefactor, but that the perfidious Ziba had taken advantage of his lameness to leave him behind and helpless, while representing to David that he was acting treasonably in the desire of putting forward his pretensions to the throne. David had in his first anger made over all Mephibosheth's lands to Ziba, and he now only revoked the grant so far as to give back half to their rightful owner, probably because Ziba, as resident steward, with his fifteen sons and twenty servants, could hardly have been dispossessed of lands in the Benjamite mountains without perilling the newly-recovered throne ; and Mephibosheth, with all the generosity of his father, acquiesced, saying, "Yea, let him take all, forasmuch as my lord the king is come again in peace to his own house."

David would have requited the hospitality of the large-hearted Barzillai by welcoming him at Jerusalem ; but the grand old pastoral chief loved his free woods and hills too well to shut himself up within the walls of a city. He said he was too old to enjoy the feasts and music of the court, but prayed that in his stead the king would take his son or grandson Chimham, and do with him what might seem good to him. There is reason to think that David rewarded Chimham with a grant of lands at his own dear Bethlehem, for the wayside halting-place there for travellers from Egypt was long after called the habitation of Chimham, and was almost certainly that inn in whose stable the great Son of David was born.

David had not for long freed himself from the rude dominion of Joab, for when a rebellion was excited by a man named Sheba, Amasa proved so slack in collecting an army against him, that David was obliged to send Abishai to quicken his movements ; and, while pursuing the rebel, Joab most treacherously murdered Amasa. David was unable to do justice on him, partly from his great influence with the army, but partly also, it is thought, because Joab was privy to the deadly secret of Uriah's murder.

Joab does seem to have had a hearty affection for his uncle, though it was the rude domineering love of a coarser nature ; and his ungodly, cruel temper could only admire David as the warrior, not as the holy man. Yet Joab did his best to save David from the last great error of his life.

The pious work of collecting marbles, cedar, gold, silver, and all that could serve to beautify the Temple that young Solomon was to raise, was the chief joy of David's later years. Now, it had been commanded by the Divine

Law that whenever a census of the people was taken, a half shekel should be paid by every man whose name was enrolled, to serve as an acknowledgment that purchase or atonement was due for his soul, and this money was appropriated to the repairs or building of the Sanctuary. Pestilence had been threatened by the law as the penalty of neglect. David, desirous both to count his fighting men and to add to the treasures preparing for the Temple, commanded a census to be taken, but Joab, probably participating in the people's sinful discontent at their king's zeal for God's house, and knowing that they would regard the numbering as an excuse for demanding the money, remonstrated against the measure which he, as captain of the host, was to carry out.

The King, however, persisted ; and Joab probably forebore to insist on the payment because of its unpopularity, for the Israelites incurred the penalty, and before the numbers were complete, the prophet Gad came to David to warn him that he had been the occasion of sin to his people, and that the penalty had been incurred. Still a choice was offered him between three years of famine, three months of devastation by the enemy, or three days of pestilence.

David's answer, " Let me now fall into the hands of the Lord, for his mercies are great ; let me not fall into the hands of man," seems to have been a refusal of the sad choice, leaving that to God alone, and thus the punishment sent was that which the original command had threatened, namely, pestilence. The deadly sickness cut off 70,000 in three days, and David absolutely beheld, on one of those dreadful days, what seems to have been the only supernatural vision of his life : he saw the Angel of Vengeance with his sword uplifted against Jerusalem !

The tribe of Benjamin had not yet been numbered. There the penalty had not yet been incurred, and David in agony prayed, " Let thy hand be on me, and on my father's house ; but, these sheep, what have they done?" The prophet Gad was sent, in answer to his prayers, with directions to offer a sacrifice of atonement to avert the plague ; and for this purpose David purchased the level space on the top of a hill just outside the walls, where Araunah, or Ornan, a great chieftain of the ancient Jebusites, was wont to tread out his corn by the feet of oxen, but which had been early hallowed by the sacrifice of Isaac. This sacred spot, with the oxen and their wooden instruments for threshing, was bought at a large price by David ; Araunah would freely have given it, but the king felt that an offering of atonement must not cost him nothing, and secured the spot, which he then designated as the place for the future temple—the dream of his life which he might not see, even as Moses trod not on the soil of the promised land.

He had yet another glad and peaceful day, when he collected all his great men from every tribe, and set before them his fair and gracious son Solomon as the chosen of the Lord to wear his crown, and fulfil his work, that holy work of building the Temple of the LORD. Chieftain and warrior, excited by the king's pious ardour, made willing offerings from their wealth to deck the edifice for glory and for beauty, and the king in the joy of his heart burst forth into the loftiest of all his songs of praise, one of those whose echo is most surely heard in Heaven :—

" Blessed be Thou, Lord God of Israel our Father, for ever and ever. Thine, O Lord, is the greatness, and the power, and the glory, and the victory, and the majesty : for all that is in the heaven and the earth is Thine ; Thine is the kingdom, O Lord, and Thou art exalted as Head above all. Both riches and honour come of Thee, and Thou reignest over all ; and in Thine hand is power and might ; and in Thine hand it is to make great, and to give strength unto all. Now therefore, our God, we thank Thee, and praise Thy glorious name. But who am I, and what is my people, that we shall be able to offer so willingly after this sort? for all things come of Thee, and of Thine own have we given Thee!"

Other equally noble words he added, which must be sought in the last chapter of the first book of Chronicles. They show how, his warfare accomplished, this great and holy man was waiting with healed wounds and peaceful spirit for the crown laid up for him in Heaven.

His life had been, in his own sweet words, "as the tender grass springing out of the earth by clear shining after rain;" and fresh hope, thankfulness, and joy had sprung out of his heaviest sorrows. He had reached the good old age, and not only saw a son of the greatest promise ready to succeed him, but knew that his throne and kingdom were secured to his lineage for ever, and that the plan of his life would be carried out after his death. Eastern monarchs had the full right to choose their successor among their sons, and indeed, Solomon had rather been God's choice than David's; but Adonijah, the eldest surviving son, as beautiful, proud, and wilful as Absalom, had been, felt himself aggrieved, and no doubt appealed to the old ungodly impatience of the cost of the Temple, for he won over to his side Joab himself, who had no feeling for the peaceful wisdom and gentleness of young Solomon, but would fain see the warlike spirit of David's younger days renewed. With him, too, was Abiathar, the fugitive Priest who had joined David after Saul's slaughter of his family, and who, not being the high priest by rightful descent, probably dreaded being displaced in favour of Zadok, the true heir. These two, and other partizans, escorted Adonijah to some gardens outside the walls of Jerusalem, and there made a sacrificial feast, evidently as an assertion of his claims to the throne. Informed by Bathsheba and Nathan, David, though very feeble, roused himself to summon his trusty and loyal servants, and cause them to take Solomon forth before the people, and there let Zadok and Nathan anoint him with the consecrating oil, and seat him on the throne. The whole city rang with glad shouts of " God save King Solomon," and the hostile party in alarm broke up, Adonijah flying to the Sanctuary on Mount Sion, where he remained till assured of pardon, while Solomon returned to his father for his blessing of thankful joy.

A strong and deep sense of justice, however, made David warn Solomon that it would be for him to inflict on Joab the punishment he himself had never been able to execute : and Joab was accordingly put to death, for this his last treason, as well as for all the crimes of his earlier life, apparently not, however, till after David's eyes had closed in his last sleep, in the 70th year of his life, the fortieth of his reign, B.C. 1014.

Where shall we find such another Worthy ? Truly it were presumptuous to seek the equal of the " man after God's own heart," save that, in the Christian times, purer light and indwelling grace has made it possible that not merely the morning, but the entire day of life, should be without clouds.

Shepherd, warrior, exile, king, lawgiver, poet, founder of a great dynasty, David in a wonderful degree unites every kind of earthly grandeur. In the minute history of his life we see his gallant outward life ; in his psalms we see the tender sensitiveness of the spirit that showed so free and dauntless. We see there why he could be happy, why he could be brave, why, after suffering, and even after crime, he could recover calm and rest, and how blessed is the soul that constantly remained in loving communion with the God of his strength.

HECTOR.

THE first of the three Worthies of the classic world chosen by our forefathers was Hector. It is strange to pass from the most true to the most uncertain, but as we are here trying to tread as far as possible in the steps of our ancestors in our study of great examples ; and also since we have just seen the highest models of the Heroic which were held up to those who lived under Divine revelation ; it is well to pass to the grandest portraits of character invented by the human mind when left to itself.

It is scarcely true, however, to say that Hector was the highest ideal of the ancients themselves. Circumstances led to his being the favourite in the Middle Ages, partly because the classic heroes had become chiefly known through Latin writings which were favourable to Hector's cause, and partly because there are elements in his nature, as originally depicted, which are more congenial to a Christian than are the dispositions of his enemies.

In order to have any understanding of the persons we have to study, it is needful to know what were the objects of their chief admiration, and therefore, together with Hector, we will try to describe the other two chief Heroes who were admired in ancient times, namely, Achilles and Ulysses, the three together perhaps making the highest perfection that the Greeks could conceive. According to the old attempts at chronology, these personages should have been placed before, instead of after, David, as they were supposed to be contemporary with Saul; but in very truth the whole of their adventures are so unhistorical, that it is a futile endeavour to assign to them any date. All that we do know is that the glorious poems of Homer which have endeared them to all ages, were current among the Greeks, and known by heart by every educated man among them, at the time when the kingdom of David had become divided, and was tottering to its fall under the apostasy and misgovernment of his degenerate descendants.

Near the gulf-indented coast of Asia Minor, towards the north-west extremity, there lies beneath the forest-clad mountains of Ida a space of undulating ground, partly woodland and partly glade, and traversed by two mountain streams, yellow, or xanthous Simoïs, and the lesser Scamander, on their way to the sea. The place has been looked on for the last 2,500 years, by every man of culture and spirit, with an affection and enthusiasm such as have centred equally on no other spot upon the earth. There was the site of the mighty city of Asiatics, which for its crimes was besieged and taken by the united forces of Greece under the leadership of her greatest heroes, and the places and scenery are so exactly described in the great poems respecting it as to be traceable even to the present hour.

The facts, thus supported, were firmly believed in, so far as they did not involve manifestly fabulous incidents, and only in late ages did any question arise of the main event. Of late, comparison has made it evident that all those imaginative nations, who have sprung from the same source as ourselves, love to believe in grand and noble forefathers, half divine, and performers of magnificent feats. Certain likenesses between these exploits and between the heroes who achieved them have further led learned men to the conclusion that they are all different traditions, of the same original story; and further investigation of the names borne by the different personages has brought some to the belief that, instead of being founded on any doings of men or women on earth, these tales arose from a sort of allegorical way of speaking of day and night, sunrise and sunset, or else that these allegorical stories fastened themselves upon some real persons or events, and embellished them, as well as confused them.

No one can now tell whether there were any kernel of reality around which the poetic and heroic tales fastened themselves that were sung of and believed by the ancient Greeks. There were many tales and songs of them that were stored in the memory of the bards or poets who went from one chief city to another, chanting them to the lyre. One of these poets, blind Homer, made his songs of such exceeding force and beauty, so grand in character and so true to nature, that they could not be forgotten. After some generations they were collected and written down, and though they only related the history of a fortnight's discord in the camp and the return of one wanderer to his home, yet all besides that can be learnt of the stories of the whole war seems little more than mere explanation of them.

And now, forgetting all that has been said of the doubtfulness of the story, let us give ourselves up to the interest of it, and look well at the three who were chiefly esteemed by the men of old Greek times.

Once upon a time, there lived at Sparta a most beautiful Queen, whose name was Helen, and who was married to a prince called Menelaus. There came to Sparta a young prince named Paris, one of the handsomest men in all the world, but selfish, cowardly, and deceitful. He returned all the kindness that Menelaus had shown to him by basely stealing his beautiful wife, and carrying her away to his own home on the shores of Asia Minor—Ilium or Troy, of which his father Priam was king.

The cruel wrong that Menelaus had suffered stirred the spirit of all the other Greeks, and they demanded that Helen should be given back, and all amends possible made to her husband ; but the Trojans chose to stand by their prince, bad as was his cause, rather than own him or themselves in the wrong. The brother of Menelaus was Agamemnon, king of Mycenæ, the chief king in all Greece, and all the princes brought together their ships and their men under his command to sail for Troy. Among them came Ulysses, the wisest of all the Greeks, from his little island of Ithaca ; and Achilles, the son of Peleus, king of Phthia, most beautiful, most brave and gifted, as befitted one who had no mortal mother, but was born of a nymph of the sea. It had been foretold that if Achilles did not go to this war, he would have a long, prosperous, but inglorious life, but that if he joined in it, his glory would be very great, but his days would be few. He chose glory rather than length of days, and with his bosom friend Patroclus, and all his brave warriors, joined the Grecian host.

Hector was the most valiant and the most beloved of all the many sons of old King Priam of Troy, far nobler than Paris, in whose cause, nevertheless, he was obliged to peril the loss of his life and throne. At first, it would seem as if the Greeks had chiefly occupied themselves in conquering the outlying possessions and the allies of Troy, but in the tenth year of the war they had their ships all drawn up on the sea-shore, close before Troy, and were living in tents in front of them, fighting whenever the Trojans sallied out against them, but not daring to scale the walls, because they were supposed to have been built by two of the gods, who would certainly take revenge on any one who assaulted them.

It is at this time that Homer's great poem of the Iliad

begins, by telling that in one of the attacks upon the coast two damsels had been carried off as slaves, and given, one to Agamemnon and the other to Achilles, as their part of the spoil. But soon after a deadly pestilence fell upon the camp, and it was made known to Agamemnon that it would not cease till he had restored his captive to her father, priest of the god Apollo, who had power over sickness and death. Agamemnon was forced to part with his prize ; but he declared in his pride that he would not lose his share, and would have instead the damsel who had been given to Achilles. This was a great insult to a king like Achilles, and especially to the very man whose bravery had won all that the Greeks had yet gained. Achilles' wrath was great. He was too dignified not to let the fair Briseis be quietly led from his tent by Ulysses and the other princes whom Agamemnon sent to bring her away, but he made a deep vow that he would not again draw his sword in the cause of Agamemnon or his brother, and would leave them to fight their battles without him.

The Greeks were the bravest warriors in the earth, but none of them was quite the equal of Achilles in strength, swiftness, or the use of their weapons. The cause of Troy began to prosper. The gallant Hector is shown as he was in his own home. Whilst the battle for a time somewhat abated outside the walls, he returned into the town to desire his mother, Queen Hecuba, to repair with her ladies to the temple of the goddess Pallas, to pray for her favour ; and he then went in search of his own wife Andromache, a princess whose family had been all killed in the course of the war, but who found that his tender affection for her made up for all she had lost. She, with her little son, Astyanax, and his nurse, had gone out to watch for her husband from the walls, and he met her returning. Then there was a most sweet and loving scene between them, while Andromache clung to him, and besought him to remember that she had none to love but him, and to take care of himself, and Hector, while fully bent upon his duty to his father and country, still spoke with sad foreboding that both he and the city were doomed, and must fall, grieving chiefly at the thought that it might be her lot to be led into captivity by some proud Greek, and pointed at as having been Hector's wife ! Then, as if to comfort her after the misgivings he had expressed, he held out his arms for his child ; but the babe did not know him in his helmet, and he had to take it off and lay it aside before he could hold the young Astyanax in his arms, and then, lifting him up towards heaven, he prayed that his boy might live and prosper, and win even a greater name than his father. Afterwards Hector went to find his brother Paris, who was idly amusing himself in Helen's apartments, as if he had not been the cause of all the evil, and, with strong upbraiding words, brought the dastard out to the battle again, though only to use his bow and arrows, which were thought cowardly weapons compared with the spear and sword.

All the great men on both sides fought in chariots— open cars, very low, and drawn by either two or three horses, which were very much prized and loved, and gene- rally driven by the nearest and dearest friend of their master. A store of spears was carried in these chariots, and launched at the enemy ; and when one of these had inflicted a wound, it was easy to leap out of the car, which was open behind, run up to him, kill him outright, and strip him of his armour. Prisoners were very seldom made in battle, and there was none of that gentler Christian feeling that has taught us to regard it as shameful to strike a man who is down, or to insult a fallen enemy. To boast over the vanquished before giving the death-blow was plainly looked on as one of the most agreeable enjoyments of a conquest, and Hector, though so gentle at home, was one of those whose tongue was most ready with these vaunts. Nor was there in those times any scruple as to attacking a sleeping enemy, nor in uttering falsehoods to deceive the foe. Certain oaths and mutual engagements were always honourably kept, at whatever cost ; but that lying was wrong in itself the Greeks never guessed, and they called many things prudence that we should call cunning.

The absence of Achilles enabled the Trojans to gain such advantages that they ventured to sleep outside their walls with their chariots beside them, and their horses tethered near, so as to be ready early the next morning to attack the rampart of earth that the Greeks had thrown up to protect their camp and ships. The Greeks were in much anxiety. A deputation was sent by Agamemnon, consisting of Ulysses, of Diomed, the fiercest of all the Greeks, and of old Phœnix, who had watched and tended the infancy of Achilles, to offer all sorts of amends, and entreat him to return to the combat. Achilles received and feasted them with his unfailing graceful courtesy, but he would not lay aside his implacable wrath. He declared his purpose of sailing back to Phthia, and kept Phœnix in his tent to return with him, while the other messengers he dismissed, in all friendship to themselves, but keeping up his bitter hatred to Agamemnon.

That night Ulysses and Diomed stole out to spy the Trojan camp, and as no watch was kept, they succeeded in making a great slaughter of sleeping men ; and moreover they came on a newly-arrived Trojan ally named Rhesus, who had never yet entered Troy, but lay asleep among his troops. This poor man they slew, and carried off his beautiful white horses, which fell to Diomed's lot.

Nevertheless, the ensuing day was a dreadful one for

the Greeks : Ulysses, Diomed, Agamemnon himself, and almost all their best champions, were wounded, and Hector with the Trojans broke through the rampart, and fought hard to set fire to the fleet. The tents and ships of Achilles were so far off that he could not see what was passing ; but the cries he heard made him send out Patroclus for tidings.   Patroclus met wounded men coming bleeding home, and tarried to bind their wounds, and at last, as worse and worse news came, he hurried back to Achilles, and besought him, if he would not fight himself, at least to let him (Patroclus) lead out his men, and save the Greeks from utter defeat and destruction.

Achilles was moved to consent. He armed Patroclus with his own armour, placed him in his own chariot, and sent him forth at the head of his troops, expressly commanding him, however, not to do more than save the camp, and not to chase the Trojans back to their own walls.

The appearance of Patroclus turned the fortune of the day ; he killed some of the most noted Trojan chiefs and their friends, and drove the rest beyond the wall; but in the ardour of the pursuit he forgot his prince's warning, and not only hunted Hector out of the camp, but followed him up to the very walls of the city, and even launched a spear against the sacred battlements, thus provoking the anger of the Sun God, Apollo, who had built them. In his wrath the god loosened the helmet of Patroclus, and rendered him dizzy and helpless ; and while he was in this state he was struck by Hector, cast to the ground, and then slain, with the usual boastful insults. Hector tore off some of his beautiful armour ; but the Greeks poured in to rescue his body, and a dreadful combat raged over it, with almost equal fortune for a long time, until the tidings were carried to Achilles. He sprang up. He had no weapons, no armour, but he hastened to the breach in the rampart, and standing there, gave a mighty battle-shout that echoed over all the plain, and so used were the Trojans to fly at his voice that they all ceased from fighting, and hurried back to their city in confusion and dread.

The friendship of Achilles and Patroclus had been most warm and tender, and when the lifeless body was borne home, Achilles' grief and lamentations were most wild and passionate. He was, indeed, suffering for his fierce anger; and in the cruel loss he had endured he was ready to forget everything but his keen desire to be revenged upon Hector. Agamemnon was willing, indeed, to return Briseis to him, with a full and manly confession of having done wrong, and large gifts by way of atonement, and Achilles with free generosity accepted his excuse, and forgave.

He would not eat nor drink till his friend had been revenged ; and when his mother had brought him new and glorious armour, forged by the divine armourer, he went forth to the deadly battle, burning with indignation. After a great slaughter of Trojans, he encountered Hector himself, and at his dreadful aspect the Trojan prince fled on foot, pursued by the swift-footed Achilles, who hunted him three times round the walls of his native city ere at length he made a stand, thinking he saw one of his brothers ready to assist him ; but it was a cruel delusion, and Achilles coming up with him, gave him a mortal blow, and stood over him as he died, refusing sternly his last entreaty that his corpse might be given back to his father.

This refusal was not so much out of cruelty, as to do honour to the funeral rites of his friend, who had been slain by Hector. But the other Greeks had not the same excuse when each in turn struck at the corpse in revenge for his former attacks, and Achilles finally dragged it to his tent, fastened by thongs through the ancles, and left it lying on the sand. Then he celebrated the obsequies of Patroclus after the Greek fashion. A huge pile was built up of trunks of trees, the body was laid on the top upon rich and costly robes, and bestrewn with fragrant spices, and fire was then set to the whole. While it was burning Achilles dragged the corpse of Hector round it behind his chariot. When the flames had burnt long enough they were quenched in wine, and the ashes of the body were placed in a golden or marble urn. Without these rites the soul was supposed to be unable to cross the dark waters that divided it from the place of rest, and therefore to remain neglected on the field was the greatest misfortune that could be imagined.

The father, mother, and wife of Hector grieved even more over the desolate state of his spirit than over his death, and at last old Priam took courage to creep at night into the camp and entreat Achilles to let him ransom his son's corpse. Achilles never appeared to greater advantage than in this interview. Sometimes, indeed, he felt stirrings of bitter hate against Priam, as the king of those who had slain his beloved Patroclus ; but when he recollected his own old father, who might soon thus grieve for him, he pitied and wept with the aged king, and seeing him spent with fasting and sorrow, made him eat and drink, and lie down to sleep on soft carpets and fleeces, and took care for his safe return with the body of his son, as well as that a truce should be granted to Troy long enough for the obsequies to be duly celebrated.

Here ends the Iliad, having shown Hector a loving and tender husband, a dutiful son, and a gallant defender of his country, though scarcely so brave as many of the Greeks besides Achilles. It is the sadness of being champion of a losing cause that has chiefly endeared him to most minds, and Achilles' own consciousness of his doom gives him much of the same interest. The tenderness of Achilles' heart, and the dignity of all he does or says, combine, too, with his generosity to make him be regarded as worthy of all honour, as well as with the admiration due to his transcendant strength, courage, and beauty. The haughty pride, the unbending anger, the bloody revenge, were thought only merits by the heathens, whose model he was ; and indeed, as Homer drew him, he had more compassion and pity than any other man of his time, so well did Homer know that the most truly brave would be the most truly gentle.

Achilles soon met his fate, being treacherously slain by an arrow from the bow of Paris. He had left a young son at home named Pyrrhus, who was just old enough to be sent for to join the Grecian host, and soon after Paris was struck by a poisoned arrow. He went back to his first love, Œnone, a shepherdess on Mount Ida, whom he had deserted for Helen, in hopes she could heal him ; but she failed to do so, and he died, leaving his name a bye-word of disgrace. Still, however, Troy held out, even though Ulysses and Diomed by night climbed the walls, and stole away a little image of the goddess Pallas, which was thought a charm to secure the city from being taken.

At last Ulysses devised a plan, according to which all the Greeks embarked and sailed away, abandoning the siege, and leaving nothing behind them but an enormous horse made of timber, which stood on the sea-shore ; and when the Trojans came rejoicing out, a stray Greek who fell into their hands informed them that it had been revealed by the gods that if they once brought this huge fabrication inside their walls it would protect them as well as the lost Palladium. Into the city then it was dragged by men, women, and children, all in raptures, and never suspecting that within it lay hidden Ulysses himself, Menelaus, Diomed, Pyrrhus, and all the boldest warriors of Greece.

When all was still they broke forth, opened the gates to their comrades, who were only hidden in the woods, and all Troy was blood and fire.

Priam was killed on his own altar; Helen was captured by her husband; poor little Astyanax was dashed headlong from the battlements of the wall; and Andromache, his mother, became the slave of Pyrrhus. No one escaped with freedom except those who followed Æneas, a prince of the royal line of Troy, who, after many wanderings and adventures, reached Italy, and was regarded as the ancestor of the founder of Rome. So savage was the Greek vengeance, so little in their reckless fury did the victors regard the holiness of the temples, that they provoked the wrath of the gods, and they encountered great misfortunes in their return.

Agamemnon was murdered by his wicked wife; Menelaus was shipwrecked on the Egyptian coast, and reached home with great difficulty; and the sufferings of Ulysses form the subject of Homer's second poem, the Odyssey.*

It would take too long to attempt to relate all the adventures and miseries that are there told. Like the Iliad, the Odyssey must be read for itself, and there are translations that give the story and the spirit of the characters so as to make them delightful, even to those who cannot read them in their own grand language. All through the poem Ulysses is shown as a grave, earnest, resolute man, so firmly attached to his small, barren, rocky home in Ithaca, and to his wife and son, that no labour or danger, no promises of ease or prosperity, could change his constant resolution to make his way back to them. He never flinched for a moment, nor lost his steady courage and resource through any variety of peril, even though

---

* So called because Odysseus is the Greek form of Ulysses.

driven by strange winds to strange coasts, where his followers fell a prey one after another, sometimes to savage natives, sometimes to the winds and waves, sometimes to their own folly, till the last ship went down, and he, the sole survivor, was cast up by the waves on the shore of a lovely and delicious island, where a sort of goddess-queen of the nymphs kept him a captive for seven years, trying to persuade him to marry her, and even offering to make him immortal like the gods.

But the faithful Ulysses refused even these temptations, for the love of his dear wife Penelope and of his beloved Ithaca, and spent all his days in gazing over the waters and longing to return, until at length a message from the great gods above forced the queen of the island to allow him to build a raft of timber and put to sea upon it. His constancy and courage, and his devout trust in the great goddess of wisdom, Pallas, who therefore loved and aided him with all her might, are most beautiful and high-minded ; but the Greek pattern of virtue did not include truth. Ulysses, in what is meant for prudence, is always paining us by what (in our English Christian judgment) is falsehood, and sometimes treachery ; and it is worthy of remark that from the first ages to the present day—even though Greece has been Christian much longer than our own country—lying has been the fault most common there ; so much so, that it would be hard to persuade a Greek that falsehood is a sin. So true is it that it is very dangerous to the character to set up an imperfect standard and then admire it.

While Ulysses was wandering, his wife Penelope was beset with difficulties. Scarcely any hope of his return was entertained, and all the young chiefs and nobles of the adjacent islands came to try to obtain her hand and her riches. She tried to put them off, by saying that it would be disgraceful to her to marry till she had spun and

F

woven a winding-sheet for old Laertes, Ulysses' father, who lived in a beautiful garden near the shore. And to prevent herself from finishing it, she every night unravelled all the work she had completed by day, until one of her slave-women betrayed her.

Meanwhile, all her suitors, to the number of fifty, had established themselves in the palace, eating and drinking with intolerable riot and revelry, and insulting every one who attempted to interfere with them, even her son Telemachus, who had grown to man's estate in the twenty years of his father's absence, but who was unable to drive them away, having no power of his own.

He had just made a voyage to Greece to ask Menelaus for tidings of his father ; and returning cautiously to avoid danger from the suitors, who would gladly have put him to death, he went first to the house of Eumæus, the slave who superintended the herds of swine which formed great part of the wealth of Ulysses. It was to this same good swine-herd's hut that Ulysses, on landing all alone in the island, had betaken himself, in order to learn whether it would be safe to go up to his own palace. He wore the disguise of a beggar ; but Telemachus did not know him till the next morning, when father and son wept in one another's arms, and counsel was taken as to how Ulysses was to recover his palace and throne, and punish the suitors.

In the first place, Telemachus went home and resumed his usual place ; and Ulysses, soon after coming up, in all appearance a beggar, was recognised by no one save by his good old hound Argos, now so utterly neglected and decrepit, but the faithful creature barely had strength to look up in his master's face, and then died for joy. The suitors, rude and lawless men, mocked at the beggar, and one of them even threw a footstool at him, and Telemachus, though with boiling anger, might not interfere to protect him more than he would have done had he been really the beggar he seemed.

Good Penelope, hearing that a shipwrecked stranger had come from a great distance, and was misused by the suitors, came down to the hall, when they had all gone to rest, to see him, and ask whether he could tell her any-thing of her husband. Ulysses told her a long feigned story, and she never suspected who he was ; but she felt much drawn towards him, and when she left him, she sent the old nurse Euryclea to offer him a bath, and wait on him with oils and unguents, as was the custom with honoured guests.

When Euryclea came to wait on the stranger, she saw to her amazement the scar on his thigh of a great gash that she well knew to have been inflicted by the tusk of a wild boar on Ulysses when quite a youth. The faithful old woman knew not whether to rejoice most at the sight of him or to lament for his forlorn condition. He insisted on her secresy, and having laid his plans with her, he slept before the hall fire.

The next morning, Penelope, who had thought of another way of baffling the suitors, came down with her husband's bow in her hand, and told them she would marry the man who could use that bow. She knew that no one save Ulysses had ever been able to bend its mighty strength, and that she was safe from any of the suitors who might attempt it. They accepted the chal-lenge, and even the beggar was to be allowed to make the effort—Telemachus, of course, gladly assenting, and Pene-lope herself feeling so drawn towards him, that though she never guessed who he was, she felt that she should far prefer his success to that of any of the suitors, who had taken advantage of her loneliness to act most vilely towards herself, her son, and their servants.

The great bow was produced, and several of the

strongest of the young men tried to bend it, among others Telemachus, who hoped, as he said, thus at least to keep his mother to himself; but though he the most nearly achieved it, the time of his full strength was not come, and he failed. The suitors, wearying of the contest, put off the trial of the rest till the banquet should be ended. In eating and drinking they were wont to consume the greater part of the day, and they sat down as usual to their feast in the hall, not perceiving that Telemachus, Eumæus, Euryclea, and another faithful slave who was in the secret, had removed all the armour and weapons that usually hung upon the walls.

In the midst of their revelry, in the height of their scoffs and jeers, the despised stranger took the bow in his hands, and its stubborn strength bent within them as though it knew its master. Then fitting an arrow to the string, he discharged it full at the throat of the most insolent of all the unbidden guests, and silenced his boasts for ever. One arrow after another followed with unerring aim, and Telemachus, Eumæus and the other slave, did their part in the deadly work. Death was most richly deserved by the suitors, and their fall was royal justice on Ulysses' part. Yet to us it seems as if their slaughter was too like the slaying of sheep in their pen—unarmed and unable to escape as they were.

When all were slain, Ulysses caused certain faithless servants whom they had corrupted to cleanse the hall from the remains of the massacre, before themselves sharing the same fate. Then Euryclea was sent to fetch her mistress, who had been shut up with the other women of the household in their own apartments while the work of vengeance was going on. Even then, Penelope was slow to know him again, so much was he changed, so long had they been parted, so greatly did she fear being deceived by an impostor. Only when he spoke of what none but himself *could* know, namely, of the living, rooted olive-stem that he had fashioned into a support for their bed, did she become convinced that she indeed beheld her husband, and gave herself up to the joy of his return.

With the happy meeting between him and his old father, and the pacifying of the parents of the slain suitors, the Odyssey leaves Ulysses to enjoy his repose, though not without hints that further toils and voyages were required of him before he returned to enjoy a peaceful old age.

Here, then, we see the three men who were looked on by Greece and Rome as among their chiefest worthies. They are men of graceful courtesy, dauntless valour, intense constancy even in the most hopeless cause, strong affections to friend, wife, and son, and, above all, to country ; and to their country's cause ready to sacrifice their lives, themselves, their all, with unflinching devotion. They all have a strong sense of honour of a certain kind, but that honour does not include either truth, pity to a fallen foe, or unwillingness to strike the defenceless : and yet they are very noble creatures, the noblest the unassisted fancy of man could frame. It is certainly curious that among the three, it should have been the vanquished one whom the Christians of the Middle Ages chose as their worthy, as if they loved suffering better than success ; but this was partly owing to the later and ruder manner in which Achilles and Ulysses were painted in Latin authors, where the one lost all his grace and was left merely ferocious, and the other had no attribute remaining but his cunning.

After all, in the next Heroes we shall treat of, we shall find that the Image of God, even in the heathen man, is more perfect than the fancy of man. The true and living Aristides, Epaminondas, and Scipio, are finer characters than the imaginary Achilles, Ulysses, and Hector, whom they admired.

ARISTIDES.

Circa B.C. 505—460.

WE have to pass on many years to find our next Worthy. In truth, for five hundred years after the reign of David we have little certainty about the name or character of any one except in the land of Israel and Judah.

At last, however, those nations which sung and loved "the tale of Troy divine," begin to come into the bright light of history, or rather they light up a candle for themselves that has shone to our own times.

When the Greeks attacked, or supposed themselves to have attacked Troy, it was as a brotherhood of little states, each of which was marked off from the rest by the mountains and seas that cut up all the Grecian lands into little isles and peninsulas, and render them most lovely and beautiful. The men who dwelt there could not help being mountaineers and sailors all in one, and had besides a most earnest and deep love for their country—first of all for their own tiny native state, and next to that for the entire land of Greece, or Hellas, as they themselves called it.

All nations sprung from that great stock which peopled Europe seem to have had among them three orders of men—a Kingly stock, whence the leaders in battle were taken, and who were thought to descend from some god; an order of Nobles, who formed his chief councillors and were leaders in his absence; and an order of Freemen, without whose consent no great law could be passed, no great criminal punished, no war or peace could be made : and beneath all these were the slaves, who were either captives taken in war, remains of conquered nations, or persons caught and sold by the men-stealing Phœnicians.

All these we find among the Greeks before Troy, but in the subsequent times matters had changed among the little states. Most of them had lost their kings, and affairs were managed by the other two orders—the nobles and the freemen. In some states one of these bodies would have more power ; in some, others ; and there were different ways of choosing who should be the chief managers of public affairs, but in general they were taken from among the nobles by the choice of the nobles and freemen. No Greek ever forgot that he belonged, not only to his own state, but to the whole of Greece ; and there were meetings at certain times at the great temple of Apollo, at Delphi, which belonged to all the Greeks together, when the affairs of the whole country were considered ; and again, there were certain grand meetings for trials of strength and skill in arms, in races, in music or poetry, when every state sent its own champion, and rejoiced in his victory as its own. Great and exquisite skill had been attained by the Greeks in these arts, and likewise in those of sculpture, painting, and building. There never was a people who cared so much for beauty, and in those times it was in a manly way, taking it as a part of perfection, and a token of strength and self-mastery in man, and a likeness to the gods, to whom their most choice and beautiful works were dedicated. Heathens as the Greeks were, and bewildered by the strange stories of their gods, the best men among them were always straining to think out for themselves the truth about the Maker and Governor of all, and their guesses formed what was called philosophy.

Foremost of all the cities both in power of thought and love of beauty was Athens, that which deemed itself to belong to Pallas Athene, goddess of sacred wisdom. It stood a little way inland, on the side of two very steep hills, and the country round was small and rugged, with a rocky sea-coast, and a sea-port called the Piræus, where the Athenians kept their ships. Beautiful temples with rows of pillars supporting pediments richly carved, on which stood statues of the gods, were beginning to adorn it, and on the top of the hill was the Acropolis, or citadel, with a sacred olive in its enclosure, said to have sprung up at the bidding of Pallas Athene herself.

The Athenians had long ago parted with their kings, and had a constitution in which the freemen or people had much power ; but the chief rule was given to nine chief magistrates, called archons, who were freshly chosen every year by the people from among those who had worked up through other offices.

It was in the days when Athens was growing to her greatness that one of the best citizens was born—one of those men who chiefly contributed to cause his city to be trusted and respected.

This was Aristides, the son of Lysimachus, a freeman of good family, though poor. We do not know anything about his early days, but all sons of Athenian gentlemen were left to their parents till they were sixteen, learning in the meantime to read, write, make speeches gracefully, and to know by heart the poems of Homer, with no doubt more or less of others, as also something of philosophy. At sixteen, the laws obliged every youth to come under the training of masters, who taught him the perfect use of his own limbs, and of all the weapons of the Greeks—the sword, the spear, the bow and helmet ; subjecting him to hard discipline to conduce to his readiness, lightness, and swiftness.

At eighteen, he had to take the military oath, never to disgrace his arms nor desert his comrade ; to fight to the death for Attica, her hearths and altars ; to leave his country in better, not in worse plight than he found it ; to respect the magistrates, and the laws and religion of his forefathers. He was then sent forth to form part of the garrison of the frontier fortresses, and be there trained in camp discipline ; and though in times of peace this service lasted only two years, he was liable till he was sixty years old to be called out to fight when there was a war. At twenty, he came to the rights of a full-grown citizen ; he might speak and vote in public assemblies, and might be elected to different magistracies as he attained the required age for them. The highest dignity was that of the archons, or judges, of whom there were nine, with one chief among them, and when after one year the archons went out of office, they were admitted to form part of the great council of state.

How Aristides climbed up through the successive dig-nities we do not know ; but the first time we find him in person, we must think of him as standing on Areopagus, or Mars Hill, the great hill of justice at Athens, so called because the god Ares, or Mars, was said to have been there tried for his crimes. Aristides there is standing under a portico of pillars of rich golden-coloured stone, dressed in the Ionic tunic, a linen garment girt round the waist, and showing freely the bare and shapely limbs of the Greek figure, and he is pleading his cause before the judges against an enemy who has done him some grievous wrong. So clear is his case, so perfect is the dependance on his uprightness, that the judges are about to pronounce sentence in his favour at once ; but on this Aristides holds out his hand and speaks up for his adversary, claiming and gaining for him the right of a free citizen to be heard in his own cause.

See Aristides again, still in his plain tunic, but with the myrtle wreath on his head that marks him as an archon, and himself seated in judgment. Two Athenians stand before him, and one of them in pleading against the other begins with his insinuating Greek persuasiveness to declare that Aristides himself has suffered many a wrong from the man before him. The archon gravely checks him, "Relate rather, good friend, what wrong he hath done to thee. For it is thy cause, not mine own, of which I sit as judge."

If such things as these seem plain enough to us now, let us remember that they were strange to the slippery Greek character, and that perhaps our sense of honour and fair play has been helped on by this uprightness of Aristides and the honour done thereto by those who recorded it. The citizens called him Aristides the Just, and held him in great honour ; but they feared his grave, stern, upright ways, and did not love him as they did those men who were more supple and easy to deal with. But there was a trial coming on Athens and all Greece that made it needful indeed to have men to serve their country who could thoroughly be trusted to love the right better than themselves.

There was always in the East some great conquering power which strove to swallow up all the nations round. At first it was Assyria, and afterwards it was Persia. Brave warriors, of the same great stock as the Greeks and as ourselves, had the mountaineers of Irân (or Persia) once been. They had come fresh and vigorous out of their mountains, and the great luxurious empire of Assyria had been given into their hands ; and though the wealth and ease they found there was fast changing their character and weakening their strength, it had not lessened their thirst for conquest. They had mastered all the great peninsula of Asia Minor, with many a city filled with Greek colonists upon its coast, and "the great king," as the Persian monarch was called in Greece, was felt to be a very dangerous neighbour. Runaways, who had been driven out of their own cities, used to take refuge at the Persian court, where their skill and ability recommended them, and by some of these wretches, as it was believed, the great king, Darius Hystaspes, was advised to conquer Greece, and to begin with Athens, the very prime of all Greek states.

He began to collect his army from "all people, nations, and languages," as his proclamations called his many subjects, and in the meantime sent heralds to all the Greek cities, calling on them to send him earth and water in token of their submission. The Athenians were at this time very much swayed by a very brave and able warrior of high birth, who had been a little king, named Miltiades, whom, though they knew him to be greedy of gain, they preferred to Aristides, probably because he was not so unlike themselves. Miltiades advised them to put the Persian envoys to death for being so bold as thus to insult them, and the Athenians had the cruelty and injustice to follow this evil counsel, although it was always the rule, as they well knew through Homer's poems, that heralds and messengers were never to be treated with violence.

This usage, of course, made Darius and his Persians doubly bitter against Athens above all the other states, except Sparta, where the same act had been committed; and, in the year B.C. 490, an immense army was collected by Darius of all the most warlike nations of the East, and placed under the command of the Median general, Datis, and of the king's own nephew, Artaphernes. On the coast of Cilicia, in Asia Minor, there was waiting for them a fleet of six hundred ships, each with three banks of rowers, besides other vessels to carry their horses; and with these they proceeded to cross the Hellespont, bearing down direct upon Attica, only pausing to lay waste the islands that lay full in their way.

Some fugitives who escaped from Eretria bore the news to Athens that the dreadful host was coming. It was a host, not only far out-numbering the Athenians, but which had never yet been defeated. Famine had, indeed, checked the Persian career on the banks of the Danube, but in no conquering expedition had they yet been defeated by force of arms ; and they were guided by Hippias, a traitor Athenian, who knew all the weak places in his own state. The brave Athenians, however, were resolved not to give themselves and their country up without an effort. Every man took up arms, and each of the ten tribes of Athens elected its own general. One of these was Aristides, another was Miltiades, and each had the right of commanding for one day. A messenger was sent off to ask the aid of the Spartans, and actually walked the whole hundred and fifty miles from Athens to Sparta in forty-eight hours ; but his speed was to no purpose, for the Spartans had a superstition which forbade them to begin an undertaking till the moon was full, and as this would not be for five days, Athens might be in ruins before they had their armour on. The messenger hastened back with the unwelcome reply ; but by the time he reached home the great Persian fleet was already in Marathon Bay, which was only separated from Athens itself by twenty-two miles of mountain road, over the ridge of Mount Pentelicus. Under the shelter of a projecting cape the ships were safely landing the army upon a broad smooth beach, six miles long and between one and two miles wide before the ground began to slope upwards, for some distance gently, but as it rose higher, the rocks became steep and rugged Hippias had no doubt directed the Persians to this spot, because it was the only one in Attica where they could make much use of their horses.

There was a council held among the ten generals, some

of them wanted to wait for the Spartans, and only defend the city. The only one among them who had fought both against and for the Persians was Miltiades, and he strongly advised that they should be attacked at once on the shore at Marathon. Aristides sided with him, and this bold measure was decided on ; and at the same time Aristides, more anxious for the welfare of his country than for glory for himself, and seeing that the army could not be properly led while the commander was continually changed, gave up his own day to Miltiades, and this good example was followed by the other eight generals ; but Miltiades was still too cautious to begin the battle until the day of his own turn, lest any general should repent of having resigned, and dispute his commands.

The little army had only ten thousand of the fully-armed men, all on foot, and wearing for protection brass helmets with horsehair crests, breastplates with a long fringe of strips of leather hanging from their lower edge, greaves of brass on their legs, and a round leathern shield guarded with brass or gold on their left arm. Each carried a heavy spear and a sword, and their slaves, more lightly armed, would supply them with fresh spears. At Marathon they met a thousand warriors sent forth to their assistance by the brave and grateful little city of Platæa, which deserved eternal honour for its promptness and patriotism. Over the mountains then they marched, and beheld, spread out before them the blue waters of the bay, filled with the curve-beaked, many-oared galleys of Ionia and Tyre, and the broad white beach bespread with the tents of the Eastern army.

Miltiades chose his quarters in a wood sacred to the god Hercules ; and causing his men to protect their front with trunks of trees against any attack from the Persian horse, he made his observations on the mighty multitude, certainly not less than a hundred thousand men, from

whom, with a tenth of their number, he had undertaken
to save his country ! In the middle lay the Persians,
well known to him by their light swift horses, their
brightly-coloured scarlet, green, carnation, or blue tunics
and loose trowsers, their pointed caps with muslin turbans rolled round them, their breastplates of metal scales,
silvered or gilt ; their wicker shields, their bows and
arrows, and short spears and swords ; and with them
were the Sacæ, fierce mountaineers, much resembling
them, but equipped with hatchets that could give terrible
wounds. There was a motley crowd besides, Arabs with
beautiful horses, heavy bournouses, and long lances ;
Indians in white cotton vests over their dark limbs ; Jews
with the hawberk of David, the spear of Joshua, or the
bow of Jonathan : but Miltiades cared little for the allies ;
the Persians who were fighting in their own cause were
the only enemies that he felt anxious about. However,
his object was to spread out his line so as to be equal in
length to the Persian, and on this account he left the
centre of his army to consist of but few ranks of men,
among whom was Aristides and his tribe, while he put all
whom he could spare to strengthen the weight, as it were,
of his wings, *i.e.* sides. Thus he drew up in order of
battle where the slope of the hill became smooth and
clear, about a mile from the enemy below him. He gave
the word to charge at a run. It was the first time that
the Greeks had ever thus made their onset ; but down the
slope they rushed, levelling their spears, and all with one
voice singing the war-song, or pæan, that cheered their
hearts and measured their tread.

Never had the Persians seen or heard the like. That
so scanty a number of men on foot should of their own
free will come hurling themselves on their own great force
would have seemed to them madness, but for that fearless
front, that disciplined step, that joyous song which made

them seem like so many gods. They came so fast that there was no time for the archers to shoot nor the horse-men to charge ; but they were themselves out of breath and out of order when they reached the Persians, and the centre where Aristides was could not stand the shock, wavered, and, though fighting hard, was driven part of the way up the hill by the Persians and Sacæ. No doubt Miltiades had known that this must happen. He knew that the allies would not resist the heavier wings for a moment, and would scatter like leaves before the blast, and he had therefore warned the men in these divisions by no means to pursue and break their ranks, but to be ready at once to close in on either hand on the Persians, who were already fighting with Aristides and the centre. It was an admirable device, and it perfectly succeeded. Down went white turban and glittering scaly breastplate, and wildly and desperately did the Persians turn and struggle to reach their ships as the only place of safety. Over the shore, into the bordering salt-marsh they rushed, into the sea—the Athenians hurrying after them and cut-ting them down, or even crowding after them into the ships. The hardest fighting of all was round the ships. Seven were dragged ashore and captured by the Athen-ians, and another was held so fast by the brother of the poet Æschylus after it was afloat, that the Persians only freed themselves by cutting off his hand with an axe.

Before evening the Bay of Marathon was clear. Every foe who had crowded it in the morning was either lying dead, or dying, on the plain, stifled in the marshes, drowned in the sea, a slave in the victor's hands, or else sailing away in the ships. But there was no rest yet. On the heights far above was seen gleaming in the setting sun something like a star, which the sharp eyes of the Athen-ians discovered to be a shield. They knew there were traitors in the land, and they suspected that this signal had been raised to show the Persians that Athens was left unguarded by all the fighting men, and that a sudden descent on her would retrieve the lost battle.

The Athenian men had fought all day for their homes and children. They were ready to hasten back ; and back over the mountain path, all the twenty-two miles, they marched again on the very evening of the battle. Only a guard was left over the huge spoil of the Persian camp, and that guard was committed to Aristides, as the most trustworthy man in all the camp, who was quite certain not to abuse his charge.

The precaution of Miltiades was not thrown away. The enemy really sailed round, and landed a few men to re-connoitre ; but they met with no encouragement, and learning that the undaunted men who had already beaten them were ready to fight them again, they took to their ships and sailed back to Cilicia, leaving Athens to her glory. The Spartans marched up just too late ; they came to see the field of battle, expressed great honour for the Athenians and regret for themselves, and returned to their homes. 6,400 Persians had been killed and only 192 Athenians.

Miltiades was for the time reckoned the first of the Athenians, but in an expedition that he soon after made to recover an island from the Persians, he failed, and was hurt in the thigh. An accusation was brought against him that he had misused the public money : and he was sentenced to pay a heavy fine and thrown into prison, where he died of his wound. Men, who felt want of integrity so great a crime as thus to treat their greatest captain, would, it might have seemed, be likely to honour above all men him whom they called "the Just ;" but Aristides was too grave and unbending to be a favourite, and he had an enemy, a plausible, ambitious citizen named Themistocles, who found so upright a man a hindrance to his schemes. The Athenians were so much afraid of any one citizen exalting himself over the rest, that they had a law that, if most of them agreed in sentencing any man to leave the city, he should be forced to go away for a term of years—generally ten. The votes were given by writing a name on a small tile, or an oyster-shell; these were cast into urns, and counted by the archons, who were forced to pronounce the person "ostracised," or banished, if they found that 8,000 had declared against him.

Seven years after the battle of Marathon, B.C. 483, Themistocles caused Aristides' name to be proposed for ostracism, and he had contrived so to poison men's minds, by whispers that the stern honesty of his rival was all pretence, that shells were not wanting to his condemnation. Aristides met one of the rough freemen of Attica who lived in the country, and was stopped by him and entreated to inscribe his shell, since he could not write.

" Whose name shall I write? "

" Whose but Aristides'?" said the countryman.

" Wherefore?" was the next question. "What has this Aristides done to deserve to be banished?"

" What he has done," said the farmer, " I cannot tell; I only know that I am weary of always hearing him called the Just."

Well pleased to find that this was his worst crime, Aristides wrote his own name down, and passed on without making himself known, and the shell went to make one of those that unjustly sentenced the best of the citizens to leave Attica within ten days. As Aristides took his last look on the Acropolis in its golden light, with the grey leaves of the sacred olive of Athene peeping over the walls, he raised his hands and prayed to the gods that his beloved city might never have cause to regret Aristides.

G.

Sore and sad it was to him to be deprived of the power of helping his country, for the great cloud from the East was gathering up for another tempest. Darius had been three years dead, but his son Xerxes had ever since been gathering together a multitude of armies with which to overwhelm the little insolent states who had dared to defy and defeat the Great King. All his doings were like those of giants or of gods ; he carried with him a crowd of tributary kings and princes ; he bridged the Hellespont for the passage of his army ; and began to sever Mount Athos from the mainland to make a way for his fleet, and he boasted as though all power on earth were given to him.

The Greeks were resolved to do their utmost, but it was with failing hearts. They might singly be better warriors than the Persians, but though it be easy to kill a dozen locusts, who can resist a swarm ? However, a council of deputies from all the states met at the isthmus of Corinth, and took measures for defence. Aristides was all this time in the island of Ægina, which lies at the entrance of the Saronic gulf that runs up to the isthmus of Corinth, between Attica and the Peloponnesus. As a banished man, he had no place in the Greek ranks ; but he used all the weight which having fought at Marathon could give him to encourage all who came in his way to be brave and stedfast.

The tidings were worse and worse. Xerxes was over the Hellespont : the Pass of Tempe, which Themistocles with the Athenian troops was sent to guard, was found untenable, and they had retreated. Thermopylæ was strewn with the corpses of the glorious Leonidas and his three hundred, and there was nothing between the enemy and the choicest provinces of Greece. The Peloponnesus, with its wild rocky coasts, and the narrow neck that joined it to the mainland, might yet be saved, and the council resolved to build a wall across the isthmus, and fight hard in defence of that, while the fleet, collected from all the states, should try to prevent a landing from the multitudinous ships gathered by Xerxes from Tyre, Zidon, Asia Minor, and Egypt. Attica was outside the wall. What was to become of her and her children ?

The fleet had all gathered in the Saronic gulf, near the isthmus, and round the island of Salamis, which lay further in than that of Ægina ; and Aristides might see each vessel making for the Piræus, the port of Attica, and returning again heavily laden with women, children, and household stores. Some came to Ægina, some sailed for Træzene, but most only went as far as Salamis, and then returned for a fresh freight. If Athens could not be saved, at least the enemy should find nothing there but rocks and empty houses on which to wreak his fury. Only a few persons refused to quit the Acropolis, and these fell a prey to the enemy. Flames and smoke rising far above the Athenian hills made only too plain to the sad watchers in Salamis and Ægina the fate of the lovely city of their pride.

All the men were on board the ships ; of which Athens possessed two hundred, while all the other states put together made up only a hundred and sixty-six. These vessels were all drawn up in that bay of the isle of Salamis which is turned towards Attica, but down along the coast were coming on the thousand ships of Persia, and six days after the burning of Athens they could be seen from Ægina, spreading their purple sails, and plying their many oars on the Archipelago, while Xerxes reviewed them from his throne on Mount Citheron. And at the same time reports reached Aristides that the captains at Salamis were so much alarmed at the notion of being caught and shut up within the Saronic gulf, that they wanted to sail away while the sea was still open. But on the evening after the review, they were still within their bay, and the Persian fleet, rowing steadily and surely, came, with all the great Phœnician ships, not only into the gulf, but into the very strait itself; and there they lay, moored in a double line along the coast of Attica, shutting the little Grecian fleet into its narrow bay, and as sure of it, apparently, as a beast of prey of the victim within its hole.

Aristides could bear inaction no longer. He must warn his fellow-citizens and die with them. At nightfall he took boat, and through the very midst of the enemy's ships he cautiously made his way, and safely gained the Greek fleet. The captains were still in council, he was told, disputing whether to sail away or give battle. He found his way to the place where the council was sitting, and sent in word that a stranger desired to speak with Themistocles. The Athenian captain came forth.

" Themistocles," said Aristides, "we are still rivals; but let our strife be which can best serve our country. I am come to tell you that it is waste of words to debate whether to fly from this place. We are surrounded. Leave it we cannot, save by cutting our way through the enemy."

Themistocles took the frank hand held out to him, and said, " I accept your rivalry, and will not be out-done by you ;" and then he exultingly confided to Aristides that this was the very news he wished for. He had no fears but that the Greeks would fight when forced to do so, and he saw the fatal error of losing all their advantages in the land-locked bay, with all its currents of wind, so puzzling to strangers ; but he had entreated and argued in vain—he had even threatened to sail off with his two hundred ships and found a new Athens in Italy ; and at last, finding himself only able to delay and lengthen out the dispute, he had feigned himself a traitor to the Greek cause, and had sent a message by a slave to Xerxes that the fleet was in a trap, and the leaders all in a state of dissension, and that now was the time to fall upon them. He declared that Aristides must take his own tidings to the council, for that if he related them they would be supposed to be an invention of his own. He had learnt the use of a man whose word was beyond a doubt. And thus, when Aristides entered among the citizens, all exiles as much as himself, his ostracism was at an end.

All doubt about the battle was over : the Greeks had only each man to repair to his ship and make it ready for action : and ere they dispersed to do this, Themistocles is said to have made them a speech reminding them of all that was noble and beautiful in the life of a free Greek compared with that of a Persian slave. Morning saw all the Greek galleys manned, the rowers at their oars, the warriors on their decks, and Xerxes repaired to his mountain throne to overlook the fight, with a scribe by his side to note down the conduct of the fleet of each ally.

At first the Greek fleet remained motionless. The truth was, that Themistocles was waiting till a breeze should spring up, which the Athenians knew was sure to come from the hills at a certain time of the day, and which would much disturb the motions of the great Phœnician vessels. And even when the Persian armament, supposing him afraid to come out, began to bear down on the line of Greeks, the vessels were backed, some say from fear, others from Themistocles' desire to draw his enemies within the horns of the bay, where their whole force could not be used. When this was done a single ship darted forward, and struck a Persian galley, and then, each man raising the mighty battle-song, the whole Greek line was impelled forward to dash against the hostile ships.

The breeze was setting in, and moreover the Persians had been at work all night, taking up their stations. They

fought bravely, but they were too close together to man-
œuvre properly : the oars of different vessels got entangled
together and broken, their foremost ships were run down
as the Greeks clashed against them, and a terror fell upon
them. The different nations of the fleet did not care for
one another ; but in their haste their ships went rushing
upon each other, heedless whom they sank so that they
might escape themselves. Two hundred Persian ships
were thus destroyed, and the whole armament routed,
scattered and confused, while the Greeks rode proudly
masters of the Saronic gulf, with the loss of only forty
vessels.

Aristides, having no ship, was not in the sea-fight. A
body of choice Persian troops had been landed on the
little island of Psyltaleia, and so soon as the battle began
to show itself to incline to the Greek cause, he collected
some soldiers and some boats, and made for the island.
The Persians were driven into a corner, and after a brave
defence were all killed, except three nephews of Xerxes,
whom Aristides sent captives to Themistocles. The belief
that human sacrifices might avail on great occasions was
not extinct among the Greeks, and at the bidding of a
soothsayer the unhappy youths were offered up to the
god Bacchus.

The Greeks were yet far from safe. The Persian fleet
still far outnumbered their own, and Xerxes still looked
down on them from the hills with his monstrous land
army, and even threatened to build a causeway across the
strait, and come to hunt them out of Salamis ; but he
was full of alarm and rage, and he let his anger fall on
the Phœnicians, whom he threatened and punished so
furiously that all the crews deserted in the night, and took
their ships home to their own cities. Without them the
fleet could do nothing. Themistocles had taken Aristides
into his counsel so completely that he proposed to him

to sail at once to the Hellespont, and there break down the bridge so as to cut Xerxes off from his own country; but Aristides represented the extreme danger of driving so dangerous an enemy to stand at bay, and the design was given up. Only the wily Themistocles contrived to give a hint of it to the Persian king, who was so terrified at the possibility, that he instantly marched off northward, and hurried home, to secure his own person, leaving however his army, under his General Mardonius, in Thessaly.

Aristides then returned with his fellow-citizens to try to build up their burnt houses and to sow their land, and all the winter they remained at peace, though very poor and suffering; but with early spring came Alexander, king of Macedon, the northern part of Greece, which the Persians had subdued. He came with a message from the Great King, proposing to rebuild the city, make the Athenians lords of all Greece, and offer no damage to their territory if they would engage to remain quiet during the coming campaign. The Spartans were so alarmed lest the Athenians should accept this proposal, that they sent off another embassy, offering a refuge to all the old people, women, and children in Lacedæmonia, and to feed them there. The answer was prompted by the high mind of Aristides. The Athenians said that they could forgive the Persians for fancying that everything could be bought with money, but that they were hurt that the Spartans could fancy that because they were in poverty *now*, they could so forget their former valour as only to serve their country for hire of bread! The treasure of the whole world, they said, was nothing to them in comparison with the freedom of Greece!

And when the Persians again marched into Attica, these brave men again placed their families in their ships and withdrew to Salamis; but the Spartans, though tardily, came to their help, and Mardonius retreated, thinking it better to fight in the plains of Thessaly than the mountains of Attica. The Greeks were mustering in full force for a decisive battle, to drive away their enemies. and Aristides was the general chosen by the Athenians to command the 8,000 men they sent to join the main army which was led by Pausanias, one of the kings of Sparta. It must have well pleased the Athenians that the place where the Persians awaited the battle was near the gallant little town of Platæa, which had so readily come to their help in their extremity. But just before the fight, the Athenians had a sharp dispute with the Tegeans, as to who had a right to the station of honour. The most honourable of all was held by the Spartans, but the second post was claimed by both Athens and Tegea, till Aristides, aware that the chief evil was dissension, came forward saying, " The time befits not for contention. The place neither takes away nor adds to honour. Whatever place the Spartans may assign to us, we will strive not to disgrace our former doings, for we are come not to differ with our friends, but to fight with our enemies; not to praise our forefathers, but to show ourselves valiant men ; and it is this battle that must show what is to be thought of each city, captain, or soldier ! "

When we find how many battles have been lost by disputes as to the place of honour, we see that there was no small wisdom and forbearance in Aristides when he thus yielded the coveted post. The Spartan king, however, decided in favour of the Athenians, knowing them to be the only Greeks who had beaten the Persians often enough to be trusted against them. At night a horseman rode up to the camp of the Athenians, and desired to speak with Aristides. He made himself known as Alexander of Macedon, and brought tidings that the Persians were resolved to fall on the Greek camp early the next morning. It was treason indeed to his Persian lords to betray these counsels ; but he was so much a Greek in heart, and in such unwilling servitude, that he could not bear to leave his countrymen unwarned. He then rode back to the Persian camp, while Aristides sent notice to Pausanias.

The battle did not after all take place the next day, for there were various marchings and counter-marchings, chiefly because Pausanias wished the Athenians to be opposed to the native Persians, and Mardonius on the other hand wished the Persians to attack the Spartans, knowing that a troop of that people had at least been slain at Thermopylæ. It ended at last in the whole brunt of the battle being between the Spartans and Persians, and between the Athenians and the Thebans, a Greek nation, who, like the Macedonians, had been forced into fighting in the Persian cause.

No other divisions of either army fought heartily, and Sparta and Athens both were completely successful, though with heavy loss, but far less than they inflicted on the enemy. Mardonius was killed, and his troops fled in all haste, making the best of their way round the northern countries towards the Hellespont. Thus the battle of Platæa completed the great work of rescuing Greece from becoming the slave of Persia. But though Pausanias held the foremost place of command, it may be doubted whether that great battle would ever have been won had the Athenians not been led by a man so patient, forbearing, and unselfish as their Aristides.

After this, there was a most joyous thanksgiving, and dedication of the choicest of the spoil to the gods, while the united fleet proceeded to deliver the Greek islets from the Persian power. It is said that Themistocles came to Aristides, and told him that he had a plan for making Athens the greatest of all Greek cities. It was, that now

all the fleets were together, to set fire to all the ships of
the other cities, so that no state save Athens would have
any power at sea. Should it be proposed to the Athenian
council? On this Aristides went back to the council, and
told them that Themistocles had a scheme which would
be much for their advantage, but that nothing could be
more dishonourable. And so much did they trust to him
that they never even asked what it was.

Indeed, all the Greeks were trusting him more than
any one else. Pausanias had been uplifted by vanity since
his victory, and was harsh and over-bearing, and the
allies all preferred placing themselves under Aristides.
But in truth the war was nearly over, and soon the
armies dispersed, and the Athenians returned to the
rebuilding of their city. Here Aristides and Themistocles
worked heartily together, and the latter, who was no
doubt the abler man of the two, did much for the grand
fortification of the Piræus, the harbour of Athens. However, Themistocles was a restless, ambitious man, always
striving to get wealth and power ; he was suspected of a
correspondence with the Persians, and was ostracised by
Athens, then exiled as a traitor by all the Greeks, without
however, one effort against him from Aristides.

He then went to the Court of Xerxes, who made much
of him, and gave him palaces, slaves, and riches, so that
he one day cried out, as he looked at the glittering feast
before him, " How much we should have lost, my children,
if we had not been ruined." Yet at heart he must have
felt his shame : and who would not rather have been
Aristides walking about Athens, the most respected man
there, though in a threadbare cloak ? All the Persian
spoil had been in his hands, but he gloried in being as
poor as when he began life.

He is believed to have died at sea, on a voyage in the
service of his country. He was so poor that the expenses

of his obsequies were paid by the state ; and, for the sake of his honoured name, his two daughters each received a marriage portion from the treasury.

What a contrast ! Themistocles loaded with riches as a disgraced exile, despised by all honourable men ; Aristides poor, and living a hard life, but at peace with himself, and honoured by all men for his lofty integrity and brave patience.

NEHEMIAH.

B.C. 456—424.

THE Persians had retreated, baffled, from the shores of Greece to their own mighty empire ; and it is among their subject nations—nay, among their palace slaves—that we must seek our next worthy, a man who, though bred up a captive and a servant, showed no less freedom of heart, courage, and love of country, than did the Just Aristides.

Strange abodes were those palaces to men of high heart and pure life. Once when the Persians had been a hardy tribe living apart on the hills of Fars, the province whence they take their name, they had shown themselves not unlike the gallant nations of the same Aryan stock, in honour, justice, and courage, so that it was said of them that the education they gave their children was that they taught them to ride, to draw the bow, and speak the truth. Nor had their faith swerved so far from the old traditions of the patriarchs as that of the Greeks. They had kept clear of the worship of images, and their only idols were the sun and fire, which they adored as emblems of the great good god, Ormuzd ; but their great error was that they supposed Ahriman, or the Evil spirit, to be a being of power equal that of the Good spirit, and to require to be propitiated. Among them were a sect called Magi, who made it their especial business to keep the religion of the people as spiritual as possible, instead of letting it fall into common idolatry. These Magi seem chiefly to have belonged to the Medes, a nation who inhabited the more fertile country on the banks of the Tigris, and who were excellent horsemen, and more civilized than the Persians. The two nations became joined together under the great Persian Khoosroo (or Cyrus), and in their fresh strength assaulted the great Babylonian empire, overthrew it, and mastered the subject races.

Then came the grandeur of the Persian empire. Reigning over countless provinces, the Great King portioned them out to his nobility, and the satrap, or governor, of each was as a king himself; only he had yearly to collect and pay into the treasury a proportion of the produce of the country—metals, corn, wine, &c.—which was either stored in great treasure cities, or appropriated to some branch of the palace expenses. One district furnished the queen's belts; another her bracelets; another was set apart for the maintenance of a certain faithful camel that had carried King Darius on the dangerous retreat from Scythia. The cities and palaces raised by the Persians were most magnificent; splendid ranks of columns, sculptures like the strange forms of Assyrian emblems, flights of steps and marble pavements of many various colours, still remain to attest the past grandeur of Persepolis, Ecbatana, Susa, and their other royal homes; and sometimes on the brick walls, sometimes on the sides of precipices, are inscriptions in wedge-shaped characters, setting forth the glories of their kings and the number of nations they had conquered.

Heirs to the overgrown, effeminate luxury of the Assyrian monarchs, the Persian kings could not fail to have their minds puffed up and their habits perverted. They were treated, from the time their temples were bound with the royal diadem—a sort of scarf set up over the forehead—as gods rather than men. Only seven nobles of the highest rank could obtain free admission to their presence ; their decrees were irrevocable, their word gave death without trial, and their summons could call together millions on millions to march at their command. Naturally gay and lively, fond of poetry and music, of story and of song, the kings could command a ceaseless round of banquets, and of slaves able to amuse them in every possible manner ; the Eastern story-teller would gravely narrate the stories that in nursery tale or Arabian night have charmed all the Aryan race ever since ; the captive or fugitive Greek would sing the sweet lyrics of his home, or rehearse the tale of Troy ; and some Jews would even sing to David's harp the song of Zion in a strange land ; for the Jews loved their Persian masters. To the great Cyrus they owed permission to return and rebuild their own city, which Nebuchadnezzar had ruined, and the trustworthiness of their nation made them preferred for all services around the king. For when the Persian kings ceased to be mountain chiefs, and turned into the mighty tyrants of half a continent, their peace of mind and trust in man or woman was gone for ever ; they might be murdered at any time, and were no longer able to look on their nobles as friends and supporters, but as dangerous, jealous spies, whom they employed in distant satrapies, surrounding themselves with slaves, who might be more entirely their own, and visiting every offence with all the cruelty inspired by fear. The horrible ingenuity of Persian tortures and punishments has never been equalled in this world. And the effect of this life was even worse for the women than the men. No Eastern monarch would have thought his dignity complete, nor his enjoyment full, unless he had an unlimited number of wives, and their slaves, jealously guarded and carefully secluded from all intercourse with other men, except when they appeared at the king's festivals. On the king's preference depended which of these women should be regarded as queen, and which of his many sons should inherit his throne ; and among these ignorant women, who thought all employment beneath their dignity, the jealousies, rivalries, and heart-burnings this hope occasioned, were beyond all our conception, and their atrocities seem like a horrible dream.

Such was the place where the ambitious designs were nursed of him whom the Greeks call Xerxes, but whose proper name was Khshayarsha—the venerable Shah or King ; and here it was that nine years after his return from Greece he was murdered by one of his captains— B.C. 456.

His third son, Artakshayarsha, the Fire Shah, was then made king at a very early age, and was called by the Greeks, Artaxerxes the Long-handed. It was this king, who, seeing his cupbearer look sad as he handed him the wine at the banquet he was sharing with the queen, demanded whether he was sick, or what ailed him.

That cupbearer was one of the royal line of the house of David, and there was a close connexion between this Great King and the subject Jews. A frightfully wicked and cruel woman, called in Greek history Amestris, had been left as the royal widow of Xerxes, and being the daughter of a Persian noble, held her elevation, and was believed by the Greeks to be the mother of the reigning king. But Persian histories say that Artaxerxes, whom they call Bahram, or the Wild Ass, was the son of a Jewish captive ; and we know that some thirty or thirty-five years back the queen-wife of Khshayarsha had so offended him, by refusing to show herself unveiled before a set of his revellers, that he had deprived her of her rank, and had collected all the fair maidens of Susa into his palace to choose a new queen from. His choice had fallen on that myrtle of the tribe of Benjamin, the gentle

Esther, whose firm, though timid intercession had saved her people from the deadly schemes arranged against them by their ancient foe, Haman. Artaxerxes was the handsomest man of his time, so that it would seem as if he had inherited from her the noble beauty of the house of Kish, to which she belonged ; but what became of her is not known, and we cannot tell whether she fell a victim to the cruelty of Amestris, or whether her son saved her and she were the queen who sat by him when he inquired the cause of the mournful looks of the Jewish cupbearer, Nehemiah.

Already had Artaxerxes, either for his mother's sake, or at her entreaty, shown himself very friendly to the Jewish people. In the seventh year of his reign, when he had scarcely reached manhood, he had sent a large number of priests, Levites, and other Jews, under the great scribe and priest Ezra, with large grants of money and provisions to proceed with the repair of Jerusalem ; but this was thirteen years since, and though it was more than a century since the great Cyrus had given permission for the return of the captives from Judea, very little had been done towards the restoration of the Holy City, and Nehemiah had been hearing a most lamentable account of its desolation.

The fact was that in the seventy years of captivity Babylonia had become a home to the Jews. The elder men might pine for their mountains, their sea, their glorious temple, but the younger generation, born in Mesopotamia, had taken root there. They fed their cattle in the rich meadows on the willow-shaded banks ; they raised grand crops of corn in the fat soil ; they watered their gardens of delicious melons with streams from the canals between slow Euphrates and swift Tigris ; or, settled in the city, they exercised many trades, and trafficked the rich stores of India for the spices of Arabia, or the purple of Phœnicia. So when Cyrus, at the instance of Daniel, issued his edict permitting the return of the captives to their native land, under the guidance of the Prince Zerubbabel and the High Priest Jeshua, those who listened to the call were the few truly religious and earnest men, the old people, who had been born in Judea, and the poor and restless, who hoped to better themselves by a change ; and so many of the wealthy remained that it was a saying that only the bran went home—the fine flour stayed at Babylon.

However, there was rare zeal and perseverance in the two leaders, and they had raised a building where the ritual could be performed, though the elder men wept to see how poor an edifice it was compared with what had shone on their childish eyes, in its glory of white marble walls and gilded dome ; and even then the prophets had rebuked the people's eagerness to build for themselves, and encouraged them not to despise the day of small things, but to look to the happy time when the desolate, fire-scathed ruins should again be streets full of merry boys and girls playing fearlessly.

A hundred years and more had passed, and still that glad day seemed as far off as ever. Jerusalem was beset with enemies : the Bedouin robbers had swarmed into the uninhabited country, and fell on the crops as soon as they were ripe ; and the mongrel race at Samaria had tried to unite with the Jews ; but having been re-jected by Zerubbabel, lest the purity of faith and of blood should be corrupted, they had become the most bitter enemies of the returned exiles, maligning them to each new King of Persia, and sometimes actually obtaining sanction from the court to the prevention of the build-ings. They had persuaded the King that if Jerusalem were once fortified, it would rebel, and that no more tribute would be paid from the west side of the Jordan ; and thus

H

the Holy City still remained a place of ruins, without gates or walls to keep out the marauders, with a scanty population of peasants, sheltering in their hovels among the remnants of grand houses, and a few priests carrying on their daily worship in a mere fragment of the once magnificent Temple.   There, by special aid of Heaven, had they repulsed the enemies whom Haman had set upon them ; and there Ezra, coming soon after with a fresh band of priests and Levites, had made some revival of hope and zeal; but this was twelve years ago.   Ezra had returned to Babylon, and things had become even worse; for Eliashib, the High Priest, had actually permitted his grandson to marry the daughter of the Moabite San-ballat, who was satrap of Samaria.   Tobiah, the governor of Ammon, once a slave, had also married into a Jewish family ; and it was plain that, unless some fresh awakening took place, the worship at the Temple would become hopelessly corrupted.

Such was the account that a traveller from Jerusalem brought to Susa, to Nehemiah, a prince of the line of David, but nevertheless a servant attending on the person of Artaxerxes.   It grieved him exceedingly, and he prayed earnestly for weeks and months, mourning and pining with grief, till at length his countenance was so worn and sad that the King remarked it as he served him with the cup of wine, and asked what ailed him, since "this is nothing else than sorrow of heart."

"Let the King live for ever," replied Nehemiah. "Why should not my countenance be sad, when the city, the place of my fathers' sepulchres, lieth waste, and the gates thereof are burned with fire?"

The King heard him graciously, and asked, "For what dost thou make request?" and Nehemiah, with an inward prayer, entreated to be sent to Jerusalem.   The King asked for how long: a time was fixed ; and Nehemiah further begged for letters to the keepers of the royal forests, permitting him to cut down timber for his repairs. Artaxerxes granted all this, and likewise gave him a guard to escort him across the desert that lay between the Euphrates and the Jordan. Nehemiah then went to Babylon, where he so upheld the cause of restoration as to make a fresh collection of volunteers for the return, with whom he set forth and safely reached Jerusalem.

The enemies of Jerusalem, the Moabite Sanballat at Samaria, the Ammonite Tobiah, and the Arab Sheik Geshem, were so influential that Nehemiah found it expedient to make his survey by night, before he spoke to any man of his purpose toward the ruined city. A terrible picture of desolation he gives in his description of that midnight ride round the spots whose cherished names had ever been so dear to him, going out through one gate burnt with fire, passing round by the grand cisterns made by Hezekiah, and finding the next gate so blocked up by ruins that he could not enter, but was obliged to return by that at which he came out, while all the wall between was a mere heap of broken rubbish.

It was a sight to make a man's heart sink; but Nehemiah collected the chiefs of the Jews, and made them an exhortation which encouraged them to do their part in rebuilding the walls of the city. Each person who had the ability took a portion of the wall, in spite of the scoffs and derision of their enemies. " What ! " said Sanballat, " will they revive the stones out of the rubbish ? " " A fox will break down all they have built," rejoined Tobiah, who seems to have been nearly connected with Sanballat ; but when they found that Nehemiah had been made by the King governor of the province, and that the defences of the city were proceeding so fast that it would soon be no longer at their mercy, they took serious counsel for their discomfiture ; and each pilgrim Jew who succeeded in reaching the home of his forefathers brought word that the fierce Bedouin and the wild Moabite and spiteful Samaritan, were arming to destroy them.

Still Nehemiah's hope was undaunted. All along his works he set sentinels on the watch; he armed the people with swords, spears, and bows, and said he, "Be not ye afraid of them. Remember the LORD, which is great and terrible, and fight for your brethren, your sons and your daughters, your wives and your houses." The Jews responded manfully, and the wall was still worked at by builders who wrought with their weapons at their side, ever on the watch. Nehemiah's own attendants divided the day between building the wall and standing on the watch, with their spears ready to hand; he himself was ever overlooking them, with a trumpeter beside him, ready to sound an alarm at the first sight of the enemy. No one was allowed to sleep out of the city, and Nehemiah himself never even put off his clothes, that he might ever be on the alert, while from their hearts came the Psalm :

> " Except the Lord build the house,
> Their labour is but lost that build it.
> Except the Lord keep the city,
> The watchman waketh but in vain."

Nehemiah, as governor, had authority to obtain provision from the people for his own household; but he thought them so heavily burdened already by the tribute due to the Great King, that he refrained from taking anything himself for the maintenance of his guards and servants, and at his own expense both supported them and kept a table daily for a hundred and fifty Jewish rulers, besides all those who came on business or on pilgrimage from other lands. This noble largeness of heart and hand contrasted with the meanness of the

wealthier Jews, who, having advanced money at an
usurious interest to enable their poor brethren to pay
their tribute, were seizing the crops, the estates, and even
the children of the debtors to be sold into slavery. This
was a clear infraction of the law ; and Nehemiah, fearless
of provoking them, openly showed his indignation, and
annulled their cruel bonds. Everything was finished in
fifty-two days, and the gates were ready to be hung
within their portals, when Sanballat and his allies sent to
invite Nehemiah to meet them amicably in a village in
the plain ; but being well aware that they designed
treachery against him, he answered that while he had so
great a work in hand he could not leave it. After four
fruitless attempts of this kind, Sanballat sent him a slave,
bearing a letter, open, as a special mark of insult, informing him that it was universally believed that his repairs of
the fortifications were made in order that he might set
himself up as King of Judah, like his ancestors ; and that
he had caused persons to feign themselves prophets and
excite the Jews to rise in his behalf. Indeed, the wily
Moabite, well knowing that nothing would be so likely
to induce the Great King to interfere as to excite his
jealousy, actually bribed a woman named Noadiah, and
several false prophets, to put forth predictions of this
kind.

Nehemiah, always firm and undaunted, answered that
all this was a mere device of Sanballat, and when a man
named Shemaiah affected great terror, and, shutting himself up in his house, advised Nehemiah to take refuge in
the Temple, he boldly answered, " Should such a man as
I flee? and who is there that, being as I am, would go into
the Temple to save his life ? I will not go in." He afterwards found that this persuasion had been another trick
of Sanballat to terrify and bring suspicion upon him : nor
was he ever free from the machinations which Tobiah

conducted by means of letters to his half-hearted kindred within the city ; but he fearlessly disregarded all, and ceased not one day from his fortifications or his watch, so that though his enemies had carried their false accusations to Artaxerxes, and obtained a letter from him desiring that the works should be put a stop to, the wall was already built, and they had no authority to throw it down.*

It is inferred that Nehemiah himself went back to Persia, either because his time was up, or because he was recalled by the King; but he must have justified himself completely, for he was soon at Jerusalem again, and with him the great scribe, Ezra, and together these two men made "the dry bones" of Judah to live again, and formed that free and constant national spirit of perfect trust and obedience which had been signally wanting to the Israel of old, but as remarkably distinguished the Jews of the restoration.   It is generally said that a subject people have much worse defects than a free one; but assuredly the Jews, for full four hundred years of being tributary, were far more blameless than they had ever been during their whole eight hundred years of liberty. Much might be owing, indeed, to their having been purified from the ten tribes, who had always been more unruly, more luxurious, and more idolatrous than the mountaineers of Judah and Benjamin : but the latter years of the kingdom of Judah had been disgraced by the loss of all virtues, save a perverse sort of courage ; and at Babylon so much of the sordid spirit of gain had grown upon them, that it had quenched all true devotion and patriotism, except that one bright flame which had warmed the hearts of the leaders of the return.

* We here adopt the view given in "Smith's Dictionary," that Ezra iv. sums up the complaints made to the Persian court, under Cambyses, Darius, Xerxes, and Artaxerxes, and that the seventh verse refers to this letter.

If Zerubbabel was as a second Solomon, Nehemiah and Ezra were the second Moses and Aaron.

The first work of Nehemiah on his return was to hang the gates, and to cause the priests to dedicate the wall by a solemn service. His brother was placed in charge of the gates, and of the watch that was to be kept over them by the citizens in turn ; and a heavy duty it must have been, for, as he pathetically says, "the city was large and great : but the people were few, and the houses were not builded." However, the enemy seems to have been silenced for a time, and the work of restoration proceeded. Ezra re-arranged the courses of priests and singing Levites, who were to minister at the Temple in turn ; and Nehemiah made an exact numbering of all the returned Jews, and found them to be only 42,360. The half shekels they gave as their ransom were applied to the further rebuilding of the Temple.

There is a beautiful story told in the second book of the Maccabees of the recovery of the sacred fire which had descended on the Ark in Moses' time, and had been always used for incense and sacrifice till the destruction of Jerusalem. It was said that the prophet Jeremiah had warned the priests to hide the Ark of the Covenant in one of the caverns of Mount Pisgah, and the sacred fire in a hollow of the Mount of the Temple. The way to the cavern of the Ark was lost, and never discovered ; but the tradition of the spot where the fire had been hidden was preserved among the priests, and search was made for it. Nothing was found but muddy water; but Nehemiah directed that this should be drawn up and poured over the sacrifice upon the altar, and so soon as the sun shone out a great flame kindled and again renewed the heavenly fire. Artaxerxes, it is further said, inquired into the matter, and much increased his gifts to the Temple in consequence of this miracle, which would indeed have specially impressed a fire-worshipper. But Nehemiah says nothing of this in his history of himself, and it is not likely that he would have passed over so signal a wonder. Indeed, it seems that these great restorers worked on in strong faith and obedience, without any supernatural token to cheer them.

The great turning-point of their work was when the Sabbath month came, the month that was kept in memory of the escape into the wilderness free from Egyptian bondage, and which likewise served as the thanksgiving-time for the ingathering of the fruits of the earth.

After the blowing of the silver trumpets on the day of the new moon that brought in the month of rest, the assembled people intreated that they might hear the Law of Moses, now grievously forgotten, and from morning till mid-day Ezra stood upon a stage of wood, reading from the Pentateuch in its original Hebrew; but as the Jews had for the most part forgotten their grand old tongue, and spoke the dialect now called Aramaic, at every pause other Levites interpreted his words. The awful tale of the cloud, the voice, the trumpet on Mount Sinai, was as a thing new to them ; and when they heard those threats in Leviticus xxvi. and the latter chapters of Deuteronomy, which they had known to be so awfully fulfilled, and knew for the first time how far they themselves fell short of the terrible purity of the standard enjoined on them, they fell on their faces praying for mercy, and weeping so bitterly that Nehemiah, Ezra, and the rest went about among them cheering them, and telling them that this was a good day of the LORD, and that they should keep the festival by joyous feasting and sending portions of their good things to the poor.

And then was kept the beautiful Feast of Tabernacles, when each family went forth and gathered long boughs of willow and pine, myrtle and palm, and wove them into booths in memory of the tents of Israel. And the dreary ruins of the streets of Jerusalem all became a succession of evergreen bowers, where the people lodged through the clear autumn nights of that pleasant week—joining early each morning in the Temple service, consisting of sacrifices at the altar and of Psalms chanted on the steps by the full body of priests and musical Levites, and waving the boughs they bore in their hands, or offering their own tithe of their produce ; then came further readings of the Scripture, and the latter part of the day was kept in joyous feastings under their bowers, when friends met from each part of the land of Judah, and pilgrims from Babylonia learnt to know the sons of their fathers' friends.

Such happy days as these had taught the people that their Law was beauteous and loving, before there came the true day of mourning, the Day of Atonement, when the High Priest confessed all their national sins, and bound them as it were on the head of the scape-goat to be borne off into the Desert, and entered alone into the Holy of Holies to make intercession for them. On that day there was true bewailing of their sin. Each person whose conscience had been touched as he heard the rule of the Law made confession of his own sin, and a grand and beautiful general confession and prayer was offered up in the name of all as they stood, or knelt, or lay prostrate on their faces in courts of the Temple. Afterwards, each man bound himself by promise, vow, and seal to keep the covenant he had newly learnt to understand, and to conform himself to those observances which had been impossible while there was no Temple. Ezra provided against the Law being ever again completely forgotten by establishing a service in every town and village to be held on the Sabbath day. Sacrifice was only permitted at the Temple, but prayers were made, Psalms sung, and the Scripture read and interpreted in these assemblies or synagogues, and this more than any other institution contributed to preserve the strong faith and hope that upheld the Jews through every later trial. Ezra likewise collected all the Books of the Prophets, compiled the Histories of the Kings from various chronicles, and gathered together and arranged the Psalms that had been composed since Josiah's time, working under the guidance of Inspiration, and leaving the Old Testament in the complete state in which we have it. Nehemiah seems to have collected the uninspired literature of the Jews into a library; but this must have been lost in the after-troubles of Jerusalem, and only a few fragments remain to us in the Apocrypha.

Nehemiah was Tirshatha for twelve years; but part of the time he must have been absent from Judea, for he tells us that in the thirty-second year of Artaxerxes he came home after an absence, and found that Eliashib, the High Priest, was preparing rooms among the priests' chambers over the Temple cloisters for Tobiah the Ammonite. Nehemiah, aware that this was against the Law, cast all Tobiah's property out; and indeed there had begun a great reformation in the matter of the Jews' marriages. For ordinary persons to marry a heathen woman was scarcely lawful, though it had been just tolerated; but a priest was expressly forbidden to contract such a union, and was thereby disqualified for his office. Many of the priests had come to Ezra when they heard this injunction, and had with tears confessed their error; and these on putting away their heathen wives were permitted to continue their office. It might seem a hard measure; but as the priesthood went from father to son, it was the only mode of preventing vain pagan fancies being breathed into the priesthood by their mothers. The son-in-law of Sanballat and grandson of the High Priest was the prime offender, and he would neither put away his wife nor quit his office until Nehemiah deposed him; whereupon he repaired to

Samaria, and Sanballat built a Temple for him on Mount
Gerizim, where Joshua had engraven the Law, and this
continued for centuries to be the place of the irregular
worship of the Samaritans.

Nehemiah's other reforms at this time consisted in
enforcing the observance of the Sabbath, preventing laden
animals from being admitted at the gates, and the Tyrian
fishermen from selling fish in their streets on that day.
He ends his own history with his oft-repeated prayer,
"Remember me, O my God, for good," and we may rest
secure that that prayer was granted to this "restorer of
the breach," this most brave and single-hearted man,
though we know no more of his history, except a tradition
that he died in Persia in an honoured old age. His
companion Ezra is said to have died on the journey
between Babylon and Jerusalem, and a tomb in the desert
is called after his name, and has never ceased to be
honoured by the Jews.

His master Artaxerxes reigned 41 years, and was much
esteemed and respected ; but he did not escape the usual
lot of Persian kings, being stabbed in his sleep in the
year 424.

Nehemiah was no warrior,—he never fought a battle ;
but the resolution with which day and night he kept his
armed watch around those shattered bulwarks with
swarms of enemies without and traitors and cowards
within, the grand perseverance which ceased not from
the work, the noble disregard of threats and treacherous
whispers, the largeness of heart that thought no sacrifice
too great for his God and his people, and the wisdom and
strength of purpose that created a new, vigorous, and
faithful spirit in a conquered, dejected, almost slavish,
race, and made them true and brave patriots—all these
qualities surely place him in the rank of the worthy and
famous men of old.

XENOPHON.

B.C. 440—350.

THE great battles of the two Persian invasions rescued Greece from all further danger from the Great King, and during the century that followed the little country was like a highly-cultivated garden, blooming with the very flower of mankind. Almost all the great works that the world has ever since looked on as models of human perfection were produced during that brief period, and chiefly at Athens.

That city herself, when rebuilt after her destruction by Xerxes, was made as beautiful and stately as art could render her. Her Parthenon, the temple to her virgin goddess Athene, stands in its ruins as a marvel of beauty, and her sculptures, even in fragments, are the treasures of museums. Schools and places of study were provided for her youth in pleasant groves and gardens, surrounded with porticoes supported on columns, where the teachers of wisdom might collect their pupils and discourse to them. It seemed to be the great study of the Athenian mind to make man's life as noble and perfect as it could be by calling out all his powers both of soul and body.

No Grecian state could equal or rival Athens, except the Peloponnesian Laconia, with its capital Sparta. Here there was no attempt at attaining to the thought, the learning, or the grace of the Athenians ; the Spartans despised all such daintinesses, and were galled and irritated that, in spite of these follies, the Athenians were no worse warriors than themselves, though they were kept under a strange, unnatural, stern discipline, which was intended to make them unflinching soldiers, and nothing else. They were as proud and savage as ignorance could make them, were harsh rulers to the other Laconian cities, and cruel masters to their slaves, and, except when actually in the camp in time of war, showed little respect to the two kings, who always reigned together in right of the twin-brothers said to be grandsons of the hero-god Heracles.

Long rivalry and dislike prevailed between the City of Wisdom and Beauty and the City of Pride and Sternness, and at last a war broke out between them for the supremacy of Greece. It is known in history as the Peloponnesian war, and lasted twenty-seven years. Many brave men fought and died in that long and deadly war, but they were scarcely such characters as to come under the denomination of Worthies. Indeed, the Greek whose history is here to be told rather deserves the title from his conduct under one great and terrible trial than from the other circumstances of his life ; and, moreover, he shows more than almost any other person the manifold powers and resources cultivated by the training of Athens in her best days, since he was at once philosopher, soldier, and historian, not in the highest order in either line, but very high in the second rank, and bearing throughout an honourable, upright character.

This personage, whose name was Xenophon, grew up in the midst of the Peloponnesian war, and was of course trained to arms. He belonged to a tribe who furnished the cavalry of Attica, and was, therefore, brought up to be a thorough horseman. Indeed, his love for the animal was so great that in after years he wrote a book upon

the management of horses. His first battle was an unfortunate one; the Athenians suffered a great defeat:
Xenophon, who must have been a mere lad, was
wounded, dropped from his horse in the flight, and
would have perished if he had not been carried for some
miles upon the shoulders of his great master, Socrates,
who, philosopher as he was, was doing his part manfully
in the battle.

Socrates was the most wonderful man in Athens—a
large, burly man, of immense personal strength, and very
ugly features, but with a depth and power of mind, a clearness of insight into truth, and a force of character, that
made him gain the mastery over the most distinguished
minds of the young men of Athens. He had been bred
as a sculptor, but his deep thought and mighty talent had
soon made him a teacher of youth; and whenever there
was a breathing time in the war, when a short truce had
been made, or the hostile armies had retired to winter
quarters in their cities, he might be seen walking in the
porticoes and gardens, instructing the young men who
thronged round him by argumentative conversations on
every subject—war, politics, learning, science. Nothing
came amiss to him, and he had something strong and
forcible to say on all matters. He strictly fulfilled his
duties as a citizen, and also what were deemed the duties
of a pious man to the gods; but he had a strong sense
that there was a Deity above and beyond the gods, the
real ruler of the universe and rewarder of just men, and
that there was a guardian to each man's life, directing
him, by an inward voice, to good, and warning him from
evil. The more this inward voice was followed, the clearer
it would be any hardship or suffering was better than
degradation through vice or weakness of spirit, and there
would surely be better things in a better life for him who
obeyed his guiding voice in this.

Three disciples who listened eagerly to the discourses of Socrates are noticeable above all. They were Plato, Xenophon, and Alcibiades. Plato laid up his master's lessons, and worked them out to the highest perfection of truth that man could reach to without direct revelation from God. Xenophon took them into active practical life, and, while Plato thought, he lived them ; and Alcibiades, the graceful, beautiful, spoilt child of Athens, received them only with his mind instead of his soul, and by his unsteadiness, caprices, and haughtiness ruined himself, and did more than any other man to ruin Athens.

For, after long contention, Athens was worsted. Her whole fleet, through the folly of her commander, was surprised by the Spartans and destroyed, together with almost all her best warriors ; the city was taken, the walls pulled down, and thirty tyrants set up over the city, who in eight months shed more blood than had been spilt through the twenty-seven years' war. This miserable year was the 404th before the Christian era, and though at the end of eight months the Athenians shook off the Thirty and restored the Archons, yet still the city was in a broken, dejected state ; and, without walls and without a fleet, could attempt no great enterprise. Spirited men, in the prime of life, such as Xenophon, would be glad to find employment elsewhere ; and, moreover, a residence at Athens was becoming a trial to a pupil of Socrates, because the populace had taken up an idea that his philosophy was overturning old fashions, and had thus led to their disgrace ; and the comic poet Aristophanes was turning it into ridicule by every possible absurdity.

Just at this time the King of Persia died, and his eldest son, Artaxerxes Mnemon, succeeded him ; but Cyrus, the next brother, who was governor of Sardis, thought that his claim was superior, as he was the eldest son born after his father came to the throne. He therefore resolved to march into Persia to dethrone his brother, and proposed to strengthen himself by taking with him a body of the best Greek troops, who were to be hired to fight in his cause. A banished Spartan, named Clearchus, who had taken refuge with Cyrus, was to be the leader, and he, together with other refugees, sent such descriptions of Cyrus's munificence, that the Greeks were wild to go. They were only told that they were to conquer and plunder the province of Pisidia ; but this seemed to them a field of glory and wealth. Young men ran away from their homes, and even wealthy and respectable men deserted their wives and children. Xenophon, who was between thirty and forty, not married, and with no present hope of honour or distinction abroad, was asked by his friend Proxenus to join the expedition ; but the Greeks had never before hired themselves out to fight for the enemies of their country, and he asked the advice of Socrates, who told him he had better consult the great oracle of Apollo at Delphi. But he had made up his mind, and instead of asking the oracle whether he should go, he asked to what god he should sacrifice for his safety in the enterprise, and was answered, to Zeus the King. Socrates very justly said the question had not been fairly put ; but the sacrifice was offered, and Xenophon started for Asia Minor. He met Proxenus, and was taken by him to Sardis and introduced to Cyrus, who received him with many compliments, and begged him to assist in the campaign against Pisidia, promising to re-lease him so soon as that should be ended. He remained accordingly, but only as a friend of Proxenus, without accepting any rank or command in the army ; and it is well for us he did so, since he it is who tells the tale.

The Greeks had for the most part assembled before Xenophon arrived. There were 11,000 heavily-armed foot soldiers, a small proportion of horsemen, of whom Xenophon was one, and 3,000 javelin throwers and bowmen : with a band of Rhodian marksmen, and with these, together with an immense force of Asiatics from his own province and Syria, Cyrus marched. They were picked men, and all armed much alike, with scarlet tunics, brazen helmets, greaves on their legs, swords and spears, and heavy shields, which, when marching, each man covered with a leathern case, and slung in his blanket at his back. The horsemen had no shields, but heavy cuirasses instead. Marching on, by long daily stages, they found themselves at Tarsus, in Cilicia, and there it became clear that they had passed Pisidia, and that instead of a campaign of a few months there, as they had been promised, they were being led into the heart of the country of their hereditary enemy, far from the sea, which gave them the only prospect of returning home. They broke out into loud cries, threw stones at Clearchus, reproached him with using them treacherously, and demanded to be led back again.

Clearchus stood before them bareheaded, and with tears in his eyes. He told them that Cyrus had been his friend and benefactor in his exile, and that he had promised their services. Faith with Cyrus or the Greeks must be broken, but he would stand by his countrymen to the last. Then he made them see how difficult even now it would be to get home if they quarrelled with Cyrus, and at last persuaded them to send to ask what was the Prince's real purpose. The answer was that he wanted to attack his enemy Abrokomas on the banks of the Euphrates ; but not a word was said about his brother. The promised pay to each man was increased ; and the Greeks, thinking it more dangerous to go back than to go forward, consented to continue the march, though believing themselves still deceived.

The Persians, though well aware of Cyrus's march, had lost so much in valour and foresight since their conquering days, that they never attempted to guard the mountain passes or river banks, and not an enemy appeared through-out the Syrian hills and valleys. At last the invaders found themselves on a broad paved causeway, along the banks of the great river, the river Euphrates, whose name in Herodotus's histories was indeed familiar to them, but more like a name of fable than reality. None of them had ever thought to see it, and they looked at it with no satisfied eyes, when, at the city of Thapsacus, they came to the place which at certain times of year was shallow enough to be forded, though it was half a mile in width. There had been ferry-boats for crossing it, but these had been destroyed; and there were no signs of Abrokomas, the enemy they had expected to meet, for, indeed, he had fled away into Syria.

Cyrus was obliged to make known the real object of his expedition; and at the same time he promised a great donation so soon as he should reach Babylon. One division of the Greeks, who had already been gained over by secret promises and presents to their captain, Menon, who had been born and bred in Persia, already plunged into the river before the interpreter had finished his speech, and as separation would certainly have been fatal, the others were forced to follow. It was now the end of summer, when the waters were low, and all crossed in safety. For nine days they marched along the bank of the river, among rich villages, where Cyrus caused supplies to be brought into his camp, in preparation for the next stage of their journey. After crossing the river Araxes, a tributary of the Euphrates, they were in Arabia, and found the country most dreary, consisting of low, heaving mounds, uncultivated, uninhabited, and with nothing growing on them but wormwood and other herbs, and with wild asses, antelopes, and ostriches careering amongst them. The Greeks had never seen such creatures before, and hunted them; but the ostriches and wild asses were excessively swift, and they only caught a few antelopes, which were a welcome prize, since food was very scarce. They were suffering much from hunger and thirst, and could only obtain provisions at a high price from the barbarians of Cyrus's part of the army. The ground, too, was very difficult ; the baggage-horses and mules were weak from want of pasture, and the waggons could not be got up the hills without being pushed by the men themselves. Cyrus ordered his Persians to assist in spite of their gay attire ; but it must have been much against the grain, for when, a few days later, there was a sharp quarrel between Menon and Clearchus about a matter of discipline, Cyrus galloped up in great haste, and warned them that if once the unity of the Greek army were broken, the Asiatics would be sure to set upon it with far more virulence than they would ever show against their enemies, the partisans of Artaxerxes. They had by this time reached a place called Pylæ, on the borders of the rich and luxuriant meadows formed by the soil washed down by the rivers—a fair, fertile, wealthy land, filled with pleasant houses, where the toils of the march were at an end ; but its dangers were coming.

Artaxerxes was reported to be near, with an' army of more than a million of men ; and Cyrus was resolved on giving battle, declaring many times that it was in the Greeks, with their courage and fidelity, that he put his trust, rather than in the whole host of cowardly, slavish, falsehearted Asiatics who followed him. Still no enemy came in sight while they marched along the bank of the river. Even when they came to a trench thirty feet broad and eighteen feet deep, which had been cut on purpose to stop them, there was no one to defend it, and they all passed safely. Cyrus began to think his brother would not fight, and meant to draw off into the farther parts of his kingdom ; but on the morning of the second day after crossing the trench at Cunaxa, only seven miles from Babylon, a Persian officer galloped up on a horse covered with foam, and reported that the king was advancing in order of battle.

Cyrus at once put on his armour, and arrayed the men. There was ample time, for only in the afternoon was a white cloud of dust seen, which presently became a dark, undefined spot, by and bye flashing with armour, and revealing the Persians, Egyptians, and scythe-armed chariots of the huge army. Cyrus rode up to the Greeks, and recommended Clearchus to fall full on the centre of the enemy, where the king was, since to defeat him would give the victory at once ; but it was a Greek maxim not to run the risk of being surrounded, and the stubborn Spartan did not choose to infringe it, and merely said he would act for the best. Cyrus then rode on to the Asiatics, whom he commanded in person, intending with them to make the charge. Just as the two armies were pausing before the attack, Xenophon rode up to him to ask if he had any last commands. There was a murmur passing among the Greeks ; Cyrus asked what it meant. Xenophon said it was the watchword, " Zeus the Preserver, and Victory." " I accept the omen," said Cyrus, and Xenophon went back to his post.

The charge began, and the Greeks rushed on with their pæan ; but where Clearchus had chosen to place himself, their rush was like using a battering-ram against sand. The Persians ran away headlong, and only two Greeks were killed, one by an arrow, and one run over by a chariot. Cyrus waited till he saw this wing successful, and then made a charge, which was so successful that Artaxerxes' guards broke ; his own rushed off in pursuit, and for a moment the two brothers were in sight of one another. They hated each other with so dire a hatred, that Cyrus, who had hitherto acted with the prudence and self-command of an

European, became a prey to Eastern fury, and crying aloud, " I see the man !" dashed forward upon him, launching a javelin, which struck him on the breast ; but the wound was slight, and Cyrus was surrounded, dragged from his horse, and killed. His Asiatics all fled away ; but the Greeks had so little communication with them that they did not find out what had happened ; but after marching in pursuit of their runaway foes as far as they thought proper, they turned back. They found their camp empty and plundered, and could get nothing for supper ; but still they remained in ignorance till the next morning, when Procles, the son of an exiled Spartan king, came and told them the truth, that the prince was killed, and his army—nowhere.

Still, Clearchus would have been no Spartan had he shown himself daunted, or repentant for his folly of the day before. He announced that he was victorious, and meant to attack Artaxerxes, and place Ariæus, Cyrus's favourite general, on the throne ; and when Artaxerxes sent the Greeks a message to lay down their arms, and submit, he answered that this was not the wont of conquerors, and that Artaxerxes had better come and take them. In the mean time the king offered a truce as long as the Greeks stayed where they were, but there was to be war if they moved onwards or backwards. Before night, messengers came from Ariæus, whose flight had brought him about a day's march behind them, saying, that it was vain to think of making him king, as he was not of royal blood, but inviting them to join him, and return with him to Asia Minor. They therefore marched back to him in the night, and he and the Greek chiefs swore to be faithful to one another. To make the oath more forcible, a bull, a wolf, a boar, and a ram were slain, their blood was mingled in the hollow of a shield, and the Persian dipping a spear into it, the Greek generals each a sword, they swore to be faithful to one another to the last. Ariæus further undertook to guide the Greeks safely back to the coast, but he said it would be better not to go by the way they had come, as they had no store of provisions to support them through the desert region they had crossed.

So at daybreak next morning they began to march, and found themselves going, not to the west, where they knew their homes lay, but to the east. They were not dismayed at this, till, in the afternoon, they found themselves almost at the outskirts of the Persian army. They then got into order, in case of attack; but no hostilities were offered though all night there was an intolerable clamour and shouting among the anxious and supperless Greeks, of which Clearchus was so much ashamed that he sent a crier round the camp in the morning to offer a reward for the discovery of the person who had let loose the ass into the camp at night. However, their shouts had been so terrible to the Persians that the most polite messages came in the morning, offering a truce; but Clearchus roughly answered that the Greeks had had nothing to eat, and dinner must come before parley.

Dinner did come, and, further, an offer to guide them to villages were food could easily be procured. This they were forced to accept, and they were taken into muddy fields and meadows, everywhere crossed by canals and ditches full of water. This looked very suspicious, since it was not the usual time for watering the fields; and Clearchus kept up the most careful discipline all the time, carrying his spear in one hand, and in the other a stick to chastise the stragglers. Thus they came to some villages, where the abundance filled them with amazement. Such corn and fruit they had never seen. Grapes, dates, melons, and palm wine, amazed and delighted Xenophon, though he records that it was at the expense of severe headaches.

While in this luxurious resting-place, the Greeks received offers from Artaxerxes, through a satrap named
Tissaphernes, that if they would undertake to offer no
damage to the country, he would have them guided home
by a track where they might always buy provisions. To this
they promised willingly to agree, and waited full twenty
days for the ratification of the agreement, becoming more
anxious as time passed on ; but at last the satrap returned,
and guided them on still eastwards ; and what made them
further uneasy was to find that Ariæus and his troops
were no longer keeping apart from their countrymen in
Tissaphernes' camp.

Thus they came to the bank of the other great river of
Assyria—the Tigris ; and though their camp was in a
beautiful wooded park, their hearts were ill at ease. However, they crossed this river also on a bridge of boats,
and continued their march, now upwards, towards the
north, in the country where they were to avoid the famine
they had suffered in the desert. Thus they came to the
banks of the river Zab, and made a halt, during which
Clearchus, Proxenus, Menon, and two other generals,
were invited to a conference with Tissaphernes. About
two hundred soldiers likewise went into the Persian camp
to make purchases, while the rest remained in their own,
which they had from the very first kept carefully to themselves, away from the barbarians.

All remained quiet here till the Greeks within saw
parties of Persian horse galloping after any stragglers who
happened to be outside the intrenchments, and they were
wondering what it meant, when one of the soldiers came
running in, bleeding, and crying out that they were betrayed, and that generals, as well as soldiers, were being
massacred. There was a purple flag on the tent where
the five had been received, and they were all killed.

The first thought of the Greeks was to put themselves

in array for defence, expecting the enemy to fall on them at once; but, instead of their being attacked, Ariæus rode up with a guard, and called for the officers Xenophon and two others came forth, and Ariæus then told them that Clearchus had been detected in a breach of the treaty, and had been put to death; but Proxenus and Menon, who had denounced him, were in high favour with the great king, "who," said Ariæus, "calls on you to surrender your arms, as they now belong to him, having formerly belonged to his slave Cyrus."

This answer brought from Xenophon an indignant reproach for Ariæus' own treason, and he soon slunk away, leaving his hearers to the full sense of the treachery that had been practised on them ever since the battle of Cunaxa, and of the truth of Cyrus's warning that *his* own Asiatics hated the foreigners far more than his enemies. They found afterwards that they had not yet learned the truth as to their generals' fate. As yet these unfortunate men were only imprisoned, and Menon, who had been a traitor all along, was in hopes of reward; but after a few days, honest, blundering Clearchus, Proxenus, and the other two were beheaded, and Menon was put to death by slow torture that lasted a whole year.

For the soldiers themselves, they were in the heart of the enemy's country. With a friendly prince, guides, interpreters, and provisions, the journey had taken them seven or eight months along the well-beaten track of the ordinary route to Persia. What was to become of them, thousands of miles from home, separated from it by enormous rivers, which they had no means of crossing; by tracts of pathless, inhospitable desert, by nations upon nations of barbarians, who, so far from affording them food, shelter, or guidance, would look on them as their natural enemies, and injure them by all possible means? A glance at the map, at the positions of Greece and of the Tigris, shows the desperate condition of this band of warriors ; and they had not even the advantage of having ever seen a map ; they had but the vaguest ideas of the relative situations of each country ; and they had been lured across the second river, and led so far astray, that the chance of retracing the former route was lost to them. Even when they had their generals with them, they had felt their case to be most perilous : and now that their chiefs—Clearchus, with his authority and ever-ready discipline ; Menon, with his experience of Eastern places and men ; Proxenus, with his persuasive reasoning, were taken from them at one fell swoop, what could be looked for but that the headless, disconnected, despairing mass would fall asunder at once, and become an easy prey to the treacherous enemy? So confidently did Artaxerxes and his Persians expect that this must be the case, that they had not attempted even to storm the camp in the first consternation, and the "poor condemned army" themselves were left to their stupor of dismay, with no one among them who had authority to command or obligation to take responsibility. Few appeared when the evening roll-call was read ; hardly a fire was lighted to cook the supper ; every man lay down to rest where he was. Yet no man could sleep for fear, sorrow, and yearning for the home and kindred he thought he never was to see again.

So Xenophon describes that piteous night ; and he further tells how he himself lay full of unrest in the dark, musing on their evil plight, until at length he fell into a doze, and thought he saw a thunderbolt fall on his father's house and set it on fire, surrounding it with a circle of flame. This dream seems one very likely to occur to a man in so dangerous a condition ; but the Greeks had rules for interpreting dreams, and on awakening he began to apply them. A light in a friendly house was a good sign ; and thunder came from Zeus, the god to whom

Xenophon had sacrificed for his own safety ; and therefore he hoped : but, on the other hand, the hedge of flame
that he could not pass was only too like the perils that
encircled him. Yet still it was a message from the father
of the gods, and it ought to rouse him. "Why do I lie
here?" he said to himself. "Night is advancing. At
daybreak the enemy will be on us, and we shall be put
to death with tortures. No man is stirring to prepare for
defence. Why do I wait for my elders, or for a man of
another city, to begin?" Here was the inward guiding
voice of which Socrates had spoken, and he obeyed it.
Starting up while it was yet dark, he sought out the captains who had served under Proxenus, and told them that
no doubt the enemy would soon be on them ; but it was
well that the treacherous peace was over, by which they
had been such losers. "The gods will be on our side," he
said, "since we have kept our oath under all temptations." Then he reminded his friends how much stronger
and braver they themselves were by nature than the
Persians, "under favour of the gods." Now, he said, the
needful thing was for some one to take the beginning on
himself, without waiting for the others to act. If one of
them would head the division, he would gladly follow
him ; but if they desired it, he would not shrink from
putting himself forward on account of his youth. All
the captains were rejoiced at his thus offering to take
the lead, except one, who regarded his proposal as mere
madness, and recommended submission to the king. But
this man had already shown himself a coward, the
holes bored in his ears marked him as born an Asiatic
instead of a free Greek, and his faint-hearted speech only
led to his being degraded. The captains then set out to
call together the surviving officers of the other divisions,
and about a hundred assembled, when, at the desire of
the senior captain of his own division, Xenophon repeated

what he had before said. Again every one was relieved to have a practicable course set before them, and it was at once agreed to elect a general for each division, instead of those who had been lost ; and, accordingly, Xenophon, who had hitherto been only a volunteer, was chosen to supply the place of his friend Proxenus ; but though he had only equal powers with the other generals, his clear head, trained intellect, ready speech, and hopeful, resolute spirit, made him the foremost man in that army. And this resolution had a true foundation, for it was real religion, to trust in the support of the just gods, so long as oaths were uprightly kept. It was as near as a heathen could get to faith in a God of Truth.

The next thing was to assemble the common soldiers, who, be it remembered, were all free citizens and volunteers, whose consent was needful to whatever their chosen officers decided. By way of keeping up their spirits, Xenophon stood forth in no dejected mien, but in his brightest armour and gayest tunic, as at one of Cyrus's reviews, and spoke of the falsehood of the Persians, the folly of trying to make treaties with such liars, and the certainty that the gods would befriend the true and faithful. Then he put them in mind of the Greek victories of old, and of their own at Cunaxa, and showed them their own strength. As to provisions, even at the best, they had had to buy them ; now, after the way they had been treated, they would take them. The rivers—they would track them to their sources, and cross them where they became shallow. They would burn their tents and waggons, and encumber themselves with nothing unnecessary ; and, above all, order, strict discipline, and obedience should be maintained, for in these alone their safety lay. " Let each man promise to aid the commanders in punishing the disobedient, and so shall we show the enemy that we have ten thousand men like Clearchus, instead of the one they have seized. If any man have anything better to suggest, let him come forward."

No one had any other plan; every one felt infinitely comforted to feel hope and honour revived, and no longer to be waiting, like sheep, for the slaughter. Every man held his hand aloft to testify his perfect approval; and Xenophon then further proposed that the camp should be at once broken up, and that they should march for some well-stored villages two miles off. They would move in an oblong mass, the baggage in the middle; the Lacedæmonian general, Cheirisophus, in the van, the post of honour; and himself and Timasion, the two youngest generals, in the place of danger, the rear-guard.

Action was of course a great relief, and the whole camp was soon in a state of preparation. A Persian envoy came up; but the Greeks had had enough of listening to the Persians, and paid no attention to him, only he carried off a few faint-hearted deserters. The river Zab, the first barrier, was crossed; and near as the Persians were, they seem to have been too much amazed to try to make any efficient attack. To them, the sight of the ten thousand, as alert and orderly as ever, must have seemed like that of a headless body going through the business of life; but soon they began to harass the Greeks by attacks of light horsemen, who cast javelins and slung stones, but never withstood a charge. In one night, however, the Greeks arranged a protecting body of fifty horse, with bowmen and slingers, who could beat off these enemies; and they altered their array from the one great mass to smaller companies, who could unite or spread themselves out as occasion served.

So they marched on, day by day, through mounds, ruins, and villages, the fragments of the great old city of Nineveh, even then a desolation; the ground, on the whole, being level, and not difficult. But the mountain summits that loomed on the horizon, as well as the arrowy rush of the Tigris, warned them of greater toils awaiting them ; and on reaching some villages full of great store-houses of grain and wine, they halted for four days to cure the many who had been wounded by the Persian missiles. They found that it did not answer to march on while the enemy were hovering round them; it was better to halt under the shelter of any village at hand, until, as the day advanced, the Persians were sure to retreat, being always anxious to sleep as far as possible from the Greeks, lest they should be attacked by night, among their horses tied by the leg. Then the Greeks would march on by night, and proceed for a good distance unmolested.

Just as they entered the hilly country, Cheirisophus saw a great body of Persians exactly on the opposite side of a valley that he must cross. He sent for Xenophon and the marksmen from the rear to join in the attack. Xeno-phon galloped up, but alone, for he had just seen another Persian multitude coming up behind, so that they were enclosed on either side. Just then Xenophon saw that by climbing a hill still higher than that the Persians occupied in front, it would be possible to charge them, and clear the forward road. He asked Cheirisophus which of the two should lead the troop to be detached for this service. Cheirisophus bade him choose, and as he was the youngest, he thought the enterprise best befitted him.

As he set out, a body of Persians perceiving his object, started to pre-occupy the height, and there was an abso-lute race up the two sides of the hill between the two detachments, each cheered on by their own army. In the midst, a soldier grumbled because Xenophon was riding, and he on foot, whereupon the general leaped down, seized the man's shield, and climbed on beneath the double weight of this and of his own breastplate ; but

the other soldiers were so much displeased with their comrade, that they drove him back to his place, and forced
Xenophon to remount, and ride till the ground became
too steep for his horse. The Greeks were on the height
the first, and their enemies seeing this, fell back, and left
the way open.

Pleasant villages were found on the other side of these
hills, and likewise numerous droves of oxen that had just
been sent across the river for the supply of the enemy.
But there was a fresh perplexity. Steep mountains were
seen rising so close to the river, hitherto the guide of the
wanderers, that it was no longer possible to continue an
orderly march along the bank ; and the stream was still
very wide, so deep that the Greeks could not feel the
bottom with their long spears, and very swift. A Rhodian
soldier suggested crossing it upon the skins of their
cattle blown up with air ; but the enemy were seen in
force on the other side, and could easily have killed the
men as they came over one by one on these skins. A
council was therefore held, and the prisoners examined.
These said that there was a road to the east, leading to
the old Persian city of Susa ; and that to the west, over
the Tigris, was the direct way to Syria and Asia Minor ;
but that if, quitting the bank, the Greeks went over the
mountain passes to the north, they would have to go
through the wild Carduchians. There, indeed, they would
not be troubled by the Persians, for no Great King had
ever been able to subdue these mountaineers, and they
had once destroyed an army of 120,000 men ; nor were
they likely to make much difference between Greeks and
Persians, but that if it were possible to get through their
country, there would be found on the other side the Persian province of Armenia, where the two great rivers might
be passed at their source, and the Euxine Sea would not
be out of reach.

This account decided the Greeks, who might hope that foes to Persia would be friends to themselves, and they pushed forward, by a midnight march, over the first mountain. They came the next evening to some villages, which had been deserted by the inhabitants, and there halted, avoiding all plunder and violence, and trying to invite the natives to traffic with them, but none would come near ; and just as Xenophon brought up the rear-guard, arrows were shot at the strangers. All night fires were seen blazing on the hills, and the Greeks augured that they should be set upon the next day. Therefore, in order to lighten their movements, they sent home all their Persian captives, and burned whatever baggage was not absolutely necessary to them. The generals stood in a narrow pass, and let nothing needless go forward ; and their precautions were, indeed, required, for the Carduchians were assembled on the heights above the long, narrow, winding valley through which they had to pass, and shot them down with terrible long arrows, of such force, that they would pierce shield and corslet, and nail the brazen helmet to the head ; and the archers were so light and nimble of foot, that they could come very near to take aim, and start away out of reach.

The second day was the worst they had had yet. There was a severe snow-storm ; the Carduchian attacks were incessant, and Cheirisophus went on so fast with the vanguard, that Xenophon, with the rear, was hurried out of the possibility of maintaining order, and reached the halting-place in dire confusion. Cheirisophus had thus hastened in hopes of gaining the steep path in front before it could be occupied by the enemy ; but it was already bristling with Carduchians, and the way was so rugged that to climb and fight at the same time seemed hopeless.

Xenophon had succeeded in capturing two prisoners, and these were interrogated whether there was any other way. They would not answer, and one actually allowed himself to be put to death rather than speak ; but when the dead body had been shown to the other, he owned that there was a longer way, easier on the whole, but with one pass that would need to be mastered, as his country-men had already guarded it.

Two thousand men were at once sent forward by night to surprise the guard and secure the pass, while Xenophon distracted the attention of the enemy in front by a feint of advancing up the road. At once the Carduchians began to roll down great rocks, which quite closed up the narrow pathway, and half the night the Greeks heard these huge masses thundering down. However, they had not been long on foot in the morning before the trumpet was heard, by which their friends were to announce that the pass was won, and the other road comparatively clear. Still, however, the Carduchians swarmed on every height, and beset them constantly, so that the seven days' march through these mountains cost them more men than all they had lost through the Persians. So strong was their feeling of duty towards their slain comrades, that, in order to give them honourable burial, they actually surrendered their guide to his countrymen in exchange for their bodies on the fourth day, and went on through these savage heights without any one to direct their course. The fatigue, peril, and suffering had been dreadful throughout this week, and had tried the stedfastness of the Greeks to the utmost, so that it was a most welcome moment when they saw a plain before them full of villages, where they could rest and discuss their adventures.

The river Kentrites was before them, and its bank, though guarded by the Persians, seemed to them as nothing after the mountains and the Carduchians, and they gallantly attempted to ford the river ; but it was 200 feet wide, more than breast high, with a bed of slippery stones, and so rapid, that they could not hold their shields against the stream, and were exposed to the Persian arrows. The passage was found impracticable ; and what was worse, the Carduchians were assembling behind them. They lay down that night in much despondency; but once more Xenophon had a dream. He thought he was in chains, and that they suddenly dropped off ; and his hopes were confirmed by two young Greeks, who came running up with the tidings that they had lighted on a ford about half a mile higher up, where the water hardly reached their middle, and the rocks on the other side were so rugged that the enemy's horse could not approach.

At once Xenophon poured out a libation in thanksgiving to the gods ; and they all got under arms and marched to the spot, where these deeply religious men traversed the stream as if performing a sacred rite. The priests offered sacrifice, and each man bound his head with a garland of leaves, reeds, or blossoms, and the pæan was shouted. Then, while Xenophon and the horse occupied the attention of the enemy by pretending to attempt to cross in the former spot, Cheirisophus and the van reached the other side, drew up in good order, and protected the passage of the baggage. Xenophon returning, found himself needed to beat off the Carduchians, who had come up, but turned out not to be dangerous in the flat country.

However, the Armenians were so much afraid of such neighbours, that for fifteen miles beyond the river the country was waste and uninhabited. The Greeks were again in a Persian province, but the governor made an agreement with them that he would not molest them provided they only took their needful food without burning the houses or offering violence to the inhabitants ; and such was the honour and self-command of these gallant men, that the agreement was strictly observed. But they had

K

another enemy to encounter, and a very dreadful one, for it was the month of December, and Armenian winters are bitterly cold. The snow lay in many places six feet deep, the north wind was cruelly piercing, and their limbs were benumbed; some were frost-bitten, others snow-blind; and as Xenophon marched with his rear-guard, he was continually coming on exhausted soldiers lying torpid in the snow, who, when he tried to rouse them, only replied by entreaties to him either to let them alone or kill them at once. The Persians, too, who had probably been watching for this moment, set upon them again; but this effectually roused the sufferers, who started up to assist in chasing them away. Darkness was coming on, and the rear-guard had to spend the night without food or fire, watching over their perishing friends. At daybreak some of the van came back to help them, with tidings that they had spent the night in a comfortable village, where they had taken the inhabitants entirely by surprise. It was now absolutely necessary to rest after their toils, and the Greeks quartered themselves in the villages, which consisted of underground houses, such as the Armenians use in the present day, as being cooler in summer and warmer in winter. There was plenty of food, both meat, cattle, vegetables, and barley wine or beer, which was kept in tubs, and sucked up through hollow reeds. Here a refreshing week was spent, and the headman of one of the villages was induced to become their guide; but he took them through so desolate a tract, that Cheirisophus doubted his faith, and beat him, so that he ran away in the night. Xenophon was vexed; and this was the only occasion on which he and his colleague ever had the least dispute throughout their months of trial and joint leadership.

Having no guide, they again followed the course of a river, till they found a steep pass held by more hostile natives. Xenophon thought it possible to creep round the hill, take them in the rear, and dislodge them. " It will be in your line," he said to Cheirisophus, " since you Spartans are trained to steal, and flogged for being found out. Let us see you steal a march." Cheirisophus retorted that the Athenians were apt to steal the public money. But this was all in good humour ; and though the attempt was made, it was thought so perilous, that neither general was risked upon it. It proved entirely successful ; the enemy were driven away, and the Greeks again descended into villages, where they found rest, plenty, and comfort, such as strengthened them to endure five days of cold and hunger as they proceeded through the country of the Taochi, a wild people, who had fled, with all their families, cattle, and provisions. At last, these were found by the Greeks, collected on a hill nearly surrounded by a river, with only one way of access, and that very steep. The supplies of the ten thousand were absolutely at an end, and dire necessity obliged them to attack the place, since it was impossible to make the natives understand that it was food only they needed. The poor creatures, no doubt thought them slave-catchers, for when the entrance was forced, the women flung their children down the precipice and leaped after them, followed by the men, so that hardly a prisoner was made ; but so much cattle was taken as supported the Greeks for the seven days during which they were fighting their way through the country of the Chalybes, the bravest warriors they had yet encountered, and not afraid, like.all the rest, to come to close quarters with the Greeks.

At last, however, they reached a city, the first rich and well-peopled place they had seen since they left Babylonia. It was called Gymnias, and they there met with friendly treatment, and obtained a guide, who promised to lead them in five days within sight of the sea ; and, at

last, while toiling up the slope of Mount Theche, the rear
of the army heard a loud shouting in front of them.
Suspecting an attack from the enemy, Xenophon galloped
forward to see what was the matter : but soon he could
hear the delighted cry, " The sea! the sea!" The sea,
to these mountain seamen, was almost as their home.
They saw, indeed, the waters of the Black Sea; but these
were the same waves that dashed round their own isles
and bays. They felt as if their miseries were over; they
wept and embraced each other for very joy, raised a cairn
of stones, with a trophy on the top, and rewarded their
guide with a horse, a silver bowl, a Persian robe, and ten
pieces of silver, besides some of their rings.

They had found a friend ; but there was still suffering
in store for them. Hostile nations still lay between
them and any place whence they could cross to Greece.
Through the first of these, the Macrones, they were
helped by a soldier, who, as he heard their shouts and
calls, told Xenophon that he believed this to be his own
country. He had been sold for a slave, when a young
child, at Athens, but had escaped, and become a warrior ;
and he still remembered enough of the language to be
able to assure his countrymen that the Greeks would do
them no harm, and wished only for a free passage and
permission to buy provisions. Thus they proceeded
prosperously through the land of the Macrones ; but the
Colchians stood up in such force that battle was necessary ; and Xenophon's speech before it was, " Sirs, these
alone are our hindrance. We must even eat them raw."

The Colchians could not resist the attack, and fled, and
the Greeks rested in their villages, where they found quantities of delicious honey, which however caused, first,
intoxication, and then severe illness. It is believed that
the honey was collected from the Azalea, which has been
found in other places to yield honey injurious to man.

Recovering from these attacks of illness, the wanderers reached the sea-shore itself, and a city inhabited by Greeks, namely, Trapezus, or Trebizond, where they received a kindly welcome ; and for the first time since they had left Tarsus, more than a year before, they knew what it was to spend thirty days at rest, both of mind and body. Still they had to maintain themselves, and this they did by forays on the Colchians, till the Trapezians arranged a treaty by which the Colchians bought peace by a contribution of bullocks. Poor as the Greeks were, they allotted a number of these animals to the fulfilment of the vows of sacrifice to the gods that they had made in their distress, and a feast was celebrated, with games after it, in the fashion of the heroes of old.

They might well look back with wonder and gratitude. Of the whole number, 12,900, who had fought at Cunaxa ten months before, after all their sufferings from heat and cold, from deserts and mountains, from hunger and unwholesome food, from wounds and accidents, there were still surviving 10,000 fighting men ; and, moreover, they had saved all the women and baggage that had gone with them. It was the longest retreat ever made by any army, and the best conducted. Never did any retreating army save so large a proportion of its numbers, and this was entirely owing to the discipline, obedience, and self-command of the warriors. To our shame be it spoken, we have never had a Christian army which has borne adversity as did these Greeks.

Still difficulties beset them which they did not all meet as nobly as those of the retreat. They were still far from home. Greek colonies, indeed, were placed on many headlands all round Asia Minor ; but these were separated by hostile tribes ; and, moreover, the 10,000 had spent all their means in buying provisions, and even their countrymen could not be expected to maintain them. Besides, as one of the soldiers said, they were sick of packing up, marching, fighting, and keeping watch. They wanted to go home by sea, and arrive at home, like their pattern wanderer Ulysses, asleep in his ship. Therefore they were delighted when Cheirisophus proposed to go to Byzantium, where a Spartan friend of his was in command, and borrow ships to take them home.

Xenophon thus remained in charge, and fearing lest his colleague might fail in obtaining vessels enough, advised borrowing a few ships of war from their hosts at Trebizond, and detaining merchant-vessels to serve them. Also, he advised sending messages to the Greek colonies on the coast, to beg them to mend their roads, in case a land march should after all be necessary ; but the very notion of this made the Greeks so angry, that he merely sent this request privately. Their subsistence could only be provided for by marauding on the Colchians and other hostile tribes. But Cheirisophus did not return ; the proceeds of their forays became more and more scanty, and the Trapezians gave broad hints that they wished to be rid of their guests. Two ships had been lent them. The captain to whom one had been confided basely used it to sail away home, and desert his comrades ; but the captain of the other had done his duty better, and had seized various vessels. Hard pressed as they were by poverty, the Greeks restored all the cargoes of these ships, and merely insisted on retaining them for a short time for their own use ; and when there were enough vessels taken to carry the women and the sick, the weary 10,000 consented to march again as far as the next Greek colony, Cerasus, the native home of cherry-trees, which take their name from it.

They waited some days in the land of cherries for Cheirisophus and his ships, but still in vain ; and poverty, hunger, and home-sickness began to break down the discipline so nobly maintained. After waiting at the next stage, Cortyora, still in vain, Xenophon began to think it would be best to seize some native city and found a new colony; and this being reported, a great tumult arose against him. Several men came forth and made accusations against him of having struck or misused them. But when their complaints were examined into, it was proved that he had only done what was needful to save them. One man who accused him loudly turned out to have been found by him burying a frost-bitten comrade alive, to save the trouble of carrying him; and his character was so entirely cleared, that for a time he was more esteemed than ever. However, the notion of their settling in Asia had so startled the rich Greek colony of Sinope, as to make it collect a good number of ships, which carried them to that city itself; and here, at last, Cheirisophus came to them, having utterly failed in his application for ships.

Disappointed, soured, and reluctant to go home penniless, the Greeks wanted to make some plundering expedition to fill their purses, and offered Xenophon the command. He was tempted by this, but, as usual, sought Divine counsel by a sacrifice to Zeus; and either conscience, prudence, or some manifestation, decided him against accepting the command, which was given to Cheirisophus. But the soldiers had become so greedy, that they expected even Greek colonies to pay them for not robbing them, and when both Cheirisophus and Xenophon refused to be the bearers of such a disgracefu. message, sent envoys of their own, who met the reception they deserved.

Xenophon, sick of the degraded state of the men, whose patience had once been so glorious, longed to leave them and take his passage alone, as would have been easy in any Greek colony; but their distress and his regard for his old comrades, still kept him with the army, to which he was the more necessary, as his faithful friend Cheirisophus, worn out with toil and anxiety, died of a fever at Calpe. The Spartan Anaxibius, who commanded at Byzantium, took a bribe from the Persians to get the wanderers out of Asia, and he transported them over the strait; but he then gave them no help, and was about to dismiss them without food or money. They were so much offended, that Xenophon could with great difficulty hinder them from sacking the town in revenge for the inhospitality with which they had been treated. He persuaded them to forbear such an outrage on the peaceable Greeks of Byzantium; but they remained in great distress, for the gates were shut against them; and Anaxibius proclaimed that if any one of them were caught inside the town he should be sold for a slave. Happily at this moment came an offer from a Thracian prince, named Scuthes, to take them into his service if they would assist in reducing some revolted tribes. He made large promises; but when, after two months' severe fighting, they had overcome his enemies, he turned them off without a farthing of payment; and Xenophon was so poor that he was forced to sell his horse, which had carried him from Armenia, where he had been forced to leave the worn-out animal that had climbed the Carduchian hills.

Again the Greeks were in grievous plight. Those who could find the means had gone home singly; and the numbers were reduced to 6,000, many of them homeless adventurers, grown reckless through the injuries they had received, and discontented with their faithful friend Xenophon, because they unjustly fancied that Scuthes had made presents to him in secret. Hurt and perplexed, Xenophon made a sacrifice to Zeus, earnestly entreating protection; and that very day came messengers from the ·Spartans, who relieved all his anxiety. A fresh war had broken out between Sparta and Persia ; and this experienced band had become so valuable, that an advance of pay was sent to secure their services, and the envoys bought back Xenophon's horse, and restored it to him. He had, however, made up his mind to return to Athens so soon as he had seen his comrades safe to Pergamos, where they were to meet the Spartan general to whom they now belonged. On the way, they heard of a very rich Persian, who lived in a fort with a large household and much wealth ; and as they were at war with his country, Xenophon had no scruple in attacking him, plundering him, making him prisoner, with his wife and friends, and putting them to a heavy ransom, which, together with the booty, replenished the purses of all the 6,000. The soldiers showed that they knew how well Xenophon had served them, for they allotted to him a very considerable portion of the spoil, so that he no longer feared returning home crestfallen and beggared. Well might they reward him, for seldom have such unselfishness, faithfulness, and patience ever been shown as he had manifested during his long trial, to say nothing of the stedfast, hopeful resolution, power of resource, and force of character that had times without number saved them from their enemies and from themselves. It was his sense of Divine protection, his habit of watching for tokens of the Divine will, his loyalty to all that a heathen could discover of true religion, that had nerved him thus to bear and forbear : and this sense of religion had been impressed on him by the great practical philosopher Socrates. To him, then, Xenophon longed to hasten with the history of his manifold trials, so soon as he had dedicated a portion of his spoil to the great Ephesian Artemis, " whom all Asia and the world worshipped."

Then he sailed for Athens ; and, after an absence of two years and a half, landed at the Piræus. But it was

to hear that his beloved master Socrates was dead, dead
only a few weeks ago ; dead, not from age or disease,
but by the sentence of the Athenians.   His teachings had
gone too deep for his people ; a charge had been raised
against him of corrupting youth, and subverting old laws
and customs.   Advantage had been taken of one of the
Thirty Tyrants having been his pupil, and the sentence
of death had been passed on him.   Plato and his other
friends could tell of his noble patience, the calm hope that
brightened his resolution as he took the hemlock draught,
and his cheerful conversation with the beloved disciples
who gathered round him in reverent grief to watch as the
deathly stupor stole over him.   But the great light of
Athens was gone, and had testified almost by a martyr-
dom to the eternal Truth that he had preached.

The grief and anger of Xenophon stand to this day
shown forth in the opening sentence of the book in which
he recorded the sayings of his beloved master.   Never could
he forgive his countrymen for having slain that great and
good man ; and no doubt he showed his feeling plainly
ere yet they had begun to repent of their crime.   He
shared in the hatred that had fallen on his master, and
unable to bear with the place that had shown itself unworthy of Socrates, he quitted Athens, and went to rejoin
his old companions in their campaign in Asia Minor.
They chose him as their commander, and he served with
them under the command of the Spartan king Agesilaus.
This king was small and lame, but an excellent general, full
of daring and hardiness, and with all the indifference to
pain and discomfort that Spartan training could produce.   Xenophon became much attached to him.   He
actually served in the Spartan army against his native
city, an act that is unworthy in any man, but which can
more nearly be excused in him than in others, when we
remember that it was no selfish offence that alienated

him, but that his fellow-citizens had forfeited his regard by their rejection and murder of the greatest man of the ancient world. The Athenians declared him an exile, and he received permission from the Spartans to settle himself near Olympia, at Scillus, a place which they had recently taken from the Eleans. Here he sent for Philesia, the wife he had married in some of his wanderings, and he obtained from the Temple of Artemis, at Ephesus, the silver which he had there dedicated. He laid it out in purchasing lands for her and building a little shrine, where he placed an image and an altar to her, all as like the Wonder of the World, and the hideous statue within it at Ephesus, as he could render it. He put up an inscription, declaring the spot sacred to Artemis, and that whoever tilled the land must offer a tithe of all the produce to her. An orchard of fruit-trees was close to the chapel, and there was pasture for herds of cattle near at hand, with a wooded mountain beyond full of game.

Xenophon lived on his own lands close by, and superintended the goddess's farm, while he attended to his own property, hunted, and wrote the history of his great retreat, and a memoir of his own time ; also a curious half fictitious history, in which he described the first great Cyrus of Persia as a perfect model for princes, statesmen, and warriors. He likewise wrote treatises on the management of horses and dogs, and altogether seems to have spent his time between study and country occupations. Agesilaus advised him to bring up his two sons in the Spartan fashion, but it does not appear whether he did so. Once a year he celebrated a great feast to Artemis, when the tithes were offered to her, and she afforded a plentiful feast to all the villagers round, consisting of barley meal, fruits, wheaten bread, meat, and venison, which last was obtained at a grand hunting-match conducted by Xenophon and his sons, and to which he loved to invite all his old friends and fellow-soldiers. Living so near the great temple at Olympia, where the games were held every three years, he was constantly visited by all that was choicest and most promising in Greece, and was often able to converse upon great questions, as well as to hear all the news of the time from the best authorities.

This happy life lasted twenty years ; and then, as Sparta lost power and Thebes gained it, the Eleans drove out the settlers from Scillus, and Xenophon had to flee to Corinth ; but peace being made between Athens and Sparta, when they made common cause against Thebes, there is reason to think he was recalled. He lost his eldest son, Gryllus, fighting in the Athenian army at the battle of Mantinea, in 362, when Xenophon was far advanced in years. He is said to have lived to be ninety years old ; but there is no record of his death, and he must have continued his record of history almost to the last, for he himself describes the fight of Mantinea, and the gallant conduct of his son. His banishment, and the cruel error of Athens, prevented the latter half of his life from being as useful or glorious as the first ; and it is impossible not to regret the prejudice and injustice he sometimes shows both towards Athens and Thebes. But take him altogether, there have been few men equal to Xenophon in the highest kind of courage, or in noble disregard of self or self-interest.

EPAMINONDAS.

Circa, B.C. 410—362.

NORTHWARD of Attica lay the state of Bœotia, a country with fewer mountains in it than most of the Greek districts, and of more fertile soil, where the inhabitants were sturdy and prosperous, well fed and easy, but less quick-witted than their southern neighbours, and with a rude dialect. It was the fashion to laugh at the Bœotians as homely and dull ; they were said to win at the great meetings for the Greek games by main strength and solid weight, instead of by skill and address, and to play only on the flute, because they could not sing to the sound of the lyre. The Athenians in especial despised their slowness, and hated them for having fought on the Persian side in the battle of Platæa. There were several cities in Bœotia, and these were wont to league themselves together in one body, and choose seven governors, whom they called Bœotarchs, and kept in office for a year, as it would seem, under the guidance of the senior or most able of the seven.

The leading city of Bœotia was Thebes. It was one of the oldest in Greece, and had some of the most wonderful of the legendary stories connected with it. The founder was said to be a Phœnician named Cadmus, who came from the East to seek his sister Europa, when Zeus, in the shape of a bull, had carried her across the sea. On his way, Apollo met Cadmus, and told him to follow a cow, who would show him the place where he was to build a city. He came to a fountain beside which lay a great dragon. He killed the monster, and buried its teeth in the ground, whereon this strange seed sprang up into fully armed warriors, who all were about to fall on him; but when he threw a large stone among them, they turned their rage on each other. Some were killed, and the survivors becoming peaceable and ordinary men, owned Cadmus as their chief, and took part in founding the city of Thebes, with the fortress that was termed the Cadmeia. The highest families among the Thebans considered themselves to be descended from this seed of the dragon's teeth, and bore the dragon as their ensign.

It is with a member of one of these dragon-sprung families that we have now to do,—Epaminondas, the son of Polymius, a man who, in spite of his noble blood, was very poor, though able to give his sons all the training of body and mind that befitted Greek gentlemen. Just as Epaminondas was old enough for deep thought, there came to Thebes an old philosopher named Lysis, who had been expelled from his own city, Tarentum, and took refuge among the Thebans. This man belonged to the brotherhood instituted by Pythagoras, the earliest of the philosophers, who had held up before his pupils so high and pure a standard of perfection, that he is thought to have learnt it from some of the favoured race of Israel. He and his disciples went as far as thought and observation could carry them into the secrets of nature and science, the relation of numbers and forms, the courses of the heavenly bodies and the like, and they came to the conclusion that there was one rule of concord running through everything in heaven and earth, and that the key to this was to be found in the musical octave. The gods, the sun, moon and stars, sea and earth, men and animals, were all meant to form one vast concert or great choir, and only crime, falsehood, treachery and violence, disturbed the human part of the great accord ; while yet there were hopes, uncertain but still earnest, that men who did their best in this life would be refined gradually after death to play their part in full perfection.

It was a large portion of the truth that Pythagoras had thus worked out, that Lysis handed on, and that Epaminondas embraced with all his heart and soul. "Virtue is the harmony of the human soul." That was his watchword and his law, and he strove all his life to act up to it. Much of his time was spent in learning, which when every book had to be separately written out on rolls of parchment or Egyptian reed, was chiefly accomplished by conversations with philosophers, by borrowing and copying books, or learning them by heart. The magnificent Athenian tragedies were now added to the poems of Homer as necessary studies for every gentleman, and Epaminondas was not contented to stop short like his countrymen with flute-playing, but learnt to chant these grand compositions to the lyre, with the perfect accent and modulation of voice and expression that was required by Greek critics. For to him lofty music and poetry were the key-notes of the universe, and all that was good and beautiful in nature or art did but chime in with those notes. Therefore he was careful to bring his own body and limbs to the utmost perfection they were capable of, and, instead of being satisfied with the clumsy weight and strength that the Bœotians tried to maintain by high feeding, he trained himself with spare and wholesome diet to the greatest swiftness, agility, and address, that he could attain, so as to have perfect power over his whole person. He kept the same watch over his mind and actions. He would not speak an untruth even in jest ; he was so modest, that it was said that no man who knew so much ever spoke so little ; and he hated all manner of fraud, injustice, and wrong.

The Spartans, as has been seen, had obtained the chief power in Greece, and they domineered over their allies in a most unbearable manner. In the year 387 they called on the Thebans to assist them in besieging the city of Mantinea, in a valley between Argos and Arcadia, and in the troop which was sent at their summons, Epaminondas marched. The Mantineans sallied forth, and there was a sharp battle, in the course of which Epaminondas saw a noble Theban youth, named Pelopidas, fighting desperately, and falling at last under seven wounds, upon a heap of slain. He sprang forward to defend and rescue the body of his countryman, and all his activity and strength were needed, for the enemy pressed him hard, and he had received a severe spear-wound in the breast, and a sword-gash in the right arm, before the Spartans made in to the rescue, and bore them both off.

Pelopidas proved to be alive, and when he found that his rescuer had been the gentle scholar Epaminondas, his gratitude was unbounded, and a warm friendship sprang up between the two, such as the Pythagorean philosophy delighted to promote. The studies and deep questions in which the elder friend delighted were indeed far beyond Pelopidas, who used to go out hunting with dogs, pole and net, when Epaminondas repaired to his books and philosophical friends ; and on the other hand, Pelopidas, who was very rich, complained that there was one man in Thebes who would take no gift from him, nor share any of the luxuries of his wealth. However, his friend's example so acted on him in this matter, that he lived as plainly as did Epaminondas, maintained numerous poor citizens out of his abundance, and when his friends remonstrated with him, he pointed to a helpless cripple, and said money was only necessary to such a man as that. .

The friends, like all other right-minded Thebans, were anxious to break off the Spartan thraldom ; and the other party in the state, fearing they would prevail, sent secret intelligence to a Spartan general who was in the neighbourhood, and when all the citizens were occupied with a great religious festival, they admitted him and his troops into the Cadmeia, whence they could overawe the city. It was a wicked act of treachery, and the Spartans were so much ashamed of it that they dismissed their general ; but nevertheless they kept the Cadmeia, put to death the Bœotarch who opposed them, and drove three hundred of the best citizens into exile. Pelopidas was among them ; but so quiet and poor a student as Epaminondas was never thought of or noticed by the Spartans and their party. He therefore remained at home ; but he kept up a correspondence with his friend, who had gone to Athens, and he cheered the hopes of the young men at home, advising them to take every opportunity of contending in warlike exercises with the Spartans of the garrison, so as to learn their modes of fighting : and thus he waited patiently for better days.

In the year 379, the fourth since the exile, urgent messages and letters came to him from Pelopidas, asking him with the other patriotic citizens to take part in a plot, by which some of the exiles, with Pelopidas at their head, were to creep into the city, go to a banquet in the disguise of women, there kill the worst of the time-serving Bœotarchs, proclaim liberty, raise the citizens, and expel the enemy from the Cadmeia. But Epaminondas, much as he loved his city, and though his heart burnt at her disgrace, was too conscientious to join in a scheme which was certainly treacherous, and might spill much innocent blood. It did not agree with the law he had made to himself, and he refused to share in it, or even to know anything about it.

L

At last, however, in the darkness of a winter night, when storms of snow came drifting in from the mountains, there was a shout throughout the city—" Freedom ! Freedom to Thebes ! Down with Spartan tyranny !" Then out leapt Epaminondas. He snatched his sword and spear from the wall, and hurried forth. All the youths he had taught and encouraged came thronging round him, and followed where his voice led them, to the place of assembly. And there, by the glare of hastily-lighted torches, under the portico of a temple, he saw his own Pelopidas, safe at home, though stained with blood, and with others of the exiles and many of the residents around him. The plot had succeeded. Twelve of the youngest and boldest exiles had crossed the country in the disguise of hunters, and entering the city one by one at nightfall, had hidden themselves in the house of one Charon. Some in long veils, as women, had gone to the banquet, to which a fellow-conspirator had lured two of the Bœotarchs, and had there slain them, and Pelopidas had killed the stoutest and bravest of all in a hard-fought combat on the threshold of his own house. All the rest of the exiles would march into the city at daybreak, and the people, who thronged fast around, were shouting that Pelopidas should be their new Bœotarch.

So many rallied round him, that he was able to blockade the garrison in the Cadmeia ; and they lost heart much sooner than was usual with Spartans, and surrendered on being allowed to march out safely. Thus Thebes was free again, but of course at the expense of a war, which she sustained by allying herself with Athens.

After six years, however, in 371, a peace was to be made and settled, and Epaminondas, who was one of the Bœotarchs, as the best speaker in Thebes, was sent to plead her cause. The little lame Spartan king, Agesilaus, reputed the best general in Greece, was there on behalf of his city; and he insisted that the Thebans should only make terms for their own single city, instead of for all Bœotia, while Epaminondas answered that he would never consent to this, unless in the same manner Sparta separated herself from all the other cities of Laconia; and he spoke so admirably, that Xenophon and the other Athenians were amazed at such eloquence in a Bœotian. However, they disliked the Thebans too much to stand by them, and as Epaminondas would not give way, Thebes was left out of the treaty of peace, and Athens looked on, well pleased to think that now the Thebans would be punished for their old offence of fighting for the Persians.

Thus were the Thebans left without allies, and Epaminondas could only hurry home to warn Bœotia to assemble in arms, for the Spartans were already marching on them; and indeed both sides acted with such haste, that, only twenty days after the conference broke up at Sparta, there were 11,000 enemies, of whom 700 were Spartans dorn, with their king Cleombrotus at their head, full in the midst of Bœotia, and on the slope of the hill opposite to them, near the little town of Leuctra, were only 6,000 Bœotians.

Nobody seemed to have any doubt how the battle must go. The Spartans had never been beaten, even by the Athenians, when their force was the larger, and many of the Bœotians did not care enough for Thebes to be depended upon : moreover, the Bœotarch whose turn it was to command was the gentle studious philosopher who was thought to know more of books than of armies. The signs drawn from the sacrifices were unfavourable to Thebes, and though Epaminondas declared he believed no omen that forbade a man to fight for his country, he was known to despise all the prognostics that were in vogue with his countrymen, and the general feeling was that it was a question whether to die honourably or submit

L 2

tamely. Only six Bœotarchs were in the camp: three were against fighting, Epaminondas and two more voted for a battle: and the seventh, coming in that evening, gave him the majority. That night Pelopidas dreamt that he had a visit from the spectre of a Theban, who had received a great injury from a Spartan at that very spot, and had so cursed it that it was sure to bring them evil, provided the Thebans would sacrifice a red virgin at the place. Though Pelopidas told his dream, men like him and Epaminondas had now come to regard human sacrifices with horror; but it was not so with the ruder Bœotians: and while the one side was arguing that the gods were no cruel demons to delight in human blood, and the other that the sole chance for Thebes would be lost unless the dream were obeyed to the letter, a beautiful young chestnut mare came cantering towards them, the soothsayer cried out that here was the red virgin, and the Bœotians were encouraged without so fearful an action to weigh on the free spirit of the friends.

Pelopidas was not a Bœotarch, but from his rank was captain of the choicest of the Theban troops, the Sacred Band of horsemen. Now, in every previous Greek battle, the two armies had spread themselves out in two great lines, and fought hand to hand. But Epaminondas thought his best hope was to take the enemy in a manner they did not expect. He would not waste his strength on the mere allies, but drew up his left wing in a column fifty men deep, to fall with full weight upon the Spartans themselves, whose order of battle was only three rows deep; and Pelopidas and his horse—the one matter in which the Thebans were superior—were to fall on the enemy and cut them down as soon as they wavered.

The Spartans were flushed with wine when the fight began, but they fought as gallantly as usual. The tremendous charge, however, was more than they were prepared for, and the wild onset of Pelopidas completed their confusion. Cleombrotus was struck down and carried off dying to the camp, the allies broke and fled, and the Thebans found themselves undoubted masters of the field! Epaminondas had gained such a victory as no other man in Greece had ever won, considering the fame and quality of his assailants. Four hundred out of the seven hundred Spartans lay dead, and about a thousand more of their allies; the rest remained in their fortified camp, which was too strong to be stormed, and at the intercession of the King of Thessaly they were allowed to march home unmolested.

Epaminondas was free from all undue elation for his wonderful victory, and merely said he was happy to think how greatly it would please his father and mother. He was entirely the leading man of Thebes, and Thebes had by this victory become the mightiest state in Greece. His desire was to lead his fellow-citizens to use their power for good, and not for evil. He hindered them from revenging themselves on the little city of Orchomenus, and he assisted in the rebuilding of Mantinea, and other cities that had been misused by Sparta, and might now act as a check on her.

Two years after the battle of Leuctra, in 369, he was Bœotarch again; and so was Pelopidas : and they together led an army into the Peloponnesus to protect their new foundations, and free a large portion of the country from the Spartan domination. For these purposes they were forced to remain there four months beyond their term of office, and when they returned, they had to defend themselves for the irregular proceeding before the public tribunal. Epaminondas spoke for both, and the deeds they had done were so full a justification, that they were both re-elected Bœotarchs.

However, Epaminondas had enemies; many thought him

far too gentle. If he took a Bœotian prisoner fighting on the enemy's side, he would put him to ransom, instead of slaying him in the approved Theban fashion; he hindered spoliation of hostile cities; and his plans for the true glory of Thebes were too noble and far-sighted for the mass of his countrymen. So, in the year 367, while Pelopidas had been sent to transact some business in Persia, the Thebans not only refused to re-elect Epaminondas as Bœotarch, but gave him the most despised office they could choose, that of superintending the cleansing of the city streets. But so far from being ashamed of it, he turned his whole might and attention to it, and fulfilled the duties in such a way that it became both important and honourable.

When Pelopidas came home, he was sent on another mission, in the course of which he was treacherously seized and thrown into prison by the tyrant Alexander of Phera, in Thessaly. A Theban force was sent to deliver him, and Epaminondas was content to march with it as a common citizen soldier; but the two Bœotarchs in command managed so badly, that they were beset by Alexander with clouds of horsemen, forced to turn back, harassed on all sides, and nearly starved. It was felt that only one man could save them, and the whole army cried out for Epaminondas to take the command. He placed himself in the rear-guard, and by his wonderful skill and foresight safely brought the army home, and was once more felt to be the only man who could uphold the Theban name.

Again chosen to his old post of Bœotarch in 365, he marched at the head of an army to rescue his friend; and the terror of his name was such that the prisoner was safely restored, and a truce was made. Alexander was a horrible tyrant, cruel beyond measure; and Pelopidas had not only suffered much personally from chains and bad nourishment, but he had heard frightful stories of the savage deeds of the wretch ; and so soon as the truce was over, in 363, he led seven thousand men into Thessaly to punish this monster. The battle was close beneath two hills called Cynocephalæ, or the Dogs' Heads ; and the Thebans had gained considerable advantage, when Pelopidas, seeing the hateful tyrant himself rallying his men, was inflamed with such a passion of furious rage, that he dashed forward, shouting his name, and defying him to fight with him. Alexander fell back in terror, his men closed in, and Pelopidas was hemmed in and killed in the thick of the battle, while his troops were rushing on the enemy, not seeing where he was.

Intense was their grief when his gallant voice was missed, and still more when his corpse was found. They piled up all the arms taken from the enemy as a trophy round it, cut their hair and their horses' manes in token of mourning, and lighted no fire, tasted no food, on that sad night of victory ; and the mourning at Thebes was no less in its degree when the brave man, thirteen times Bœotarch, was borne home for his funeral rites.

He to whom the loss was most severe, Epaminondas, was at sea, conducting the fleet which had been raised by his counsel. In his absence the Thebans took their barbarous vengeance on Orchomenus, the city he had once protected ; and his return from his eight or nine months' voyage must have been a very sorrowful one. But he was not destined long to survive his friend. In the summer of 362 he was sent with a Theban army to the Peloponnesus, to defend the allies there from the attacks of Sparta. He had almost taken the city of Sparta itself, but that the army, with old King Agesilaus, hastened back before he could surprise it ; and then both armies marched upon Mantinea, the very place of Epaminondas' first battle and his rescue of Pelopidas.

The battle was a fierce, well-contested one. At length the Spartan forces began to break. Epaminondas was singled out by the foremost, and darts were showered on him, some of which he turned off with his shield, others he grasped and hurled back at the foe. The rout of the enemy had just begun when a spear struck him full in the breast, and as he fell, it broke, leaving the point fixed in the wound. His comrades held him up and bore him back, and the whole army stood still in consternation, not making another step forward in pursuit of the flying enemy.

He was taken, in great pain, with his hand on the fatal spear, to a hillside, where he recovered enough to ask if his shield were safe, for to lose it was reckoned a great disgrace. It was held up to him by his armourbearer, and he gazed anxiously down on the flying Spartans, and knew the day was his; and then, as the surgeons pronounced that death would probably follow on the extraction of the spear, he bade them wait till he could speak with the two next in command. He was told they were both killed. " Then," he said, sadly, " you must make peace with the enemy." But seeing his friends' tears, he added, cheerfully, " This day is not the end of my life, but the beginning of my happiness and completion of my glory ;" and as they mourned for his death, unmarried and childless, he said, " Leuctra and Mantinea are daughters enough to keep my name alive." Then, while others faltered, unable to bear to remove the dart, he drew it forth with a firm hand, and the gush of blood soon closed the life that may almost be called holy. As we have seen, he died in the trust that new bliss was beginning for him, and that his part in the great harmony of the Divine will would become more clear and perfect. And surely none can doubt that one who had so " worked righteousness" by the imperfect light vouchsafed him was accepted before Him who had seen him walking after the law that he was unto himself.

The broken-hearted Thebans buried him where he had died, and raised a column on the spot, bearing the figure of a dragon, in token of his lineage from one of the heroes of the dragon's tooth. It was the tomb of their own greatness. They never prospered after the grand fifteen years of the influence of their great Pythagorean soldier.

ALEXANDER.

B.C. 356—323.

THE Worthy next to be spoken of is one whose transcendent achievements have raised him to the foremost place in the memory of the world. Probably more persons during the last two thousand years, both in the East and West, have heard of the fame of Alexander than of that of any other man, though in many cases without knowing any of his real exploits, and while making him the hero of a fabulous tale of wild, romantic wonders.

Those forefathers of ours who placed him the second in their list of heathen Worthies had probably no very clear notion of his actual life ; and his errors were so great that his claim to be reckoned among them will be disputed by many. Not only, however, are we bound to dwell on the chosen name of old, but we think there were noble and peculiar elements of "worthiness" in Alexander, apart from his unrivalled prowess ; and that, if his faults were great, his virtues were also magnificent ; and both are seen by a more than wonted lustre, which brings into full display many flaws that no doubt existed in other characters that seem more faultless, because less closely examined.

We have seen how the admirable Epaminondas had raised his native state of Thebes to the leadership of Greece, and how when he fell at Mantinea he left not his like behind him. The power of Thebes fell with him, and thc old struggles between Athens and Sparta continued in full force; but both cities seemed to be exhausted, and there was no warrior of mark among them to stay the progress of that northern kingdom which they had hitherto despised as barbarous.

Macedon lies at the head of the Ægean Sea, extending about halfway along the northern coast, and stretching as far as the Bermian mountains to the west. Mountains cut it off on the north from the savage Scythians, and on the south from the Thessalians, and the great three-fingered peninsula of Chalcidica gave it many admirable harbours. The people were bold, hardy mountaineers, who spoke a sort of Greek, but neither well-pronounced nor grammatical ; they had never been reckoned as members of the Greek federation, and in the "Iliad" they are shown as fighting on the side of Troy. After this, however, when the Greek cities were changing from kingdoms to republics, a prince, who traced his descent from the demi-god Hercules, fled from Argos, and contrived to be made king of the barbarous Macedonians, who gradually became more civilized under the influence of his family and descendants, and began to build cities in their fine ports. The great desire of their kings was to be considered as free of the commonwealth of Greece, and to be allowed to contend in the Olympic games ; and when this at last was granted to them, it was because they proved their birthright as citizens of Argos, not because they were kings of Macedon.

This grant was made to Alexander II., whom we have seen obliged to serve in the Persian army, but still so entirely a Greek at heart that he came to warn Aristides before the battle of Platææ. His son was a man of taste and learning, and though a time succeeded full of fierce feuds and factions, the princes partook more and more of Greek culture. One of the young princes, named Philippos,

or, as we call it, Philip, was sent to Thebes either as a
pledge for the payment of a debt, or else was carried
thither by Pelopidas, to secure him from his enemies at
home. He was lodged in the house of the father of
Epaminondas, and became infinitely impressed by the
great example he saw in the noblest of the Thebans. It
was not, however, the beautiful harmony of virtue that
struck him in Epaminondas so much as his genius, both
for war and government. He laid up many lessons for
future use, not intending to employ them for the public
good, like his model, but for his own advancement; and,
likewise, he had no intention of fettering himself by
scruples as to justice or sincerity.

In 360, two years before the battle of Mantinea, he
heard of the death of his elder brother, and returning
home obtained the kingdom. He so dealt with his people
as to enable them to be both brave and educated enough
to take advantage of the wasted condition of Greece. He
disciplined his army to perfection, and improved the
Greek fashion of drawing up the men into what was
called the Macedonian phalanx. This was a body of
heavily-armed foot-soldiers, each with a spear twenty-four
feet long, and a heavy shield. In advancing, their shields
could be carried so as to form an impenetrable wall, and
when they stood in battle array, the ranks were so near
together that each man in the foremost row had four
spear-points projecting before him. There was a great
purpose in Philip's mind. This tremendous phalanx was
to make Macedon the leading power in Greece, and then
all Greece was to be united, and to dash at the great foe in
Asia. Xenophon and his 10,000 had probed the weakness
of that enormous empire of slaves, and where bands of
mercenaries, betrayed and headless, had come out unscathed, a disciplined, well-led army would assuredly
conquer.

In his own days, or his son's, the work might be done.
The mother of that son was a beautiful, imperious woman,
named Olympias, who was the daughter of the King of
Epirus, and thus deduced her lineage from Pyrrhus, the
only son of Achilles. She was an enthusiast in the wild
worship of the wine-god, Dionysos, and the first time
Philip saw her was at Samothrace, wreathed with ivy
and vine, dancing fearlessly among great serpents, which
twisted about the maidens' vine-crowned staves, in their
golden baskets of figs, and even in the garlands on their
hair. These orgies were lawless and almost frenzied, and
they accorded so well with the passionate nature of the
Epirot princess, that her ecstatic beauty so impressed Philip
that he asked her in marriage so soon as he was established upon the throne.

In 356 was born, at Pella, the son of this marriage,
amid dreams and portents that were thought to mark his
greatness. On the day of his birth the wonder of the
world, the temple of Artemis at Ephesus, was burnt down;
a great battle was won by Philip's general, Parmenio; and
a horse of his breeding won the race at the Olympic
games.

Philip is said to have at once written to Aristotle, the
chief philosopher of his time, telling him that not only
was he happy in having a son, but in the possibility
of that son's having such a tutor as Aristotle. This
great man was a Macedonian by birth, and acted for
many years as the chief physician at court. He was
a great student of nature, and a most powerful reasoner,
working out a grand theory of thought and morals to
be carried into practical life, and he was well pleased
to have a young prince to bring up to be his model
king. As Pythagoras thought harmony the key to the
world and guide of man, and Socrates trusted to the
guidance of the inner voice inspired by the Deity, so

Aristotle believed in the rule of Law, and would have man subject himself completely to the laws of Virtue that conduced to perfection, and taught that there was one universal God, manifested in different forms in divers countries.

He seems to have merely directed his pupil's education at first. His maxim was that for seven years the boy should be trained in body instead of mind, only guarded from all that might taint eye or ear ; kept from intercourse with vulgar obsequious slaves, made active by running, leaping, and climbing, and hardy by moderate diet, cold bathing, and light clothing. A noble lady, named Lanike, seems to have had the charge of Alexander at this time, and he remained all his life most warmly attached to her. Probably, too, this regimen had a great effect on his bodily frame, in diminishing the slight blemish with which he was born, namely, the neck being somewhat inclined towards the left shoulder ; but his grace and activity were such that this never interfered with his majestic appearance. Otherwise, although rather below the middle size, he was of perfectly symmetrical form and extremely beautiful features, fair and ruddy, and with exquisite melting eyes.

A tutor named Lysimachus then took charge of him, and at once taught him the Homeric poems, to which the boy became so fervently attached that to the end of his life he carried a copy of the " Iliad " about with him, and loved to think of rivalling his ancestor, Achilles. His tutor used to call him by that glorious name, his father Peleus, and himself Phœnix. When Alexander was ten years old, some Athenian envoys came to Pella, and, after they had been banquetted, the prince was called on to play on the harp and sing some lyric poetry, and to go through a scene from a drama with another lad. The performance, however, did not come up to the code of

Athenian taste, and the visitors went away laughing at his incorrect accent.

He was more successful when a few years after a horse was brought for sale to his father, most beautiful, but so spirited that no one dared to mount him. He was being led away as useless, when Alexander exclaimed, "What a pity to lose such a horse for want of courage and skill to manage him!" His father rebuked him for blaming persons older and wiser than himself. "I believe," said Alexander, "that I could deal with this horse better than any of you."

His father consented to his trying, and he began by turning the creature's head gently to the sun, having perceived that his antics had been caused by fear of his own shadow, and then stroking and caressing him, as he held the reins, he gently dropped his own fluttering mantle, and vaulted on his back, sitting firm through all the fiery starts and rearings, but using neither whip nor spur, and gradually straitening the rein, till at last the creature obeyed perfectly his voice and heel. It was such a gallant exploit that Philip embraced him with tears of joy, and the horse, called Bucephalus, or the Bullhead, because he had a white mark like a bull's face, remained through life a favourite companion of his young master, the only person who could control him.

Alexander was now thirteen, but he had shown himself so manly in his understanding and forbearance in this matter, that his father placed him under the immediate tuition of Aristotle three years earlier than the age fixed by that great man for the beginning of the course of philosophy. Alexander, whose heart was as great as his intellect, fervently loved and admired his master, and seems to have imbibed from him a largeness of views and power of doing justice to persons of different breeding from his own, which eminently fitted him for the task in store for him ; also a deep and curious interest in all the wonders of nature. But Aristotle did not aim at making him either philosopher, poet, or scientific man, knowing well that though intelligent interest in all things is needful to a king, yet that his prime duty is to be practical. The one thing Aristotle did not teach his pupil was self-control ; but probably this was not the fault of the philosopher, but of the heathen's want of any principle strong enough to curb the fiery temper which Alexander had inherited from his mother Olympias, and the licentiousness and overweening ambition that he derived from his father.

Already had he begun to understand Philip's views, and, while still a mere boy, would complain on hearing of a fresh city conquered, that his father would leave him nothing to do. At sixteen he was permitted to join an army which was to meet the Athenians and Thebans in a last desperate struggle for their liberty, to which Athens was constantly excited by her great orator, Demosthenes, the most eloquent of men.

The place of battle was Chæronea, on the borders of Bœotia, where 500 years after an old tree was still called Alexander's Oak, from the tradition that his tent had there been pitched. Philip commanded against the Athenians, and Alexander against the Thebans. At first the Athenians' spirited charge almost broke their enemies, but superior discipline was now on the Macedonian side, and Philip wore them out by his firm unflinching resistance ; while in the other wing Alexander gained a well-fought though not so difficult a victory over the Thebans, and entirely destroyed their Sacred Band. Chæronea, fought in the year B.C. 338, was the ruin of the independence of the Greeks, Athens and Thebes were too much shattered for further resistance, and Sparta alone refused to acknowledge the supremacy of the northern barbarian.

Peace was made, and Alexander's spirit and wisdom

amazed the envoys of the cities, and must have proved to them that in his time there was little hope of their shaking off the yoke. The king was beginning to prepare for his second great object, the invasion of Persia, but his vices became his hindrance. The true high-bred Greeks were contented with one wife, kept indeed in a dull, decorous, inferior position, yet still their only spouse; but the Macedonian princes were so much infected by Eastern licence as to take several wives, and Olympias, with her violent temper, her serpent dances, and domineering ways, had become so distasteful to him that, after the birth of a daughter, Cleopatra, he espoused several other women. Alexander, who was fervently attached to his mother, chafed in secret, until Philip actually deposed Olympias from her position as chief wife and queen, and placed his last favourite in her stead.

At the marriage banquet, a relation of this lady, when half intoxicated, proposed to drink to the hope that she might bear a son to be heir to the throne, and this insult so enraged Alexander that he threw a goblet at the man, using fierce words that incensed his father, who leapt up, sword in hand, to chastise his son, but, between rage and wine, fell prostrate on the pavement.

"See," said Alexander, "a man preparing to cross from Europe to Asia cannot step safely from one couch to another!"

He then left the apartment, conducted his mother to her native home in Epirus, and went to Illyria; but after some months, Philip, hearing that his son was arranging for a marriage he thought inferior, recalled him, but still kept him in a sort of disgrace, and surrounded himself with the kinsmen of the new queen, whose newborn son might thus become a dangerous rival. No justice could be procured by persons who suffered injuries from these men; and when the aggrieved complained to Olympias,

M

she fiercely asked them why they did not revenge themselves. Alexander himself, when told of these wicked
acts and of the insulting demeanour of the young queen,
could not refrain from quoting a terrible line from a
Greek tragedy, where a forsaken wife vows to be revenged

"On husband, wife, and him who gave the bride."

Except for this quotation, Alexander was guiltless of what
followed. His own sister, Cleopatra, was to be given in
marriage to the King of Epirus, whom Philip hoped thus
to detach from Alexander's interests, and in the height of
the festivity, as Philip majestically entered the theatre
in a white garment many paces before his guards, one of
the offended persons dashed forward and thrust a sword
through his body, then fled so rapidly that he would have
escaped had not his foot been entangled in the vine stocks,
so that the guards came up with him and cut him to pieces
on the spot. Alexander was immediately conducted to the
palace and proclaimed king, when he stood forth before
the people, and expressed his hopes that he should so
govern, that they should feel that their king was changed
only in name. He severely punished the conspirators,
whom he believed to have been secretly instigated by
the Persians, and with all his heart he took up the project
of his father for attacking them in their seat of empire.

He was only twenty years old, but his abilities
were those of a man of much greater years, or, rather,
such genius as his was no matter of age, and daring as
were his exploits, they were never rash, for they never
exceeded his powers. The first necessity was to leave
everything secure behind him : moreover, his great desire,
and one which was never accomplished, was to be
heartily accepted by Greece as her champion : and at
present terror alone could force the old republican states
to endure the supremacy of Macedon.

He accordingly marched into Thessaly, where he was elected chief of the nation, and then went on to Thermopylæ, where the Amphictyons were assembled, who accepted him as one of their number. At Corinth again he met deputies from all the little states, who, having no power of resistance, were forced to elect him Captain General of the Greek Confederation. All consented save the Spartans, who said it was their custom to lead and not to follow; while the Athenians pretended to submit, but watched anxiously for an opportunity of shaking off the yoke. Then he turned northwards, to subdue the wild Thracians on the Danube and in the Hæmus mountains. It was a dangerous expedition, which lasted four months; and the Greeks, hearing nothing of him, fancied him slain, and encouraged the Thebans to proclaim their independence of the power of Macedon.

No sooner did the news reach Alexander than he hurried back from Thrace, so speedily, that the first news his enemies had of his being alive was finding him among them at the head of an army.

He offered favourable terms to the Thebans if they would submit, but they hoped for another Leuctra, and refused. He assaulted the city, and the battle was fought from street to street with a terrible slaughter: and still more dreadful was the vengeance. Alexander had been much exasperated, and was resolved to make an example. All the Thebans who were not connected by ties of hospitality with him or his father were sold into slavery, their city was pulled down, all save the temples, and the territory divided between two other Bœotian cities, one being Orchomenus, which had been so ill-treated by Thebes in the absence of Epaminondas. In after years, Alexander often regretted this dreadful act of severity, and as Thebes was the especial city of the wine-god, Dionysos, he viewed it as an effect of the vengeance of the deity that any excess in wine was wont to blind him with ungovernable fury.

Intimidated by the fate of Thebes, all Greece, except Sparta, again sent deputies to meet Alexander at Corinth, to accept his leadership and accede to his demands for the men, money, and stores each was to supply for that triumph over Asia that was to console them for the loss of their own freedom. Every one was subservient, with only one exception. This was Diogenes, a disciple of a pupil of Socrates, who had exaggerated all his master's lessons till he had made them into caricatures, so that Diogenes was called the Mad Socrates. Utter indifference to all the pomps, honours, or pleasures of earth, was professed by these men, who were called Cynics, either from their first place of teaching, or from Cyon, a dog, because of their currish habits, as they seldom washed, went about in rags, and slept in any wretched lair in the open streets. Diogenes used to roll in burning sand in summer, and embrace marble statues in winter, and his dwelling-place was a huge earthenware tub that belonged to the temple of the Mother of the Gods at Corinth. All these extravagances were of course a protest against the over-refinement and elegance, the softness and polish, in which the Greek cities were losing their freedom and courage. Alexander was struck with the stories of the fearless and sharp sayings of Diogenes, now nearly eighty years of age, and went to see him. The old philosopher lay basking in the sunshine before his tub, and as he took no notice of the princely youth who stood before him, his visitor introduced himself:

"I am Alexander the King."

"And I am Diogenes the Cynic," was the answer, in a tone of perfect equality.

Alexander then asked him questions about his system of philosophy, and heard his theory of the equality of the souls of men, and his scorn of the body and its needs. There must have been a rugged greatness about the old man, which contrasted favourably with the supple complaisance of the Greek deputies, for Alexander was impressed, and, on taking leave, asked what he could do for the philosopher.

"Only to stand out of my sunshine," was the famous answer ; and as Alexander complied, he said, "If I were not Alexander, I would be Diogenes." If he could not, as he hoped, master all earthly things, he would rather despise them than be mastered by them. Twelve years later Diogenes, then past ninety, was one morning found dead in his tub, after having the night before supped on the raw leg of an ox ; and, strangely enough, it proved to be the very day of the death of Alexander.

These years, which the old man had spent as one day in sunning himself and deriding the weakness of the world, had to the young man been the most wonderful ever spent by man on earth. All was now clear behind him for the fulfilment of his great scheme, one of the mightiest that ever entered a human brain, since his intention was not merely to conquer the East, but to make that hitherto barbarous region no longer the abode of mere vulgar magnificence, savage luxury, and abject slavery, but intelligent, active, and free, even as Greece itself. There was much in the state of Persia to render the time suitable. That Artaxerxes II. who had hoped to destroy the Ten Thousand had died at ninety-four years old, B.C. 356, leaving 116 children. There were civil wars and revolts all through the reign of his successor, who was a ferocious and wicked man, in whom the direct line of Persian kings ended. He chose, as his successor, Codomanus, the grandson of a brother of Artaxerxes II. and of Cyrus, a man of some reputation for courage and ability, and who came to the throne in 336, the same year as did Alexander. He took the royal name of Darius, by which he is always known in history.

Since the Great Retreat, many Greeks had hired themselves to fight in Persian wars, and Alexander had many opportunities of learning where lay the strength and weakness of the empire while he was spending the winter at Ægæ in preparations. The days when each Greek citizen was ready to fight the battles of his country were at an end. Men who had a taste for war learnt fighting as a trade, and took wages of those who remained at home, to fight in their stead ; and these formed themselves into bands of soldiers, who received payment from such cities as chose to hire them ; and were of course superior in skill and training to the citizen warrior, without having his loftier qualities. Alexander had 5,000 of these soldiers, and 7,000 collected from the Greek cities, but his main reliance was on his own Macedonians, who, always hardy and used to warfare with their Thracian neighbours, had been trained by Philip into the most efficient soldiers the world then contained. Of these there were 12,000 infantry, trained to act in the terrible phalanx of sixteen men deep, armed with the enormous spear : and there were also 5,000 well-trained horsemen, for the Macedonians were excellent horsemen ; some heavily equipped, others more lightly, but all most formidable, from their arms and their address in using them. There was a body-guard of youths whom Philip had bred up in his court, lads of the best families, who had eaten at his own table, never were beaten except by his order, and were trained in learning and military discipline. These were always around Alexander, and were accustomed to live almost on terms of equality with him ; his chief friends were among these, and several of them imbibed something of his own wonderful genius. There were, besides, a number of

Thracian bowmen and slingers. But his whole army was only altogether 34,500 men—a wonderfully small number with which to launch himself against an empire reaching from the Archipelago to the wilds of Tartary, from the Black Sea to the deserts of Africa ; and such had been the expenses of his outfit, and so large his gifts to his officers, that when he was asked what he had left for himself, he made answer, " My hopes."

He left his kingdom under charge of his father's trusty counsellor, Antipater, and took leave of his mother and of his native country early in the spring of 334—the home he was never to see again. He passed the Hellespont in April, steering his own vessel, and was the first to leap on the Asiatic shore ; after which he made his way to view the plain of Troy, which he looked upon as the first point of Greek enterprise in Asia. With a manuscript of the " Iliad," corrected by Aristotle, in his bosom, he went over the scenes so perfectly described by Homer ; and lest Priam should bring evil upon him, as a descendant of Pyrrhus, he offered victims to the shade of the old king, and, with more enthusiasm, sacrificed and performed gymnastic exercises at the mound that was said to contain the urn of his ancestor and model, Achilles. His dearest friend, Hephæstion, went through the same observances in honour of Patroclus. A temple of Pallas still stood on the site of Troy, and here Alexander, dedicating a suit of his own armour, took down one which was said to have been worn by one of the Grecian heroes of the " Iliad." The armour itself was probably too large for him, but the shield was always carried before him by one of his armour-bearers. He was told that the harp of Paris was preserved in a neighbouring city, but he said " he thought it not worth looking at, but he should be glad to have seen that of Achilles, which had resounded to songs of heroes."

The ablest general in the Persian service was a Rhodian captain, named Memnon, but he was not the satrap ; and when he recommended starving out the enemy by burning and destroying everything before him, the Phrygian satrap Arsites declared that not a house in his government should be burnt ; nor would he listen to Memnon's other suggestion of sending an army to attack Macedonia, and thus force the invader to return. The Persian army consisted of an immense force of cavalry and 20,000 infantry, chiefly Greek hirelings, and with these the satraps of the provinces of Asia Minor resolved to contest the passage of the river Granicus, a mountain stream rising in Mount Ida, and flowing into the Black Sea. Alexander was well pleased at the prospect of a pitched battle, knowing that here Greek discipline always had the advantage ; but the troops were somewhat daunted, because they did not regard the month of June as a lucky one. However, he told them that they must consider it as a second May ; and when his father's experienced general, Parmenio, made the more reasonable objection that the banks of the river were steep, and that it was swollen by the melting snows, he said " he should disgrace the Hellespont did he fear the Granicus." He gave the command of the left wing to Parmenio, and put himself at the head of the right. Both armies stood on the opposite sides of the rushing stream in a pause of expectation ere the clash of arms should begin between the East and the West, every one gazing towards the young king, who was easily recognised by the white plume in his helmet and the glittering of his armour. He leapt upon his horse, and then spoke a few heart-stirring words to his men, calling on them to follow him and prove themselves good warriors.

" Where's the coward that would not dare to fight for such a
    king ? "

In a slanting direction he led his wing down to the river, amid trumpet cries and battle hymns, and the whole army proceeded at the same time, trying to keep as much as possible in line ; but the struggle was desperate as they tried to climb the opposite bank, where the Persians stood firm, and the horsemen were jammed together in one struggling mass. Here it was the strength of the Macedonian pike that prevailed, and forced back the enemy up the slope to the level ground above. Here there was still hard fighting ; Alexander broke his pike, and calling to his groom to give him another, was shown by the man that only a fragment remained to him also. Another officer, however, handed the king one, with which he soon after slew two Persian nobles, and before he could draw it back from the corpse of the last he was saved from a deadly blow by Cleitus, the brother of his nurse Lanike. The light Persian javelins and scimitars were of little avail against the stout Greek armour ; and seeing this, the defenders broke and fled, without having killed more than 115 Macedonians altogether. Their loss was not more than 1,000 slain and 2,000 prisoners, for Alexander forbade pursuit, and kept his army together. The Persians, in their terror, dispersed so entirely, that no army remained in Asia Minor to attempt any opposition, and Arsites killed himself in despair on recollecting his fatal interference with Memnon.

Alexander buried the dead on either side with full honours, visited all his wounded, talking kindly to each man, and sent home 300 suits of Persian armour to be dedicated to Pallas Athene, in her Parthenon at Athens. All spoil or plunder he forbade; he viewed the country as his own, and the inhabitants as his subjects : he only changed the governors of the provinces and cities from Persians to Greeks. Sardis, the rich and splendid purple-weaving, gold-hoarding city, where Crœsus had been

warned by Solon and conquered by Cyrus, was surrendered to him without a blow, though the citadel, built on
a triangular rock, was wellnigh impregnable. The treasures he here found were of no small service in his
onward march, which led him to another of those great
cities whose names had so familiar a sound in Greek ears
—Ephesus, the great Ionian city, whose glorious Temple
to Artemis, the wonder of the world, had received Xenophon's votive offerings, and had perished by fire on
Alexander's birthnight, only twenty-two years before.
It was already partly rebuilt, and Alexander granted the
whole tribute which had hitherto been paid to the Persian
kings to carry it on ; and he caused the black and
hideous statue, said to have fallen from heaven, to be
carried at the head of a procession of himself and his
troops.

The first resistance he met was at Miletus. Memnon,
who had fled there with many of his officers, had obtained
authority from the King of Persia to carry on the war, and
the Persian fleet was on its way, but did not come in time.
Alexander was forced to besiege the town, and the capture
cost him many men.

On coming into Caria, the Greeks were reminded of
that spirited Artemisia, the widowed queen, who had
fought for Xerxes at Salamis, and whose tomb to her
husband Mausolus was another of the seven wonders of
the world. That tomb, after giving its name to all such
monuments, now reposes in the British Museum, but then
was doubtless in full splendour, and was duly gazed at by
the Macedonians. Another widowed queen of the same
family, named Ada, came to meet Alexander with complaints of having been expelled from her throne by her
brother-in-law, and was restored by him. She adopted
him as her son, and was called by him mother ; and her
care for him was so great that, in dismay at his hardy and

simple habits, she sent him a rich banquet every day that he spent at her city of Alinda, and on his departure she offered him her best cooks and confectioners to provide his meals for the future. He thanked her, but said his tutor had supplied him with cooks far superior, namely, a march before daybreak as sauce for his dinner, and a light dinner as the relish for his supper. He said, too, that this same tutor was wont to turn over his baggage, lest his own mother Olympias should have put in too soft or luxurious a cloak or bed for him.

Yet his strict habits did not make him forgetful of the enjoyment of others. All the young men in his army who had been married just before the campaign were sent home by him to spend the winter with their brides, and at the same time to excite their friends by the history of their victories, so as to return to him in the spring with numerous and willing comrades. Nor was he idle during their absence. He continued to take possession of cities, and, while relieving them of their obligations to the Persians, to gather them into the great Empire of the East that was his dream : and most willing was his reception. The old free Greeks of Athens, Sparta, or Thebes, might chafe at his yoke ; but to the colonies he was a deliverer—a native Greek lord was infinitely preferable to a barbaric Persian.

And to the Greeks these Asian realms were a sort of living dreamland, the site of as many familiar legends, the home of as many heroes and poets, as Greece itself. Here was Phrygia, with its capital Gordium, respecting which a strange wild tale was current. A Phrygian peasant, it was said, was ploughing in his field, when an eagle flew down and settled on the yoke to which his oxen were fastened. Such a portent could not be neglected, and he therefore went to consult an oracle, and on his way met a young girl, who gave him advice as to the manner of conducting the sacrifice, and finally became his wife. Their infant son, Midas, was marked out as the wealthiest of mankind by the ants, which carried grains of corn to his mouth as he lay on the ground. He was grown to manhood when he and his parents set forth to the place of popular assembly in Phrygia in a cart, to which the eagle's yoke was attached by a complicated knot made of a with of cornel-tree. They were hailed by loud cries, that here was the King of Phrygia ; for an oracle had declared to the people that it was thus that their king should come to them ! Accordingly, Gordius and Midas reigned in the capital still called Gordium, and there it was, quoth tradition, that Midas won from the god Dionysos his imprudent wish that his touch should change all things to gold, and there, when hunger and thirst had brought him to beseech that the fatal gift should be removed, he wore the badge of his folly for ever in the long ears of an ass. The father and son had dedicated their waggon in the temple-keep of Gordium, and there it actually remained with the wonderful cornel-twisted knot, already many hundred years old. It was said that the oracle had declared that he who could loose that knot should be Lord of Asia, and Alexander must needs fulfil the oracle. He ascended to the cell, and the knot was parted. Some say that in his impatience he hewed it through with his sword ; but a follower who wrote his history says that on pulling out the pin he detected the strands of the knot, and really unravelled it by skill : and, curiously enough, while the first story, giving rise to the proverb about cutting the Gordian knot, suits with the vulgar estimate of his character as a fierce, violent conqueror, the second is in accordance with the fact that he was really more acute and more persevering than other men, and that no difficulty could baffle him.

Yet his career was wellnigh stopped by a foe against which man could do nothing. In the early spring of 333 he was again on the march, to turn as it were the corner between Asia Minor and Syria, where the Taurus mountains, with their many swift torrents cutting up the province of Cilicia, rendered the way so difficult and perilous, that the very weakest defence would seem capable of turning back an army at almost any point ; and as Memnon was known to be rallying his forces, it was his desire to hurry through these wild passes ere the Persian troops should be ready to assail him. A report reached him that the Persians were about to burn the city of Tarsus that he might find no harbour there, and he therefore dashed forward with his cavalry, over hill and through ravine, and coming down into the plain already parched by the glowing Levantine sun, hurried into the city in time to save it. He was heated, spent, wearied, and covered with dust, and before him rushed the clear crystal waters of the river Cydnus. He at once obeyed the impulse that led him to throw aside his garments and plunge into it. The stream was cold as ice, coming freshly from the melting snows of the Taurus hills above, and, in the exhausted condition of Alexander's frame, the shock of the chill was wellnigh fatal. A violent fever came on, and he was soon in the extremity of danger, which was increased by the Macedonian custom of putting the physician to death if his patient died under his hands, so that all hung back, unwilling to administer any strong remedy. At last one named Philippus undertook to give him a draught that might relieve him, but, just as it was ready, a letter was brought to him from his general, Parmenio, informing him that it was said that Philippus had been bribed by the Persians to poison him. When the physician entered, Alexander held out the letter to him with one hand, took the cup in the other, and drank the potion while Philippus read the letter. At first this confidence was hardly tested, for his sufferings increased, and fainting fits came on that seemed like death ; but at length the crisis passed, and he began to recover, though it was some time before his strength returned sufficiently to resume his march, and he was obliged to send Parmenio forward to secure the pass of the Issus to Syria.

He himself turned westward along the coast as soon as he was capable of a slow movement, and visited the ruins of an ancient city, where the remnant of a royal statue existed with the hands in the act of being clapped together, and an inscription in Assyrian characters, which the Greeks thus interpreted :—

"Sardanapalus, son of Anacyndaraxes, built Anchialus and Tarsus in one day:

"But thou, O stranger, eat, drink, and be merry;
All other pursuits of man are worth this,"

—*i.e.* the clap of the hands. The Greeks believed this to be the Sardanapalus of Nineveh they knew in their histories as having adorned himself like a woman, and lived in the utmost luxury until his doom overtook him and he burnt himself, his wives, slaves, treasures, and palace, in one vast funeral pile. They looked at his inscription with contempt, as only fit for an Oriental insensible to true glory. Meantime, divisions detached from the main army had reduced the rest of Asia Minor, and at Soli the full conquest and the complete recovery of the conqueror were celebrated by games, by a procession of the army in honour of the physician-god Asclepius, and by a race with torches at night.

But the victory was far from being yet achieved. The Persian monarch himself was advancing through Syria, dispirited indeed by the loss of Memnon, who died in the midst of his exertions, but greatly encouraged by exaggerated accounts of Alexander's illness and of his subsequent slow westward march ; and thinking he had turned back to Greece, was determined to catch him in Cilicia and decide his fate ere he could escape. Darius' army included not only his own Immortal band of Persian cavalry, but a very formidable body of Greek infantry from Sparta and other cities, who were willing to side with the Great King out of their intense hatred to Macedonian supremacy.

The march of the Persians when the king himself was in presence was a magnificent procession. True worshippers of Mithras, or the Sun, they displayed a crystal disc to represent him over the monarch's tent, and never moved till sunrise, when a trumpet summoned them before the royal tent.

Their order of march was as follows :—Silver altars, bearing the sacred fire, were borne first, followed by Magian priests singing hymns, and accompanied by a band of youths, one for each day in the year, and followed by the Chariot of the Sun, drawn by white horses. A horse dedicated to the Sun followed, led by white-robed attendants with golden rods, and ten more chariots completed their sacred and mystical vanguard.

Then came the cavalry from twelve nations, and the famous Immortal band, wearing robes covered with gold, and silver-handled lances. The king's own chariot was adorned with two statues representing War and Peace, with a golden eagle between them. The chariot was very high, and on it sat the Great King in a robe of purple striped with silver, and a mantle crusted with precious stones, representing two falcons pecking at each other, and on his head his tiara, encircled with a blue and white fillet. Guards of different ranks followed, and then came the chariots of his mother Sisygambis, his wife Statira, his two daughters and one son, three hundred and sixty inferior wives, and an immense troop of their guards and slaves, with no less than 600 mules and 300 camels to carry the baggage and treasure.

Most of the treasure was left at Damascus with the families of the satraps, but Darius moved on in all his cumbrous state, while every one, even of the Greeks in the Persian army, thought that the Macedonians *must* be crushed, and at Athens there was rejoicing beforehand in their destruction. The host, hoping to catch Alexander in Cilicia, while yet enfeebled by his illness, came pouring over the passes of the Taurus into Cilicia by the road of Mount Amanus, and descended into the town of Issus; but when there, they found that Alexander had in the meantime entered Syria by the western pass, and had only left behind him a few sick and wounded, on whom Codomanus took a cruel revenge at the instigation of his grandees, killing some and cutting off the arms of others. So great was the alarm that Alexander's treasurer gave up all for lost, and fled back from Tarsus into Macedonia.

The few who could escape from Issus fled eighteen miles onward to Alexander's army, and brought word that the Great King was behind him! He could not believe it till he had sent a ship along the coast, whence the multitudes were easily to be seen; and he then acted as promptly as ever. He marched back at the head of his troops to the narrow mountain-pass through which he had gone two days before, reached it at midnight, and, to his great relief, found that the enemy had not secured it. Going up the side of the mountain, he looked down on the country all ablaze with Persian watchfires, and after offering sacrifice to the tutelary deities, halted for rest, food, and daylight.

At dawn he was moving again down the single narrow pass, where his men had to move between rocks in almost single file ; and here was his greatest danger : but by and by it widened, and opened upon the seashore, so that he could extend his army in battle array, with the sea protecting the left wing and the river Pinarus flowing between the two armies.

The Persians, on learning that their enemy was turning back on them, drew up and prepared for the battle, intending to dispute the passage of the river ; but there were too many for the narrow ground, and only a small number could actually fight with the Macedonians. Darius himself mounted his chariot, and placed himself in the centre of his line, watching as the Greeks slowly moved towards the river, under a hail of arrows. Then, with a sudden change of movement, Alexander dashed forward at the head of his right wing, and, long before they expected it, the Persians found him and his Macedonian pikes at their throats. They broke and fled, hotly pursued, and Darius in a panic turned his chariot, and fled headlong towards the Amanus pass. When the ground grew too rough for his chariot, he left it, and with it his robe, sword, and bow, mounted a horse, and never rested till he was on the other side of the Euphrates.

Yet the deserted Persians and the Greek mercenaries behaved bravely, and there was hot fighting before they were driven from the field ; many Macedonians were killed, and Alexander himself received a gash in the thigh ; but he was not disabled, and hurried on in the pursuit, where there was so horrible a slaughter that he actually crossed a narrow ravine upon a ghastly bridge of dead bodies. In the evening he came back towards the camp of the Persians, and was led at once to the royal tents, which had been carefully guarded as his right. He took off his armour, and, smiling, said he would try the bath of Darius—a very different bath from his perilous one in the Cydnus. A spacious curtained hall, vessels of wrought

N

gold and silver, delicious odours, sweet unguents, vials, caskets, a thousand articles undreamt of in Greece, and a multitude of abject slaves, awaited him, and made him laugh as he said to his comrades, " So this is what it was to be a king !"

Having bathed and had his wound dressed, he sat down to make proof of a Persian supper; but at that moment he heard a loud and mournful wailing close at hand, and asking the cause, was told that the royal robe of Darius had been brought to the captive princesses, and that they were lamenting the death of their lord. He immediately sent to inform them that Darius had escaped, and added that they should have no fears, for they should retain all their honours and titles. The next day he offered a visit to Sisygambis, the mother of Darius. The wife, Statira, he would not attempt to see, since he knew that the very sight of her would be an insult and injury to her husband; nor did he wish to be tempted to make her his own by the sight or even the report of her beauty, which was said to excel that of any woman in Asia.

The old princess Sisygambis beheld two simply-dressed and armed Greek gentlemen enter her tent side by side, looking much as any soldiers hired into the Persian force had looked in her eyes. Yet one of these must be the terrible warrior who had twice overthrown the hosts of the Eastern Empire, and at whose mercy they all lay. How would he treat her—an aged woman, who had known little gentleness or courtesy even from those who were nearest and closest to her? She could only drop on her face at the feet of the tallest.

But the tallest drew back, and her attendants hastily pointed to the lesser man, whose fair young face, so full of gentleness and pity, had seemed to her no visage for king or conqueror; and he, stepping forward to raise her from the ground, said gently, "Be not dismayed, mother ; for Hephæstion is Alexander's other self." Never had the poor old lady experienced the generous courtesy she met with from the stranger, and a relation almost of mother and son sprang up between them. He also was very kind to the young prince, whom he took in his arms, auguring that he would make a bolder warrior than his father. After this, Alexander attended the funeral obsequies of those he had lost in the battle, and caused the Persian officers to be buried according to the directions of the queen-mother, while three altars were raised on the banks of the Pinarus as tokens of thanks to the gods.

As the Granicus had given Alexander Asia Minor, so the Issus gave him Syria, and his further march was but a taking possession. Darius sent an embassy to him full of complaints, and demanding the restoration of his family ; to which Alexander replied by a blunt and businesslike letter, in which he went through the injuries his father had received from the Persians, declaring that he would reply to no communication that was not addressed to him as King of Asia, and that Darius could obtain nothing of him but by personal supplication. "If, however," he concluded, "you still intend to dispute the dominion with me, fly no more, but stand and fight, for I will attack you wherever you may be."

For the present, however, Darius was beyond the two great rivers, and Alexander was too wise to follow him thither till all to the west had been reduced. Syria was his ; but there still remained both Palestine and Egypt, which, having been won by Nebuchadnezzar, had followed the fortunes of the Empire of the East when the Lion of Daniel's vision had given place to the Ram. And now the He-goat, the ensign of Macedon, was forced to pause in his rushing course on the northern border of the moun-

tainous strip which held such indomitable tribes in its
valleys and on its seaboard.

The first whom he had to encounter were the Phœnicians, the tempters of Israel, and the merchants of the
world. A cluster of small independent states, their cities
lay with their backs against Mounts Carmel and Lebanon,
and their faces to the sea, where their sailors roamed far
and wide, and exchanged the riches of the East and
West.

Their religion—that of Baal, the sun god ; Moloch, the
star to whom infants were burnt in the furnace ; Ashtaroth, the sensual queen of heaven—was a fierce and
corrupt one, and their national character was at once
courageous but treacherous, enterprising but luxurious.
They were needed by the West as traders, but hated as
men-stealers and deceivers. Their adhesion to the Persian Empire had been but loose ; it had been limited to
paying a tribute that had been but a slight burden on
their wealth, and to sending their galleys to fight his
battles by sea, when no doubt there were opportunities of
plunder that made the expeditions welcome. Aware that
in Alexander they should find a real master, they were
less willing to submit to him; but their ships of war were
absent with the Persian fleet, and so Sidon and the other
cities submitted to him. Even the Tyrians, though they
had once endured a thirteen years' siege from Nebuchadnezzar, and had since raised their city in greater
strength than ever, on an island half a mile from the
shore, felt that they must own the power of Alexander as
far as they had owned that of Darius, and sent him a
golden chaplet and an oriental offer of doing all he should
require of them.

His requirement was to be admitted to march through
the city in solemn procession with his army to pay his
devotions at the shrine of Moloch, whom the Greeks

chose to identify with the demigod Hercules, and who was thus claimed as an ancestor by the kings of Macedon ; but the Tyrians, knowing that if the Macedonian army were once within their walls a garrison would be left there for ever, made answer that Alexander's sacrifice to his forefather could be performed at an ancient temple on the mainland, but that they were resolved not to admit any Macedonian within their walls, as they had never admitted any Persian.

So far were they from suspecting Moloch of any inclination to his *soi-disant* descendant, that they even set him to keep Apollo in order by chaining up to his image a little statue of the Greek god, which had been sent to them as the spoil of a city in Sicily. Alexander, on the other hand, related to his soldiers a dream of having been led by the hand by Hercules and placed within the city. Certainly the attempt to take it was a labour worthy of Hercules, for only in his spirit could a king with merely a land army have attempted to take an island city with the finest fleet then in existence.

His first measure was to raise a mound so as to form a causeway across the strait between the isle and the mainland, obtaining piles from the forests of Mount Lebanon, driving them into the sand, and filling up the space between with stones and rubbish from the old deserted Tyre. The work prospered till the mound had advanced about half way across the strait, but there the bottom became much deeper, and, moreover, the workmen were within reach of missiles from the walls, whence they were assailed with stones, arrows, and darts bearing wisps of burning tow. Alexander erected two towers and hung their sides with wet hides ; but this protection did not avail them long, for the Tyrians towed a burning ship, filled with combustible materials, against the mound, set fire to the timbers, and totally destroyed it.

Upon this the work was recommenced on a larger scale, so as to present a wider front to the enemy, and in the meantime he set forth on an expedition to chastise the robber tribes, who from time immemorial had infested the mountains of Northern Palestine. With him went the old tutor, Lysimachus, who had loved to call him Achilles and himself Phœnix. It was the depth of winter, and the snows of the Hermon mountains made the weather most bitter. Night came on while the party was still entangled in the rugged ground, where the robbers might start out of any bush. They were forced to dismount from their horses, and make their way on foot; and by and by it was plain that the aged Lysimachus could not struggle on, and must soon sink from fatigue. His pupil called a halt, but the chill of the winter night threatened to be as fatal to the old man as fatigue would have been. All around were to be seen fires where the robbers were resting and refreshing themselves, and Alexander, springing up, dashed like the swift-footed Achilles himself towards the nearest of the watchfires, and flashing out of the darkness before the eyes of the amazed robbers, cut down two who attempted to resist him, snatched a burning log from the fire and bore it back to his own followers. A large pile was soon collected and kindled, and old Lysimachus was safely cherished till morning. In eleven days all the robbers had submitted, and Alexander descended to Sidon.

Winter had brought home the fleet to Sidon and the other Phœnician cities, and these were placed at the disposal of Alexander; also from the island of Cyprus another fleet had come, which had probably been waiting to take part till he should prove to be successful: and thus he reappeared before the walls of Tyre with a fleet of two hundred and twenty ships.

Still the task was a fearful one, for the walls towards the strait were a hundred and twenty feet high, and there were two harbours full of shipping and defended with chain-cables. Alexander's machines came to the edge of the mound, his vessels attacked from the water; but still the Tyrian defence was valiant, and the hot sand that was poured down on the Greeks, getting under their clothes, caused intolerable suffering. A great seafight, however, in which Alexander's galley was brought up at the decisive moment, destroyed most of the Tyrian fleet, and crippled the defence. Then there was a general assault, and after many hours of terrible hand-to-hand fighting the Greeks were masters of the great merchant city. There was a frightful slaughter, but the Phœnician allies saved many fugitives in their ships, and the king, with all who had taken refuge in the temple of Moloch, were spared. This was in the spring of 332. The siege had lasted five months, and Alexander was prouder of the achievement than of either of his pitched battles.

Again Darius sent an embassy to him. It is said that, on hearing how scrupulously Alexander had respected the dignity of his family, he had prayed aloud that, if he were to lose Asia, Alexander might be his successor; and his proposals were, this time, that Alexander should reign over all to the west of the Euphrates, and marry one of his daughters. " I would take his offer if I were Alexander," said Parmenio. " So would I, if I were Parmenio," replied Alexander; and this second proposal met with a still haughtier reply—Alexander could marry one of the daughters whenever he pleased, nor would he take a part where the whole, he said, belonged to him.

On then he went along the coast to the country of the Philistines, those warlike foes who had so beset the land

of Judah, but who had long lain quiet beneath the great
Eastern dominion.   Four out of the five cities readily
submitted, but the fifth, Gaza, was governed by a high-
spirited black eunuch, named Batis, who, against all hope,
was resolved to hold out the city to the last, and called in
a band of Arabians, who seconded the Philistine valour
with all their native ferocity.

During a sacrifice at the outset of the siege, a vulture,
flying overhead, dropped a small stone on Alexander's
shoulder, and the soothsayers thereupon predicted that
the siege would be successful ; but that the king himself
would not escape without injury.   The augurs were more
sanguine than the engineers, who had declared the place
impregnable ; but Alexander set resolutely to work, raised
a mound with great labour, battered the city with his
mighty machines, and cast stones into it from his cata-
pults.   In the midst, however, a stone from the defenders
struck him between the breastplate and shoulder-piece,
and inflicted a very painful wound, the healing of which
was tedious.   During his recovery, he caused mines to be
carried beneath the walls, and sent for further instruments
of war from Tyre, and at last the assault was made.   Full
three times the attack was repulsed by the gallant Philistines and Arabs, and only at the fourth—led by a relative
of Alexander—was the brave defence overcome, the garrison all slain at their posts, and the governor Batis taken,
still breathing, though severely wounded.   Some narra-
tives declare that Alexander, in imitation of his ancestor
and example Achilles, pierced the ankles of the brave
black while yet alive, and, putting thongs through them,
dragged him round the walls ; but this would have been
an act of barbarity beyond that of the Homeric Achilles,
who dragged a senseless corpse round the pile of his
friend ; and, moreover, Alexander was still disabled by
his wound,—so that, as the story is omitted by his best

and most correct biographer, we may believe that he could respect the unusual courage even of a negro slave.

Gaza proved to be stored with quantities of balm and spice, ready probably for exportation, and the sight reminded Alexander of an occasion when, in his boyhood, he had thrown handfuls of incense upon the sacrifice, and had been reprimanded by his stern and frugal old governor Leonnatus. So he packed up bales on bales of myrrh and spice, and sent them to his old friend, with a playful note that now he begged of Leonnatus to be more liberal to the gods.

Still another province remained to be subdued before Alexander could safely enter Egypt—a city, like Tyre, destroyed by Nebuchadnezzar, and built up by its citizens with the sanction of Cyrus, after seventy years, and noted for the fierceness, constancy, and exclusiveness of the inhabitants, who had made their walls wellnigh impregnable, in the face of the utmost difficulties. Would their religion, which was said to be bare, morose, and stern, lead them to a resistance as violent as that of Tyre and Gaza, which had between them detained Alexander nine months, and cost him the hardest fighting he ever encountered in his life?

Ready then for a fierce combat, Alexander marched up the rocky road to the city of Jerusalem on her precipitous hill. But, behold, as he came to the spot whence first the city could be discerned, he beheld a whole host pouring forth from it—not, however, armed. Not a sword was among them, all marched in measured procession, wearing flowing white robes bordered with a broad ribbon of blue, and led by white-turbaned priests with white scarfs crossed over raiment of blue and scarlet, with silver trumpets, harps, and other instruments in their hands, leading a sweet, measured chant that echoed back from the mountains ; while at their head walked a magnificent figure, with a long beard, garments of bright blue and scarlet, the border hung with golden bells and pomegranates, his bosom glittering with a breast-plate of gold and precious stones, and on his brow a glorious mitre of beaten gold, bearing the inscription, " Holiness unto the LORD."

The Phœnicians in the army were ready to laugh this demonstration to scorn, and hoped to slake their vengeance in the sack of Jerusalem; but Alexander, after watching this grand spectacle with ardent eyes, as it at length came near him, flung himself from his horse, fell on his face before the leader of the procession, and stretched out his hands in adoration. Then rising, he saluted the high priest, and was soon surrounded by the chief of his followers, whom he received courteously and respectfully.

His officers could not believe their eyes, and Parmenio remonstrated with him on this prostration to the high priest of the Jews. " It was not to him," said Alexander, " but to the Name of God on his brow "—for no doubt he had become familiar enough with Phœnician characters to recognise the Holy Name on the mitre. He further added, that long ago, at Dium in Macedonia, when he was considering of his expedition into Asia, he had in a dream beheld exactly such a majestic form, which bade him not hesitate, for he would lead him into Persia and deliver the empire over to him.

Having thus explained himself, Alexander took the high priest Jaddua by the hand, and with him entered the sacred city, where he went up with him to the temple, to the outer court of the Gentiles, and worshipped while the priests offered sacrifices. Then Jaddua, returning with the rolls of prophecy, assured him that he was already expected, and, unfolding his parchment volume, told him how a son of their ancient kings, who lived and died as both slave and prime minister in the palaces of Nebuchadnezzar and Cyrus, had seen in a vision a he-goat, the very ensign of Macedon, "come from the west on the face of the whole earth"—so swiftly as not to touch the ground—and smite the two-horned ram of the Medes and Persians, and stamp him even to the ground. Yea, and an angel had explained that rough goat to be the King of Grecia, and the great horn to be the first king. And there was another roll, the writing of one of the captives whom Cyrus had sent home, and who had kept up his country-men's courage in those hard days when their temple and city were being rebuilt. Had not he written that Tyre did build herself a stronghold, and heaped up silver as the dust, and fine gold as the mire of the streets, but that the LORD should cast her out, and smite her power in the sea, and she should be devoured with fire; that Ashkelon should see it and fear, Gaza also should see it and be very sorrowful?

Was not this Alexander's own campaign? And there was a promise, too, of safety for Jerusalem, which to Jaddua the high priest had been clenched—in the hour of distress and alarm on the tidings of the fall of Gaza—by an appearance by night, which bade him fearlessly open the gates, and go out to welcome the conqueror as one appointed by God for His work. But the oracles did not end there. They told, that when it waxed strong, the great horn should be broken. Alexander accepted the first part of the augury with gratitude. If he failed en-tirely to learn that the God whose Name he had bowed before was the only God in heaven and earth, the God who had raised him up to fulfil His own purposes, the God who had already declared how quickly the great horn should be broken, yet still he was impressed and touched by the grand purity he beheld; and with all his greatness of soul he respected the Jewish people, and gladly ac-cepted a band of them to march with his armies.

It was Alexander's desire to be regarded as the deliverer and friend of each nation that had been subjugated by the Persians, to adapt himself to their notions, restore their cherished laws, and then gradually to infuse into them that high-toned Greek spirit of philosophy and morality that should lift and ennoble them. Only at Jerusalem was it that he was mistaken in thinking what he brought superior to what he found ; and though partly from his own defects, partly from those of his subjects, and partly from the briefness of his career, his grand idea failed, yet he carried out enough of it to spread Greek culture and character throughout the Levant, and thus to be one of the chief agents—if not the chief of all—in smoothing the way for the spread of the Gospel.

The gates of Egypt were unlocked when Judæa submitted, and in the old kingdom of the Pharaohs the Persians were so much hated that Alexander was hailed, as he wished, as a rescuer. Unlike the Magians, who had loathed and insulted the quaint symbols of divinity worshipped by the Egyptians, Alexander flattered the inhabitants by adoring the bull Apis and all his animal train, and became instantly popular. The treasures of Egypt were immense, and the sight of that most wonderful and fertile country inspired him with the intention of rendering it as Græcized as he could in his usual manner, namely, by planting a colony to extend Greek civilization around it. The spot he chose was on the Delta of the Nile, a most commodious harbour, whence it would be easy to transport the wheat and fine linen of Egypt to the west, and to keep up the intimate connexion between the Greek settlers and the mother-country. He called the city, that was to be, Alexandria, and caused his engineers to trace the ground-plan before his eyes. Chalk not being at hand for the purpose, flour was used, and as fast as it was scattered was eaten up by flocks of wild seabirds, which came up in multitudes at the sight. The augur immediately foretold that the new city should be a great mart, enjoying and dispersing a profusion of corn. Never has augury been more completely realized than in the mighty and wealthy Alexandria, which has for these twenty-two centuries remained, as the great founder foresaw, the great point of contact between the East and West. Alexander filled it with a mixed population of Egyptians, Greeks, and Jews, the latter of whom he invited, with promises of special privileges, to settle there. Not small was the effect that Alexandria was destined to produce on the tone of thought among both Jews and Greeks. His taste for building, and the ample means at his disposal, made Alexander desirous of completing the Temple of Ephesus at his own sole expense, and inscribing his name as the founder upon the portal ; but the Ephesians were too proud to allow their great national shrine to be turned to the glorification of one conqueror, and they politely answered that it did not become one deity to raise a temple to another.

For that Alexander was a hero or demigod—such as belonged to the age of myths, and such as the Greeks deemed their ancestors—began really to be believed. Here he stood, at the age of twenty-four, the victor of the East, having accomplished deeds such as no man in the sober pages of Herodotus or Thucydides had ever achieved, but such as decked the names of Dionysos, Hercules, or Theseus. Was he not, indeed, another of that race of godlike men, born into later times, and not verily the son of Philip of Macedon, but of Zeus himself —like those great heroes of old ? The imagination crept into his heart, and he decided on an expedition to the most mysterious and inaccessible of oracles in order to satisfy his mind on this strange suspicion.

On an oasis in the very midst of the Lybian desert

there had stood from the most ancient times a temple to
a ram-god, or god with a ram's head, called Ammon, with
an oracle that was regarded as infallible.   The Greek
colony in Cyrene had spread the fame of this divinity,
and the old legends of Perseus and of Hercules both
represented them as seeking counsel at this wondrous
shrine, which was supposed by the Greeks to belong to
their own Zeus, and was thought of by them as a place
of wonder and of dread.   In historical times, the wild
Persian Cambyses, the insulter of Egyptian gods, had set
out to plunder the Temple of Ammon, but his army had
perished by the way under whirling columns of sand.
This of course enhanced the fame of Ammon, and increased Alexander's desire to visit the shrine.   He set
out with a small select band, and made his way thither,
amid strange portents, that seemed to assure him of the
special favour of the gods—wonders that are recorded by
the most sober of the historians.

Sudden showers spared the band from thirst in the
sandy waste, a raven appeared at their utmost need and
acted as their guide, and when the path had been lost in
the drifting sand, two huge serpents came forth and
crawled along direct for the oasis, a lovely island in the
waste, about six miles across, and rich with laurels, myr-
tles, and palms, among which rose the mysterious temple.

As the Greek travellers approached, they saw gold
glittering from among the trees—as it were a sun of rain-
bow light, sparkling down on them.   It was a symbol of
the god—a disc encrusted with precious stones, and placed
in an enormous golden ship, which was borne on the
shoulders of eighty priests, and accompanied by dancing
maidens, who sang a chant entreating the god to be pro-
pitious.   Alexander was conducted even to the innermost
sanctuary, and there remained alone.   He never disclosed
what passed there, only saying that the answers to his

questions had been satisfactory. No doubt they were more pleasing oracles than those the high priest had shown him at Jerusalem; in which it had been foretold that the great horn was to be broken in his might. These there can be little doubt added to the overweening pride that his wonderful course had already inspired; and thenceforth began a certain inflation of tone, which marred the brave simplicity and hardihood of his earlier course. His whole conduct favoured the belief that Zeus Ammon had verily owned him for his offspring, and he accepted the flatteries that so hailed him.

After arranging the government of Egypt, Alexander returned by sea to Tyre, in order to prepare for following Darius into the further East. He celebrated a great sacrifice and games in honour of Hercules—as he chose to call Moloch; and, in the spring of 331, set forth with 40,000 foot and 7,000 horse on the track, untrodden by any Greek, save as an exile, a captive, a slave, or a hired soldier of the Persian, whereas Alexander carried with him the captured family of the Great King.

A body of troops were sent forward to throw a bridge over the Euphrates, hitherto the barrier of the East, at Thapsacus; and the Persian guard retreating on the advance of the Greeks, the river was safely passed, and Alexander held on his way towards the north-west, where there was no great heat, no enemies, and plenty of provisions; but the rugged ground, and the many streams that were to be crossed, made the journey so toilsome, that it occupied at least two months, and seems to have worn out and caused the death of Statira, the beautiful wife of Darius, whom Alexander had never chosen to behold.

She died just as the invaders had crossed the Tigris, the foot-soldiers wading with the water up to their breasts and their shields held on high over their heads. On the other side, Darius was known to be waiting with "all people, nations, and languages" from the far East—the boldest of the Persians, the hardy mountaineers of the Caucasus and Himalayas, the fierce desert horsemen—all assembled to meet the enemy, who was seeking them in their very homes.   To some, at least, the Great King was the native chief, not the foreign conqueror ; many were bold and dashing warriors, and this battle—with the rivers behind them—in the heart of the enemy's country—was, in truth, the most perilous that had yet been fought by the Greeks.

Some hearts among them which were disposed to quail were much dismayed by an eclipse of the moon, which took place the night after the Tigris was crossed ; but the ingenious soothsayer contrived to assure them that the sun meant Macedon, and the moon Persia, and therefore that her darkness only boded good to the Greeks.

For four days the army marched along the banks of the Tigris without seeing an enemy, but late in the afternoon of the fifth they came in sight of the Persian host, drawn up in battle array about four miles off, and extending as far as the eye could reach.

It was so near night that Alexander resolved to defer the attack till morning, but he set everything in order, directing his generals, and exhorting his men, ere he went to rest in as much security as if his handful of men were not wellnigh enclosed within the multitude of foes all around.   The varied cries and shouts, the clang of arms, trampling of horses and treading of feet, from the whole vast circuit, was like the ground swell of the ocean before a storm ; and Parmenio, becoming anxious, followed his king to his tent to recommend that, against such tremendous odds, a night attack should be the resource.   All the answer he received was, " It would be base to steal a victory ;" and when in the morning he brought word to the royal tent that the army were on the alert and all drawn up, he found Alexander fast asleep.

"How can you sleep so calmly," he exclaimed, "with one of the greatest battles in the world before you?"

"How could we not be calm," replied Alexander, "since the enemy is coming to deliver himself into our hands?"

He then arrayed himself in a short tunic closely girt round him, and over it, not metal armour such as had been crushed into his shoulder at Gaza, but a breastplate of strongly-quilted linen, girt with a broad belt of leather, encrusted with massy gold figures of exquisite workmanship, and sustaining a light sharp sword. His helmet was of polished steel, with a gorget of precious stones, and a white plume; light greaves rose to his knees, a shield was on his left arm, and his long Macedonian spear in his right hand. And so he went forth, in all the alertness and vigour of his five and twenty years, to oppose Codomanus, who, though not greatly his elder, was encumbered with the trappings of oriental royalty, helpless from long custom, and enervated in spirit by his luxurious life.

Two hundred chariots, armed with scythes, and fifteen trained elephants, protected the towering chariot of Darius in the centre of his army, and he talked grandly of charging the Greeks in full front, and letting his wings close in on them at the same time, so as to squeeze them like an insect in the hand.

Alexander, divining this intention, had instructed his troops to be ready to face about on whatever side they were attacked, and he likewise sent light-armed men in among the chariots, to cut the traces, and kill the horses, so as to make this covering cloud of no effect. He himself, instead of spreading his main body to meet the Persian charge in full front, drew it up in a wedgelike shape, and pushed forward obliquely into the very heart of the Immortal band as they charged, so that their order was broken ; they began to scatter, and he was on the verge of pouncing on Darius, when tidings came that the right Persian wing, brave mountain tribes, and horsemen of the desert, had broken the troops of Parmenio, and were threatening the camp. The Persian prisoners there were all in commotion, and hurrying to their queen-mother, Sisygambis, told her that their rescue had come, and she had only to fly to regain her freedom. But either she did not believe it, or Persian liberty was less sweet to her than Greek bondage, for she never stirred from her carpet, never spoke a word nor unclosed her lips, but apparently took no notice of the tidings.

Alexander had already secured the victory by putting the Immortals and their king to flight, but he was forced to turn to Parmenio's assistance, and it was not without some hard fighting that these brave men were dispersed, and he was free to endeavour to overtake Darius, who had mounted a fleet mare, and was galloping away headlong towards the Armenian mountains. It was said that he refused to let the bridges be broken down behind him, lest his followers should thus be cut off from escape ; but such an act of consideration was scarcely like a Persian king.

Alexander followed him forty miles, as far as Arbela, the city which gave name to the battle, where he arrived at midnight. The gates were shut, and he was forced to halt, but only to enter the next day, and find there the sword and bow of the royal fugitive.

The battle of Arbela gave Alexander the very heart of the empire. Babylon was ready to surrender to him. Babylon, the centre of all ambition in the ancient world, as its name has been the proverb for the heights of worldly glory in the modern ; Babylon, the city of Nebuchadnezzar, the place of Daniel's visions, the pride of the East, the far-off marvel of the West, was opening her gates to the Goat of Macedon!

There, in the midst of her waters, surrounded by her massive walls, lifting up her terraced gardens, pointing aloft with her temple of Bel, she lay in majesty, tarnished indeed, but still unrivalled, and eager to own her conqueror. The streets were strewn with flowers, and bordered with silver altars steaming with perfumes, and the Chaldean priests came forth, in sumptuous procession, escorting splendid horses and cages of leopards and lions as presents to the conqueror. Alexander accepted them graciously, and was well pleased to converse with the Chaldeans, who had preserved the discoveries of the first astronomers in the world, who had given the names by which we still know the stars. The registers of their observations ranged back for 1903 years, and copies of them were a welcome treasure, which Alexander despatched to his old master, Aristotle. He also wondered at the naphtha which was collected from a cave near Babylon, and which, being dropped along a street, and then lighted at night, made a wonderful illumination. In a dried state this naphtha became· bitumen, and had cemented the walls of Babylon and the towering temple of Bel. Xerxes, the great foe of all worship save the Magian, had done his best to ruin this temple, but Alexander, who regarded all religions with a certain curiosity, interest, and respect, secured the hearts of the Chaldeans by decreeing that it should be restored by the hands of the inhabitants. Many of these were, however, Jews, and as they not only knew it to be an idol temple, but regarded it as the original Tower of Babel, they petitioned Alexander that they might be exempted from the work; and he consented. He spent thirty days at Babylon, by way of giving his wearied men repose; but he did not then begin to establish there a new and mightier Empire of the East : he had other cities first to win and review.

Susa came first : "Shushan the palace," where Daniel prayed on the banks of the Ulai, and where he lies buried ; where Esther had interceded for her people, and Nehemiah had borne the cup. Her palaces, with their marble pavements and incalculable stores of riches, the accumulated tribute-money of three centuries, were all surrendered to him ; and there, too, were found the trophies of Xerxes' invasion of Greece, the brazen statues of the two deliverers of Athens, Harmodius and Aristogeiton, which he had carried from the Acropolis as tokens of his success. These, with many treasures, Alexander despatched to their home, trusting that at last Athens would feel that by him Greece was revenged.

While at Susa, Alexander received letters from his home, and presents of garments, spun, woven, and worked by the loving hands of his mother and sisters. He took them to show to his captive, Sisygambis, and when she admired them, offered to have her grandchildren taught the same arts, but to his surprise she began to weep bitterly, and he found that to a Persian princess any employment seemed servile, so that she thought he was no longer going to treat her as a queen, but that a harsh slavery would be the lot of her family. He reassured her, and told her how Greek ladies deemed the loom the honourable tribute of even a goddess, and how deeply he loved and esteemed the mother who had thus worked for him. He had indeed a most fond affection for Olympias—more perhaps than she deserved, though it was so great a grace in him. His regent, Antipater, had written many complaints of her haughty interference. "He knows not," said Alexander, "that one tear of a mother will blot out ten such letters." No doubt it was this strong reverence for his own mother that made him so filial towards his aged captive, whom he now installed in her own palace at Susa, whilst he set forth on a severe winter campaign in the mountains.

He had now to push into Fars, the original rocky nest of the once hardy Persians, and to make his way through tremendous defiles, where, but for his skill and the want of skill in his adversaries, his army could have been reduced to great straits. His object was Persepolis, the cradle of the Persian kings, and fuller of treasure than even Susa ; and he pushed on the faster because of a report that the inhabitants were about to pillage the treasure themselves. As he advanced to the stately city enclosed by precipitous rocks, carved in wedge-shaped characters with the boastful records of many a Persian prince, he was greeted by a miserable band of Greek captives, with noses, lips, hands, or feet cut off, and eyes thrust out, by command of the masters who had taken them from the cities of Asia Minor. To Greeks, who so highly esteemed the dignity of the body and who never tortured, the spectacle was abhorrent. The king burst into tears, and promised that he would send them to their homes with all the compensation possible ; but almost all declared that they should be ashamed to show themselves to their friends, and begged that he would rather assign them a maintenance in their present dwelling-place, which he did with the utmost readiness.

The sight greatly embittered the spirit of Alexander. Hitherto he had treated the places he entered as captive countries to be liberated from the Persian yoke, but already at Susa he had shown that he considered himself to be in an enemy's country, and Persepolis— the seat of the Magian religion and the Achæmenid dynasty—which had attacked the gods of Greece in their most sacred shrines, he deemed the right spot for retribution ; and he therefore came to the resolution of giving it up to plunder. Parmenio interceded for the beautiful city, the storehouse of the Persian kings, representing that he would be destroying his own property; but in vain. One story declares that it was at a banquet, when Alexander was inflamed with wine, and by the fierce battle songs of

> " Timotheus placed on high
> Among the tuneful choir,"

that he was worked up by the impassioned discourse of a beautiful Athenian lady, named Thais, to make another Troy of Persepolis, and himself to apply a torch to the palace, an example that was but too speedily followed. The burning, however, was soon stopped by his command, but there was a terrible massacre of all the men; the women were made slaves, and the private property shared by the ferocious soldiery, while a huge amount of royal treasure was secured for Alexander himself. It was one of the few savage actions that blot his memory, whether prompted by passion or by policy, whether he was carrying out the character of Neoptolemus, revenging the wrongs of the Grecian name, rewarding his soldiers, or impressing terror upon the Eastern people, which last cause he assigned in a letter of his own. The other Greeks certainly felt all these impulses. A Corinthian shed tears at seeing him on the Persian throne, exclaiming, " What joy have those Greeks missed who have not seen Alexander on the throne of Darius!"

Alexander, after visiting the tomb of Cyrus, pushed on in pursuit of Codomanus to the Median capital, Ecbatana; but again he found that his prey had fled at his approach, and was gone northward into the mountains. Again Alexander set forth to hunt down his victim, but in the meantime despair and treason were doing their work among the troops of the miserable fugitive. Bessus, satrap of Bactra, and his companions were resolved to wrest the command from the incapable hands of Darius, and, taking the leadership themselves, to make a desperate defence among their native hills; and though the Greek mercenaries still remained faithful, their numbers were not sufficient to protect the king from being seized, bound with golden chains, and placed in a covered chariot. On hearing of this revolt, Alexander dashed on headlong with his fleetest horsemen, riding all night, only halting in the noonday heat, and then again hastening forward. The last twenty-five miles were across a desert without water, so as to meet the Persians, who were following the ordinary road around it. At daybreak he beheld the Persian army moving along like a confused crowd. He charged them, and there was a general flight.

Presently there was a cry that Darius was taken, and Alexander flew to the spot. But it was only to find the unhappy monarch lying on the ground, pierced with javelins, speechless, if not already dead.

> " Deserted at his utmost need
> By those his former bounty fed;
> On the bare earth exposed he lies,
> Without a friend to close his eyes."

Bessus and the others had tried to place him on a horse and take him with them in their flight; but he had refused to go as a prisoner, and they, being resolved that Alexander should not have him alive to use his name against them, flung their darts at him, and abandoned them. A Macedonian soldier had found him, given him some drink, and gathered up his faltering accents of gratitude to Alexander for his treatment of his family, of trust that the conqueror would avenge his murder—as the common cause of kings—and a hope that so great a man might be the sovereign of the world. He died almost as Alexander came up, and the Greek monarch could only testify his respect by throwing his own mantle over the body, which he caused to be embalmed, and sent to Sisygambis to be interred with royal pomp in the mighty sepulchre of the thirteen Achæmenid kings, whose race was utterly crushed, their very nation, as it were, extinguished for full six hundred years.

The pursuit of Darius had been terribly exhausting ; many men and horses had sunk under the fatigue ; and when Alexander led his army to rest in a place that the Greeks called the City of the Hundred Gates, he found that they imagined that, now Darius was dead, their work was done, and that they were already preparing to carry home their spoil and enjoy it in Greece. Such was far from their prince's purpose. He did not, like them, want to make Greece a spot whence to receive tribute, or else to plunder and punish the world. His idea was to make the world one great Greece, imbuing every place with all the best and noblest that it could receive from the land of Homer, Plato, and Aristotle ; and to be himself, not the King of Macedon treading down the East, but the all-beneficent monarch of East and West alike, ruling, reforming, improving from the central home of greatness, power, and conquest, upon the mighty rivers of Assyria. It was the grandest and most nearly executed human dream that the world has seen. But he was obliged to exert all his eloquence and ascendency over his soldiers to retain them, for unwilling followers he would not have ; and he actually dismissed his Greek auxiliaries with pay, gifts, and honours, such as might tempt those at home to join him in their stead ; and though his Macedonians professed themselves ready to follow him to the ends of the earth, the numbers he retained only amounted to 20,000 foot and 3,000 horse ; and he, therefore, necessarily must rule as Persian sovereign, and secure Eastern deference by the appendages that the oriental mind deems essential to sovereignty.

So he took the Eastern title, Shah-in-Shah, King of Kings, and the head that had hitherto been crowned only by its own majesty and heroic descent was encircled by the tiara, the simple Greek robe gave place to the sweeping garments of the oriental on all state occasions, and the Persians owned in him their half-divine sovereign. Even Artabazus, the faithful satrap, who had held by Codomanus to the last, now gave in his submission in his 95th year. His age and fidelity were so much honoured by Alexander, that when he accompanied the army, the king, though always by preference walking, would mount his horse, that the old man might not be ashamed to do so.

But what impressed the Persians was hateful and ridiculous to the Greeks, who saw in this assumption of royal trappings only ridiculous pride and vanity, and resented the distance at which their master's elevation placed them, when they were used to treat him only as the first among equals. Mischievous murmurs went about, and were in danger of ripening into a plot, when Alexander made an example, and a fearful one. Reports came to him that his father's old general, Parmenio, and his son, Philotas, were constantly speaking of him contemptuously as " the boy," and actually were guilty of forming a plot for his destruction. The tale was carried to him by malignant whispers, and it is not certain whether it was true or not, but Alexander acted at once upon it. Philotas alone was present in his camp, and he caused him to be arrested and tried before the soldiers, he himself acting as his accuser. Philotas was a proud, selfish, unpopular man, and the soldiers by acclamation condemned him to die, and would have stoned him at once ; but his testimony was needed to condemn his father, and he was carried away and put to the torture, superintended by Hephæstion and Cratinus, while Alexander was not too far off to hear his cries.   He was made to say whatever his tormentors chose, and then slain, while messengers were sent to Ecbatana there to kill old Parmenio, and to bring his head to Alexander. It was a grievous affair : nor is it possible to say how stringent was the necessity, nor how far Alexander was justified in thus sacrificing his father's old friend ; whether there were really treason on the part of father and son, whether there were mere suspicion, or whether in the inflation of Eastern despotism he had become unable to brook Macedonian freedom of speech.

It was Alexander's present object to complete his victory by hunting down and destroying Bessus, and for this purpose he had to penetrate into those wild and wintry regions around the Hindoo Koosh, which are now chiefly inhabited by Kurdish tribes, and have never been trodden by any other civilized conqueror.   There were grievous sufferings from cold, and the difficulties of the march were impeded by the soldiers' solicitude about their baggage, which the plunder of Persepolis had rendered unwieldy.   Seeing this, Alexander caused all, including his own, to be brought forward and burnt, thus recalling his men to a sense of the discipline they had forgotten.

For two months in the depth of winter he was forced to halt at a place that must have been near Cabul, and then, in the spring of B.C. 329, struggled on through the snow to the banks of the river Oxus, which was half a mile broad, and so deep that he could only accomplish crossing it, after the fashion of the old Assyrians, on floats of hides inflated with air or stuffed with straw.   This occupied five days, and the remnant of Bessus' army, on learning that this last barrier was passed, seized and imprisoned their satrap just as he had done by Darius. Alexander therefore sent his general, Ptolemy, forwards,

and he soon returned with the miserable man, who was
led into Alexander's presence naked and with a clog
round his neck. He was sent away under the charge of
a brother of Darius to suffer a punishment so cruel as to
savour far too much of Eastern barbarity.

Still the fierce population refused to submit, having
never really known a master, though the seven fine towns
in the delicious country around the Jaxartes were considered to be Persian, in contradistinction to the country of
the wild Scythians or Tartars on the other side of the
river. Alexander did not obtain possession of these
without much severe fighting, and was twice wounded—
by an arrow in the leg at Samarkand, and by a stone at
Cyropolis, which, falling on the nape of his neck, confused his sight for several days. His mood at the time was
fierce and bitter. An unfortunate Greek population, whose
fathers had given up the treasures of the Temple of Apollo
to Xerxes, and had been transplanted by him 150 years
before, were all massacred by way of retribution, and
the punishments that fell on a Persian province that
endeavoured to revolt were terrible. He also entered on
a war with the savage and independent Scythians, and
had one sharp battle with them, in which he put them to
flight; but, in the heat of the pursuit, a draught from a
brackish and unwholesome spring took such an effect
on him that he was carried back to the camp more dead
than alive, and becoming convinced that no good could
be done by trying to reduce a houseless race in an inhospitable region, he accepted a species of submission from
the Khan, and returned to Samarkand. He had been in
an irritable and suspicious state, apparently, ever since the
information that led to Parmenio's ruin, and at Samarkand this temper broke out in a most lamentable manner.
It was the feast-day of Dionysos, but Alexander chose to
dedicate it to Castor and Pollux, and after the sacrifices

held one of those " banquets of wine " which were a Persian
custom, and into which he had fallen only too readily,
forgetting the terrible degradation to which drunkenness
had brought his father. His brain was also probably
the more easily disturbed in consequence of the blow at
Cyropolis, which had evidently produced concussion. His
Macedonian officers partook of the general licence, and
when his flatterers began to exalt him beyond the twin
heroes of the day, and to talk of his divine parentage,
Cleitus, his nurse's brother, burst out wrathfully in rebuke
of their falsity and Alexander's boastfulness. " Listen to
truth," he said, " or else ask no freemen to join you, but
surround yourself with slaves ! "

These words enraged Alexander to such a pitch that
he sprang up and felt for his dagger to slay Cleitus ; but
the weapon had been removed, and he was withheld
by Ptolemy and the others, while some strove to force
Cleitus out of the room. But Cleitus was not to be
kept back, and Alexander struggled furiously, declaring that he was chained like Darius and only the name
of king left him, until he shook off the detaining hands,
snatched a pike from a soldier, and laid Cleitus dead at
his feet.

Remorse followed the next moment. He had almost
thrown himself on the point of the same lance at once, and,
when withheld, flung himself into his chamber and gave
way to an agony of lamentation and self-reproach, without tasting food for three days. His flatterers at last
framed the plea for him that Dionysos had produced the
frenzy in revenge for the neglect of his festival, and Alexander so far accepted it as to make grand sacrifices in
honour of the wine-god. But there was much angry
feeling among his attendants, and the Greek hatred to
the observances exacted by Persian royalty was strongly
kept up by a philosopher named Callisthenes, a pupil of

Aristotle, one of the learned men whom Alexander carried with him to study the sciences, learning, geography, and natural history of these new and strange climes. To Callisthenes, moreover, was entrusted the education of the young men who acted as pages to the king, supplied him with weapons in battle or in hunting, waited on him, and watched his bed by turns at night. Callisthenes was a proud man, who hated all forms of observance ; and when at the banquet Alexander sent his golden cup round among Persians and Greeks—after which each advanced in turn, bent to the ground, and then was kissed by the king—Callisthenes took the cup, but omitted the obeisance. Hephæstion directed the king's attention to this lack of courtesy, and Alexander turned away, whereupon the philosopher contemptuously observed, " I go away the poorer by a kiss."

A man of this independent temper naturally infused the like spirit into the young noblemen, who were already impatient of the oriental abject habits of courtesy ; and there was much inclination to discontent and insubordination among the young pages. At Bactra, whither Alexander moved upon leaving Samarkand, he found himself near one of the huge parks or forests for wild beasts that the Persian princes had kept for hunting-grounds. There he found magnificent sport ; it was the very native home of lions, tigers, and wild beasts of all kinds, and Alexander himself had a single encounter with an enormous lion, whose fearful leap he received with the hunting-spear, so perfectly directed, and so steadily held, that the animal was instantly pierced to the heart. The Macedonians, however, were so dismayed at the fearfulness of the danger, that they decreed in council of war that the king should never hunt alone on foot again. In one of these chases, Hermolaus, one of the most apt pupils in Callisthenes' school of democratic independence, rushed

rudely before the king to give the finishing stroke to a
wild boar; and the misdemeanour was punished by a
flogging and the deprivation of his horse. It is not clear
whether this were the ordinary chastisement of a presumptuous boy, or a real outrage upon a free noble; but
to Hermolaus and some of his hot-blooded comrades it
appeared to be an inexpiable offence, and they laid a plot
for murdering their master in his sleep the first night all
the conspirators were on guard together. That night,
however, Alexander, acting on a mysterious warning sent
through a Syrian witch, sat up till after the watch of pages
was changed, and the next morning one of the lads,
seized with terror and remorse, told his brother of the
plot, and the brother carried it to Ptolemy, one of the
chief officers.

The unhappy youths were arrested and put to the
torture, when they made full confession of their own
intentions, Hermolaus even justifying them as a glorious
mode of ridding the world of a tyrant; but they declared
no one else to have been aware of them, and expressly
denied that Callisthenes had any complicity, persisting
in this reply when brought out to be stoned by the whole
army, by whom their sentence had been pronounced.
The philosopher, however, was so fully regarded as having
been the author of the mischief by his violent language
that he was taken into custody, where one author says
that he died, another that he was tortured and hanged.
Aristotle had long ago warned him of the peril of unguarded declamation by quoting the line—

" Short date of life, my son, these words forebode."

It is hard to judge Alexander in these matters, since
nothing but the most visible greatness and authority will
keep Eastern nations submissive, and any show of dis-
respect from the Greeks would have been ruinous to him,

unless he had chosen to make them a dominant caste, which would have been cruel and unjust to the Persians.

Thus had three years passed in securing Persia, and it was in B.C. 328 that, having decided against molesting the savage hordes of Scythians in the unknown North, he turned to explore, rather than subdue, a country of almost fabulous fame to Western ears—of which even the Phœnician sailor and the Jewish merchant could scarcely speak—the wondrous land of India ; where a few wild myths spoke of the triumphal course of Dionysos and Hercules, but which the conquering kings of Persia themselves had never attempted.

That rugged band of mountains—interspersed with beauteous table-lands and valleys—which lies as a barrier between Persia and Hindostan, has been impenetrable to every victor save this greatest of all. The high-spirited and ferocious inhabitants have used all their advantages of ground, and have been free from the earliest ages. Neither from the north nor the south have any attacks been availing to subdue them, and the only passage ever forced through them was that of Alexander, whose name their tradition still holds in veneration. It was only through severe fighting, and terrible sufferings from snow, ice, and rugged roads, however, that the Greek army accomplished this unrivalled expedition— which we cannot trace, for want of the power of surveying the mountains ; and in the spring of 327 he came down through the long and dangerous Khyber Pass to the banks of the Indus.

Here he found himself in a wonderful land, with literature, art, and philosophy more ancient than even that of the Greeks, and not yet blighted by the foreign invasions of duller races. The religion of the country—derived from the same source as that of the Greeks—showed such analogies, that it was possible to imagine that he had really come on those traces of the conquests of Dionysos. He was, indeed, only on the outskirts of India, in what we now term the Punjaub, or land of five rivers ; but he had come into contact with true specimens of the grand old Hindoo race—dignified, refined, thoughtful, and brave without being aggressive.   In especial was noted a king on the banks of the Jhelum, called by the Greeks Porus, and probably named Parusha (or the hero).   He bravely disputed with Alexander the passage of the river, leading a large army, supported by a number of trained elephants. On one of these he rode, conspicuous by his noble stature, and the silver scales of his beautiful armour covering all save the right arm, which was kept free to strike.   It was the best contested battle that Alexander had fought, and the victory was not decided till two o'clock in the after-noon, when two of Porus's sons had been killed and the king himself wounded in the shoulder.   Alexander was anxious to save so brave a foe, and sent messenger after messenger, until at last one of his Indian allies persuaded the valiant old man to surrender.   He was refreshed and rested, and then was led to the victor, when he advanced without bating a jot of his royal dignity, greeting Alex-ander, not as a suppliant, but as a brother monarch. There was a silence as these two grand specimens of the sons of the East and the West surveyed one another with dauntless eyes, and then Alexander asked whether his brother prince had any request to make.

" None, save to be treated as a king," said Parusha.

" That," said Alexander, " I shall do for my own sake. Is there nothing more you would ask ? "

" All is included therein," said the Eastern hero.   The two understood each other from that moment, and became fast friends ; Alexander not only restored Porus's kingdom, but enlarged its borders at the expense of more refractory princes ; in fact, he carved and cut and disposed of the lands about him to such a degree, that the natives of the Punjaub still call a river that alters their landmarks by changing its course " an Alexander." He still fought his way, and drove away another Parusha, whom the Greeks termed Porus the Coward ; he defeated a wild tribe of Tartars, whom his people termed Cathaians ; and received the submission of thirty-five cities, all full of inhabitants. In the midst of them he founded two more, one of which he named Bucephaleïa, in honour of his beloved steed, which died here in the midst of a battle, without a wound. Wherever Alexander had been, had been planted colonies of Greeks, so as to form the germ of a city, whence civilization might spread to the adjacent parts and communication be kept up with the mother-country.

He soon found, however, that he was merely on the outskirts of the land of wonder. The Ganges, the sacred river of India, still lay far beyond, and there he was told of a city—supposed to be Patna—eight miles long, with five hundred and seventy towers and sixty-four gates, and full of riches of every description. No temples had he yet seen, and only two of the Brahmin Yogis, or ascetics, who must have put him much in mind of his old acquaintance Diogenes—for one refused all shelter from sun and rain, and the other took no repose but by leaning on his staff. He invited some others to show themselves, but they would not come ; and he only heard from his officers of fifteen men, all naked, and immoveable in their positions.

Everything excited his curiosity and drew him onward, but his men were daunted by the very expectations that allured him. Were they to be wanderers for ever, and never place their prizes in security, or amaze their friends at home with the narration of wonders such as Homer had never sung ? Nay, if they were to find a Porus in

P

every prince, they might never get back at all! These Hindoos were more warlike than the Persians, and better disciplined than the mountain tribes; and the Greeks were not stimulated by the chance of finding themselves equally matched. The rainy season, too, made them discontented and miserable; and when they reached the banks of the Sutlej, they came to a resolution to place no more rivers between themselves and their home.

Alexander, fearing that the camp was full of murmurs, assembled the officers and addressed them publicly. He reminded them of all they had done, assured them that they should soon reach the Eastern Ocean (which must perforce be the bound of their expedition), held out to them the hope of unrivalled fame, and promised ample rewards.

He was met by a deep silence, which was only broken by the oldest of his generals, who represented to him how he had never carried unwilling troops with him before, represented the fatigues and trials his present soldiers had undergone, and their longing wish to see home once more, and himself recommended him to revisit his home and his mother, and then collect a fresh army, with which to carry his conquests to the utmost bounds of earth. Thus would he be showing the moderation in prosperity which was honourable above all things.

This speech received the eager applause that Alexander's own had lacked. He was bitterly mortified and disappointed, and broke up the council abruptly. The next day he summoned it again, and declared that he should proceed, but only with those who followed him willingly; the rest might go home, and say they had left Alexander in the midst of his enemies.

This appeal produced no reaction of enthusiasm in his favour, though he shut himself up in his tent, and waited three days in hopes of a change in the minds of his followers. He then sacrificed, and the augurs pronounced the omens unfavourable to his advance, which gave him an excuse for yielding to the compulsion that for once his army had exercised on him.

He assured the council that he would advance no further, and endured the rapture expressed by all the troops. It was in the summer of 326, in his thirtieth year, that Alexander was thus turned back, on the borders of the Sutlej, in his unrivalled career of conquest. He marked the spot by the erection of twelve towers, in the shape of altars, on which he offered mighty sacrifices, and then applied himself to prepare for his return, not through the mountain passes by which he had come, but by building a fleet, in which to coast upwards, even to the mouth of the Euphrates.

The river on which the ships were constructed was the Hydaspes, or, as we now call it, the Jhelum, which made its way down to the Indus through tracts of fine forests of fir, cedar, and pine. These had hitherto been the home of multitudes of monkeys and baboons ; and these creatures, collecting at the top of a hill, presented an appearance so like that of an army, that the Greeks were actually beginning to arm in their own defence, when the Indians explained the matter.

While the ships were being built, Alexander made expeditions into the surrounding regions, and collected curiosities, both in animals and in native produce. One rajah brought him some of the still famous hunting dogs of Sindh, and another three hundred pounds' weight of wootz, or highly tempered steel ; a large number of elephants were likewise collected ; and he made acquaintance with that Indian plant which " instead of fruit produces wool, of which the Indians make their clothes."

At last the fleet was ready. There were eighty vessels of war, and a great quantity of smaller craft which had been collected from the natives. But a large portion of the army was still to go by land, a division marching along each bank of the river, while the ships, with Alexander on board, were to sail down in the middle.

Before he went, he installed Porus as king of seven nations and two thousand cities, and appointed his general, Philippus, satrap of the country west of the Indus. Then grand sacrifices were offered to Poseidon, and all the watery gods; and, standing on the prow of his own ship, Alexander poured a libation from a golden cup to propitiate Hydaspes, the supposed river god of the Jhelum, invoking both him and his superior, the Indus. The trumpet sounded, and the entire fleet moved on to the sound of music, every oar sounding in time, and the rowers chanting to their strokes. The sight and sound were both magnificent, and crowds of natives rushed down to admire, and to give them good speed with songs and wild dances which the Greeks supposed that Dionysos had taught them.

There are rapids where the Jhelum falls into the Chenab, and the ships had some difficulty in passing them. The lesser ships got through safely, but the larger vessels broke their oars, and two ran foul of one another, and sunk, with all their crews.

Here, too, a hostile people was encountered. Two tribes, called the Malli and Oxydracæ, though habitually at war, united against the invader, and Alexander landed with a division of his army to defeat them. He pursued the Malli to their city on the banks of the Hydraotes, or Ravee. The place still bears the name of Mooltan, and is curiously like what Alexander found it, being still a fort surrounded with a strong outer wall, inside which fruit trees may be seen growing. The king had actually pursued the flying army of the Malli across the river, there 500 yards broad, and, after resting for a night, attacked them in their stronghold. The garrison deserted the wall and rushed into the fort, while Alexander called loudly for scaling ladders, and seizing the first, placed it against the wall and hurried up. Others crowded after him, but the ladder broke, and he stood on the top of the wall, conspicuous from his armour, entirely alone, and a mark for every weapon the enemy could aim at him. His guards stretched out their arms to entreat him to leap back to them, but, scorning this as like flight, he sprang down within the wall among the enemy, who fell back for a moment in sheer amazement; but finding that he was absolutely alone, they rallied, and rushed like hounds on a lion at bay. He set his back against the wall, under a fig-tree, and slew the foremost assailant with his sword, driving back the others with large stones, so that, afraid to approach, they formed a semicircle, and shot at him with huge barbed arrows from bows six feet long. Three more men had, when the ladder broke, been near enough to the top to cling to it, and climb up after a long struggle ; and these now jumped down by him, and fought in front of him : but one dropped almost immediately with an arrow piercing his brow, and the next moment another of these deadly weapons was quivering in Alexander's breast. For some minutes he did not give way, but fought on until pain and loss of blood so overpowered him that he sunk down in a kneeling posture, his forehead on the rim of his shield so as to shelter himself behind it, while his officers held their shields over him, regardless of the wounds they themselves received.

The Macedonians, maddened by losing sight of their king, were scrambling up the wall, driving pegs in, climbing on each other's shoulders, breaking through the bolts of a little gate; but when at last they rushed in, they found Alexander lying as one dead, and his brave friends well nigh exhausted. Believing him slain, the furious troops burst into the little fort, and slaughtered every living thing they found there, while his friends lifted up the unconscious king, laid him on the Grecian's rightful bier, his own broad shield, and carried him to his tent. On the way he gave signs of life, and when the long shaft of the arrow was cut off, and it was found that the point was firmly fixed in his breast bone, he was so much himself as to call his friend Perdiccas to cut a gash sufficient to allow the barbs of the arrow to pass before withdrawing it. And his power of will was such that he endured this operation in perfect stillness, allowing no one to hold him; but by the time it was completed he had again fallen into a swoon, and for many hours lay between life and death, while the whole evening and night the soldiers watched under arms, and in deep silence, refusing to stir until at length they heard that he had fallen into a quiet sleep.

He was in great danger. The wound had touched his lungs, and he continued unable to bear any motion for a whole week; while in the meantime the main body of his army, believing him dead, gave way to constant sighs and lamentations, both for his loss and their own fate, and the Indian tribes, believing the same report, were preparing to rise.

Alexander could afford to waste no more time on a sick bed, and therefore caused himself to be carried on board a galley, and lay there under an awning as the vessel sailed down the Ravee to the camp on the Chenab. At first sight the Macedonians there deemed the prostrate figure was their king's corpse; and when he sat up and waved his hand to them, the whole air rang with shouts of delight mingled with sobs of joy. A litter was brought to the landing place, but, invigorated by the joy of his welcome, he asked for his horse and rode slowly through the crowd, who ran together in ecstasy to make sure that he was among them again. When he came near his tent, he desired to be lifted down, and walked, leaning on his two nearest friends, who, with all their gladness at his recovery, could not help reprimanding him with all their old friendly freedom for having so recklessly exposed the life which was safety to all. One old Bœotian, however, said, "O Alexander! deeds show the man," and quoted the line—

> " He who strikes must also bleed."

Alexander smiled, as well pleased with these words as with the fervent cries of joy, invocations of blessings, and the wreaths and garlands that the common soldiers were lavishing on him. He still was obliged to give himself rest for many days to come; and these were employed in the construction of fresh ships from the woods around, where the Greeks wondered at a banyan-tree, beneath which fifty horsemen could take shelter at the same time. Meantime he sent out parties to secure the submission of the country round, and having nearly recovered, he again set forth and reached first the Indus itself, and then the city now called Hyderabad, but which the Greeks found to be called Patala, a name which they considered to mean the same as Delta, this being the spot where the delta of the Indus does in fact commence. Here he seems to have established another merchant city like that which already bore his name in the Delta of Egypt; and in the meantime he set out to survey the Indus, and follow its course down to the sea. After having gone beside these utterly unknown banks for about sixty miles, the welcome smell of sea air was recognised by the Greek sailors, and Alexander sprang up with all the joy of a successful explorer, and in due time he actually beheld the open sea of the Indian Ocean, from an estuary twelve miles broad. His delight was extreme;

the broad fresh salt waves were dear to the Grecian soul, and this moreover was an ocean absolutely new to all the European world. Strange, too, it was and perilous, to men accustomed to the tideless Mediterranean, for the waves were coming in with such force that the little vessels had to take refuge in a creek, where the next morning they found themselves high and dry, but the water returning upon them from a distance in the same wonderful manner.

Alexander remained for two or three days studying the marvels of the coast, and offered the sacrifice of a bull to Poseidon, accompanied not only by libations of wine, but by the cups and bowls whence these were poured. Then returning to Patala, he arranged for his march. His ships, under a Cretan commander, Nearchus, were to sail along the coast, while he himself at the head of his land army was to force a passage inland, since, from the small size of the ships and the imperfect state of navigation, it would have been impossible for them to proceed without continually repairing to the shore; and thus secure landing places must be provided, and wells dug where springs were not on the surface,—setting out two months beforehand.

This expedition of Alexander is perfectly unparalleled in classic times. No other Greek or Roman seems to have had his curiosity respecting unknown climes; and the journeys of the early discoverers in America, half explorers, half victors, are the only things like it in history. But, alas! the pupil of Aristotle was a more beneficent and less greedy conqueror than were Cortes and Pizarro.

The desert of Gedrosia, or Makran, which lay first in his way, has scarcely been trodden since his time. It lies between the mouths of the Indus and the Persian Gulf, and even to the present day only the northern portion is considered passable, and that not without great difficulty. Of the part which Alexander crossed we have no modern account. He found it overgrown with aromatic herbs and shrubs, which diffused a pleasant odour when trodden upon; but there were also poisonous bushes like laurels, the taste of whose leaves killed the cattle, and some species of Euphorbia, with a milky juice that if spurted into the eye caused blindness. Many dangerous serpents lurked in this scant vegetation, the wells were few and far between, and the sun was burning. The whole sea border was encumbered with such rugged rocks that Alexander was forced to keep far inland, led by a few guides who professed to know the way. He sent a small party down to the shore to see what provision there was for the fleet, and they reported that they found nothing but desolation. There were indeed a few miserable fishermen on the coast, but they lived on nothing but fish, drank brackish water from holes scraped in the sand, and built their hovels of shells and sand, with roofs of fishbone rafters.

Alexander meantime had halted at a more fertile spot in the desert, and on hearing this report he sent a convoy of provisions to the shore; but the men lost their way, and were obliged to consume what they brought. A second, however, met with better success; but it was a perilous thing for the land army to part with their stores in this rainless region of shifting sand, which hung in masses like wreaths of driven snow, and soon became utterly impassable for the wheeled carriages. The men could hardly stagger through them, and the heat and thirst were intolerable. A few brackish springs there were, and these were the halting places. Around them the panting host would rest till the heat of the day was over, and then proceed by night, not stopping again until another pool was reached, even if they had to march on in the fearful noontide heat. Numbers dropped from sleep or faintness, and rose no more ; and many more paused to kill the beasts of burthen they were driving and devour them,—and the sick or helpless were thus utterly lost. When water was reported to be near, there was a general maddened dash forwards to it, and often into it ; and these hasty and excessive draughts led to so many deaths that Alexander was forced to cause his scouts to keep the discovery of water a secret from the army, which he halted out of sight of it, and then had it served out by trusty officers. He could not be severe on these breaches of discipline, but he shared the privations of his soldiers to the utmost, and when once—in the terrible heat of a noonday sun—a little water, found with great difficulty, was brought him in a helmet as he plodded through the scorching sand, parched with thirst, he thanked the bringer with all his heart, and then, in the sight of all, poured the whole away into the sands, as being resolved not to take to himself what all could not share. And in the midst of their two months of misery from thirst they were one night almost drowned, for they encamped in the stony bare wady, or valley, of an exhausted torrent ; and a sudden tempest somewhere in the mountains above so swelled it that the floods, rushing violently down, bore away almost all the remaining animals, drowned many women and children, carried off Alexander's own equipage, and reduced many who had almost died of thirst in the evening to swim for their lives before morning.

Whispers went about the host that Cyrus had once tried this march, and had appeared at the end with only seven men ; and alarm came to the utmost when the guides declared themselves to have entirely lost their way—the shifting sand-heaps to which they had trusted as landmarks had changed their form, and they had no conception either of the onward route, or where there was any likelihood of finding water. The Macedonian army would assuredly have left their bones to whiten the desert, or to form houses for the fish-eaters of the coast, had they not had a veritably great man at their head. Aware that the coast must be to the southward, and able to guide his course by the sun and stars, he took with him a party of horsemen, and set forth to find his way to the coast; but such were the sufferings of this exploration that only five were with him when at length the sea greeted his eyes. He dug into the sandy beach, and at once came upon pure fresh water. He sent back for the rest of the army, and for seven days was himself their pioneer along the beach, until the guides came to a spot which they recognised, and brought the much diminished army after this dreadful march of sixty days to Para, the capital of Gedrosia, which appears to be the modern Bunpore.

Gedrosia was part of the Persian empire, and no more really severe difficulties remained in his way to Kerman or Caramania, which he entered as much after the fashion of the triumphal procession of Dionysos as could be contrived by splendid chariots adorned with Indian hangings and boughs of trees, and likewise by the continued revelry of the soldiers, to whom universal licence was permitted, to make up for their past miseries. Still there was much uneasiness respecting the fleet: but soon after he had resumed his march, he was told that Nearchus and five men were arrived; and they were brought to him, pale, lean, and so like ghosts, that every one supposed them to be the sole survivors out of all the crews, and the king even began to condole with the commander, when Nearchus exclaimed, "Thanks to the gods, O king! your fleet is not lost." It was safely moored at the isle of Ormuz, where Nearchus had heard a report of Alexander's being within a few days' journey, and had hurried up to report himself. He had a strange tale to tell of the perils he had run from starvation, and the mutinies it led to, as well as from whales, or more probably sharks and sepias, and even from the enchantments of a wonderful island ; and Alexander was so excited by it as to plan finishing his next intended expedition to India by trying to find the way round far to the south, and to return to the Mediterranean by the pillars of Hercules—the voyage sketched out by Greek fancy as having been made in his latter days by Ulysses. Meantime he wished Nearchus to remain with him and rest from his anxious toils, while some one else conducted the fleet to the Persian Gulf; but the Cretan, a sailor to the backbone, would not relinquish the glory of his voyage of discovery. He afterwards wrote an account of it, which underwent the usual fate of travellers' wonders, and was derided as incredible by stay-at-home Greeks.

Alexander sent Hephæstion to march along the shore to provide for the security of the fleet, since there was now no further difficulty in that quarter, and his own presence was required at Persepolis, where the Persian satrap left in charge had been incapable or unfaithful, and the Macedonians had been insubordinate. Moreover, the great tomb of Cyrus, which had been only reverently visited by the king himself, had been broken up and plundered. Severe executions followed, the more distasteful to the army because they believed the king to be influenced by Bagoas, the eunuch, who had been in favour with Darius ; and when the new satrap, Peukestes, one of the three who had saved Alexander's life at Mooltan, adopted Persian state and ornaments, they looked on in contempt at what they believed to be either personal vanity or servility to the king, as usual not understanding that, in the East, a little outward show might save a great deal of bloodshed.   It was a time when

Alexander was forced to be very severe. Many of the governors he had left had reckoned on his perishing in India, and had plundered the treasuries and the people in fancied security, and the Greeks he had left in charge at Ecbatana had actually gone off with the gold to excite Sparta and Athens to revolt. Heavy punishments of course followed, alike to Greek and Persian, and in like manner rewards were impartially distributed among both nations, and to amalgamate them more completely he held an enormous wedding feast at " Shusan the palace," amid Ahasuerus' hangings and pavements, when eighty Greek nobles married eighty Persian and Median ladies.

Alexander himself married Statira, the eldest daughter of Darius, and gave her sister to Hephæstion, saying he wished their children to be as nearly allied in blood as themselves in friendship; and each of the other great officers found a bride among the satraps' daughters. The Persian laws required all marriages to be solemnized in the spring, and it was in the beginning of the year 324 that this great ceremony took place. Eighty double seats were placed in one great hall, where the eighty bridegrooms feasted ; then the eighty brides entered, wearing jewelled turbans, beneath which streamed their long locks, wide linen drawers, silken tunics with long trains, and broad flounced belts set with jewels. Alexander advanced and took his princess by the hand. Each of his officers followed his example, led his lady to her seat, kissed her, and placed her upon it. This was the whole Persian nuptial ceremony ; but to this the Macedonian rite was added, by which the husband took a loaf of bread, cut it in two, gave half to the wife, then poured out a libation of wine, and ate and drank with her. However, the bridal was celebrated by five days of festivity, with recitals by the poets. Every bride received a marriage portion from the king, and every soldier who would take a Persian wife a donation; and the Persian ladies were so beautiful and lively that the Greek contempt for "barbarian women" might well be overcome. Of the marriages whose history can be traced, some ended tragically, others were very happy; but the difficulties of blending Macedonians and Persians continued to increase. A large number of young Persians had by the king's command been trained up in Greek discipline and in the use of Greek arms, and these were now ready for service, to the great annoyance of the jealous veterans; and when soon after Alexander offered to discharge all his original warriors, who had become disabled by age, wounds, or sickness, there was an absolute mutiny, the whole army cried out to him to dismiss them all, and try what he could do with the help of his new father, Ammon, alone.

Alexander was forced to hurry in among them, cause the ringleaders to be seized, and then make them a spirited speech, in which he showed them both what their nation had been before the time of his father, and what it now was, as well as that all the gain and the glory was as much theirs as his. Even then they did not submit, but remained sullen and silent for two whole days, while Alexander was collecting his trustworthy officers and the Persian troops to reduce them. At last they were overawed, and before a blow was struck sent a message of submission, and entreated the king to come among them again.

He came, and they knelt round him weeping, entreating his pardon, and showing such a passion of affection to him, that the tears came into his eyes. But when he asked what was their grievance, there was a silence: they hung their heads, and no answer was made till at last an old captain contrived to say, "The Macedonians are chiefly grieved that you have allowed Persians to be called your kinsmen !"

"Henceforth," said Alexander, "you are all my kinsmen !" and he kissed the speaker. This fully appeased the now ashamed multitude, and a great reconciliation took place, which was celebrated by an enormous banquet, to which the most distinguished soldiers—9,000 Greeks and Persians—were invited! Augurs and Magi celebrated their separate rites ; 9,000 hands at once poured a libation of wine, 9,000 voices joined in the pæan, or hymn of joy; and then all sat down to the feast under awnings arranged in concentric circles, the king in the centre, then the Macedonians, then the Persians, and beyond them the persons of other nations.

The pride and jealousy of the Greeks having been thus pacified, there was an examination of the troops, and no less than 10,000 were found to be too much worn out for further service. To each of them was given his full pay till he should reach home, and a talent over and above; and when they took leave of their king—not without many tears of warm affection—their leader was the king's intimate friend Craterus, whose health had begun to fail, and who was sent home to take the government of Macedon, while Antipater was to come out in his place to join the king.

Alexander himself was not ready for a return. His object was to consolidate the empire he had won, and unite it by threads of common interest, using the seventy cities he had founded as stations for learning, civilization, and trade, and uniting around him at one of the great central cities all that was best, wisest, greatest, or most beautiful of every land, according to the theory of his master, Aristotle, that the gods manifested themselves in different ways in every nation. It was another Babel of intellect and power mounting up to heaven, and raised by one who demanded the honours of a god.

But the end was at hand. The hardships and exertions of body, and the extraordinary strain of mind, undergone in the last ten years, could not but exhaust the powers. Almost all the Greeks who had come with Alexander from home had either died or been forced to retire, and his closest and dearest friend, "his other self," Hephæstion, was seized with fever, neglected it at first, then suddenly became worse, and died before Alexander could hurry to his side. This was at Ecbatana ; and Alexander fell into an agony of grief, directing all to mourn for Hephæstion as a prince or king, when, in Persian fashion, not only were men shorn of their beards, but the horses and mules of their manes and tails, and the towns of their battlements. The corpse was sent to Babylon to be burnt upon the costliest of piles, with the most splendid of games, and an embassy was even sent to Ammon to ask the oracle whether Hephæstion might not be adored as a hero-god. At these games and funeral feasts the king himself was to be present; but he first had to cut off a robber tribe around the sources of the Tigris ; and when he met a deputation from the Chaldean priests entreating him not to enter the-city, as their soothsayers foretold that evil awaited him there, Alexander lightly answered, that he did not believe in predictions, and in fact he suspected that the priests were afraid of his inquiries into their tardiness in rebuilding the Temple of Bel : but the prediction hung heavy on his mind, all the more so as it agreed with a warning from a Greek augur, and with the last words of one of the Hindoo Yogis, who had followed him from India, and finding his health decline had, to the great horror of all the Greeks, insisted on burning himself to death on a pile of wood, calmly uttering predictions, one of which was that Alexander should die at Babylon.

And above and beyond all these, nay, perhaps inspiring them all, were the words of Daniel, that when the " Goat waxed strong, the notable horn between his eyes should be broken."

But no city was so suitable as Babylon for the centre of the intended Empire, and into it accordingly Alexander marched, and there he kept his state seated on the golden throne of the Persian shahs, with a gold vine, with fruit of emeralds and carbuncles, behind him, and guarded by circles on circles of devoted subjects,—Greeks in their well-ordered simplicity of arms and raiment, Persians in flame colour or scarlet, with azure sashes, and elephants beyond all. There he received ambassadors from all quarters—Greeks with wreathed brows and incense in honour of his pretensions to deity, merchant kinsmen of the Phœnicians from Africa, Hindoos, Scythians, and a grave, resolute-looking party of men from the far West, in simple white garments edged with purple, who came to confer with him upon some quarrels with the Greek colonies in Italy, and looked on his magnificence with a certain rough scorn as unworthy of so brave a man, and little thought that their struggling city was destined to spread her conquests wellnigh as far as Macedon had done.

To render Babylon all that his mind's eye saw it, it was needful to repair the damage that had been increasing ever since Nebuchadnezzar had looked on "this great Babylon." The arrangements for irrigation so carefully arranged by the Assyrians had been suffered to fall into decay, and the floodings of the Euphrates formed pools and marshes such as rendered one principal gate unusable, and bred fevers and agues among the inhabitants.

To survey these and set the canals to work again was Alexander's occupation ; and his plans were in course of being carried out, when, as he was steering his own boat among the sluggish waters, a sudden gust of wind caught the light broad-brimmed hat which he wore to protect his head from the heat, with the royal diadem wreathed round it, and carried it among some weeds and weeping willows that grew around an old neglected tomb of some Assyrian king. A sailor swam to fetch it, and, to avoid wetting it, put it on his own head as he returned. The king rewarded him with a talent, but had him flogged, to preserve the awful respect for the diadem. But the lodgment of the crown upon a tomb was viewed as an omen of danger, while the real danger was probably in the exposure of the bare head—so recently shorn of its clustering locks for Hephæstion's sake—to the glare of the Eastern sun, amid those malarious marshes.

An expedition into Arabia was intended, and the king offered a grand sacrifice for its success. The next night fever came on. Common report ascribes it to his having drained an enormous goblet of wine, called the Cup of Hercules, after which he fell down like one dead; but as this was unlike his usual habit, which, though not entirely abstemious, certainly showed no tendency to such boisterous foolhardiness, and as no such excess has been mentioned by the physician whose diary of his illness has been preserved, the story may fairly be believed to be only one of the many that were always current against Alexander among the republican Greeks, who hated him so bitterly.

He struggled against the increasing illness with all his might. Day after day the journal records his taking cold baths, being carried on his couch to take part in the daily sacrifices, and afterwards conferring with his generals and giving orders for the intended expedition; but ever at night the fever returned with increasing violence. On the seventh day he was with difficulty able to bear to be carried to the altar of sacrifice; on the next, though he just accomplished this, he could not speak, although he showed that he knew his officers; and for three days more he lay so extremely ill, that when his soldiers, in the utmost anxiety, insisted on being admitted to see whether he were yet alive, he could only raise his head and acknowledge them with his eyes. Speaking seemed to have become very difficult to him from the first, and after the disease had once put it beyond his power to keep up the effort, he seems to have sunk into a sort of lethargy. His constitution must have been exhausted by the alternations of cold and heat, the tremendous bodily labours and never-ceasing weight of anxiety and care, the severe wounds, especially the concussion of the brain and the injury to the lungs; and though but thirty-three years of age, he was worn out, and sank rapidly under this malarious fever, just as his friend Hephæstion had done before him.

When they saw that their wonderful chief was passing away, the generals became very anxious and perplexed as to their own future, and that of the vast dominions he had conquered, and they watched anxiously for some indication of his will; but either his tongue or his mind refused themselves to the task, and very little dropped from him. Once he said something that they interpreted into declaring that his empire would pass to the strongest; and again he said, " there would be fierce contests at his funeral games," but nothing further; no reference to the child whom a few months would bring into the world; no choice of guardians for his helpless family. That mightiest of intellects, which had been full of world-wide projects a few short days before, was incapable of a single expression of will as concerned mother, wife, or child. Only at the very last, when in the very death-struggle, he placed his signet-ring upon the finger of Perdiccas, the nearest and dearest of his friends since Hephæstion was dead and Craterus was gone; and therewith he expired.

Weeping and wailing, mourning and lamentation, spread from the palace to the army ; from the army to the city ; from the city to the provinces. None withheld their tears save the men of Greece. Otherwise, never was conqueror so mourned by a conquered people, to whom he had brought not subjection, but the freedom of the civilized European instead of slavery under an Eastern despot. Every one bewailed him as their glory, their friend, their patron, their hope, their defender. Old Queen Sisygambis, his captive, who had never been so kindly treated as by him, covered her face, sat down in a corner, and lamented, " Alas ! where shall we find another Alexander ?" and accepted no food, until in a few days she followed him to the grave.

And Persian affection so clung around his memory, that tradition, though preserving his name, made him no foreign victor, but a native prince ; and even the wild tribes of the Cabul mountains actually imagine themselves descendants from his men.

When his officers met, and Perdiccas laid down the ring upon the empty throne, there was a great blank, indeed, that never has been filled up. Earth has never since produced a man equal to Alexander of Macedon.

For two years the officials at Babylon were preparing his corpse for interment. It was intended by his mother to place it in the temple of Ammon ; but as it was imagined that, wherever it lay, prosperity would follow, every one contended for the keeping of it. At last, however, it was brought to Egypt, with a most superb train of chariots adorned with sculpture ; but it was never taken to the oasis of Ammon, for Ptolemy, who in the great break-up of the Empire obtained the kingdom of Egypt, built a temple to receive it at Alexandria, and there offered his master the honours of a hero-god.

So lived and died Alexander the Great. He had more

visible faults than the three Greeks we have dwelt on before ; but he had greater trials, and he lived in a glare of light that brings his errors into full display. But none can deny him the title of pre-eminently Great ; not only for his victories, but for his vast designs, and for his unflinching constancy and unfailing resource. And as little can he be denied the title of " Worthy," for the magnificent justice and beneficence that distinguished him above every other conqueror led him to make it his great object to improve, raise, and ennoble alike all the nations of the world.

MARCUS CURIUS DENTATUS.

B.C. 360—270.

AMONG the ambassadors that met Alexander at Babylon
in the last year of his life there was, it has been said,
a deputation of grave, earnest-looking men, with coun-
tenances set and serious, and of resolute demeanour, without the smiles and gaiety, the grace and cultivation, of
the Greek, but with no lack of strong practical sense,
and of simplicity and hardihood equal to those of any
Spartan. The garment in which they appeared on solemn occasions was an immense semicircular cloak, which
almost entirely enveloped the figure, hanging down like
a gown in front, but so arranged as to form a deep
bosom, leaving one arm free. This very inconvenient
dress was called a toga: it was of white homespun wool,
edged with purple, more broadly or more narrowly,
according to the rank of the wearer and the offices he
had borne.

These homely but resolute men, who gazed half in
wonder, half in contempt, at the barbarian magnificence
of the East, and at the small, slight, finished gentleman
who had subdued it all, came from the peninsula in the
West, which the Greeks were in the habit of regarding
as quite as despicably barbarous as Persia, and more
rude and savage, but furnishing good ground for the

settlement of colonies when their own cities wished to throw out swarms, with a greater chance of real freedom than could be found in Asia. Many of these existed in the adjacent isle of Sicily ; and the extreme south of the peninsula of Hesperia, the land of the Evening Star, as they termed it, was so full of these settlements as to be sometimes called Greater Greece.

Hesperia itself was called by its natives Italia. It was, like Greece itself, a land of mountain and seacoast, with bright streams rushing down to lovely valleys ; and like Greece it was divided into numerous little states, but with more diversity of feeling, and forming many different unions of tribes, hostile to one another.

Near the centre of the western side of the long narrow peninsula, where the tawny waters of the Tyber came rapidly winding between the low skirts of the Apennine hills towards the sea, a city had risen up in the narrow ravines, the houses crowding the slopes, the temples and fortresses crowning the hills, the market-place spreading into the wide intersection of the valleys, and the walls girding in the whole with blocks of stone of huge size and wonderful architecture, only to be compared with that of the drainage beneath, which, strange to say, did not correspond with the situation of the houses above, as if a more intelligent people than the present inhabitants had made them.

However that might be, these present inhabitants were very terrible people to their neighbours. They were, in quiet times, hard-working farmers, each tilling his own little piece of land in the rich flat country that spread around the hills, keeping his own sheep, kine, and goats, driving his plough in his rough sheepskin coat and broad hat, and gathering and treading his own grapes, while his wife and daughters spun and wove his garments, ground, kneaded, and baked his corn, pressed his cheeses, and sealed up his wine in pointed earthenware jars or goatskins. · All this was done with much religion too. The guardian gods of boundaries hallowed the landmarks between the fields, the gods of seedtime and harvest were invoked to bless the sowing and the ingathering, the gods of the hearth and of the family had their altar in the court, round which the sheds forming the house were built, and every meal began with the pouring out of a libation or drink-offering to them. Above all, every man looked to the sacred city, where a holy fire was tended night and day by virgins dedicated for the purpose to the goddess Vesta, where the ancestral stern father-god, Mars, was worshipped, and where the citadel or capitol was sacred to the great universal father of the light and day, the sky-god, thundering Jupiter ; and especially that city herself, his sacred Rome, was the object of his intensest affection ; so that for her safety, her greatness, and her glory, he would without hesitation willingly give, not only his little piece of land, but his sons, his life, nay, more than life, if he had had it to give.

Let him put on his white homespun toga and walk bareheaded into the Forum or market-place, that valley surrounded with the low booths that served for shops, and this peasant farmer showed himself a statesman. If he had a gold ring on his finger, he would prove himself an exceedingly proud, haughty noble, or patrician, jealous of the rank and privileges of his order ; and probably tracing his descent from some god or hero, generally a fugitive Trojan : if he wore none, he would be equally proud of his family, and of belonging to the sturdy commons, the plebs, who were always treading on the heels of the patricians, and never of one mind with them except in dealing with the enemies of Rome.

If his toga were resplendent with a rubbing of chalk, the Roman was asking the votes of his fellow-citizens to raise him to one of the magistracies. These offices only lasted one year, and those who had served them might be known by the broader edge of their toga; and such as had been in the highest thereby entered the Senate, or council of elders, which was composed of the heads of the great patrician families, together with those who had served the great offices of state.

Chief of all these was the consulate. There were always two consuls, equal in rank, and for their year of office almost kingly in their power and privileges. Embroidered purple togas and ivory chairs distinguished them, and each was attended by a pair of lictors, or executioners, bearing an axe and bundle of rods to execute prompt justice on any transgressor of the law. But the consulate over, the office-bearer returned to his farm, and, except for his seat in the Senate, was what he had been before. Neither had consuls nor senators power to make any law, or decide upon any public measure, unless the people were satisfied ; and hot and fierce were the struggles for power between the patrician and plebeian races, so that at home they often seemed ready to tear each other to pieces, but at the sound of war all were as one man in their determination to uphold the strength and glory of their beloved Rome.

Then out came all the freemen of Rome according to their tribes ; and officers appointed for the purpose, who were called tribunes, chose out the fittest men for arms, and formed them into legions, the plebeians fighting on foot and the patricians on horseback. One consul was supposed to lead them to battle, and the other to stay at home and govern Rome, but often both were called into the field at once. There the discipline was perfectly strict. However turbulent a man might be as a citizen of Rome, in the camp, as a soldier, he was as obedient as a slave, and did not even value his own honour and glory in comparison with the good of his country.

Such iron resolution might well make the Romans formidable foes to deal with, and they had fought their way by slow degrees to be the chief power in the north and middle of Italy. Grand stories had come down of the elder heroes of their history, but they had been a rude and far from studious people, and when, B.C. 389, the great invasion of the Gauls had for a time endangered even the existence of Rome itself, such records as they had were all lost, so that it is not till after that era that enough can be collected about one man to be able to describe him as a Worthy.

Yet there was much to make a Roman as worthy as a heathen could be. He was not a thinker, like the Greeks, and had no notion of living out schemes of philosophy, like Xenophon, Epaminondas, and Alexander; but the original law of right and wrong was written deeply on his heart, and the ancient code of Rome was grand and pure. It consecrated marriage with solemn rites of sacrifice, and taught the matron to be faithful, resolute, simple, and devoted to her husband and children, giving her far more honour than did the Greek. It made sons submissive and dutiful to their parents, and the whole nation resolute and faithful to their country, their oaths, and their gods, with a great sternness and pride, but still with many high and noble traits of character.

Among these ancient Worthies of the earlier and more unmixed days of Rome, perhaps the best to choose as representing the class of men to which he belonged will be Marcus Curius Dentatus, as he not only was in himself a very fine specimen of the old Roman character, but was connected with other men of the same high nature, and lived at a turning-point in the history of his city.

He must have been born somewhere about the middle of the third century before the Christian era. He belonged to a Latin town, where the people were fellow-citizens with Rome, and belonged to the plebeian race, called the Curian gens, in right of which he inherited the family name of Curius; and it seems that it was because he had teeth when he was born that the nick-name of Dentatus, or the Toothed, was given to him. It remained with him all his life, and was made honour-able by him. His first name of Marcus was that by which he was registered as Marcus Curius at seventeen years old; when he put on the white toga of the full-grown, and took rank as a citizen and soldier, having by that time learnt to read and write, and practised himself in speaking fluently, as well as in the use of the short Roman sword and heavy spear.

Nothing is known of his early life, but the wars in which the city was then engaged must have been those in which he was trained to arms, at the very time when Alexander was conquering in the East.

The north of Italy had been nearly all subdued by the Romans, but in the south, among the steep limestone hills now called the Matese, a spur of the Apennines, dwelt a fierce Italian race called the Samnites. Their home was on the mountain side, with snowclad peaks above, woods of beech and chestnut clothing the slopes, and valleys of rich grass watered by clear streams. Bold and high-spirited as the Romans themselves, these mountaineers had been at war with them for half a century, and with varying success.

The combats between these two nations were at their height during the youth of Dentatus, and desperate were some of the conflicts in the plains of Campania. It was in B.C. 325 that, the reigning consul having fallen sick, a Dictator was appointed to supply his place, and the wise old general Lucius Papirius was chosen; but being obliged to return to Rome for a short time, he left the command of the army in Samnium to his lieutenant, Quintus Fabius, with strict orders to remain on the defensive, and attempt no battle until his return.

Fabius was a high-spirited young patrician of a family highly esteemed among the Romans, and of remarkable strength and ability. Growing impatient of the delay, and fearing an advantageous moment might be missed, he attacked the Samnites, and found them more firm and resolute than he had expected. Thereupon he caused the horsemen to take off the bridles, and charge the enemy at the full speed of their horses. The shock was tremendous. Numbers of the Samnites were slain, and the victory was complete; but Fabius in his exultation neglected his duty to the Dictator, sent notice only to the Senate, and burnt all the spoil lest it should adorn the triumph of Papirius.

Roman discipline could not endure such insubordination, and Papirius set forth in haste to call his lieutenant to account; but in the meantime Fabius persuaded the army that every one of them was as much to blame as himself, and when Papirius arrived, and, drawing them all up before his tribunal, called on Fabius to explain his breach of duty, they were all on the side of the accused. The Dictator sternly sentenced his disobedient officer to be seized by the lictors, stripped, bound, and executed; but Fabius contrived by the help of the veteran soldiers of the front rank to slip away among them and escape to Rome, to be tried by the Senate, instead of by the person he had most offended.

His father had been three times consul and once Dictator, and was so much respected that he readily obtained of the Senate to meet at once, in hopes of their acquitting his son before Papirius was come; but in the midst of their sitting a great noise was heard, and in came the Dictator, full of rage, commanding his lictors to seize the escaped criminal.

The oldest senators interceded in vain, the Dictator was inexorable, and all that was left to the elder Fabius was to appeal to the whole people assembled in the Forum. There then they met, and Papirius ascended the rostrum or pulpit, shaped like the beak of a ship, whence speakers were wont to address the people. The two Fabii were following thither, when he angrily commanded the accused to be pulled down. Then the old man, following his son, called to gods and men to witness the effects of jealous cruelty, and throwing his arms round his son's neck, wept a flood of tears.

Every one was touched; but when Papirius spoke of the evils of transgression of law, and the mischief that might be done by the example of one successful breach of discipline, there was no one who ventured to dispute that the life of Fabius was in his hands, and deserved to be forfeited; but the whole assembly became suppliants for the life of the gallant young man, and entreated for his pardon. The Dictator was satisfied. "Quintus Fabius is pardoned," he said, "at the intercession of the Roman people. Live then, though guilty of a crime which your own father in my place could not have forgiven. The best return you can make to those who have saved your life is to show that this day has taught you obedience, whether in peace or war."

So Fabius was saved, and with no loss of rank, for he became consul the next year, and gained another victory which was entirely his own. But in 320 the Samnites chose as their captain an exceedingly able man, named Caius Pontius, who contrived to spread a false report that the Samnite army was besieging the city of Luceria in Apulia, and thus led the whole Roman army with both the consuls, Veturius and Postumius, to march through the gorges of the Apennines to the rescue. Thus they came to the opening of a valley which is shut in by rocky and woody slopes, very narrow at either entrance, and with a marshy meadow in the midst, through which the track lay. As the Romans approached the further issue, they beheld it blocked up with huge stones and trunks of trees, and at the same moment the once solitary wooded heights began to swarm with enemies. The order was given to turn back, but no sooner had the rearguard passed than the Samnites had in like manner blocked the other opening. The Romans were caught in a trap, and stood gazing on one another. Then the consul's tent was pitched, and the usual arrangements were made for encamping, digging a trench, and raising an embankment around the tents; but meantime the hills rang with the laughter of their adversaries, who knew that a few days must starve the enemy into accepting whatever terms they chose. Meantime the Samnites could not agree among themselves how to dispose of their grand capture, and sent to consult Herennius Pontius, the father of their general. His answer was, "Do no harm to the Romans, but let them go freely." This generosity, however, seemed beyond the power of the Samnites, and they sent to consult him again. This time he replied, "Spare not the life of one Roman."

Thinking there must be some error, they sent again, to invite him to the camp to explain himself. He then told them that by free generosity and magnanimity they might obtain the alliance and friendship of Rome; but if they could not resolve upon this, it would be better to cut off as many of such formidable enemies as possible at one blow. He was for no half-measures: but his countrymen were less wise and resolute.

The half-starved Romans had in the meantime sent an

embassy to offer to treat, which had been scornfully refused; and their officers held mournful deliberation in the
consul's tent.   Like brave men they came to the conclusion that, though to their own feelings it might seem nobler
to rush on the Samnite spears and sell their lives dearly,
yet, as they were the strength and defence of their city,
they ought to submit to any terms that would preserve
them to their country.

And Caius Pontius offered terms that were on the whole
lenient.   He required of them an oath to restore the
towns and lands they had conquered, and to establish
a secure peace, upon which he would let them go, merely
yielding up their arms and passing before the army as
prisoners.

The consuls consented—as consent they must ; and as
the proper Roman officer whose business it was to swear
to treaties was not in the camp, the consuls and all the
officers swore to the treaty, and six hundred young
equites or horsemen were given up as hostages.

Then the Romans marched out of the camp.   It was a
miserable humiliation, for the clothing left them was but
a single garment, a sort of kilt; and the consuls were
as much exposed as the commonest men : spear, sword,
helmet, cuirass, and war cloaks were taken from them,
and they had in this manner to pass singly beneath
three spears set up like a doorway, called a yoke, fork, or
gallows, the token of absolute surrender.   The spot was
called the Caudine Forks, and a village named Forchia
still marks it.

Terrible was the sense of degradation to these proud
men.   Their allies in Campania came out to clothe and
comfort them, and provide fresh tokens of honour for their
consuls ; but they would not raise their eyes, and marched
on in moody bitterness of soul.   On their own territory
they dispersed in silence to their homes, and the consuls

shut themselves up in their houses, as unable to act for the rest of the year of office : and though the defeat had been bloodless, the whole nation went into mourning ; there were neither feasts nor marriages, and the patricians left off their gold rings and purple hems.

At the end of the year old Papirius was one of the new consuls, and a debate was held whether the treaty should be accepted. Postumius, one of the late consuls, stood up and strongly gave his opinion that the people should not accept the treaty that had been wrung from the army in their dire distress. But he declared that he and his colleague Veturius were willing to be delivered up to the vengeance of the Samnites for having undertaken what they could not perform. This was likewise giving up the safety of the six hundred hostages, who were mostly the sons of senators; but Romans never weighed their own feelings against the good of the state, or when they thought its glory concerned. So the late consuls, and all the rest who had sworn the oath, were conducted by the priest of the public faith, whose office it was to confirm treaties, to Samnium. There they appeared before the Samnites, the priest in his long robes, his hair bound with a white band and twisted with sacred herbs ; but the late consuls and their companions in the half-naked state in which they had passed under the yoke, and bound hand and foot. The priest declared to Pontius and his colleagues that these men had promised what they had no power to perform, and that Rome, refusing to confirm the treaty, delivered them up to be dealt with as the Samnites thought fit. Then Postumius, striking the priest with his knee, cried aloud that he, a slave of the Samnites, had done violence to the person of a priest of the faith, and called on the Romans to avenge the insult. But for this last trick the proceeding would have been grand, and Pontius had magnanimity enough to declare that the treaty was broken by Rome, not by these men, and therefore to restore them safely to their homes.

This great disaster must have happened in the first childhood of Dentatus, and all through his youth and early manhood the Samnite war was the one thought of Rome. His first appearance in history was, however, in matters of state, not of war. About the year 299 he was chosen tribune of the people. This was an office always held by a plebeian, and had been instituted to guard their rights against the encroachments of the patricians. Thus it was that Marcus Curius Dentatus had to stand forth, when a factious and turbulent personage, named Appius Claudius, who was holding the elections for the next year, refused—contrary to the law—to receive votes for plebeian candidates. The resolution of the tribune was successful, and the Senate passed a decree that rendered such injustice impossible for the future.

There were other magistracies to be held, but the patricians still kept them in their own hands, except that one of the consuls was always a plebeian; and in 290 this dignity was conferred upon Dentatus. The last year had been one of great success. Fabius, the same who had been spared at his father's intercession, had become the most able captain of his time, and had long ago won for himself the surname of Maximus, or, the Greatest. Strangely enough, his son likewise erred in his first command, and was forgiven on his father's intercession and promise that, if the consulship were continued to him, he would himself serve under him as legate, or lieutenant, and conduct all his proceedings. Under this generalship a decisive blow was at length dealt to the Samnite power, and Pontius was made prisoner thirty years after the matter of the Caudine Forks. One of the grand triumphs entered Rome, the soldiers marching joyously, singing songs of victory, and carrying their standards wreathed

R

with laurel, or displaying the spoil ; the officers on horse-back ; and the consul himself in a chariot drawn by white horses, his head crowned with laurel, and his face painted with vermilion, driving along the Sacred Way, and then climbing to the Capitol hill to lay down his laurel-wreath on the knees of the great Jupiter. It was young Fabius who received these honours, while his father rode behind him, rejoicing in the glory he had won for his son ; but the triumph was, as usual, stained by the slaughter of the chief prisoner. The brave Pontius was led to the dungeon beneath the Capitoline hill, and there beheaded while Fabius offered his wreath. His mercy to the consuls long ago won no mercy for himself.

The next year, Marcus Curius Dentatus entered on his office, in company with Publius Cornelius Rufinus, and followed up the victories of the Fabii with such success, that the Samnites were reduced to sue for peace. The story goes that when their deputies came to seek for the consul, they found him, after the old Roman simple fashion, sitting on a wooden stool by the fire, cooking a few roots for his dinner, and that they offered him a large sum of money to obtain favourable terms for them. " So," said the sturdy, rustic consul, " you think poverty must be to be bought. You are wrong. I had rather command rich men, than be rich. Take back the metal, the bane of men, and tell your fellows that I am as hard to bribe as to beat." The Samnites were obliged to take the terms Curius imposed : and thus ended a war of forty-nine years. He had his triumph, but this was scarcely over before he was called out by a revolt of the Sabines ; and, for reducing this, had a second triumph. This was the first time two such glories had ever accrued to a consul in a single year ; but his stern plainness was not affected by it, and he became the great champion of the poor. It was a time of terrible distress, for there had been a severe

pestilence, and the people of the city were in a state of
the utmost despondency, until a ship arrived, commanded
by one Agulinus, bringing a huge serpent, which had
come out of a hole at the foot of the statue of the god of
medicine (Æsculapius) at Epidaurus, and had entered the
vessel to be brought to Rome, where it took up its abode
in an island on the Tyber. Here a temple was built,
where the sick resorted for advice, given in dreams
by the god; and the subsidence of the malady was
attributed to the wonderful visitor. It had, however,
left much poverty; and the customs of Rome, by which
the wealthy lent out money on usury, and then made
slaves of those who could not redeem the debt, led to
horrible misery. The son of Titus Veturius—one of
the unfortunate consuls of the Caudine Forks—a fine,
handsome, well-educated youth, was actually sold into
slavery for the debt he had incurred to pay the expenses
of his father's funeral; and, having been severely flogged,
made his escape, all bleeding, and showed himself to
the people.

Upon this there was a great tumult, and the law permitting free citizens to be sold for debt as slaves was
repealed. Dentatus likewise proposed that the lands
which he had just won should be used to relieve the
general distress, and that each citizen should be allotted
seven acres. The patricians made a violent opposition,
for there was nothing they hated so much as enriching
the plebeians with the lands of the vanquished; and his
life was at one time in so much danger, that 800 young
men, probably his former soldiers, formed themselves into
a body-guard, watched round him, and would fain have
decided the quarrel by the sword; but no act of violence
seems to have been committed on either side, and the
edict was carried, which, for a time, relieved the general
distress. But a far more dangerous enemy than any

which the Republic had yet encountered was about to descend upon Italy.

When Alexander died at Babylon, without any one to succeed to his empty throne, his huge conquests were broken up between his officers, and the fierce and ambitious struggles that arose between semi-Greeks, half orientalized, were no school for Worthies. Moreover, Egypt, Syria, and Macedon occupied one another so entirely by their strife, that there was no time nor thought of further conquests. The kingdom of Epirus, however, on the shores of the Adriatic, stood in the same sort of relation to Greece as Macedon had formerly done, and like it contained a semi-barbarous people, ruled over by a royal family with high pretensions to a heroic Greek ancestry. It was from thence that Olympias, the mother of Alexander, had come; it was through her that he derived his claim to be the descendant of Achilles; and here—among the children of her kinsman, Æacides—there was born a young prince, named Pyrrhus, who, after obtaining the throne of his father through countless dangers, formed the design of emulating the fame of Alexander by conquests directed towards the West rather than the East.

Southern Italy was full of Greek settlements, which had always kept up their connexion with the parent states. The climate of the coast of those deep bays, which give the form of a boot to the peninsula, has always been enervating, and most unfavourable to the growth of anything resolute or courageous; nor was Tarentum, the leading city in the third century before our era, an exception to the prevailing love of ease and dissipation. The Tarentines had all the Greek cultivation and refinement, and looked down on their rude, hardy Italian neighbours as mere clumsy barbarians; but they were by no means sorry to have so determined a race as the

Samnites between them and the Romans, and when these gallant mountaineers were crushed and Pontius slain, they began to stir up fresh enemies to the dangerous city on the banks of the Tyber.

About six years after the double triumph of Dentatus, the Tarentines—though themselves keeping in the background—had formed a league of the remains of the Samnites with the Etruscans and several other Italian tribes, and the Etruscans took into their pay a large number of the Gallic tribe called Senones, though the bulk of the nation was at peace with Rome. In the first battle the Roman general was killed, great multitudes of his men killed, and the rest made prisoners; and three ambassadors, who were sent to remonstrate with the chiefs of the Senones at home, were murdered and hewn in pieces—an outrage which was held to place the person guilty of it beyond the pale of mercy.

Dentatus was, of course, no longer consul: but he was appointed Prætor, the next highest office, by which a man was judge at home, and general abroad; and, in concert with the two consuls, he took a terrible vengeance upon the savage Senones. Their men were defeated in battle, and the survivors slew themselves in despair; the women and children were sold for slaves; and their country was occupied by a Roman colony. Caius Fabricius Luscinus, another plain, homely, country warrior like Dentatus, gained several battles against the other allies; but as it was quite certain that the Tarentines were the true authors of the mischief, it was resolved to send ten ships of war to watch their movements.

On the afternoon of the grand festival of Dionysos, the wine-god, when, in the open theatre which faced the sea, the whole of the Tarentines were assembled to witness the tragic songs and dances appropriate to the day, they suddenly beheld ten vessels sailing round the headland into the narrow gulf that ran into the heart of the city and formed their harbour. They rose in fury at the insult, and hurried down to their ships, and being far more numerous and better accustomed sailors than the Romans, they sunk four ships and took one, when they killed the soldiers and sold the rowers for slaves.

For this and for their other violences in time of apparent peace the Romans sent Lucius Postumus with an embassy to demand an explanation, but, on their first appearance in the street, he was set upon by a disorderly rabble of foolish conceited Greeks, who hooted at the white purple-bordered toga as an absurd and clumsy dress, and mocked the sturdy rustic bearing of the Romans. Thus they were brought to the theatre as the place of public assembly, but the whole populace were so possessed with contempt for them, that when Postumus began to address them in Greek, they broke out in shouts of laughter at his foreign pronunciation and grammatical blunders, while through the whole the Roman gravely and calmly rehearsed his speech, without so much as seeming to hear or see their insolence, until at length a drunken wretch came up and threw dirt upon the trailing skirt of the white toga. He held it up to the assembly, but they only shrieked with laughter, clapped their hands, and yelled out their mockery.

" Laugh on, Tarentines," said Postumus, " laugh while ye may. The time is coming when ye shall weep. The stain on this toga shall only be washed in blood."

The Tarentines felt that they had in their mad folly committed an unpardonable offence against the majesty of that barbarian city of proud warriors, and, a good deal terrified, they sent off an embassy to young Pyrrhus, King of Epirus, in the name of all the Greek colonies of Italy, to invite him to chastise the rude but overweening city that began to make them uneasy.

Pyrrhus readily accepted the invitation. He was an active, able, and spirited man, who delighted to believe that he resembled Alexander, but who only did so in a few externals. He had neither Alexander's transcendent talents, nor his wide grandeur of benevolence, nor had he even the more common gift of perseverance and steadiness of purpose to guide his ambition, but as a well-trained Greek captain he was far superior to any one whom either the Tarentines or Romans had yet seen.

He arrived at Tarentum in the depth of the winter of 281, a shipwrecked battered man, who only gradually collected his dispersed fortunes ; but no sooner was he in the city than these merry revellers found their laughter already checked, for he shut up the theatres, forced every one to be exercised in arms and guard the walls in turn, and put a stop to the riotous banquets held in public. Those who did not like this discipline tried to escape, but he set a guard at the gates and stopped them as deserters, and he punished seditious language severely, until the Tarentines heartily repented of their invitation. They did not all get off so easily as the youth, who, being asked by Pyrrhus if he had really abused him as reported, answered, "Yes, truly, king ; and we should have said much more against you if the wine had not failed us." Meantime his army was gradually crossing from Epirus, and it not only included 25,000 foot, disciplined in Macedonian mode of warfare, able to form the irresistible phalanx and use the mighty lance of Alexander, with a large number of horsemen, archers, and slingers, but likewise seventy trained elephants, which the Macedonians had, since their Eastern expedition, been accustomed to procure from India and to use in their battles, though the creatures seem to have been chiefly serviceable as giving a certain grandeur of appearance which inspired barbaric terror, and often rendered the horses unmanageable.

The consuls that year were Publius Valerius Lævinus and Tiberius Coruncanius, and very hard and perilous was their task in encountering an invasion of the best disciplined troops then existing, led by a prince of no mean ability, and inheriting the traditions of the conqueror of the world. Every nation hostile to Rome in all Italy was ready to rise and join him, and it was necessary to choose into the Roman legions every available fighting man, if the independence of Rome were to be preserved. The host was divided; Coruncanius being sent to watch the Etruscans, while Lævinus marched southward into Lucania, intending to fight with Pyrrhus before he should receive reinforcements from home, or be joined by the Samnites.

Thereupon Pyrrhus left Tarentum to meet him, sending first this haughty letter :—

" PYRRHUS TO LÆVINUS.—Health ! I am informed that you command an army against the Tarentines. Disband it without delay, and come and plead before me. When I have heard both parties, I will give judgment ; and I know how to make myself obeyed."

The answer was :—

" LÆVINUS TO PYRRHUS. — Know that we neither accept you as a judge nor fear you as an enemy. Does it become you to call yourself a judge, after having injured us by landing in Italy without our consent? We will take no arbitrator save Mars, the parent of our race and guardian of our arms."

After this defiance had passed, Pyrrhus advanced towards the Roman camp, which lay on the further side of the river Siris, which flows into the Tarentine Gulf. He crossed the river Aciris, which runs nearly parallel with

it, about three miles off, so as to have the plain between
as a battle-field, and then rode forward to inspect the
appearance of the despicable clowns that the Tarentines
had described to him.

When he had gazed at the orderly lines of the camp,
and the regular entrenchments, with sentries posted at
each opening, he turned to one of his friends, saying,
" Megacles, this order of the barbarians is not barbarian.
We shall see what they can do in fight."

This view, however, made him wish to wait for reinforcements, and he stationed a guard to prevent the
enemy from crossing ; but the water was shallow enough
to allow of their marching steadily across. The guard
fell back, and Pyrrhus found himself obliged to give
orders to his army to draw up in battle array, whilst
he himself with the cavalry rode forward, hoping to
fall on the legions while in the confusion of climbing
the bank.

He found them, however, all drawn up, their long
shields forming an embattled line, their pikes projecting
before them, and their horse in front ready to receive the
attack. The fight was sharp, and Pyrrhus' beautiful
armour and scarlet mantle marked him out for general
attack. One of the Italian allies so pursued him, that a
Macedonian called out to him to beware of the barbarian
on the black horse with the white feet.

" What must be, must be," called back Pyrrhus ; " but
not the stoutest soldier in Italy shall encounter with me
for nothing."

The Italian dashed at him and killed his horse, but he
was instantly remounted by his attendants and his brave
foe killed, while he fell back on his infantry, hastily ex-
changing his too conspicuous attire with Megacles. It is
curious that a most exquisite pair of bronze shoulder-
pieces should have been discovered on the field of Siris,

so beautiful and costly in their engraving, as to render it very probable that they were dropped by Pyrrhus in this hasty change of garb. Megacles became the object of general attack, and was soon slain, his royal array being brandished by the Romans in triumph, so that Pyrrhus was forced to ride bareheaded along his own line to convince them that he was alive. It was a tremendous battle. Seven times the Romans were forced back from their ground, seven times they gained it again, and at last Lævinus brought forward a chosen body of cavalry, which he had kept in reserve, hoping that a charge of fresh troops must disperse the Greeks, exhausted by such hard fighting. But now the elephants—never before beheld by any Roman—were brought forward in imposing array. The horses grew mad with terror, and turned about, treading down the infantry, and the rout was complete : indeed the Romans would have been totally destroyed, had it not chanced that one of the elephants having been wounded in the trunk came thundering back on the Greeks, and so disordered them, that the remnant of the Roman army had time to cross the river and retreat in something like order.

But Pyrrhus felt that he could not afford to win many more such battles. He had lost 4,000 men, many of them his best friends and generals, and he could not have been much delighted with the Tarentines. Moreover, the weather was dreadful. A storm so severe happened soon after the battle of Siris, that in one small division of the Roman army thirty-four men were knocked down and twenty-two nearly killed. And all seemed so unfavourable that Pyrrhus decided on offering terms to the Romans. If they would make peace with Tarentum, restore all they had taken from the Samnites and other Italian tribes, and declare all the Greek colonies independent, he would leave Italy and enter into an alliance with them.

He sent Kineas, a Thessalian philosopher, to Rome to propose these terms. He was a man of much wit and brilliancy of speech, and had such a memory that the day after his arrival at Rome he could address every senator by his proper name ; and he likewise brought with him numerous elegant and costly Greek ornaments as presents to the ladies, in hopes that they would dispose their husbands favourably. Some writers boast that they were all refused, others say that more than one senator was swayed by them, but at any rate a day was appointed for Kineas to have an audience in the Senate House, and set forth his proposals before the Conscript Fathers—the official title of the Senate.

After all the folly the Tarentines had uttered, the Greek was greatly struck by the majestic scene that the Temple presented where the Senate assembled. The carvings might indeed be rude, and the pillars clumsy, but there, in their seats of office, sat rows of grave, solid-looking men, in their long white robes, and ivory wands, each of them having won his place by ruling in the city, and commanding in the field, and each as ready to obey as to command—all actuated by one will, and that the glory of their city.

Kineas stood up, and began to address them with the fluent tongue which was said to win as many cities for Epirus as the sword of Pyrrhus. In the midst there was a hush. Some of the senators went down the steps, and then the whole of the Conscript Fathers rose as they returned, leading in a blind old man, in the extremity of age, and placed him on his curule chair. He was Appius Claudius, formerly a factious, turbulent politician, the great enemy of Dentatus, but wholly a Roman in heart, and unable to stay away from a debate touching the honour of the Republic. When he spoke from his chair of the shame of allowing a foreign king to intrude himself into judging of the quarrels of Rome, or requiring her conquests to be relinquished, the whole Senate was led by his words.   There was perfect silence as long as his voice was heard ; and when he ceased, the senators with one accord voted that the answer should be, that they would make no terms with Pyrrhus as long as he remained on Italian soil, but that they would oppose him with all their might, even though he should vanquish a thousand Lævini.

Kineas left Rome the next day, and went back to his master at Tarentum.   Pyrrhus asked what he thought of the city.   He replied, " Rome is a Temple, and the Senate an assembly of kings ;" and he likewise added that to fight with such a people was like fighting with the hundred-headed hydra, whose heads grew again as fast as they were cut off.

The new consuls of B.C. 278 were Publius Sulpicius Saverrio and Publius Decius Mus ; the latter the son and grandson of the two men who had both sacrificed themselves for their country : and preparations for the campaign proceeded.   Meantime (though there is some doubt as to the year) three Romans, of whom Caius Fabricius was the most noted, were sent to Pyrrhus to arrange for an exchange of prisoners.

Fabricius was one of the sturdiest and plainest of Romans, and Pyrrhus had heard that he was exceedingly poor, and was remarkable for his honesty and integrity. So, according to the Roman writers, the king desired a private interview with him, in which he declared that he needed nothing so much as an honest man in his service, and would give any price for him, offering large payment in the hope of securing one at least of this nation of kings to act under him among his faithless degenerate Greeks. But Fabricius smiled at the proffer, and declared that his little farm, cultivated by his own hands, supplied all his wants, he needed neither gold nor silver, and no king could do anything for him—he cared only for a good conscience and honest fame.

Pyrrhus then tried rather a childish experiment on his self-possession, by drawing aside a curtain suddenly, and showing his biggest elephant close behind, flourishing its trunk and trumpeting terrifically; whereat Fabricius only smiled, and told the king that he took no more account of his great beast than of his gold and silver.

The Roman ambassadors were invited to a banquet, where Greek luxury was displayed before their eyes in hopes of eliciting some wonder and admiration ; and Kineas was further set to discourse on philosophy. That which he had embraced was that of Epicurus, who held that enjoyment was the great purpose of existence, and the wisest man was he who most consulted his own pleasure. It was the favourite sophistry then common among the Greeks, and it was well wrapped in specious wordiness ; but no sooner did the soldierly Fabricius make out its drift than he quaintly cried, " O Hercules ! may Pyrrhus and the Tarentines be heartily of this sect while they are at war with us !"

This made Pyrrhus wish all the more to persuade Fabricius to become his friend, and go home with him. " Nay," said the Roman humourously, "take care when your subjects know me ; they may want me for king in your stead !" The result of the interview was that though the captives were not exchanged, they were allowed on the word of honour of Fabricius to go and celebrate a religious festival at Rome.

Another battle was approaching. Pyrrhus was besieging Asculum when both consuls advanced to raise the siege, and it was reported that Decius Mus intended to imitate his father and grandfather by throwing himself on the spears as a sacrifice to the nine gods. Pyrrhus accordingly warned his soldiers that if they saw any one arrayed in the purple embroidered toga, such as had been worn by the two preceding Decii on those occasions, they should not kill him, but take him alive; and he sent word to the consuls that if he should take any Roman practising such a trick, he should put him to death as an impostor. The consuls answered that they needed no such help, for that Roman courage was sufficient.

But it did not prove itself equal to the impossible task of breaking through the hedge of levelled pikes that protected the phalanx. In vain the Romans hewed at them with their swords, or tried to thrust them aside with their hands.

> " The stubborn spearmen still made good
> The tough impenetrable wood,"

and the legions perished without being able to inflict a wound. Decius the consul fell, they gave way, and then the elephants charged, and drove them off the field; but in the meantime the faithless Italians had been plundering the camp of Pyrrhus, and it is even said that he himself was wounded while driving them out.

The winter set in, and Pyrrhus became more and more disgusted with his enterprise and his allies, more especially when he received the following letter from Fabricius, who had been appointed consul in company with Quintus Æmilius :—

"CAIUS FABRICIUS AND QUINTUS ÆMILIUS TO KING PYRRHUS.—Health ! Thou choosest ill both friends and foes. When thou hast read this letter sent us by one of your own people, thou wilt see that thou makest war with the good and honest, and trustest the base and wicked. We warn thee not for our own sake, nor to make our court to thee, but to avoid the shame thy death would bring on us, if, for want of strength and courage, we used treachery."

Therewith was sent a letter from Pyrrhus' own physician, endeavouring to obtain a reward from the consuls for poisoning his master.

Pyrrhus exclaimed, "This is that Fabricius who can no more be turned from justice and generosity than can the sun from his course." To show his gratitude he newly clothed all the Roman prisoners, and released them without ransom; and the proud Republic, not choosing to incur an obligation, conferred the same benefit on an equal number of his Tarentine and Samnite allies. He was beginning much to prefer the Romans to his allies, and sent Kineas again to propose a treaty, but the Senate would accept none as long as his troops remained in Italy.   .

However, a project of delivering the Greek colonies in Sicily from the dominion of the Carthaginians called Pyrrhus off, and he sailed thither, still, however, keeping up his support of the Italians, to whom, after two years, he returned, B.C. 276, late in the autumn, with numerous reinforcements, making as formidable an appearance as on his first arrival.

The Romans felt the moment critical, and chose a second time to the consulate the brave Curius Dentatus in company with Lucius Cornelius Lentulus. The Senate was as resolute as ever, but the terrible losses of the battles of the Siris and Asculum had dismayed the populace; the Greeks seemed to them invincible; and moreover there had lately been a severe attack of some infectious disease throughout the city, so that a depressed temper prevailed, and when legions were to be raised for the war, men hung back reluctant.

Stern Curius saw that prompt severity was needed. The tribes were summoned to the Campus Martius, the field of Mars, or muster place; the sacrifices were made; they were sprinkled with the sacred water of lustration;

and then the names of all the tribes were thrown into an urn, whence they were to be drawn forth by a young child. The first tribe drawn was the Pollian gens. All the names of the men of that tribe who were of fit age to serve were then thrown into a vase and drawn again. The first that came up belonged to an insolent young man, who replied by refusing to take the oath that bound him to serve and obey.

Curius thereupon commanded the property he would not fight for to be sold by auction, according to an old law, which, however, had so seldom been put in operation that Pollius appealed to the tribunes of the people to protect him, but they would not interfere; and Curius proceeded to command the man to be sold as well as his lands, saying "the Republic did not want fellows who refused obedience."

After this no one refused to answer to his name, and two armies were soon formed, with one of which he marched into Samnium, while Lentulus entered Lucania. Pyrrhus himself came out to encounter Curius, who had taken up his position on some steep, rugged ground near the city of Beneventum. There he lay entrenched, and finding that the Epirot king was coming in person against him, sent to summon his colleague to join forces with him; but Pyrrhus, hoping to surprise him before this could take place, set forth by torchlight, meaning to fall on him in early morning. The way, however, was full of steep hills and valleys, rugged with rocks, and encumbered with woods, so that his men's progress was slow; the lights burnt out, and many straggled, so that by daybreak the wearied army was in full view upon the slope of the hill above the camp.

Curius drew out his men to attack them; and as on the rugged ground it was impossible to form the impenetrable phalanx, he was already gaining great advantage when one of the elephants was wounded, and, as usual, rushing back among the troops among whom it marched, did much mischief to them. Another was killed, and eight more were driven into such a narrow place among the rocks that their drivers, seeing no escape, surrendered them to the Romans. After this skirmish, Dentatus descended into the open plain to fight a pitched battle with the enemy. One side had the advantage from the first. The other was forced backwards by the charge of the elephants into the camp; but there gathering up darts and javelins, they hurled them at the unwieldy monsters, while others dashed out on them with flaming torches. The poor beasts were wild with terror, and, hurrying back, trod down all behind them. One young one, which was much hurt, screamed frightfully, and this maddened its mother, who thundered hither and thither, effectually ruining the whole order of the Greek army, so that the Romans, getting between the long spears, used their short swords with terrible advantage. The victory was complete : Pyrrhus could only retreat into Tarentum with the remnant of his army, leaving his whole camp to the plunder of the Romans, and, what was more, to their study, for they learnt many useful lessons from its arrangement, and much improved their own method of encamping.

Pyrrhus found matters so hopeless in Italy that he sailed at once for his own kingdom, leaving an officer named Milo in Tarentum, and promising to return when he should have raised a fresh army. Meantime, Marcus Curius Dentatus returned to hold his triumph, which was the grandest that had ever passed along the Sacred Way, since the spoil of Pyrrhus consisted of all that Greek art combined with Eastern luxury could produce. There were vases of gold and silver, purple carpets and hangings, beautiful statues and pictures, and, most wonderful of all, the captured elephants padded along with their towers upon their backs. All this spoil was given up to the public treasury without reserve; such was then early Roman honour. The Senate wanted to reward Dentatus with fifty acres of the lands of the Tarentines, but he had always held that it was a crime for the generals to enrich themselves out of what he viewed as a provision for the poor citizens, who ought to receive allotments before those already possessed of enough to live upon. So he answered that he was content with his own seven acres. Thereupon, some of the greedier sort, who hated this example of disinterestedness, declared that this was all pretence, for that he had helped himself largely to the spoil of Pyrrhus. He was called upon to make oath before the Senate that he had taken nothing of the plunder. He bethought himself for a moment, and then confessed that verily he had taken something. He had picked up one wooden bowl, wherewith to make a libation to the gods, and had carried it home!

The Roman people elected him consul for a second year —his third consulate—and he marched out to drive the Samnites into their mountains; after which he went back to his little farm till his country should again need him. In the course of the next year he was made censor; that is, he had to take charge of the public buildings, as well as to inquire into the qualifications of every citizen for voting or standing for a magistracy. This gave him an opportunity of proposing a worthy manner of disposing of the booty of Beneventum. It was, to spend it in bringing water into Rome, by building an aqueduct to conduct a stream from the river Anio into the city, so as to keep it constantly supplied with pure fresh water. He likewise dug a canal to bring the water of the lake Velinus to refresh the town of Reate, after which the stream had to leap down a rock 140 feet high into the river Nar.

For two thousand years has it thus been dashing down the rock, so that those who gaze upon the beautiful cascade, now called of Terni, forget that it is not the work of Nature, but of one of the large-hearted, simple-mannered men of the time when Rome was a temple, and her Senate all kings.

The aqueduct of the Anio was a work of time; and Curius was appointed to another magistracy in 270, that he might superintend its completion. But he died only five days after the choice was made, leaving his family so poor that the state gave a dowry to his daughter, but bequeathing to them a name held in eternal honour for simple uprightness, honesty, and patriotism, the qualities which not only marked him and his friend Fabricius, but many others of the high-minded men whose constancy drove Pyrrhus out of Italy.

That poor imitation of Alexander never returned. He became involved in wars nearer home, and in 272 was killed in besieging the city of Argos, by a woman who, seeing him about to strike her son, threw down a heavy stone on his head. The Samnites, learning his death, fought one last desperate battle, and then, after their wars of seventy-two years, gave up their independence; the city of Tarentum surrendered; and before many years were past the whole of Southern Italy was in effect subject to Rome, the all-conquering.

CLEOMENES.

B.C. 252—220.

WE must turn for a time from the contemplation of thriving, brilliant, and prosperous nations in early youth, and look at the picture of Worthies as staunch and true, but fallen upon sadder times. After having seen how Nehemiah, under Divine aid, brought back the old constitution to his fallen city, we must now see the brave struggle of two young Greeks to revive the severe and noble days of their ancient state.

Sparta had become thoroughly degenerate. Her ancient discipline was gone; and though her two kings remained to her, the government was in the hands of five ephors, or elective judges, who held the whole power in the city. They were shamefully corrupt, and the whole of the system of Lycurgus was utterly disregarded. Indeed, the Greek states existed and retained their freedom only through the rivalries of the four great powers into which Alexander's empire had split up—Macedon, Thrace, Syria, and Egypt. Leonidas, one of the two kings, had spent several years at the court of Seleucus, King of Syria, who held all the Eastern conquests of Alexander, and at whose court there was a strange and most unwholesome mixture of Greek intellect and Oriental luxury, an atmosphere full of corruption. There Leonidas had married, and on his return tried to introduce the pomp and splendour of an Eastern prince, when all real power and freedom were gone from the country he ruled in name. The other king, Eudamidas, was equally averse to hardihood, and was, besides, avaricious, so that on his death, B.C. 244, his widow and his mother were said to possess more gold than all the rest of the Lacedæmonians put together. His son, Agis, was, however, of very different mould. He had read the histories of his nation, and longed to be worthy of his forefathers. Even as a boy he renounced whatever Lycurgus had forbidden, wore the simplest dress and ate the plainest fare, declaring that he would not care to be king were it not for the hope of reviving the ancient discipline of Sparta.

After his father's death, when he was but nineteen, he continued his plain and hardy habits; and while the elder king wore the diadem, and the purple, and the jewels of an Eastern potentate, the younger proudly uplifted his head uncovered, like Leonidas and Agesilaus of old, and used all his influence to resume the public meals, baths, and lodgings, and all the rules which, if harsh and unnatural, were to his mind identified with all that was virtuous, glorious, and self-sacrificing. But reforms must go deep. The proud old native Dorian Spartans had dwindled to 700; and only about 100 of these had preserved their hereditary possessions, while all the rest were starving. To bring back the old law and make a redistribution of lands was in the young king's mind the only remedy. He knew he must begin at home, and his persuasions brought his mother and grandmother to consent freely to throw all their enormous wealth into the common stock as the first sacrifice. Moreover, his mother talked over her brother Agesilaus, which was the more easily done because he was so much in debt that he could only be the gainer by any arrangement.

The wealth of Sparta was, it was said, chiefly in the

hands of women, and their dismay at the young king's proposal was extreme. They loudly clamoured to his colleague, and entreated him to check such madness and robbery; but Leonidas, though bitterly angry, could not make open opposition, since Agis had on his side all the men of high birth who had been brought to poverty by the working of the later law.

An assembly was held, and Lysander, one of the ephors, who always had more power than the kings, brought forward the measures proposed, and showed how by the violation of her old laws their city had fallen from her supremacy and become degraded, whereas their revival might yet bring back her valour and self-respect. For it was moral greatness, not breadth of conquest, that a true Greek valued.

Then Agis, in the name of himself, his mother, and grandmother, gave up his wide tracts of land and heaps of gold and silver! Leonidas, of course, spoke in opposition, but Agis was ready with many a maxim of philosopher and poet, and won over, not merely all the needy, but all the high-minded and enthusiastic, among them a youth nearly related in birth, named Cleombrotus, who was married to Cheilonis, the daughter of Leonidas. But the elder king had so strong a party among the rich that the reformers felt that he must be removed if they were to make any progress; and accordingly they brought forward an ancient law, which deprived any son of Hercules of the kingly office if he espoused a foreign woman.

On hearing of this, Leonidas took sanctuary in the temple of Athene, while his daughter came to supplicate for him; but as he did not appear when the ephors summoned him, they deposed him, and appointed Cleombrotus in his stead. The two young kings acted in their impatience with some violence; for when Lysander and his friends went out of office, and a less favourable set

of ephors came in, they went with drawn swords and
turned them out, putting in a new set, including Agesilaus: but they shed no blood; and Agis, hearing that his
uncle meant to have the dethroned prince assassinated,
took care to have him escorted safely to Tegea with his
daughter Cheilonis, who clung to him in misfortune.

This uncle, Agesilaus, was an unprincipled and mischievous person. All he really wanted was to be quit
of his debts, and he persuaded his nephew that till all
these were cancelled it was impossible to redistribute
the lands. So all the bonds were brought into the place
of assembly and burnt, while Agesilaus cried out "he
had never seen so fine a fire." Then, having gained his
object, he was resolved not to part with his lands, and
managed to delay until a summons came to Sparta from
their neighbours the Achaians, who were trying to maintain the old dignity of Greece, to march against the Æto-
lians. Agis went out at the head of an army, consisting
of all the best and bravest of the Spartans, and though
the youngest man in his camp, and surrounded by no
pomp, he was so much respected and implicitly obeyed,
and his troops were so orderly, that the allies looked on
as if the Spartans of old history had risen from their
graves at Thermopylæ. Owing to the excellent tactics of
Aratus, the general of the Achaians, there was no fighting; and when Agis returned to Sparta, he found that
his absence had been ruinous to his reforms.

Probably few really wished for them, though his ardour
had prevailed over the spirits of some for a time; and
Agesilaus had been disgracing his cause by deeds of violence and avarice, till he was in so much danger that he
had been obliged to raise a guard of soldiers to secure
his life. His conduct made people distrust Agis, and the
opposite party prevailed to have Leonidas recalled so
suddenly, that, while Agesilaus fled, Agis was forced to

shelter himself in the temple of Athene, and Cleombrotus in that of Poseidon, where he was found by his wife Cheilonis, whose heart was always with the unfortunate. There her father found her and her two little children, as if to protect her husband. She threw herself before him, in a mourning dress and streaming hair, and pleaded hard for Cleombrotus, until her father gave way and granted his life, provided he would go into exile. She would not consent to remain with Leonidas ; but after kneeling in thanksgiving to the goddess, left the city with her husband.

Agiatis, the young wife of Agis, loved her husband as devotedly, but she could not join him in the temple, for her firstborn infant was born in these days of suspense. Agis remained for some little time living in the temple, where no one could touch him, and only leaving it to go to the baths, escorted by a band of armed fiends. Two of these were at last bribed by Leonidas to betray him, as they were passing the street. One seized him, crying, "Agis, I must conduct you to the ephors " The other threw his mantle over him to muffle and ercumber him ; while Leonidas came up with a foreign guard of hired soldiers ; and the brave youth was forced into the prison just at nightfall.

Thither at once came the ephors to interrogate him. One, hoping to save him, asked if he had not been forced to all his strange proceedings by the compulsion of his uncle.

"No," he said ; "by the example of Lycurgus alone."

"Did he repent ?"

"I can never repent of virtue, in the very face of death."

Sentence of death was at once pronounced, and the guards were ordered to remove him to the dungeon where criminals were usually strangled. Even the foreign soldiers hung back from laying hands on the kingly young man, not yet twenty-four years old, and it was the traitorous friend who seized on him and dragged him to the dungeon. Meanwhile, sounds of deliverance drew near ; the people, whose champion he had been, were clamouring at the doors, torches gleamed in the streets, and his mother and grandmother were hurrying from one to another, imploring that the King of Sparta might at least plead his cause in open day before the citizens.

These sounds only hastened the proceedings of his enemies. The executioners were sent at once to perform their office. One absolutely shed tears, but Agis calmly said, " Weep not, my friend ; 1 am far happier than those who condemn me," and held out his neck for the rope, which strangled him almost at the moment that his mother and grandmother entered the prison to see him. The grandmother was instantly strangled ; the mother simply said, " May this be for the good of Sparta ! " straightened the limbs of the two corpses, and presented her neck to the same cord. The three corpses were exposed to public view, and the young wife Agiatis, and her babe, were carried to the house of Leonidas, while Archidamas, the brother of Agis, fled to Messene.

Thus in 240, after three years, did the noble scheme of Agis apparently end in horrible violence, and the grand thoughts acted up to are wholly without fruit ; but the spirit of Agis still lived, though his infant child was soon poisoned in the house of his enemy. The poor young wife, Agiatis, was treated as a captive, till, much against her will, she was compelled to marry Cleomenes, the son of the murderer of her husband and child. He was a mere boy, guiltless of his father's crimes ; and though Agiatis always remained grave and stern towards her hateful father-in-law, his wife Cratesiclea was kind and good. She softened towards the lad, who had the same loving heart as his mother, and who looked up to her with reverent affection and admiration, for she was said to be the most beautiful, stately, and wise of the ladies of Greece. He never ceased to ask her questions about Agis and his designs : and thus, in the very house of Leonidas, she was bringing up a true scholar and imitator of the brave young husband who had been cut off in the bud of his hopes.

Moreover, Leonidas had sent his son to listen to Sphærus, who was teaching philosophy according to the fashion of the later Greeks, who thought no education complete without at least the theory of some system or other. Sphærus was of the Stoic school, so called from Stoa, a porch or portico. It was graver and sterner than the former systems, and declared Virtue to be the supreme good, in quest of which no sacrifice was too great, and that he only was worthy who would devote himself solely to Virtue, without thought of reward here or hereafter. It was a most sublime thought, truly above and beyond the powers of human nature ; and this hopeless faith was the stimulus and support of the greatest spirits of these dark and weary days, spirits the greater perhaps for their very hopelessness.

To Leonidas it was a mere high-sounding jargon ; and he little thought that it was becoming the principle of his young son's life, or that Stoic philosophy was nerving the boy to become a second Agis, and to strive with his whole soul to bring back to Sparta a virtue, uprightness, and resolution that his imagination ascribed to her in her severest age.

Leonidas died in 236, and Cleomenes became the sole king, since Archidamas, the only survivor of the other line, was a fugitive. Still he was entirely powerless, for the ephors usurped the whole government ; and all he could do was to live as a true disciple of Lycurgus, and study the example of Agis from those who had known him best. His hope was in taking the field at the head of an army, and it was not long before an opportunity was afforded him. The little cities of Achaia had banded themselves together in what was called the Achaian League; and under the guidance of Aratus, a statesman and general of considerable ability, had rendered themselves so formidable that the brave old days of Greece seemed almost reviving in them. They wanted to become supreme in the Peloponnesus, and were very jealous of Sparta. So, without any provocation, Aratus led a party at night to surprise Tegea and Orchomenus, Arcadian towns in alliance with Sparta. However, warning was sent in time to Lacedæmon; and Cleomenes, with full consent of the ephors, reinforced the garrisons of the towns, and marched out himself to a place called the Athenæum, which commanded one of the passes into Laconia.

Aratus failed in his attempt: whereupon Cleomenes sent a letter to ask the purpose of his night march; to which Aratus replied, that he meant to prevent the fortification of the Athenæum. "What, then," demanded Cleomenes, "was the use of the torches and scaling ladders?"

Aratus laughed, and asked a Spartan exile what kind of youth this was.

"If you have any designs on Lacedæmon," was the answer, "begin them before the game-chicken's spurs are grown."

However, the spurs were grown enough to have made themselves felt in Arcadia before the ephors summoned him back; but they soon had to send him out again, with 5,000 men, into Argolis. The Achaians offered battle, and with very superior numbers; but Aratus, arriving in the camp, commanded a retreat—for what reason is not known. But the army were much elated, and Cleomenes proudly reminded them of the old saying that the Spartans never asked about their enemies how many they were, but where they were. And soon he gained a most brilliant victory; for coming up with the Achaians at Mount Lycæum, he routed them so utterly that for some days it was not known whether Aratus were dead or alive.

The doubt was solved, however, by the wily old leader suddenly appearing at Mantinea, and capturing it : and this material loss gave the ephors occasion to cry down their young king's success and call him home. Feeling himself hampered on every side by their opposition, he hoped to be stronger by the support of his fellow-king, Archidamas, and sent to invite him to share the throne ; but the ephors, fearing their united strength, caused the royal youth to be stabbed immediately on his arrival : and the enemies of Cleomenes contrived to cast the blame of both this murder and that of the infant child of Agis upon him. His mother, Cratesiclea, who, if she were the Græco-Syrian wife of Leonidas, had become a true Spartan at heart, did all she could to further her son's cause, and even married again to gain a partizan for him. Once more his ardent wish was fulfilled ; he again was sent out with an army, and gained another victory over Aratus and the Achaians.

He felt assured that he could raise Sparta to her old place if he were but free to act, unfettered by the ephors. And most conveniently for him, one of the ephors having gone to sleep in a temple, according to the habit of those who sought revelations from the gods, saw four of the chairs of his colleagues removed, and heard a voice say, "This is best for Sparta." Upon this, Cleomenes, having arranged matters with his friends, led out an army containing most of the persons most averse to reform. He took them on long marches, and at last, when they were wearied out, encamped at a great distance from home, and there leaving them, he and a trusty party of friends hurried home without exciting suspicion, for Cleomenes never could bear to stay long away from his beloved wife, and was in the habit of galloping home to see her whenever he could be spared.

He and his friends beset the ephors at supper. Four were killed—and this must be charged against Cleomenes—but there was no other blood shed; and when the people were assembled in the morning, the king clearly demonstrated that the ephors' overweening power had been usurped, and that after their most illegal murder of Agis without a trial it had been needful to use strong measures. Almost all his opponents were fled or absent, and the people eagerly agreed to his proposals for reformation. The cancelling of debts and redistribution of property were carried out; Cleomenes resigned his own estates, and the division was made, reserving a share for the exiles, who he promised should return when the reform was safely established. And as the other line of kings was now extinct, he raised his younger brother, Eucleidas, to the throne.

Thus, for a time, Sparta was renovated—Agis' work was done—and the severity of their manners restored. Strict military discipline was established throughout the city; the young men were always on duty; and the meals were plain and simple—though, indeed, when one of his zealous imitators entertained some strangers with black broth and pulse, Cleomenes reproved him, saying that it would not do to be exact Spartans when entertaining visitors. No sports of the theatre were allowed, only athletic training; and Cleomenes himself was the hardiest and simplest of all in his demeanour. Men used to the Eastern pomp of the successful Macedonians remarked, that while these upstart princes wore purple robes and splendid diadems, lounged on piles of cushions, and never received or answered a petition but through

a host of attendants and slaves, when visitors came to
Sparta, the lineal descendant of Hercules, whose ancestry
counted back through thirty-one kings, came simply forward to meet them in person uncrowned, and clad like
any other Greek, attended to what they said, and showed
his true nobleness in gracious demeanour. And the contrast, though partly the effect of the smallness of his
kingdom, did no small good to the cause of the last of the
Heracleids.

Mantinea turned out the Achaians and invited Cleomenes back ; and all Peloponnesus felt that the question
was whether the Achaians or Spartans should be their
chief. After another Spartan victory, a conference was
proposed, at which, according to promise, the Achaians
were to have made peace, and declare Cleomenes head of
the League of Peloponnesus ; but he had overtaxed his
strength by the Spartan discipline, and after having excessively fatigued himself by long marches, and chilled
himself by drinking cold water, he broke a blood-vessel,
and was forced to be carried back to Sparta to be nursed
by his wife. The first thing he did on his arrival was to
command all the Achaian prisoners to be set at liberty, in
confidence that his illness had only deferred the fulfilment
of the treaty.

But it gave Aratus time to send an embassy to Antigonus, King of Macedon. To him it seemed that dependence
on the northern state was better than the alliance with
Sparta. The glory of his youth had been the freeing his
country from Macedon : now he was ready, out of sheer
rivalry, to put himself under the yoke again. He invited
Antigonus to Greece, promising that the Achaians and their
allies would receive him, if only Sparta might be put down.

However, Cleomenes, on his recovery, most gallantly
took Argos ; and soon after the Corinthians drove Aratus
away, and surrendered to Sparta ; and the king showed his

generosity by protecting all the property of Aratus which he found there. But, however great his activity, his doom was sealed. What could 5,000 Spartans do against the whole force of Macedon?

Antigonus was soon at the isthmus; and the recently-won towns surrendered, the allies deserted, and at Tegea, in the midst of a retreat, Cleomenes heard the tidings of the death of his ardently-beloved Agiatis. With the resolution he had learnt from the Stoic he commanded his countenance and voice, gave orders for the defence of Tegea, and then, marching all night, returned to his home and gave way to the passionate grief of his Greek nature, with his mother and his little children.

Then, looking out upon his danger and difficulty, he saw that his only hope lay in an alliance with another Macedonian king, the rival of Antigonus, namely with Ptolemy, called Euergetes, the grandson of the Ptolemy who had secured Egypt. To him, therefore, Cleomenes applied for aid in men and money. The reply was a grievous one. Ptolemy would only send succour on condition of the young king, whose heart was still bleeding at the loss of his wife, sending his little children and his mother to Egypt as hostages for his fidelity.

Cleomenes, who had none of the hardness of the old Spartan, was distressed exceedingly. The only hope of his country was in Ptolemy, yet he could not bear to send all he loved to the risks of a foreign land; and he could not even bring himself to speak of the proposal to his mother, till she, perceiving that something was on his mind, asked his friends what preyed on him. When he was thus forced to tell, the brave old lady laughed aloud. "Was this the thing," she said, "that you feared to tell me? Why do you not put me on shipboard, and send this carcase where it may be most serviceable to Sparta, before age wastes it unprofitably here?"

Thus, having given her free consent, Cratesiclea and her little grandsons were escorted on foot along the rocky road to Tænarus by Cleomenes at the head of his whole army. There the temple of the sea-god Poseidon looked forth from the promontory on the deep, and into this the mother, son, and babes retired for their farewell. Cleomenes was almost broken-hearted, but his mother's spirit rose. " Go to, King of Sparta," she said ; " when we are without door, let none see us weep, or show any passion beneath the honour and dignity of Sparta ! That alone is in our own power, while success or failure depends on the gods."

And thus she parted with him with full composure, while he, with such calmness as Spartan temper and Stoical philosophy could enable him to wear, turned back to his desolate home to fight out the last struggle. During the winter Antigonus had received the title of Chief of the League, which Cleomenes had so nearly attained ; his statues had been set up, and even—after the profane fashion begun by Alexander in his exaltation and carried on by his successors—feasts were decreed in honour of this Macedonian king as a god, and Aratus, once a patriot, led the pæan and the dance of this most corrupt idol. Such was the work of envy.

Only Laconia held out, the passes all garrisoned in the spirit of Thermopylæ, though little efficient aid even in money came from Egypt, only a letter from brave old Cratesiclea bidding her son do whatever was most profitable to his country, without regard to offending Ptolemy, for the sake of an old woman and a child. Nor did his courage or energy fail for a moment. He raised money by letting the slaves buy their freedom, and enlisted 2,000 troops from among them. With this reinforcement he surprised the Achaian town of Megalopolis. The inhabitants fled, and he offered to give them back their city provided they would ally themselves with him; but when they refused, he collected all the plunder, and laid the place completely in ruins, as a warning to other Peloponnesians. But in the next year, 221, when he invaded Argolis and beat down the standing corn with large wooden swords to cut off supplies from his enemies, he would not allow a place full of sacred monuments to be burnt, and expressed his grief for having done so much harm at Megalopolis. The long struggle was nearly over; Antigonus had collected his troops for an invasion of Laconia, and Cleomenes, having fortified all the other passes, placed himself on the road near Sellasia, where the river Ænus flowed between two hills named Evas and Olympus. On the first he placed his young brother Eucleidas, on the other himself, and his cavalry in the middle. His numbers were 20,000, those of Antigonus full a third more; and among these was a young Megalopolitan named Philopœmen, who himself lived to be the last champion of his country, and must have bitterly lamented the rivalry that ranked the noblest spirits of Greece against one another, instead of binding them together.

Young Eucleidas was not equal to his post. He did not avail himself of the advantage of his ground to charge down the hill on his enemies, but let himself be driven backwards upon the precipices, and there perished with his men. The cavalry were beaten by Philopœmen, who fought to the last, though both his legs were transfixed by a javelin; and Cleomenes, making a desperate attempt on the phalanx, found the numbers and weight utterly impenetrable; his own 6,000 of the choicest Spartan troops were borne down, and, though they fought with desperation, only 200 survived.

Cleomenes found himself one of the survivors, and rode with them to Sparta, where he stood still in the market-

T

place, and firmly told the citizens that all was lost; adding, that they had better receive Antigonus, and make the best terms they could, and that wherever he was he would endeavour to serve Sparta; they should decide whether his life or death were best for them.

Perhaps there is no more pathetic scene in all history than that which Plutarch here gives—of all his fellow-fugitives welcomed by their wives, mothers, and children, running out to rejoice in their safety, take their arms, or bring them drink; while the king, now utterly solitary, turned towards his empty and bereaved house to wait while the citizens decided his fate. A slave woman, taken at Megalopolis, came out to offer to wait on him and bring him drink; but he would taste nothing, nor even enter beyond the portico; only, being wearied out, he laid his arm sideways against a pillar, rested his head against it, and leant there in silence until word came to him that the citizens wished him to provide for his own safety.

Thereupon he stood up, and the last of the line of Hercules slowly walked from the home of his fathers, and embarked at Gythium with a few friends. He had reigned fifteen years, and must have been a year or two above thirty when the noble designs of his youth were thus crushed, and himself driven out as a wanderer. His beloved city was kindly treated by Antigonus, who did not long survive the battle.

Cleomenes touched at the island of Ægilea, where Plutarch reports a curious dialogue between him and one of his followers, who, after condoling with him that "death in battle, which is the most glorious of all, we have let go," tried to persuade him that the only course for a brave man was to die by his own hand—far better than showing himself to his mother a defeated man, an exile, and a slave.

But Cleomenes replied that he saw no bravery, only

cowardice, in such an action, and that "it was base to live or die only to ourselves;" neither did he yet despair of his country.

Thus, full of steadfastness, he reached Egypt, rejoined his mother, and was welcomed by Ptolemy Euergetes at Alexandria. Never was one city a greater contrast to another than Alexandria to Sparta; not only sea with rock, but wealth with plainness, learning with ignorance, splendour with simplicity. The trade of Tyre and the philosophy of Athens alike had found a home there; the choicest endowments of all nations were lavished there, in a setting of the strange old Egyptian marvels. The population of Jews, Greeks, Egyptians, Tyrians, swarmed in every street, intent on trade, on study, on philosophy, on pleasure; and the court was a scene of wonderful luxury and splendour, full of every indulgence and refine- ment that East or West could produce—all that Cleomenes had learnt to despise.

However, the old Macedonian vigour had not quite died out of Ptolemy Euergetes, who had been a brave warrior in his youth, and was able to appreciate Cleomenes. At first he was short and cold with the exiled son of a hun- dred kings, who would not cringe as a suppliant; but after a while he was struck with the strong sense and judgment and brief Laconic irony of his guest, and saw that his grave self-contained equality of demeanour was a nobler thing than flattery. He treated him as a brother king, promised him men and ships to recover Greece, and allowed him a pension of twenty-four talents a year. The frugal Cleomenes and his mother used very little of this for their own needs, and with the rest maintained crowds of Greeks banished like themselves.

Unfortunately his plans were only just formed when Euergetes died; and his son, Ptolemy Philopator, was a miserable voluptuary, heedless of all but his vicious pleasures and his selfish security. Once he did consult Cleomenes whether it was safe to leave his brother Magas alive and at large.

"I should think," said the Greek, "that it would be better for your security, if you had more brothers."

"Yes," said one of the favourites, speaking for his master, abashed, "only the king can never trust the hired soldiers while Magas lives."

"Never fear for that," said Cleomenes; "among them are 3,000 Peloponnesians, whom I can rule with a nod."

This was a communication to horrify the Egyptians, and Cleomenes was hated and dreaded from that day forth. Moreover, as the court grew more foolishly and wantonly depraved, he walked about in his simple garb, with his thoughts far away, and his stern sad face, till the Alexandrians in their gaiety shuddered at him and called him a lion in a sheepfold.

The army and fleet once promised were refused; but when the tidings came of Antigonus' death, he longed to depart with only his own friends. The king would not see him, the ministers thought it dangerous to let him go, and he found himself watched and kept, a prisoner at large.

Just at this time, when he was burning to be at home, and was walking on the quay, straining his eyes towards his beloved Greece, he was saluted by a man named Nicegoras, of whom he had bought an estate, but had been prevented by his misfortunes from paying for it. He now asked what brought him to Egypt.

"I have brought war-horses for the king," he said.

"Dancing girls would be more to the purpose," bitterly said Cleomenes.

The man applied again for the payment of his debt, and, finding that Cleomenes was penniless, went in malice and reported his irony to the minister, and the two concerted an accusation against him that he was plotting to seize the island of Cyrene.

On this the king ordered him and his friends to be invited into a large room and there kept. At first he fancied it a mere freak of the king, and endured with patient scorn as usual; but having followed a visitor to the door, he overheard a sharp reprimand to the guard for not " better watching such a savage beast."

This seems to have maddened him, and at the first opportunity, when the guards were asleep in the heat of noon, he and his friends, thirteen in number, rushed furiously out with drawn swords into the streets, crying " Liberty!" with perhaps some frantic hope that Greek blood might be stirred by the cry, and at least they might fight their way to a ship. But finding that no one stirred in their cause, and that they were hemmed in, though no one dared to touch them, they did that which in a cooler moment Cleomenes had denounced as cowardly —they fell on their own swords. One, named Panteus, re-mained to the last, composed the body of his king, kissed him, and then killed himself over the body.

Even Cleomenes' little son was infected by the frenzy, and, running to the top of the house, threw himself down, and was taken up severely bruised, and lamenting at not having killed himself like his father. But in the midst of the grief of Cratesiclea came tidings that the savage Ptolemy had commanded that all the women and children should be put to death. Among them was the young bride of Panteus, who had actually fled from home to join him after the battle of Sellasia. She was tall, strong, and very beautiful, and she supported Cratesiclea on her way to death. The high-spirited matron had no fears, but only begged to die before her grandchildren. The soldiers, however, denied this last request, and killed both the little boys before her eyes. She cried out, " Oh, children ! whither are you gone ?" and so died with them. Panteus' wife laid out the body, then bound her robes round her own limbs and held out her neck.

Cleomenes' body was flayed and hung on a cross, until, to the general amaze, a serpent was seen coiled round it. This portent so struck the. Egyptians that the body not only received due rites, but was by Ptolemy's command treated as that of a divine hero.

So closed the Spartan history ; so ended the long lines of the twin sons of Hercules, each with a true hero ; so piteously ended the brave efforts of two kingly youths to bring back valour and virtue ; so closed a young life which, but for the one act of almost justifiable violence on the ephors, and for the last frenzy that belied his previous noble patience, was as grand and stainless as that of any of the great heroic figures of ancient time.

Tender and brave, resolute and vigorous, perhaps the. Stoic philosophy never had a better representative than in Cleomenes, last King of Sparta.

SCIPIO AFRICANUS.

B.C. 234—183.

IN the year 218, four years after Cleomenes perished in Egypt, a young Roman of noble blood set out on his first campaign—immediately after the family festival which always took place when a youth reached his seventeenth year, put off the boyish tunic and the bulla or round gold amulet he had hitherto worn, put on the full, long, white woollen toga of a citizen, became liable to serve in the army, and was enrolled by his individual name among the members of his family and clan.

The clan to which the boy belonged was the Cornelian, a very old patrician race of the purest Roman lineage ; and the subdivision or family in which he was born was further named Scipio, or "the Staff," in recollection, it was said, of a young Cornelius who was often seen acting as a staff to his blind old father. The name conferred on the youth was Publius, the same which was already borne by his father, as in fact it seems to have been always chosen for the eldest son of the house of Scipio. Young Publius Cornelius Scipio was bred up to more of learning and cultivation than the rugged old Romans of two generations back; he belonged to a family in easy circumstances, with a house in Rome built round a square court, with an altar to the household gods in the midst, and little dens for slaves, clients, and shopkeepers clustered outside on the walls. He was taught reading, writing, and public speaking, and the Greek language, although the custom of keeping Greek tutors for young men had not then set in. And in the Campus Martius, or Field of Mars, he was wont to be exercised among all the other youths of Rome in all soldierly exercises, using the sword and spear, and manœuvring on foot and on horseback with discipline and regularity, but especially on horseback, as this was the manner in which his patrician birth entitled him to serve. In all these he had borne his full part ; and he was further remarkable among the lads of his own age for a deep devotional feeling, which led him to seek for divine direction in whatever he did. At any great turn in his life, or on any fresh undertaking, he was wont to climb the steep hill of the Capitol, and, entering the temple of the great sky-god Jupiter, or Diespiter (father of day), there to remain in deep thought and prayer until, as he deemed, the divine will was made known to him. And when we mark the tenor of his course through life, we can scarcely doubt that the true Father of Lights whom he thus ignorantly worshipped guided this honest and upright heart in the paths of obedience, justice, mercy, and purity.

Young Publius' first campaign promised to be a gallant one, for he was to accompany his father, who had newly been elected consul, and had chosen Spain as the place of his command in the war that had just been proclaimed in defence of the allies of Rome.

This war was with the great Phœnician, or, as the Romans shortened the word, Punic, city of Carthage, originally an offshoot from Tyre and Sidon, planted on the rich northern shore of Africa, but, having flourished unscathed while the parent cities were taken by one Eastern conqueror after another, now far more rich and

,owerful than they had ever been, and the one dangerous rival of Greece.

Probably we shall form the best notion of the Phœnicians by thinking of them as greatly resembling the Jews in language, habits, and customs, and in the framework of their character; but as Jews without the Law and the Prophets, with no knowledge or aspirations towards a Perfect God, and instead, with a religion infinitely more mischievous than that of Greece or Rome. The faith of these great states was the outcome of natural and traditional religion acting on thoughtful minds and honest consciences; but there was an element of wickedness in the very foundation of the Phœnician faith, which seems as if the Evil Spirit had influenced its formation. Baal, the sun-god, and Ashtaroth, the queen of heaven, or moon-goddess, were supposed to be adored by absolutely criminal acts; while "Moloch, horrid king, besmeared with blood," was propitiated by placing live infants between the brazen hands of his colossal statue to be dropped into the furnace beneath. Thus all the sins against which the Israelites were unceasingly warned grew unchecked among the Phœnicians—the avarice, the treachery, and the sensuality; so that not only the Scripture, but the heathen nations of the West, condemned them for their want of honour and morality, their cruelty and their baseness, and "Punic faith" became a byword.

They had to the full the aptitude of the Jews for gardening, farming, bargaining, and likewise for the higher branches of commerce, so that wherever they fixed themselves the country became beautiful for tillage; their streets were full of shops, and their harbours of merchant ships, which carried on the greater part of the trade of the whole world; and on this account they established settlements, which soon became cities, all along the

Mediterranean—places where native produce could be collected and exchanged for treasures brought from other places. There was none of the love of glory and prowess for their own sake that actuated the Greeks and Romans in the Phœnician nation ; they preferred peace for the benefit of their trade, but neither greatly loved nor esteemed military glory, though they were no cowards ; as sailors they were the boldest in existence ; and they would fight doggedly on occasion, as the Romans had already learnt in a war which lasted from 264 to 241, and ended only three years before the birth of the young Scipio.

The Carthaginian settlements were dotted about over the islands and coasts of the Mediterranean, where also were a good many Greek colonies ; and as the Greeks, in the decay of their nation, were turning their minds to commerce, there was plenty of rivalship and many quarrels. The Greeks having no one in their parent state capable of aiding them, asked the help of the Romans; and the first Punic war had resulted in the expulsion of the Carthaginians from Sicily, an offence that they remembered with great bitterness. Twenty-three years had since passed, and there had been a great civil war at Carthage among the elders and judges (who seem to have had the same sort of power as the persons called by similar titles in the Bible). When this was over, however, the great family of Hamilcar Barca, or Barak, "the Lightning Chief," the only Carthaginians who had any real warlike fire or passion for enterprise, began to push forward the dominion of Carthage in Spain, which was then a region filled with savage Celtic tribes, fringed round with Greek and Phœnician colonies, attracted by the fertile slopes towards the west, and by the silver and other mineral wealth of the mountains.

Hamilcar Barca had taken his little son, Hannibal, or "the Grace of Baal," with him to Spain at nine years old, after having first made him swear to be at enmity with the Romans as long as he should live. That oath was taken the very year that young Publius Scipio was born; and in the meantime Hamilcar, after distinguishing himself greatly, had died; but the oppression of himself, his son, and brother-in-law, on the Greek cities was so severe that they entreated aid from Rome, war had been declared against Carthage, and all preparations were being made.

Three armies were raised; one to keep guard under a prætor in Italy, one to go to Sicily under the other consul, Tiberius Sempronius Longus, and perhaps to make a descent upon Carthage, and the third, under Publius Cornelius Scipio, to meet the enemy in Spain. This, however, seems to have been thought the least imminent matter; Scipio's army was the last to be raised, and it was not till late in the summer that he was ready to set out with two legions, each numbering 6,000 men, 156,000 Italian allies, and 60 quinquiremes, or great galleys, of five benches of rowers, one above the other. These met Scipio and his land army at Pisa, where a rumour was confirmed which had already reached him on his march, that the audacious young Hannibal was actually preparing to march round the gulf, traverse two mountain chains, and descend upon Italy from the Alps.

Scipio could hardly believe in so wild an enterprise, but he embarked his men at Pisa, expecting to be in time to meet the Carthaginian leader in Spain and turn him back; but his troops suffered much from sea-sickness, and when at length he arrived at the great Greek colony of Massilia (now Marseilles), for Roman navigation did not even venture to go direct from Italy to Spain, he found the place in consternation. Hannibal, with 50,000 picked troops and 9,000 horse, besides elephants, was across the Pyrenees, and in Gaul.

Scipio, therefore, landed his men on the banks of the Rhone, intending to give them a short respite to recover from the voyage, and then to march up the river and fight a battle when the enemy tried to cross it.   But another rumour came in through the Gauls that, on the very day of his landing, this wondrously active foe had actually crossed the Rhone much higher up than he had expected, and beaten off the natives, who, being attached to the Massilians, had tried to oppose their passage.   Still incredulous, Scipio sent out 300 horsemen, guided by a body of Gauls, to ascertain the truth.   By and by they came in sight of a body of horsemen, dark lithe figures, clad in white garments with glittering coats of mail.   These were the Numidians, the native population of North Africa, the same whom we now know as Moors, and who have always been famous for their grace and lightness as riders and for their skill in wielding their long slender lances.   There were several petty kingdoms of these in alliance with or else tributary to Carthage, and they supplied a large portion of Hannibal's cavalry.   The two reconnoitring parties encountered, and the shock of the heavy Roman horse was such as to overwhelm the lighter Africans, full 160 of whom were left dead, while the others galloped away at headlong speed on their light Barbary steeds, followed closely by the Romans, who only drew rein when they had seen the fugitives received into a great fortified camp, formed after the regular Greek fashion, and upon the east side of the Rhone.

They could only come back to the consul with the account, who at once decided to give up the attempt to come up with Hannibal in Gaul, and to return himself to Italy by sea, and take the command of the army that was already in the northern province under the prætor, Lucius Manlius Vulso, so as to meet the Carthaginians on their descent from the Alps, and take them when exhausted by their journey, if indeed they ever succeeded in traversing what had hitherto been deemed a barrier impenetrable to all save the light-footed and savage mountaineers of Gaul. Meanwhile, he sent the consular army he had raised into Spain, under the command of his brother, Cnæus Cornelius Scipio, commonly called Calvus, or " the Bald," so as to keep the Carthaginians occupied there, and prevent them from concentrating their whole force upon Italy ;— and to this measure Rome probably owed her preservation.

The whole of what' we now call Lombardy and Piedmont was then known as Cisalpine Gaul, and was inhabited by Celts who, though subject to Rome, and furnishing large contingents as horsemen and javelin men to her armies, were far from patient of her dominion, and were ready to rise and take part with any enemy of hers. To keep these in check, Scipio felt his own presence required ; and he therefore took ship with only his son and his immediate attendants, and, landing at Pisa, hastened to assume the command of the prætorian army of 25,000 men at Placentia. He had scarcely arrived before he learnt that Hannibal had safely performed that wonder of history, his passage of the Alps, and was actually in Italy with 12,000 African and 8,000 Spanish foot and 6,000 horse, besides the elephants, and that the Gauls were everywhere favourable to him.

Scipio pushed on to meet him, so as to prevent a general rising of the Gauls, and throwing a bridge of boats across the Ticinus, he found himself moving on a parallel line with Hannibal in the angle between that river and the Eridanus. Both generals rode out at the head of their cavalry to reconnoitre, and, as before on the Rhone, there was an encounter ; but on this occasion Hannibal had with him his Carthaginian horse, who were heavily armed, and equal to resist the shock of the Roman horsemen.

Scipio himself was grievously wounded, and while his troop were staggered by his fall, the heavy Carthaginian cavalry thundered on them in front, and they were suddenly hailed upon in flank and rear by the Numidian darts, as the swift horsemen wheeled round them, launching their javelins, or cutting down with their sabres whoever fell in their way. The startled and discomfited Romans lost all semblance of order and fled wildly to their camp, pursued by the Numidians like swarms of angry wasps, while the wounded consul would have been left to his fate, but for the brave young son who stayed by him, upheld him, defended him, and at length brought him into the camp, sorely hurt, but still able to think for his army.

The cavalry was as good as lost, and the consul therefore decided that the camp must be broken up at once, since without horsemen, and in a country fast becoming hostile, it would have been impossible to march safely so near the enemy. Therefore the army moved at once, crossing the Ticinus, and leaving 600 men to destroy the bridge of boats. They succeeded in doing this before Hannibal came up and made them prisoners ; and this delayed his advance, so that there was time for Scipio to be joined by his fellow-consul, Sempronius, who had been summoned from Sicily, and brought a fresh army, before Hannibal arrived in front of the Roman army on the opposite side of the little river Trebia.

It was now far on in the winter, and Scipio was of opinion that it would be the wisest measure to watch and harass the enemy, and let them waste under the inclemency of the season, while the Romans were trained to meet their mode of warfare, and the Gauls grew tired of them as guests. Sempronius, however, was eager to fight a battle both before his term of consulship should expire and likewise whilst the entire glory of the day would be his own, since his colleague was still disabled by his wound, and forced to remain within the camp.

The two armies were five miles apart, with the pebbly bed of the Trebia between, a watercourse almost dry in summer, but in winter filled with a broad and swift torrent. Here in the early morning a skirmish between the light troops on either side began, and Sempronius, eager for the battle, ordered out the legions to support the cavalry before they had had time to eat, and caused them to wade through the river, which, swollen and chilled by a recent snowstorm, reached up to their breasts. Drenched and shivering, they were drawn up on the bank, while their opponents had eaten their morning meal, oiled their limbs, and put on their armour by their fires ; and, moreover, Hannibal had placed an ambush in a narrow ravine under his younger brother, Mago, ready to fall on the enemy at the critical moment. The darts and arrows of the Roman light infantry, who had long ago begun the battle, were soon used up, and they were quickly driven back ; the cavalry were beaten by the African horse and elephants ; and though the legions fought with all their steadiness and hardihood, the sudden onset of Mago and his ambush broke them, the elephants closed in on them, and the rout was complete. Those who retained some order marched under Sempronius straight on for Placentia, while the rest dashed back through the river to the camp. The enemy would have followed them, but the cold, which had but numbed the hardy Romans for a time, was absolutely fatal to the more southerly men of Carthage, and many men and horses perished, as well as nearly all the elephants brought across the mountains with such frightful labour. Scipio, on learning the flight of his comrade, assumed the command of the fugitives, and a second time left the camp by night, led the remnant of the army across the river, and passing unseen the entrenchments of his enemies, arrived at Placentia.

Thence the dejected Romans retreated in two divisions, Scipio to Ariminium and Sempronius into Etruria; while the winter set in so severely that Hannibal, who attempted to cross the Apennines, was fairly beaten back by the wind, which rushed so furiously through the gorges that neither man nor beast could stand against it, more of his poor elephants were destroyed by the cold, and he himself became blind in one eye.

In this respite Sempronius returned to Rome, and held the election for the two new consuls of the incoming year, 217. As soon as the newly-elected consul, Servilius Geminus, arrived at Ariminium, Scipio, with the dignity of proconsul, departed to take the command in Spain, where his brother Cnæus was doing good service; but he left behind him his brave young son Publius, who was already an officer in the cohorts of horse attached to the legions at Ariminium.

Meantime, the other consul, Consul Flaminius, imprudently meeting Hannibal in the defile of Lake Thrasymenus, there perished, with the loss of all his army, and Rome was in an agony of grief, though neither of terror nor despair. To supply the loss of the consul the wise and prudent Quintus Fabius was elected Dictator. His principle was to avoid pitched battles, and in their stead to watch and harass the enemy, laying all waste before him in the hope of starving him out; but this system was very distasteful to the Romans, who were always anxious to try their fortune in the field, were suffering much from the devastation of their lands, and could not bear to see Hannibal march all the way from Cisalpine Gaul to Samnium loaded with plunder and prisoners.

Their two fresh consuls of 216, Lucius Æmilius Paullus and Caius Terentius Varro, were to follow an entirely

different system. They were thorough representatives of
the two orders—Æmilius a proud, refined, and much disliked patrician, but a good officer ; and Varro a butcher's
son, able but impetuous, and always inclined to pull
against his noble colleague. It was scarcely well to send
out two such adverse spirits together, at so critical a
moment, to take the command of the army on alternate
days.

Hannibal had just come out of his winter quarters and
taken the city of Cannæ, on the river Aufidius, containing
great stores of grain and commanding all the corn-
growing country around, so that the harvest lay at his
mercy. It was the end of June, when the wheat was
nearly ripe, that young Scipio, who had, though only
nineteen years old, become tribune of a legion, a rank
answering to that of colonel of a regiment, went out in
the great army of 90,000 men, which was led by the two
consuls, to meet the enemy. Probably he owed his early
promotion, not only to his personal merits, but to the
grievous losses Rome had already sustained, for the
legions were no longer of hardy, practised soldiers, but
of the lowest of the people, too poor to arm themselves
perfectly.

Æmilius would fain have followed the policy of Fabius,
or, at least, if there was to be a battle, have withdrawn
among the hills, where Hannibal's dreadful cavalry could
not be so effective, more especially since the Roman horse
had already suffered so much that they were more crippled
in this branch than in any other respect. But Varro,
commanding on alternate days, forced on a meeting on
the banks of the Aufidius, and, on the morning of a long
summer day, hoisted the red flag, the signal of battle, on
his tent.

The legions, drawn up in close order, stood in the
centre, the red and white crests of dyed horsehair rising

U

high above their helmets, and their shields almost touching one another. The front of their line was very narrow, the flanks lengthened, and on Varro's word to advance they were driven on with tremendous impetus through the very centre of Hannibal's array, like a bold hand thrust in to split open a tree. But if the hand cannot at once rend asunder the wood, the recoil will crush it with fatal force ; and thus it befell the legions. Their cavalry, all of young patricians, had been, as usual, dispersed by the Spaniards and Numidians ; and these now rode in on their flanks. There was no room to fight ; the Romans stood literally wedged into the midst of their enemies, unable to fight or retreat, struggling blindly, as they were hewn down on all sides with an unexampled butchery, neither asking nor receiving quarter.

Publius Scipio—fighting step by step—found himself at last, with some few men, clear of the horrible throng, and, well accustomed now to lost battles, for this was his third within two years, he restored some sort of order, and made his way to the town of Canusium, where he remained to take breath and gather the fugitives, who came in on foot or on horseback, singly or in parties, with direful histories of slaughter and ruin. Lentulus, another tribune, came in telling how he had met with the consul Æmilius, sitting on a stone, covered with blood, and how he replied, to all entreaties to try to escape, that he had no mind to answer to the Senate for this day's work, nor to accuse his colleague, but that Lentulus must carry word to Rome to prepare for a siege, and tell Fabius that he had tried to follow his advice to the last. Thereupon a flood of flying Romans and pursuing enemies swept Lentulus away, and he believed Æmilius to have fallen under their darts. Of the other consul nothing was known, even by the 6,000 men who marched in last, having cut their way out of the camp, where they with as many more had been left in reserve to attack the Carthaginian camp while the battle was being fought.

Out of 90,000 men only 10,000 remained, and no officer higher in rank than the four tribunes who found themselves together, Scipio, Lentulus, a youth called Appius Claudius Pulcher, or "the Fair," and one other. There was nothing to hinder Hannibal from thundering at the gates of Rome! The legionaries elected Scipio and Claudius to command them; but the other young patricians, in terror and despair, proposed to make for the coast, embark for Spain, and there join Scipio's father, who was gaining great advantages.

In the midst of their plans, however, Publius Scipio stood among them : "I swear," said he, drawing his sword, "never to forsake the Republic, nor to suffer any of her citizens to do so. I call the great Jupiter to witness this my oath." Then turning to the young gentleman whom he knew to be the chief of the despairing conspirators, he added, "You, Metellus, and all present, take the same oath, or not a man of you shall escape this sword."

Ashamed and dismayed, each obeyed; and this resolution prevented a defection that would have been more fatal to Rome than even the slaughter of Cannæ. And ere long Varro appeared at Canusium, having escaped with seventy horse to Venusia. After a few days of terrible suspense it was found that Hannibal had not advanced on Rome, but was remaining in Apulia, expecting all the Italians to rise and join him, and trying to secure the south of Italy, whence he could best communicate with Carthage. There was time, therefore, for the broken forces to rally, and though a whole bushel of gold rings from the corpses of patricians had been gathered from the field of Cannæ, still the spirit of Rome had not died with them, and there was a brave little remnant of the

U 2

army left at Canusium, under charge of Marcus Marcellus and Publius Scipio, while Varro went back to face boldly the ordeal that Æmilius had shrunk from. So far from blaming him, the whole Senate came out to meet him and thank him for not having despaired of the Republic, knowing that to bear a failure is a greater thing than to gain a success.

Thenceforth the maxims of wary old Fabius, which Æmilius had in vain tried to follow, were carried out, and, instead of giving battle, the Romans watched and harassed Hannibal, besetting him wherever he went. A winter in the luscious climate of Campania, amid the various luxuries of the city of Capua, was thought to have demoralized that terrible army of his; and from the jealousies which prevailed at Carthage, as well as the employment given to the Punic armies in Spain by the two Scipiones, he never received reinforcements to make up for his losses in the march and in his four battles;—so that, though he continued in Italy, the peril of Rome was never again so imminent as when Publius Scipio prevented the desertion of her young nobles after the battle of Cannæ.

That the Romans appreciated his behaviour on this occasion was shown by their electing him four years later, in his twenty-third year, curule ædile, the first magistracy to which a patrician was eligible, and which made him superintendent of the paving and cleansing of the streets, of the selling of slaves, and of some of the grand religious athletic exercises. He was still under the legal age, though probably by this time married to Æmilia, the daughter of his old general, who had died at Cannæ; but when the censors objected to him, he replied, that, if the Romans chose him, that gave him sufficient age.

His year of office was scarcely over before tidings arrived from Spain that his father and uncle, who had been gaining great successes for the last five years, had been betrayed by the Spaniards, and both killed in two battles following immediately one after the other, and that the remnant of the army was held together by their lieutenant, Titus Fonteius, and an eques, or plebeian rich enough to serve on horseback, called Lucius Marcius.

The prætor, Caius Claudius Nero, who had been greatly distinguishing himself in the siege of Capua, whence the Carthaginians were at length forced, was at once sent out to take the command : but the Romans determined on sending a larger force ; and as the consuls must remain to watch Hannibal, that a proconsul must be selected to command it.

The treachery of the Spaniards and the forlorn aspect of affairs had so discouraged the Romans, that no man offered himself, until the eldest son of the slaughtered pro-consul, though only twenty-four years old, stood forth in the rostrum overhanging the Forum, and declared himself convinced that there was still a way to retrieve the cause of Rome in Spain, and that he could do it, if they would elect him in his father's place. No doubt he had received letters and messages from his father which had given him some knowledge of the situation; and, moreover, he had held his mysterious communings with the deity in the temple of Jupiter : at any rate, young as he was, and untried save by terrible reverses, the Romans unanimously elected Publius Cornelius Scipio proconsul of Spain.

He took with him his only brother, by name Lucius, to whom he was much attached. Lucius Scipio is the only one of the family of whose features we have any representation, and that only on a coin, which shows a spirited though not very handsome head, bearded, with parted lips, a raised brow, and rather retreating forehead, not very high. The great Publius is, however, said to have been a man with fine features and engaging expression, and long hair flowing down his back, of goodly presence, and no doubt the fire of genius looked forth through his eager eyes, and inspired both terror and confidence; for he seems to have been as much dreaded and hated by one party as beloved and esteemed by the other. His was a strong and determined nature, always going straight to the point, and little inclined to heed the many legal checks that the Roman constitution had invented to prevent the encroachments of the ambitious, but which often clogged the actions of the patriotic; and thus he was always most popular when furthest from home.

His other companions were his earliest and nearest friend, Caius Lælius, to whom he gave the command of the fleet of thirty quinquiremes, and Marcus Junius Silanus, who was to be pro-prætor in the place of Nero. Coasting along, as he had begun doing with his father seven years before, he arrived at Emporiæ in the autumn of 210, a colony of the Massilian Greeks on the Spanish side of the Pyrenees, and there, disembarking his seasick soldiers, marched them by land to Tarraco, where he spent the winter in treating with the Spaniards, or Keltiberians, a grave, resolute, but indolent people, not very unlike the same nation at the present day. Like the Gauls, they were divided into clans, and had petty chiefs; but the Greek and Carthaginian colonies had taught them some of the habits of civilization, and they grew wheat, olives, and vines, besides working their silver mines in the Sierra Morena and its spurs towards the south.

The coast of the Mediterranean was thickly studded with colonies. Those to the north of the river Ebro, being Greek, held with Rome; those to the south were Punic,—and the chief of these was the great seaport of New Carthage, or, as it is still called, Cartagena. On this place Scipio determined to make his first attack as swiftly and suddenly as possible; and as soon as the winter storms were over, he sent forward his fleet, while he conveyed his army in a wonderful march of a single week to the borders of the narrow neck of land that alone connected the city with the continent, for the marsh which now lies behind the city was then made a lagoon, filled with seawater, and only crossed by an isthmus.

Just as Scipio had fortified his camp the Carthaginians made a sally along the isthmus, and there was a sharp battle, ending by their being forced back into the town, while the Romans planted their ladders and tried to scale the walls ; but the ladders were too short, and evening obliged them to give up the attempt. Next morning Scipio told them that Neptune, the god of the sea, had appeared to him and promised his help; and it seemed a fulfilment of the dream when the ebb tide, slight as it was, left the bed of the lagoon uncovered, so that five hundred men could be sent across it to attempt the walls in another place, while Scipio himself, with the main body, stormed the walls again with ladders, now lengthened.

The five hundred found a spot where no defenders were stationed, climbed the walls, rushed to the gate, threw it open, and the Roman army poured in, slaughtering every creature that came in their way, till Scipio, with a thousand picked men, having obtained the formal surrender of the citadel and governor, made a signal to stop the carnage, for he was a man of much greater humanity than was usual with Romans. His discipline forced the soldiers to leave the houses, and, putting all the spoil together in the market-place, return to their posts and wait for the morning's distribution of the plunder.

The next day he reviewed his prisoners. The free citizens he restored uninjured to their homes, and the mechanics and artisans were promised full liberty when the war was over, if they would serve Rome faithfully in the meantime; and the same promise was given to the fishermen and sailors whom he drafted into the fleet. Eighteen Carthaginian galleys were in the harbour, and he manned these for Rome, placing in each vessel a crew consisting of two-thirds of Romans and one of the prisoners. Quantities of corn were likewise taken, stores of arms and abundance of treasure, all which he sent off by Lælius to Rome, requesting to have some supplies returned to him. The Carthaginian officers were likewise sent to Rome as prisoners. But there were taken at the same time a great number of hostages kept by the Carthaginians to secure the fidelity of the clans of Keltiberians.

A tall, majestic-looking lady came forward, and, with tears in her eyes, said she was the wife of Mardonius the chieftain, now in the camp of the enemy, and had been seized with her daughters and nieces by Asdrubal Gisco, the Carthaginian commander in Spain, for her husband's non-payment of a debt. She hoped, she said, that the Romans would be more civil than the Carthaginians. She was too high-spirited to utter further complaints, but Scipio assured her that his own sisters should not be more carefully protected than she and her maidens. Another beautiful young girl among the hostages was betrothed to a chief named Allucius. He sent for him and for her father, who brought a great ransom for her; but Scipio immediately handed it over with the lady as her dowry to Allucius: and the consequence was that the young chief joined him with 1,400 horsemen, such as had been so terrible on the other side. The other hostages, 300 in number, received presents, and were told to write word that they should be returned to their homes if their kindred would become allies of Rome. Meantime he took them back with him to Tarraco, treating them with great kindness, and restoring them as fast as their clans submitted. The Spanish lady's husband and his brother deserted Asdrubal, and brought their very powerful tribe to join him ; and though the Carthaginian commanders contemptuously declared that the young Roman was proud of his one town, but that they would quickly teach him to remember his father and uncle, they soon felt that the magic of his name was such that no Keltiberian army could be trusted when he was in the field.

Another Asdrubal, the brother of Hannibal, had come into Spain to collect reinforcements and supplies for the army in Italy, and hoped to gather the Spanish tribes once so warmly attached to his family, and to fight a battle so as to crush Scipio before returning to Italy. Scarcely a Spaniard, however, would stir ; all were devoted to the gracious and kindly Roman ; and Scipio advanced to the banks of the Guadalquivir in such strength as to force him to retreat to save himself from being stormed in his camp. Some accounts declare that he was defeated in a great battle; but the above was the report of the matter given in his old age by Lælius, the greatest friend of Scipio, and is, of course, the more trustworthy. Asdrubal retreated into the west, crossed the Tagus, and collected the more northerly and westerly Spaniards, who had not yet heard of the beneficence of Scipio, crossed the Pyrenees, made his way over the Alps, and was full on his way to join his brother when he was encountered on the river Metaurus by Claudius Nero, who was now consul: his army was cut to pieces, and he himself died in the battle. Nero, a true member of the fair-faced, cruel-hearted, Claudian family, caused Asdrubal's head to be cast down in scorn before his brother's camp.

Meantime the retreat of Asdrubal and the kindness of Scipio had such an effect on the Keltiberians of the east and south that they, with one voice, as they stood round him, saluted Scipio, as their king. But royalty was a hateful sound to Roman ears, and though thanking them heartily, he made answer, that he valued no title so much as that of Imperator, or victorious commander, which his soldiers gave him, and if they thought a royal soul the grandest endowment of man they might think of him as they pleased, but never call him king.

Hannibal's other brother, Mago, was also in Spain, whither he had brought troops from the Balearic isles, as being less likely to desert than the Keltiberians. A Numidian prince, named Massinissa, who had been educated at Carthage, had likewise brought a large reinforcement of his fierce horsemen : and these uniting with Asdrubal Gisco, determined to meet the young Roman imperator, crush his presumption, and restore the allegiance of the Spaniards. They numbered altogether 70,000 foot, 4,000 horse, and 32 elephants ; while Scipio, between Romans and natives, had only 45,000 foot and 3,000 horse ; nor did the fate of his father and uncle dispose him to feel secure that the fickle men of Spain might not fail him in his need. He therefore endeavoured to avail himself of them more for show than for use ; and after having in the evening reviewed his army, with them on the wings and the Romans in the centre, he suddenly altered their disposition in the night, placing them in the centre and the Romans on the wings, so as to disconcert the counter-arrangement of the enemy. He himself took the command of the right wing, giving the other to Silanus ; and after the whole line had advanced evenly together, he caused the centre to halt, while the two wings rushed forward with the greatest impetus and utterly defeated and destroyed those opposed to them, after which they were free to fall on the best troops in the centre, who made such a brave resistance that Scipio was forced to throw himself on them, sword in hand, before his men succeeded in breaking them. Then, trodden down by their own elephants, and slaughtered on either side, they fled to the camp only 6,000 in number ; and there Scipio would have pursued them, but that a violent storm forced his troops to seek shelter : and in the night they retreated, some to their garrisons, and others embarked at Gades for Africa. This great battle was fought, B.C. 206, at a place called Silpia, probably in the province of Seville, but the spot cannot be identified. It gave Scipio the supremacy of Spain ; and when he sent his brother Lucius with tidings to Rome, it was to say that there was now not an enemy in the field between the Pyrenees and the Pillars of Hercules. Such had been his work in four years, while he was still under twenty-eight.

Massinissa, before returning to Africa, is said to have seen the pro-prætor Silanus, and to have promised him to desert the cause of Carthage. Nothing could so effectually cripple the Carthaginians as to deprive them of the alliance of the Numidians ; and, besides, Scipio had made up his mind to endeavour to strike the Punic city at her heart, and to free Italy from Hannibal's presence by recalling him to defend his native home,—and for this relations with the Numidians must pave the way. These people were it seems divided into two tribes, the Massilians to the eastward, of whom Massinissa's father was king, and a more powerful tribe to the west called the Masæsylii (at least so the Romans construed the words), under a king, by name Syphax, who had already been in correspondence with Scipio's father, and was reported to be favourable to the Romans. Accordingly Scipio sent Lælius to Africa to confer with him, and when the ambassador returned with tidings that Syphax would treat with no one but Scipio in person, he embarked at New Carthage in a quinquireme, and, with only one other ship in attendance, crossed over to Africa with a swift and favourable wind. Strange to say, he found, newly arrived in the harbour, seven ships which had just come with Asdrubal Gisco for the purpose of securing Syphax to Carthage.   It was a curious encounter : the two generals met in the presence of the prince, who feasted them at the same banquet, and listened to their conversation with admiration.   Asdrubal was exceedingly struck with the courtesy, readiness, and wisdom of his rival, who, he said, seemed to him more dangerous in peace than in war, so that he had ceased to wonder how Spain had been won. Syphax likewise seemed much pleased with the Roman, and made him fair promises, so that he returned well satisfied with his mission.

On his return he performed a vow he had made in honour of the souls of his father and uncle, by celebrating games at New Carthage.   These in the Roman fashion consisted of fights of gladiators or trained swordsmen, sometimes slaves kept for the purpose, sometimes hired warriors; and on this occasion two Keltiberian princes fought together, with a chieftainship for their prize. These shows became a horrible abuse, but their worst form had not then begun

But Scipio's work was not yet done.   Syphax in his absence had been won over to Carthage by the promise of marrying Sophonisba, the beautiful daughter of Asdrubal, and Scipio's journey had further slackened the allegiance of the fickle Spaniards.   Two cities, named Illiturgi and Castulo, had maltreated the fugitives after the defeat of the two elder Scipiones, and these were to be besieged and punished.   There was a terrible massacre at the first, which was taken by assault, but Castulo surrendered and was pardoned.   Immediately after Scipio returned to New Carthage, being apparently forced to rest by the approach of illness, while Marcius proceeded to besiege the town of Astapia, a fierce community whose natives had always been foes to the Romans.   They were resolved to accept no terms, but raised a pile in the middle of the city, placed their wives and children on it, put fifty men to watch, and then sallied out to die fighting to the last. Then the fifty set fire to the pile, killed the women and children, and falling on their own swords, threw themselves into the flames.

Meanwhile Scipio lay at New Carthage, fast becoming so desperately ill that the report went forth through Spain that he was dying, or dead. The effect on the whole country showed that he had unintentionally won partisans rather to himself than to Rome, for the Keltiberians, shamed perhaps by the fierce patriotism of Astapia, began to revolt, and even Indibilis and Mardonius, the brother chiefs, showed themselves unfaithful, and, what was far more serious, 8,000 Romans and Italians, who were in a camp on the banks of the river Sucro, or Xucar, rose in mutiny, insisting on receiving their pay and being sent home to Italy. They drove out their tribunes, and elected as their leaders two common soldiers, Italians, named Atrius and Albius, who arrayed themselves as consuls, and caused the lictors with their bundles of rods to go before them. They even proposed to go to Campania, seize a city there, and plunder the country round ; and Mago, in the Carthaginian garrison at Gades, or Cadiz, secretly sent them supplies, rejoicing in the embarrassment that thus should be caused to Rome.

Such was the condition of affairs when Scipio was again able to attend to business. The first thing he did was to send seven officers to the mutineers to ask their grievances, promise them their pay, and invite them into New Carthage to receive it ; and at the same time preparations were made for the immediate march of Silanus, with all the faithful troops, to chastise Indibilis; so that the proconsul would seem to be left at their mercy. The whole eight thousand marched in, and went to their quarters, the seven officers each inviting five of the ring-leaders to supper. They came unsuspiciously, and were quietly seized and imprisoned without being able to communicate with their supporters.

In the morning Silanus' troops were summoned to march, but they were in reality sent round to secure the gates of the city, while the malcontents were invited to meet the general in the market-place. Thither they all hurried, without their arms, and there they first missed their leaders in rebellion, while they beheld on the tribunal, or judgment-seat, in his official dress, the lictors with their rods and axes on each side of him, their proconsul, pale, grave, sad, and terrible in the silence with which he looked down on them.

There was an awful time of suspense until the crier proclaimed silence ; and then Scipio stood up and spoke to them on the baseness and folly, the shamefulness and ingratitude, of their behaviour, in thus turning against their country, simply because, as he said, "their general was sick, and could not give them their pay at the usual time !" They hung their heads, sensible that they had in their recklessness committed the fault most unpardonable in the Roman mind. None of their noisy leaders were visible to encourage them ; but they heard the clash of arms, and saw every street full of their faithful comrades, whom they expected to slaughter them according to their legal deserts. "But," added Scipio, "the multitude who were led astray are freely pardoned. Justice is satisfied by the punishment of the ringleaders, who have been tried by the council of war."

This was in fact what he had been waiting for. A court of officers had been trying and sentencing the prisoners, and the crier proceeded to call over the names of the thirty-five. Each was led forth, already stripped to the waist, bound to the stake, beaten with rods by the lictors, and then beheaded. Some were old soldiers of the elder Scipio, and the young general looked on with tears at their sufferings; but on this severity depended the safety of the army: and as soon as the terrible scene was over the corpses were dragged away. Water and sand effaced the blood, and Scipio rose again and swore that he freely pardoned the rest. Then one by one each was called, renewed his oath to serve as a soldier, and received his full arrears of pay. Thus pardoned, the attachment of the troops to Scipio became stronger than ever; and it was needed, for Indibilis and Mardonius, with a huge multitude of Keltiberians, were plundering the Roman possessions north of the Ebro. Scipio felt this defection bitterly, and in his speech to his troops called the Spaniards nothing better than robbers and ingrates. The soldier fully shared his feeling, and in ten days he had brought them to the banks of the Ebro; in four days more had gained a complete victory : 4,000 Spanish slain encumbered the ground, many more escaped, and the two chiefs came into the camp, and, throwing themselves on the ground before the general, implored his pardon, throwing all the blame on the report of his death, which had changed the minds of the people.

Scipio, always merciful, but stern, answered, "You have deserved to die, but you owe your lives to Roman clemency. I shall not disarm you. That would look as if I feared you. If you rebel again, I shall not punish your faithless hostages, but yourselves. So consider whether you prefer our mercy in peace or our severity in war."

Nor did he inflict any punishment on them, except the payment of a large sum of money from their silver mines, which no doubt was exceedingly needed, since Rome had too much on her hands to supply him with more than permission to use the stores of Spain to support the war.

After this Scipio made an expedition to the immediate neighbourhood of Gades, for the purpose of holding a meeting with the Numidian prince, Massinissa, who had notified his great desire of seeing the renowned Roman, and who was at that last Punic stronghold with Mago. A plundering sally was so arranged that Massinissa might secretly fall in with the proconsul ; and the effect on him of Scipio's appearance and manner was more complete than it had been upon Syphax. The dark, high-spirited Moorish prince had been highly educated, and could better appreciate the nobleness, grace, and strength of the Roman ; he attached himself warmly to him on the spot, invited him to Africa, and promised him his assistance against Carthage. At present, however, he kept terms with his old allies, and returned to Gades, whence Hannibal soon after summoned his brother. Mago, anxious to collect treasure for the Italian war, plundered the temples, and used such extortion that he alienated the citizens, though they were mostly of Tyrian origin ; and as soon as he was gone they had surrendered to the Romans; so that Scipio had in five years absolutely driven the Carthaginians out of the peninsula, and well redeemed his promise to the Roman people.

On his way back to Tarraco, after receiving the submission of Gades, Scipio was met by two new proconsuls who had come out to relieve him, his five years of office being over. He therefore took leave of his Spanish army, and, with his brother Lucius and his friend Lælius, sailed for Italy. No sooner was he gone than there was another Keltiberian revolt, which was only put down by the death of the two fickle and untrustworthy chiefs.

In the meantime Scipio with his ten ships arrived at Ostia, and thence proceeded to the gates of Rome, where, according to custom, he waited till he should receive from the Senate leave to enter. He could not have a triumph, because he had never been a consul ; but the Senate came out to the temple of Bellona to meet him, and hear the number of victories, and sieges, and the tribes he had subdued, and how, having found four Carthaginian generals with their armies in Spain, he had not left one single soldier there on their side ; and he brought home a considerable amount of gold and silver, which, as he entered Rome, was carried before him to the treasury.

It was the time of election for the consulate of 204, and though he was still two years under the legal age of thirty, the whole people unanimously elected him consul, together with Publius Licinius Crassus. This was in his eyes only a step to his great scheme of attacking the Carthaginians at home. There was Hannibal, driven up, indeed, into Bruttium, the extreme end of the peninsula of Italy, and very ill supported from home, but still there, and waiting till the tide should turn in his favour at Carthage to burst forth with all the terrors of his wonderful genius. There was no way, as Scipio believed, to deliver the Italian soil from him but attacking his native country, and, standing forth in the Senate, the young consul eagerly explained his views, and demanded an army to take to Africa. So vehement was he, and, from long absence, so little aware of the temper of his hearers, that he declared that, if the Senate would not consent, he would appeal to the people, who would gladly accord their sanction.

Nothing could be more offensive to the old fathers of the Senate than these words from a man who would not have been among them at all if he had not been sent to a province that nobody else would take, and there had five years of unchecked power, which they believed to have rendered him rash, headstrong, and conceited. Above all was shocked old Quintus Fabius. His grand-

X

father had won the surname of Maximus by harassing and wearing out Pyrrhus, and he himself had, by the same tactics carried on with more caution and weariness, prevented another Cannæ, shut Hannibal up in Bruttium, and obtained for himself the additional surname of Cunctator or "the Hinderer." He was now the senior senator, or, as it was termed, Father of the Senate ; and he rose in great displeasure to put down the presumptuous young general, who, as he said, had not come to the years of his son, while he himself had been twice dictator and five times consul. He dilated on all the disasters that had ever happened from rashness, especially the loss of Regulus in Africa, and concluded, after praising his own prudence to a great extent, by saying, " My opinion, Conscript Fathers, is that Publius Cornelius was created consul, not for his own sake, but that of the Republic, and that our armies were raised for the defence of Rome and Italy, not that consuls, like kings, should out of pride carry them into whatever countries they list."

Scipio kept his temper as Roman dignity required, and contented himself with arguing the point ; but he had set the Senate against him by talking of an appeal to the people, and instead of being answered, he was desired to state whether this was his intention. He said he should do what was for the welfare of the state, and would make no further answer ; but finding that the tribunes of the people would not support him, he promised to submit to the decision of the Senate. The other consul also held the office of Pontifex Maximus, or chief priest, and therefore could not serve out of Italy ; and thus the Fabian party could not prevent Scipio from being the commander in Sicily ; but though they gave him leave to cross to Africa if it were for the good of the state, they would not allow him to raise an army in Rome.

Still he worked energetically, and his popularity with

the Italian soldiers was so great, that many, from all the Italian nations in alliance with Rome, volunteered to join him, and though the old Cunctator at Rome prevented any supplies from being granted to him, he obtained assistance from the cities in alliance, cut down timber from the mountain slopes of Sicily, and built thirty new galleys. Massinissa, too, came to visit him, and urged him to cross into Africa, assuring him of a welcome ; but on the other hand Syphax as strongly dissuaded him from coming.

While thus engaged, he still had time to enjoy his residence at Syracuse, one of the most cultivated and learned of Grecian cities, and still redolent of the fame of Archimedes, the greatest of ancient mathematicians and engineers, who had been killed in the sack of the place by the Romans only seven years before. Scipio, who had only hitherto been able to glean fragments of the Greek harvest of wisdom, poetry, science, and art in the remote colonies of Gaul, threw himself into the study of all that Syracuse could offer of training, both for mind and body, in her books or her theatres—even in the midst of his ardent preparations for the voyage to Africa ; but his year of consulship sped quickly by, and his only deed of arms was the taking of the small city of the Locrians, on the opposite shore of Rhegium, from Hannibal's garrison, and putting in a legate called Quintus Pleminius, who behaved with shameful ferocity to the unfortunate inhabitants.

It was Scipio's hope that, though his year of consulship was over, he might be continued as proconsul in Sicily, and carry out his views ; but no sooner were the two new consuls established for the year 203 than ten deputies from Locri, in shabby garments, with olive branches in their hands, arrived at Rome, and came before the Senate with lamentable complaints of the barbarous usage they had received from Pleminius. Fabius asked whether they had appealed to the consul, whose officer he was.

" Yes, indeed ; but he was too busy about his preparations for war to hear them. Besides, he had already shown unjust favour to Pleminius."

The deputies were heard and pitied, and then up stood Marcus Porcius Cato, a young man, but belonging to the elder party, who wanted to keep Rome the stern old plain city of peasant kings she had once been. Dentatus was his model. He spent his time in war, farming, and statesmanship, lived in poverty, disapproved of all but the barest rudiments of learning, despised foreign customs, and dreaded any accession of territory, lest the old Roman manners should be spoilt by luxury. He had been sent as quæstor with Scipio into Sicily, and had there remonstrated against his expenditure, to which all the reply he obtained was, " It was of victories, not money, that an account should be rendered to the Republic."

He now described what he deemed the great and useless expenses of Scipio, and his love of the Greek theatre and gymnastic sports : " Worthy of a boy whose business was to celebrate games instead of making war," said the rough Cato.

Other senators added, that the proconsul had discarded the toga for the Greek mantle and sandals ; that he was always reading Greek, and amusing himself ; and that his army was as bad as himself, and more terrible to friends than to foes.

" Born to ruin military discipline," declared old Fabius, " he lost as much by sedition as by war in Spain. One while he indulges his soldiers in licence, and another he tyrannizes over them like a king and stranger."

Therefore Fabius proposed that Scipio should be recalled, and deposed from the proconsulate with ignominy, that Pleminius should be brought in chains to Rome for punishment, and that ample amends should be made to the Locrians.

However, the debate had lasted so long that the votes of the Senate had to be taken the next day ; and this gave time to Quintus Cæcilius Metellus, who, perhaps, owed Scipio some gratitude for having saved him from abandoning his country, to induce the Conscript Fathers to send commissioners to examine into Scipio's conduct, and only bring him back to Rome if they found him deserving of such disgrace.

Accordingly the embassy proceeded to Locri, where the first aspect of Pleminius somewhat cooled their pity for his accusers, for it proved that they had taken the law into their own hands and had cut off his nose and ears. However, they sent him off to Rome, and went on to Sicily, where to their surprise they found a fine new fleet, a splendid army in perfect discipline, a contented province, and an alert, active proconsul, who, if he did speak and read Greek, showed no traces of any of that effeminacy of which Cato and Fabius accused him, far less of ferocity. They were quite satisfied. Pleminius had indeed been a bad man, but the cruelty exercised on himself had made it needful for Scipio to support him, as representing Rome, and the more respectable Locrians themselves quite exonerated the proconsul from anything but unwillingness to believe in the guilt of a fellow-soldier who had been savagely used. The commissioners, so far from sending Scipio home, gave him their full sanction for his expedition. " Go," they said, " and the gods give you that success which the Roman people promise themselves from your virtue and abilities."

So, in the year 203, Scipio was at length able to sail for Africa, starting from Lilybæum with the army he had been forming for nearly two years, many of them old soldiers who had fled from Cannæ, and burnt to retrieve their fame. The number of his army is uncertain.

He embarked with solemn prayer, and landed near Utica, a city in a bay very near the great harbour of Carthage. Asdrubal Gisco, after having long played off the two young Moorish princes, Syphax and Massinissa, against one another, by alluring them with the charms of his daughter Sophonisba, had at last given her to Syphax, and had then attacked Massinissa with such effect as to drive him from his home, and force him to lurk about the country with a few followers, until on the news of Scipio's landing he joined the Romans, and 2,000 of his brave horsemen flocked together round him.

Scipio's first endeavour was to besiege Utica, but he was forced to desist by the advance of Asdrubal and Syphax with an immense army. Both parties encamped for the winter; the Carthaginians in huts of wood, the Numidians of reeds. On these Scipio made a sudden descent, set the camp on fire, and in the confusion killed 40,000 enemies and dispersed the rest. They united once more, and were again defeated and scattered; and then, while Scipio remained to besiege the cities on the coast, he sent his friend Lælius with Massinissa to pursue Syphax into his own country.

They met him in battle, defeated him, and made him prisoner; and then Massinissa, hurrying on to Cyrtha in advance of the Romans, there found the beautiful Sophonisba, the bride he had been defrauded of, a high-spirited woman of the proud determined Phœnician stamp, who hated the Romans with the direful hate of Hannibal, and whose first entreaty was that her captor would save her from falling alive into Roman hands.

Massinissa, who had long loved her, instantly decided that to marry her himself was the only mode of protecting her, and the Carthaginian rite had just been performed when Lælius arrived, and was much displeased, since the lady was Scipio's captive, and in Roman eyes was the destined ornament of his triumph. The real danger was the influence her beauty and resolution were sure to give, for when Syphax arrived at Scipio's camp in chains, he told the general, with some bitterness, that it was she who had driven him into opposition to the Romans, and foretold that she would act in the same way by Massinissa.

Thus when that prince arrived, after having completed the subjugation of the Massilians, Scipio received him with grave displeasure, reminding him how careful he had himself been in Spain to protect the wives and families of his prisoners as sacred possessions, and showing him that he had neither been a generous enemy to Syphax nor a true ally to the Roman people, since to them alone belonged the right of disposing of a royal captive.

Massinissa was confounded. All he did was to murmur something about his promise to Sophonisba that she should not be delivered alive to the Romans. Then retiring, he shut himself up in his tent, whence his sobs and groans were heard; and finally he sent a trusty slave to Sophonisba, with a dose of poison, telling her it was the only way left him of redeeming his promise. She said, " I accept this marriage-gift; he could do nothing kinder;" drank it, and died.

It was no doubt what Scipio intended. Of gentler mould than most of his nation, he did not delight in the cruel insults of dragging princes and princesses along at the wheels of his car to be murdered at the close of the procession. Even Syphax was spared this humiliation, and kindly treated, though kept a prisoner. And when self-destruction was deemed no crime, he no doubt thought it real generosity to leave Sophonisba to die voluntarily, rather than be rent from her husband and cast into the imprisonment she hated. Syphax was sent to Italy under the charge of Lælius.

These losses so alarmed the judges and elders of Carthage, that they resolved to negotiate with their enemies, and gain time for the recall of Hannibal and Mago from Italy. They sent ambassadors, who threw themselves at Scipio's feet, and besought him to grant them terms of peace. He answered at first that he was not come to treat with Carthage, but to conquer it, and he proposed terms that he thought impossible for them to accept; but as they only wanted to gain time, they pretended to take them into consideration, and thus obtained a truce, during which they sent orders to Hannibal to return to their defence, B.C. 202.

It was sixteen years since Hannibal had forced his way over the Alps, and, by unexampled skill, defeated the Romans on their own ground again and again, and threatened their proud city with imminent ruin. Ever since, with patience and constancy almost unrivalled, he had kept his army together, obtained support, and bided his time for a decisive attack;—but that time had never come. Jealousy of his family had prevented his countrymen from supporting him, for though they had a bitter malevolence against Rome, it was not active enough to lead them to make any great exertion against her, and they had none of the love of martial glory which would have fired them with zeal to push on the conquest. They merely let him stay in Italy and maintain himself as best he might, until they needed his services, and then they ordered him home, with no feeling save that he was likely to be their best defender. "The Romans," he said, almost with tears, "have not vanquished Hannibal. It is the Carthaginians!" And he prepared to quit the soil of Italy with as much grief and reluctance as an exile going into banishment—sorrow not a little increased by the loss of his brave brother Mago, who was mortally wounded in a sea fight on his homeward voyage, and died in the island of Sardinia. Hannibal thus re-entered Carthage almost as a stranger, for he had never set foot there since he had left it with his father at nine years old, and now returned at forty-five, with manners, tastes, and sentiments far more Greek than Phœnician, but with the implacable hatred to Rome that he had sworn before Baal's altar only increased by the death of his two brothers.

Rome was in an ecstasy of joy, although old Fabius Cunctator was certain that the fate of Regulus awaited Publius Cornelius as soon as Hannibal should once come within reach of him, and further declared that "the Republic had never been in a more deplorable state." But it was his last croak; he died in the course of the same year; and the greater part of the Senate, who had been won over to the side of the brave proconsul by the failure of Cato's accusations, appointed Lælius his quæstor, and finding that one of the consuls, Servilius Cæpio, was intending to go to Africa to obtain the final honour of the victory, they appointed a dictator on purpose to prevent him from interfering with Scipio.

As to the victory, it was indeed no certain matter, for successful as Scipio had been, it had been only against inferior generals, and Hannibal was the victor in every one of the eight battles in which he had been engaged; he had defeated nine consuls, singly or in pairs, the choicest soldiers of Rome, of whom no less than four had been slain; and the only previous Roman expedition into Africa had been lamentably unsuccessful. Yet when an embassy came from Carthage to propose the terms of peace that had been laid before Scipio, the Senate rejected them, and granted reinforcements to be sent out by Lælius.

The truce was broken by the Carthaginians as soon as

Hannibal had landed at Leptis, contrary, it would seem, to his opinion, for he saw that the loss of a battle in the present state of things would be utter ruin, and, consummate general as he was, he had only the few old soldiers he had brought from Italy to whom he could entirely trust, and those magnificent horsemen who had done him such signal service. Spanish and Numidian were now all on the other side. But as Scipio was ravaging the highly-cultivated fields and gardens of the Carthaginians, multitudes flocked to oppose him, and the number of Hannibal's army soon far exceeded that of the Roman.

A Carthaginian spy was taken prisoner, when, instead of hanging him, Scipio caused him to be led round the beautifully-ordered camp, and sent him back to report what he had seen. This gave Hannibal an opportunity of begging for a personal interview, and the two generals marched their armies to the neighbourhood of the city of Zama, where there was an open plain between the camps. Into the centre of this the two rode, each accompanied by an equal number of guards, and, after respectful salutations, remained for a while contemplating each other in silence. There is no description of Hannibal's appearance, but he may be thought of as a man of middle age, rugged, worn, and weatherbeaten, with keen Eastern features, and the loss of an eye; while Scipio was in the prime of manhood, and full of agile grace and courtesy, his long hair flowing beneath his helmet. Hannibal had always striven to show that his hate of Rome was not hate of individual Romans, and he spoke to Scipio with great respect, offering honourable terms of peace; but none of these would Scipio accept, alleging that the Carthaginians having broken the truce, could not expect to escape without a penalty, and therefore that he could only impose terms far severer than those that had been before presented. Thus the two great captains parted to prepare for one of the most notable battles in the world, not only because of the great interests there at stake, but because it was the collision of two of the most skilful generals of the whole of time.

It was the 19th of October, 202, that they were thus to measure their strength. The number of men on either side is not known, but Hannibal certainly had the greater force, although Scipio, in addition to his own troops, was supported by Massinissa with the Numidian cavalry.

Hannibal had eighty elephants, which he ranged in front; behind them he placed his hired troops, the Gauls, Moors, and Baleares; in the next line the Carthaginians, and a body of mercenary Greeks; and in reserve his tried veterans from Italy, placing the Carthaginian horse on one wing and the few Numidians remaining to him on the other.

Scipio drew up his legions after the usual fashion, except that he kept a sort of lane between their compact masses, as a place of retreat for the light troops in case of their being discomfited by the elephants, instead of being obliged to run back on the spears of their comrades. He placed the Italian horse under Lælius to the left, the Numidians with Massinissa on the right.

Skirmishes began between the Numidians on each side; then Hannibal ordered his elephants to advance; but the Roman shouts and trumpets rendered some of them restive, and, turning back on the Numidians, they broke their line, and Massinissa thus had an easy success. Others did the same work for Lælius, but the centre ones would have much damaged the light spears but for the lanes, down which these retreated behind the heavy infantry, and the beasts, following them, were captured. Then came the great fight between the legionaries and the foot soldiers on the other side. The first line of these was the hired soldiers, and as soon as they began to give way, they fancied it was for want of support from those behind, and fell upon them in a rage, so that, after fighting bravely, they fled. They would have fallen back upon Hannibal's reserve, but these held out their bristling spears, and drove them off in other directions. Then came the real brunt of the battle, between the veteran remnant of the conquerors of eight Roman armies and the legionaries of Scipio. It was well and steadily fought, and was decided at last by the arrival of Lælius and Massinissa, who galloped up from the pursuit while victory was still doubtful, and so entirely turned the scale, that Hannibal was forced to ride at full speed to Adrumentum, closely followed by Massinissa, and Scipio stood on the field, victor, in the greatest battle that Rome had yet fought. Twenty thousand enemies were slain, and the might of Carthage was crippled for ever.

After the obsequies of the 2,000 Roman slain, Scipio went on board ship, and sailed towards the harbour of Carthage, leaving his army to march thither by land. Soon a galley decked with olive branches came out to meet him, containing deputies who sued for peace. He replied by laying on them conditions far harder. No possessions beyond the African coast should be allowed them; the kingdom of Massinissa should be made independent; no war should be entered into without Rome's permission; no elephants might be trained for war; and 10,000 talents of gold were to be paid by instalments to Rome within fifty years.

Terribly hard terms were these, but Hannibal himself saw the hopelessness of the situation, and advised his countrymen to submit. Indeed, he gave such offence by his promptness of speech, that he was obliged to apologise for having no acquaintance with the forms of public speaking current in the city. Nay, grievous as were the conditions, the consul Publius Cornelius Lentulus, a relation of Scipio's, thought them too mild, and wanted to come out to Africa, to supersede the proconsul, and utterly destroy the city; but this the Senate prevented, and, though they could not keep him from going to Africa, decreed that the management of the treaty and the bringing home of the army were the right of Scipio. Accordingly the peace was concluded, the ships, elephants, and prisoners made over to the Romans, and the first instalment of the tribute paid. When the amount which each Carthaginian was to contribute was read in the public assembly, the whole of those present burst into tears, except Hannibal, and he fell into a fit of laughter. They turned on him in anger. " My laughter," he said, " is as far from mirth as your tears. You wept not for the loss of our arms and our ships ; but for a little money you weep as though our city were going to her burial."

Meantime Scipio placed Massinissa on the throne of all Numidia, and then set out for Rome, where he was received with rapture. All his enemies were for the time silenced by gratitude to one who had been the deliverer of his country. The triumph that ended the second Punic war, B.C. 200, was the most magnificent hitherto seen, enriched as it was with the splendours of the Carthaginians, with a huge amount of treasure, and with the unwieldy march of the trained elephants. The people were so enthusiastic in their exultation, that they proposed to nominate Scipio consul and dictator for life, and to set up his statue in all the public places ; but he was too wise to seek honours that would have been inconsistent with the constitution of the state, and the only reward which he accepted for his services was the surname of Africanus, or the African, to be hereditary in his family.

However, in 198, he was made Prince of the Senate, and likewise elected censor, and four years later was a second time consul. During this time Marcus Porcius Cato was proconsul in Spain, where there had been another revolt, and though he had proved himself a good general, and thoroughly disinterested, had been so ferocious and cruel that he had become the misery and terror of the Keltiberians; for, indeed, it was his boast that he had destroyed more cities than he had spent days in that unhappy country. Scipio, who could not but have a great regard for the country where his first successes had been won, and a people whose hearts he had held in his hand, accused Cato before the Senate, and procured his recall, and his own nomination to the province for his proconsulate.

But when Cato returned, it was with a long list of conquered tribes and besieged towns, and with a huge amount of brass, iron, gold, and silver. Men's minds turned in his favour: the indignation of Scipio passed for personal spite; the common sort of Romans had no feelings for the sufferings of subject or rebel tribes, and Cato and his officers had plenty to say of the desperate perfidy, violence, and savagery of the tribes they had hunted down. Instead of censuring or reversing his acts, the Senate decreed a thanksgiving of three days, and Scipio, finding that if he went to Spain he should have no power to do anything but tread down the remnant of his old friends in continuation of Cato's barbarous policy, chose to remain at home; and thus Rome lost one opportunity of being taught to be less merciless. However, his cousin and friend, the son of his bald-headed uncle Lucius, Publius Cornelius Scipio Nasica, or "the Long-nosed," a young man of great promise, was well maintaining the fame and the love of the name of Scipio in the further province, which was always governed by an ex-prætor.

There was evidently a jealousy of the united strength of the great Cornelian Gens, for all the interest of Africanus could not secure Nasica from being defeated when he stood for the consulate on his return to Rome in 193. However, on a quarrel between Massinissa and Carthage, Scipio was sent to mediate, and two years later on another embassy.

Whatever Cato and the plain old Romans might wish, the city had not found it possible to stand still and cease from aggressive wars. Every fresh conquest led to fresh relations, and even before the second Punic war was over there were complications with the Greek powers that led to alliances with some and contests with others. Already in the efforts made by Philopœmen of Megalopolis to undo the mischief that he had joined Aratus in doing, and to free Greece from Macedon, Rome had been called in, and in alliance with the Greeks had tamed the pride of Macedon, and taken the whole country under a sort of protection that was not far from subjugation. This brought them into collision with Antiochus the Great, the sixth of the Macedonian dynasty who ruled in Syria, and held great part of Asia Minor, as well as many of the islands of the Ægean and the Thracian Chersonese. His dominions, including Assyria and all the boundless resources of the wide East, made him deem himself able to cope with Rome, whilst Hannibal, whose life had become unbearable among the sordid cabals of Carthage, had fled to his court, and, thinking him the most promising enemy of Rome, stirred him up to enterprise.

The Chersonese was the subject of dispute, and a Roman embassy was despatched to debate the point and make terms, or else declare war. Scipio Africanus thus had the opportunity of passing through Greece, and beholding the exquisite buildings and works of art, and the historical scenes that he had always loved to dwell on; and on arriving at Ephesus, with all her glories of temple, theatre, harbour, and palace, he there found what interested him far more than Eastern splendour, his own great rival, Hannibal.

Again the two national foes met as personal friends, and much did they walk and talk together in the porticoes and gardens of Ephesus. Only one of their conversations has, however, been recorded. In it Scipio is said to have asked whom his companion regarded as the greatest of generals.

"Alexander, for he did the mightiest of deeds with a handful of men," said Hannibal, looking on the very scene of some.

"Who the next greatest?" asked Scipio.

"Pyrrhus, for he conciliated and kept together the Italian allies," answered Hannibal, who was a good judge what a task this was.

"And the third?"

"Myself."

"Then where would you rank yourself if you had conquered me?"

"Above Alexander," returned Hannibal, perhaps in irony.

The two were hoping soon to be again measuring their skill one against the other, but the base fancies of the Syrian Greeks led them to think the intimacy between the two generous rivals was a sign of treachery on Hannibal's part. The news of the death of Antiochus' son gave him a pretext for breaking up the conference; he dismissed the Romans without an answer, and though he commenced hostilities soon after, he only gave Hannibal the command of some ships, in which he was inexperienced, so that he was beaten by the Rhodians.

Meantime Scipio Nasica had obtained his election, and the next year Lucius Scipio with Caius Lælius sat together. On the expiration of their year, the proconsulate of Greece and Asia and the conduct of the war with Antiochus was naturally the portion of Lucius ; but some hesitation was shown as to whether he was capable of such a charge ; whereupon his brother Africanus offered to go with him as legate, which proposal was most thankfully acceded to. The two brothers embarked at Brundusium, and Scipio took with him certainly his youngest son, Cnæus, and probably his eldest, Publius, to whom he was giving an exceedingly learned education in all Greek literature, the only line of distinction open to the lad, who, though his father's equal in abilities, had health too delicate for a soldier's or statesman's life. They were probably left at Athens, which in her decay was becoming a kind of university for the youths of Greece and Asia ; their father and uncle proceeding to Philippi, the court of the young king Philip of Macedon, whose battles the Romans professed to be fighting.

Philip entertained his allies most courteously, and, as usual, the charm of Africanus' manners was felt, so that the king willingly accompanied the army to the shore of the Hellespont, whence they were to carry the war into Asia Minor.

Here there was a short delay, because it was the feast of the *Ancilia*, or Golden Shields. The first of these shields had been found in the palace of Numa, who was reckoned as the second king of Rome, and eleven more had been made by a wonderful smith, such as is to be found in all mythologies, named Mamurius Veturius ; and twelve priests of Mars were appointed, who bore them through Rome on the calends of the month of Mars, clad in a mystic dress, singing hymns in honour of the smith, and keeping time by beating the shields with rods as they danced along in solemn procession, and were therefore called Salii, or the dancers. Such an office

Y

seems to us curious for the greatest generals of a state; but Africanus was one of these dancing Salii, and though he could not perform in the streets, and was absent from his shield, it would have been sacrilege for him to march while the festival lasted, and he was one of the most pious of men.

He joined the army again by the time they had reached the plain of Troy, which they loved and rejoiced to see; but not, as Alexander had done, for the sake of Achilles. They deemed themselves the sons of the fugitive Trojans; looked at Mount Ida as the cradle of their race; loved the memory of Hector; and offered a sacrifice to Pallas Athene, whose image, the palladium, had been stolen from the citadel, and safety with it, by Ulysses and Diomed.

Soon after an embassy met them, proposing conditions of peace from Antiochus, and with a secret message to Africanus that his youngest son, Cnæus, had been captured, probably by pirates, when boating from one part of the island of Eubœa to another, and was now in the hands of Antiochus, who offered to restore him, provided the influence of the legate were used for a favourable peace. To this Scipio could only return the answer that any honourable man must make, that no private concerns could make any difference to his actions in his country's service; but either anxiety or the feverish atmosphere of the Levant affected his health, and at Elea he fell seriously ill, and had to be left behind, while both sides were in the midst of preparations for a battle.

Antiochus had some generosity about him, and in a few days the boy appeared at his father's bedside, released without any conditions. Scipio held him for a long time in his arms, and then looking up to the persons who had brought him, said smiling, " Thank the king from me, and tell him, the only token of gratitude I can send him is to desire him not to fight till I am in the camp."

Antiochus seems to have intended to act on this message, whatever it meant, and retreated upon Mount Sipylus, where he fortified his camp ; but Lucius Scipio followed hard after him, as if resolved to force on the combat and have the glory without his brother. He had sixteen of the Carthaginian elephants, but these were inferior, both in size and intelligence, to the thirty-four from India that Antiochus had, which carried towers on their backs, each holding four men, and had plumes of feathers on their heads, with purple and gold trappings. The Syrian army had, indeed, much of the old Persian splendour, but likewise of the Persian cumbrousness, and though there were Greeks enough to make a brave resistance, the defeat was entire. Antiochus fled to Antioch, and thence humbly entreated for peace.

Scipio Africanus never showed any jealousy of his brother's success, and assisted him in receiving the embassy. Antiochus was to give up Asia as far as Mount Taurus ; to send his second surviving son as a hostage to Rome ; and to cease to harbour Hannibal, who thereupon fled to Crete, and afterwards went to the court of Prusias, king of Bithynia.

The brothers returned home, and Lucius entered Rome in triumph, and received the surname of Asiagenes, or Asiaticus. But the hostility of the opposite faction could not long be silent. In 187 two tribunes of the people, instigated by Cato, demanded that Lucius should be called to account by the Senate for the sums of money received from Antiochus, and the spoil, which they alleged he had not paid faithfully over to the public treasury.

The Senate met, and Lucius, standing before them, took a roll from his bosom. " Here," he said, " is the account of all the moneys I have received and paid."

" Read it," said the senators.

" He shall not put such an affront on himself," said Africanus, and snatching the roll from his hand he tore it in pieces.

It was a foolish act of passion, and only excited more suspicion. Another tribune, named Marcus Nævius, indicted Africanus himself, but merely accused him of overweening presumption unfit for a citizen; of having acted towards his brother more like a dictator than a legate ; and of having received his son from Antiochus ; besides the old stories about Syracuse and Locri.

" Romans," said Scipio, " this is the anniversary of the battle of Zama ; it ill becomes us to spend it in wrangling. Come to the temple and return thanks."

Every creature followed him except the tribune and the crier, and no one ventured to accuse him again. But the investigation of Lucius' accounts was insisted on ; he was found guilty, and was about to be thrown into prison till he should pay an enormous fine. Scipio, with his usual vehemence, rescued him from the officers of the law, and went off to his own estate at Liternum, not far from Naples. The hostile party now insisted that a day should be fixed for the trial of this presumptuous offender ; but one of the tribunes, Tiberius Sempronius Gracchus, who had hitherto been an enemy to the brothers, came forward and said, that to treat Publius Scipio as an enemy was a dishonour to the Roman people. Was no merit to become a sanctuary to great men ? If Publius Scipio were brought to Rome, he should, as tribune, stop the trial ; and as to Lucius, he would never see a Roman general imprisoned in the very dungeon whither he had himself brought the enemies of Rome.

This speech brought the people of Rome back to their senses. Moreover, in exculpation of Lucius, it was found that his whole property was far less than the fine imposed on him, and such a subscription was raised, that his fortune would have been made had he not chosen to accept no more than enough for his maintenance. However Cato, as censor, at the next review deprived him of the horse with which he appeared as a patrician and a senator, because of the story of the bribes of Antiochus ; at the same time taking away other horses, because their masters were too fat to serve in battle.

Scipio showed his gratitude to Gracchus by giving him, plebeian as he was, his beautiful, learned, and excellent daughter Cornelia as a wife ; but the Roman ingratitude he could not forget, and he never returned to the city, but spent his latter days on his estate at Liternum, and there died in 183, when only forty-eight years old, desiring to be buried there instead of in the grand sepulchre of his family. His statue, however, adorned it, together with that of his brother Lucius.

His younger son grew up unworthy ; the elder was very much respected, but was too sickly for public life, and having no children, adopted the son of one of his sisters, who had married an Æmilius. This son, known as Publius Cornelius Scipio Æmilianus, completed the conquest of Carthage, and won for himself a second time the title of Africanus. But it was Cornelia, the mother of the Gracchi, as she loved to be called, who was the brightest glory of the great Scipio family, the representatives of Roman manners, just at the turning-point between rudeness and luxury, and of Roman valour, before bravery in self-defence had entirely degenerated into lust of conquest.

JUDAS MACCABÆUS.

B.C. 190—180.

THE roll of Worthies would be so utterly incomplete without the mention of the noble Jew whom our ancestors seem to have respected and admired most of all, that we must not omit his biography, although most of it has been anticipated in the Golden Deeds ; and after having seen the vain endeavours of such men as Agis, Cleomenes, and Hannibal to raise up a falling state, to awaken dormant patriotism, and infuse new life into decaying limbs, it may be well to contemplate another patriot, who perished, indeed, but who did not fail, and who awakened new life as they could not do, for the very reason that he had to do with a living body, they with a dead one.

The victory of Scipio Asiaticus at Mount Sipylus had resulted in Antiochus of Syria being obliged to send his son, of the same name as himself, to be educated at Rome. There Antiochus Epiphanes, or "the Illustrious," as he surnamed himself, remained for thirteen years, and became imbued with admiration for the grand and stately simplicity of the citizens. There was a reaction in his mind from the Eastern pomp that the Syro-Greeks affected, and he became thoroughly Latinized, lived on free terms with the Romans of his own age, wore the same dress, esteemed those homely practical offices by which they rose to the highest dignities as far superior to his family's royalty, and even became enthusiastic for the Roman gods, infinitely preferring the Jupiter of the Capitol to the Grecian Zeus with whom he was identified.

From his residence at Rome he was recalled, B.C. 175, by his brother Seleucus, the reigning monarch, who, wanting to employ him, sent his own son, a mere boy, to serve as a hostage in his stead ; but on his journey homeward, at Athens, he was met by the tidings that Seleucus had been poisoned by a favourite named Heliodorus, in the hope of obtaining the throne while both the heirs were out of the way.

Upon this Antiochus turned aside to the King of Pergamus in Asia Minor, whom he induced to assist him with his forces ; and, entering Syria, he met with no opposition, but peaceably obtained possession of that most beautiful and luxurious of the Greek cities planted in the East—Antioch.

There his Roman customs soon brought him into contempt among the minds so long accustomed to connect power with pomp. Had he been a great man, really able to appreciate and transplant the grandeur of simplicity, it would have been a critical experiment ; but he was a mere hot-headed dissolute youth, and it was the freedom, not the severity, of Roman manners that he imitated, and without any discretion. With almost despotic power in his hands, he would go from street to street in the white toga of a candidate for office, soliciting votes ; and having got himself elected as ædile or tribune, would cause such matters as would have come before those magistrates at Rome to be brought before him, by which proceeding he made himself simply ridiculous in the eyes of the satirical Greeks of Antioch. They resented, too, his custom of mingling freely with all companies, and his delight in conversing with craftsmen in gold and gems. Moreover, he was a drunkard, and would be seen in the wreath of roses, which the Romans wore at banquets to keep the brain cool, hurrying about the streets, flinging money to the populace, and crying "Catch who catch can !" At other times, when his mind was full of the Roman custom of going out alone, and without state, he would carry stones in his toga, and pelt every one who attempted to follow him ; and by such proceedings he soon brought the men of Antioch, who were famous for their love of nicknames, to call him, not Epiphanes, or "the Illustrious," but Epimanes, or "the Madman."

Just at this time there arrived a traveller from Jerusalem, which after having belonged to the Ptolemies of Egypt in the first partition of Alexander's empire, had, partly by conquest, partly by treachery, been transferred to the Syrians in the time of Antiochus the Great. The new-comer had but little of the Jew about him ; he wore the Greek tunic, and called himself Jason—a Greek name, in which none would have detected the old glorious Joshua which had been bestowed upon him at his circumcision. For he was one of those Jews who had begun to imagine that adherence to the law of Moses made them behindhand with the world ; and he further wanted to propitiate the King of Syria by flattering his tastes. He was the second son of the late high priest, Simon, the brother of the present, Onias, and he coveted the office, not for its sanctity, but because it brought in much wealth and conferred a good deal of political power.

So, through the medium of the courtiers, he offered Antiochus a bribe of 440 silver talents, provided he should be placed in his brother's office ; and, with still more shameful ingenuity, begged to pay 150 more talents for permission to set up a gymnasium, or place of public athletic shows, at Jerusalem, and for permission to call the inhabitants of Jerusalem Antiochians, thus charming the pride of the Syrian prince.

Such a petitioner was sure to be heard ; and the faithful Jews had the grief of seeing their good high priest deposed in favour of this disgrace to the sons of Aaron, who, bent on taking rank with Greek statesmen and gentlemen, looked on his holy office as only the remnant of an obsolete superstition, involving a few ceremonies that he must perform to content the people till he could wean them to higher philosophy. In the valley, at the foot of the tall fortress on Mount Sion beside the temple, was built one of those gymnasia, where the Greeks were wont to contend naked in the race, the wrestling match, or throwing the disc, and always in honour of their deities—things that were a shame and a horror to the imagination of a devout and modest Israelite. The chief young men, led away by the comparison of what was called their own narrow-minded barbarism with Greek learning, splendour, and beauty, followed Jason, adopted Greek fashions, and wore the broad hat, the mark of the Grecian soldier. The priests themselves grew afraid or ashamed to keep up their constant chant of psalms ; they neglected the sacrifices, despised the altars, and hurried to seek distinction by displaying themselves in the arena like the heathen, " not setting by the honours of their fathers, but liking the glory of the Grecians best of all."

Since Alexander's adoption of the Tyrian Moloch into his own ancestor Hercules, the festival of that abhorrent deity (probably without the immolation of the children) had been very popular throughout the Græcized East, and games were held in his honour every five years. By way of preserving his favour, Jason sent 300 drachmas of silver as an offering to this festival, though they were spent not on the sacrifices, but on the fleet ; and when King Antiochus himself visited Palestine, Jason received him at Jerusalem with a torchlight procession, loaded him with gifts, and accompanied him to Phœnicia.

Again, three years after, he sent fresh presents to Antiochus by Menelaus, who is said by some writers to have
been his nephew, by others a Benjamite, but who by
his flatteries, and promises of a yet larger tribute than
Jason's, gained the ear of Antiochus, and was assured of
the priesthood. Jason fled to the Ammonites, and this
still more wicked wretch came in, and committed many
murders in the hope of securing himself in his post, and
robbed the temple of some of the golden vessels. He
even obtained the person of the good Onias by treachery,
and murdered him; and so gained over the courtiers of
Epiphanes, that when three of the Sanhedrim went to
meet the king at Tyre to complain, they were absolutely
put to death for venturing to murmur—a cruelty the
Tyrians so resented as to bury them with all honours.

However, Antiochus shortly after went to Egypt, and, on
a false report of his death, Jason returned, and by the
assistance of his partizans obtained possession of part of
the city; but Menelaus kept the fortress on Mount Sion,
and there was an incessant warfare in the streets, with
much bloodshed, until, on the tidings that Antiochus was
returning, Jason fled and took refuge in Sparta, where he
died miserably.

The tidings of the revolt, however, greatly enraged Antiochus, or he may have only made it a pretext for making
a violent attack upon Jerusalem, which he entered as a
place taken by assault, giving licence to his troops to
plunder and massacre, so that in three days 80,000 were
slain, and many more taken to be sold as slaves. The
king himself entered the holy place in the temple, with
Menelaus the apostate as his guide, plundered it of a
great treasure in gold and silver, and carried off the shew-
bread table, the golden altar of incense, and the seven-
branched candlestick, with many others of the sacred
vessels, and the veil of the sanctuary.

He seems to have deemed this a fit moment for destroying the individuality and nationality of the Jews, and all the purity of faith and morality that seemed an insult to men stained with every sort of sensuality, but expecting divine honours from their subjects. He treated the Samaritans at Gerizim in the same manner, and in each place put a Syrian governor, who cruelly oppressed the people.

In 168, two years later, he proceeded to more stringent measures, sending his collector of tributes, Apollonius, with orders to destroy the city itself. The wretch waited until the Sabbath to put his commands into execution, and then, when the whole population was assembled in the courts of the temple, he surrounded them with his troops, butchered all the men, and secured the women and children to be sold as slaves ; then rifled the houses, and set fire to many parts of the city. Only the walls of the temple and the fortress on Mount Sion were spared ; and this last was greatly strengthened, and garrisoned by a savage band of soldiers. No sacrifice was permitted to take place within the temple, and if a Jew were seen stealing thither to worship in those desolated courts, he was instantly pursued and slain.

Shortly after an edict was published at Antioch, commanding all nations in the dominions of Antiochus Epiphanes to cease from their own private laws and religion, and to adore the same gods after the same manner as their illustrious master. In pursuance of this command, an altar to Jupiter, as defender of strangers, was set up in the schismatical temple at Gerizim, and another to Jupiter Olympius was placed upon the great altar of burnt-offerings in the true temple at Jerusalem.

An old man named Athenæus was sent to instruct the Jews in the new rites that were to be imposed on them, and stringent commands came forth against offering sacrifice, observing the Sabbath or any other holy day, or circumcising children. Every book of the Law to be found was burnt, and Greek festivals were instituted, especially the procession when ivy was carried in honour of Dionysos and the sacrifices on the king's birthday. The young men who had been led astray by Jason, and other persons who had learnt to care for favour rather than for faith, were content, but terror prevailed with many more. A synagogue full of worshippers on the Sabbath was burnt, and two women who had circumcised their children were hanged with their babes round their necks ; other resolute Israelites were unmercifully put to death ; and outwardly the king's commands were executed, and the chosen people were in a more lamentable condition than ever before. Never had paganism so triumphed, for though Nebuchadnezzar had ruined the temple, he had never set up a rival god there, and the Jews had freely professed their own faith at his very court, with their priesthood still to lead them, whereas now the high priests had been the first to apostatize, and were in exile or slain.

No country is, however, so hard to deal with as a land of mountains like Judæa. Small as the district was, it was a toilsome and dangerous journey from one city to another, and it was scarcely possible to seize an outlaw among the network of narrow ravines that intersected it.

Thus, even when Jerusalem, in her state of desolation, Joppa, Jericho, and the other cities, had been forced into obedience to the edict of Antiochus, still there was a remnant of faithful men left in the mountains, who still clave steadfastly to God, and poured out their lamentations in psalms wrung from the Levites long ago, when they in like manner were hiding from the sacrilege of Ahaz. With greater force than even these Levites could they cry :—

" We see not our tokens, there is not one prophet more :
No, not one is there among us that understandeth any more."

And in the prophetic books of Daniel they plainly read
the prophecy of all that was come upon them; of the
horns of the Macedonian goat, that came up on the
breaking of the great horn; and of that little horn which
had waxed so great as to cast down some of the stars
from heaven : nay, further, the detailed history of the wars
and alliances they had themselves seen between Syria
and Egypt, even to the "vile person," whom they must
but too well have recognised as their present master ; for
had he not "polluted the sanctuary of strength, and
taken away the daily sacrifice, and placed the abomination
that maketh desolate" upon the altar, as had been foretold, "corrupting many by flatteries"?

All this had been long ago foreseen; so, dreadful as it
was, it did but prove the perfect foreknowledge of the
Almighty, and strengthen the faith of the true-hearted.
"The people that do know their God shall be strong and
do exploits," said the roll of prophecy ; and in one little
city, lying in the rugged hills around the desecrated Jerusalem, a priestly family had taken refuge, who were
resolute against the general apostasy.   They were of the
family or course of Chashmon, whence, in the softened
Greek in which their history is recorded, they were called
Asmoneans, and they consisted of an aged father named
Mattathias, and five sons, Johanan, Simon, Judas, Eleazar,
and Jonathan, all of them full of that high and fiery spirit
which had been so strong in Levi himself, and ever and
anon had broken out in his offspring, in spite of their
dedication.

Modin, their home, seems to have stood on a high
ridge between the Mediterranean and Jerusalem, and
here they withdrew themselves, mourning in a sort of
psalm for the ruin they beheld—

" Woe is me ! wherefore was I born, to see this misery of my
 people ?
Behold our sanctuary, even our beauty and our glory,
It is laid waste, and the Gentiles have profaned it."

They put on sackcloth, fasted and lamented ; but in the
midst came a summons from the authorities to all the
men of the place, to meet in the market-place at Modin,
where they found the royal officers and the Greek priests
prepared with garlands, victims, and incense, intending
to compel every man among the assembly to offer sacrifice
to the gods of the king's choice.

Mattathias being the principal person present, the
officer first addressed him : " Thou art a ruler, and an
honourable and great man in this city, strong in sons and
brethren. Now, therefore, come thou first, and fulfil the
king's commandment, like all other nations and the Jews
likewise. So shalt thou and thy children be among the
king's friends, and be honoured with silver and gold, and
many rewards."

But the old priest stood forth and made answer :—

" Though every nation in the king's dominions should
obey him by falling from their fathers' religion, yet will I,
and my sons and brethren, walk in the covenant of our
fathers. God forbid that we should forsake the Law and
Ordinances ! We will not hearken to the king's words,
nor swerve from our religion either to the right hand or to
the left."

While thus Mattathias stood defying the Greek officer
by the brave confession of his faith, another Jew of Modin
came up, and, accepting the wreath, was about to cast
incense on the sacrifice. At this shameful sight the old
ruler's wrath burnt so hotly, that, shuddering with anger,
he sprang forward and slew the apostate at the altar, and
in the tumult that ensued he, his sons, kinsmen, and the
other faithful Modinites were so strong that they slew the

king's officer, cleared the place of his soldiers, and threw down the altar; but well knowing that he could not hold out the place against the garrison of Jerusalem, Mattathias resolved to betake himself to the mountains, like David and his valiant men of old; so he proclaimed in a loud voice, " Whosoever is zealous for the Law, and maintaineth the Covenant, let him follow me."

Then, at the head of his five sons, he left the town, and entering on those wild deeply-caverned heights which grimly border the Dead Sea, was there in an almost impregnable fastness, whither faithful Jews flocked to join him, bringing with them their wives, children, and cattle. One large body who were on their way to join them, consisting of many armed men, with their women, children, and cattle, were beset by the enemy on the Sabbath Day, and summoned to surrender, with the promise of their lives if they would obey the king; but they utterly refused, and likewise, deeming it contrary to the Fourth Commandment either to fight or fortify their encampment, they made no attempt to defend themselves, but were all massacred, to the number of a thousand. In courage and firmness they resembled the Phœnicians of Aletta, but here there was the true patience of the saints— no ferocity, no self-murder. However, when the priest Mattathias and his sons heard of their fate, they held counsel together, and decided that it was evidently the will of God that the Sabbath should not be so observed as to lead to unresisting slaughter, but that when attacked on that day they would fight for their lives.

So many now began to come in to the assistance of the family of Mattathias, that he gained numerous victories over outlying parties of the Syrian army and drove them back into the principal cities. The idolatrous altars were pulled down wherever he found them ; children received circumcision ; fresh copies of the Law were written out, to supply the place of those that had been burnt; and where it was not safe to read them in the synagogues on the Sabbath Day, rolls of the prophets were substituted, so that it became the custom to read one lesson from the Law and another from the Prophets.

The winter in the wild hills of Judah, which David had dreaded for his aged parents, is always very inclement, and it seems to have been too much for the aged Mattathias, for in B.C. 166, the year after his gallant exploit at Modin, he found himself dying. His last exhortation to his five sons is a recapitulation of the heroes of Hebrew history, and encouragement for the sake of their constancy in evil times. Abraham, faithful under his trial; Joseph, proof against temptation; Phineas, their own ancestor, zealous for the Lord; Joshua, true to the word; Caleb, a faithful witness before a furious host; David, long persecuted; Elijah, fervent against idolatry; the Three Children who were preserved in the fire, and Daniel from the lions, all are referred to by the dying man, to prove that, "throughout all ages, none that put their trust in the Lord shall be overcome. Fear not then," he said, "the words of a sinful man, for his glory shall be as dung and worms. To-day he shall be lifted up, and to-morrow he shall not be found, because he is returned into his dust, and his thought is come to nothing. Wherefore ye, my sons, be valiant, and show yourselves men in the behalf of the Law, for by it ye shall obtain glory."

He then appointed his son Simon to be their chief counsellor and as a father unto them; and Judas Maccabæus, the third brother, who had been strong and valiant from his youth, to be their captain. He then blessed them, died, and by the valour of his sons was buried in the sepulchre of his fathers at Modin, near as it was to the enemy.

The surname of Maccabæus here given to Judas appears to mean " the Hammerer," though it is said by some to have been assumed afterwards, from the initial letters of the Hebrew words, " Who is like unto Thee, O God," which he bore on his banner ; but as all the brothers had surnames to distinguish their very common names, the first is by far the most probable. In his own tongue he would have been Judah Maccabi. He would commonly have spoken the Syriac or Aramaic, which the Jews had learnt in Babylon ; but as a priest he would have been familiar with Hebrew, and as an educated man of a ruling family must have spoken and written Greek. What we gather of his character from the books of the Maccabees, the only authority for his history, would show him to have been a more adventurous and simple-hearted man than any of his brothers, excepting the younger, Eleazar, with less of craft and policy and more of dashing and desperate valour, sprung of a deep conviction that any death or suffering was better than leaving his people to the enemies of God, and the " glorious land" to be defiled by idols. It was not the joyous hopeful valour of Joshua and David, full of direct inspiration, and backed by absolute tangible aid from Heaven ; there were no present prophecies, no miraculous interpositions, to support the warrior-priest ; and even the old prophecies on which the faithful leant were sad and mournful, and told of " falling by the sword, and by flame, and by captivity, and by spoil many days ;" and that even those of understanding should fall, that they might be tried, and purged, and made white. And when Zechariah had spoken of the sons of Sion contending with the sons of Greece, and being " as the sword of a mighty man," though there was assurance of glory, it was vague and distant—distant as the great promises on which all Judah fed. Thus it was in a grave, melancholy valour and constancy that Judas

z

Maccabæus girded on his sword ; sure, indeed, that God was with him, and that resistance was his bounden duty, but far from sure that the result, as regarded himself or the present generation, would be victory or success. And yet, in this happier than the men we have seen striving against the decay of virtue in Greece, he knew that the utmost he could endure would be only to make him white and purify him, and that for his people and himself the year of the redeemed would come, and that he should see it—whether here, or from beyond a bloody grave.

At first, while he was assuming the leadership very like that of the judges of old, there was a little respite, for Antiochus was celebrating a great festival at Daphne, near Antioch, where it is said that his absurdities were so great as to scandalize all the beholders from Greece and Rome. His persecuting governor at Jerusalem, Apollonius, endeavoured to put down the rising of the Jews, but was overthrown by Judas and slain. His sword was brought to Judas, and served him through the rest of his life. Another Syrian captain, named Seron, led a considerable army to attack Judas in his mountain stronghold with very superior numbers. There were some Jews who showed much alarm, but Judas made answer, that it is as easy to the God of heaven to deliver by few as by many. " They fight for violence and for spoil," he said ; " but we fight for our lives and for our laws."

And all along the steep descent of Bethhoron he chased and slew his foes, and though the sun stood not still at his word, as at that of Joshua, the victory was as complete, and the Lion of Judah once more lifted his head.

Antiochus was roused from his amusements at Daphne by the tidings of this great revolt. In a great fury he assembled his army, intending to put an end to the very name of this rebellious people ; but he found his treasury exhausted : he had squandered huge sums on the games ;

he gave lavishly to his favourites, and had a heavy tribute to pay to Rome ; besides which, the wealthy provinces of the far east were becoming remiss in the payment of their tribute. As Tacitus, the Roman historian, puts it, " A Parthian war prevented him from reforming a most repulsive people ;" for in that light were the staunch virtues and spiritual worship of the Jews regarded by the heathen world.

So while he himself set out for Persia to secure the source of his wealth, he sent his relative, Lysias, with an army to do his best against the repulsive people, with half his army, and a supply of elephants, which one would have thought not very available in so mountainous a country, where even horses were of very doubtful advantage ; but the terror of their appearance and name was the great point.

A huge force was accordingly placed under the command of Ptolemy and Nicanor ; and so certain was the destruction of the Jews regarded, that a great number of slave merchants accompanied the army, who had already bargained with Nicanor to give him one talent for eighty Jews, by which means he expected to raise the sum needed by the king for his tribute to the Romans, and they to make their fortune, since the trustworthiness and skilfulness of the Hebrew race rendered them very valuable slaves ; and with this host he encamped at Emmaus, very near Jerusalem.

There was great consternation in Judæa, and the more timid fled from the country ; nor could Maccabæus collect more than 6,000 warriors, but he encouraged his friends with all his might. " They trust in their weapons and boldness," he said, " but our confidence is in the Almighty God, who at a beck can cast down both them that come against us, and also all the world."

In this confidence he collected his army at Maspha, as

they now called Mizpeh, where Samuel had long ago rallied Israel against the Philistines, and there, looking to the holy mountain of God, as it lay desolate, the thin thread of smoke of an idolatrous sacrifice rising up from it, and David's tower, the stronghold of the enemy, they fasted, put on sackcloth, and prayed aloud. Eleazar, the youngest brother, read out the Book of the Law to the weeping people, and then Judas made the old proclamation that only the strong and unencumbered should go to battle, but the busy, the newly married, and the faint-hearted should go to their homes. Six thousand remained with him, whom he divided into four bodies, giving the command to himself and his three brothers, and choosing as his watchword " Eleazar, the help of God !" the name of his brother, he made his final exhortation : " Arm yourselves and be valiant men, and see that ye be in readiness in the morning, that ye may fight with these nations that are assembled against us to destroy our sanctuary ; for it is better for us to die in battle than to behold the calamities of our people and our sanctuary. Nevertheless, as the will of God is in heaven, so let Him do."

After this steadfast but mournful summons, Maccabæus dismissed his men to their tents. But immediately after he received intelligence that 5,000 foot and 1,000 horse had left the main body at Emmaus, intending to fall on him at Mizpeh and destroy him by a night attack. He at once called up his troops, and himself quitted the camp with the 3,000 under his command, so that Gorgias found nothing but the tents and entrenchments, and proceeded in pursuit of the Jews, as he supposed, into the gorges of the mountains.

However, Judas, instead of flying, had marched straight on the camp at Emmaus, and arriving at daybreak, offered battle, sounding his trumpets and making so un-expected an attack that in a short time they were masters of the field, and the enemy were flying in all directions. Here Judas showed himself an admirable general. " Be not greedy of the spoil," he proclaimed, " inasmuch as there is a battle before us, and Gorgias and his host are here by us in the mountain ; but stand ye now against the enemies and overcome them; and after that ye may boldly take the spoils."

While he was speaking, some of the division of Gorgias were seen looking down from the mountain passes, but when they saw their own camp on fire and the Jews in good order, they were panic-struck and fled in disorder, while the Jews collected a great booty of silver, gold, blue silk, and " purple of the sea," and returning to Mizpeh sung hymns of thanksgiving, keeping a most joyful Sabbath of rest on the following day ; and then, after setting apart a portion of the prey for widows, orphans, sick, and maimed, they divided the remainder among themselves.

Two more lieutenants of Lysias were defeated, and Lysias himself advancing from Idumea was so completely beaten at Bethsura, that Judea was absolutely cleared from all the Græco-Syrians for the time, except in the garrisons in the chief towns, and in the tower on Mount Sion ; and this happy interval was employed by Maccabæus in cleansing the temple. When the faithful Jews entered and beheld the sanctuary desolate, the altar profaned, the courts overgrown with a forest of shrubs, they rent their clothes, made great lamentation, and threw ashes on their heads, falling on their faces to the earth, while the trumpets blew an alarm.

Then Judas appointed a part of his army to watch the enemy in the tower of David, while he superintended the purifying of the temple. He and his brothers were too much of warriors to fulfil their priestly office ; but he chose faithful men from among the priesthood, who cleansed the holy place, and carried out the defiled stones, restoring all things that could be replaced.   The great altar of burnt-offerings which had been profaned by sacrifices to Jupiter they took down, and hid the stones in one of the many mountain caves till some prophet should arise to tell them what ought to be done with them, and after building a new one, they dedicated it with great joy, with the beloved old songs of the Levites which had been so long unheard, and with a renewal of the sacrifices that had ceased so long.   He also so strengthened the walls as to make it a strong fortress of defence.

Such was the glory and the joy of Judas Maccabæus ; and it was followed up by many successes over the neighbouring heathen nations, who were always ready to assault and fall upon the Jews, so that the nation began to acquire a fame such as it had scarcely known since the days of Jehoshaphat.   The three years since the revolt of Mattathias had changed Judæa from a downtrodden province to a valiant and independent country.

Antiochus had in the meantime been penetrating into Persia, and arrived at Elymais, where was a temple that was reported to abound in treasure.   He had no respect for Persian worship, and was about to plunder this temple like the Jewish sanctuary, but the Persians ran together fully armed, and beat him off with such success as filled him with rage and fury ; but finding he could not maintain his ground there, he withdrew to Ecbatana.

There he was met by messengers from Judæa with an account of the defeat of his army.   In a still greater fury he set out to punish the rebellion, and on his way through Babylonia met the further report of the battle of Bethsura, and of the recovery of the temple.   He fell into a violent passion, and commanded the utmost speed, uttering loud threats, and declaring that he would make Jerusalem the burying-place of the whole Jewish nation.

Almost as he spoke an agonizing pain seized him, but

defying his suffering he still called to the driver to press forward, until, losing his balance, he fell and was terribly bruised. He was placed in a litter, but still insisted on being carried forward, although his disease became frightful and disgusting to the last degree. At last a conviction flashed on him that his misery was the reward of his sacrilege ; and sometimes he groaned out vows that he would turn Jew himself, restore the temple and load it with gifts, while at others he thought he saw avenging spectres reproaching him with trying to violate the temple of Elymais. In this condition he died miserably, B.C. 164, leaving a son of nine years old, called Antiochus Eupator, to the regency of his favourite Philip ; but the government was seized by Lysias, who, weary of the unsuccessful war with the Jews, offered them peace, and promised them liberty to observe their own laws, which was eagerly accepted. Judas now applied himself to fortifying Bethsura as a defence against the Idumeans.

The peace was, however, soon broken. The Syrians and Greeks in the cities committed all manner of violence. The men of Joppa in especial drowned full two hundred Jews, whom they had decoyed into their boats ; and Judas was called upon to avenge them, as verily he did, by setting fire to all the ships in the harbour at night. Timotheus, his former enemy, now invaded Judea, but only to meet with another complete repulse, with the loss of 30,000 men. The Jews were gratified further by hearing that their apostate high priest, Menelaus, the author of all the mischief, had fallen into disgrace at Antioch, and had been smothered in a tower filled with ashes.

But in 163 Lysias, taking with him his young king and an enormous army, with thirty-two elephants, descended from the Idumean frontier upon Palestine, where Judas was still endeavouring to take the fortress upon

Mount Sion. The Jews received the tidings with a general fast and supplication, lying prostrate on their faces in the temple, and then armed themselves to relieve Bethsura, which was the first place attacked by the Syrians. The Jews marched to a place called Bathzacharias, an excellent place of defence, being a sort of peninsula of rock with a narrow isthmus behind, and with valleys overgrown with thickets on either side.

The historian of the Maccabees gives a most effective picture of the Græco-Syrian host and of the elephants. " To the end they might provoke the elephants to fight, they showed them the blood of grapes and of mulberries ; moreover, they divided the beasts among the armies, and for every elephant they appointed a thousand men, armed with coats of mail, and with helmets of brass on their heads ; and besides this, for every beast were ordained five hundred horsemen of the best. And upon the beasts were there strong towers of wood, which covered every one of them, and were girt fast unto them with devices ; there were also upon every one two-and-thirty strong men that fought upon them, besides the Indian that ruled him. Now when the sun shone upon the shields of gold and brass, the mountains glistered therewith, and shined like lamps of fire ; so part of the king's army being spread on the high mountains, and part in the valleys below, they marched on safely and surely."

Against this tremendous-looking host Judas, having chosen one of his beautiful watchwords, " Victory is of God," went forth at night with some picked men, caused great confusion, and killed four elephants, departing by the break of day. But this " taste of the manliness of the Jews," as the Second Book of the Maccabees calls it, does not seem to have prevented a great battle the next day, in which the patriot army were defeated, in spite of their desperate valour. It was in this battle that Eleazar, the brother of Judas, perceiving an elephant larger and more adorned than the rest, fancied that the king must be on it, and creeping under it thrust his sword into it from below, regardless of his own inevitable death under the falling weight ; and from this exploit he was ever after known as Avaran, or Savaran, from a word meaning to pierce an animal behind. He was buried in the tomb of his forefathers at Modin.

Judas was obliged to retreat, and leave Bethsura to capitulate for want of provisions, which had not been stored in consequence of a Sabbatical year. The same cause made the siege of the temple fortress at Jerusalem almost successful; the Jewish garrison was reduced to great straits, and the army could not be kept together without stores. The enemy had almost obtained possession of the holy mountain, when tidings came that Philip, the regent appointed by the late king, was on his way to assert his claim ; and Lysias, wishing to be free to turn all his strength against him, offered peace to the Jews, and even dismantled the fortress on the Hill of Sion.

There was another respite for Jerusalem, while the Syrian princes were disputing at Antioch. In 162 that Demetrius, son of Seleucus, whom he had sent as a boy to be a hostage at Rome in the stead of Antiochus Epiphanes, made his escape, and being supposed by the army and nation to have come backed up by the Roman power, all joined him, and offered to give up to him his young cousin Eupator and the regent Lysias. " Let me not see their faces," he said ; and the army took the delicate hint, and saved him the pain of condemning them.

Demetrius, coming fresh from Rome, had no experience of Jewish valour and constancy, and he lent a willing ear to Alcimus, a Græcized Jewish prisoner, on whom Lysias had conferred the title of high priest upon the execution of Menelaus, and who now persuaded the new king to send an army to reinstate him and punish the Jews, whom he represented as rebellious against their lawful high priest.

He was really nearer to the direct line of Aaron than were the Asmonean family, and this fact made a large body of the Assideans, as the more precisely orthodox Jews were called, go over to him; but they soon found out their error, for he caused sixty of them to be massacred in one day, and showed great cruelty to all who had followed the Maccabæan standard. Upon this Judas took the field again; whereupon the intruder hurried back to the king with his complaints, and Nicanor, " the master of the elephants," was again sent into Judæa, with orders to seize Maccabæus, and send him in chains to Antioch, and to ravage the country. Policy was Nicanor's instrument this time. He appointed a peaceable interview with Judas, to which each was to come with a few attendants: but it soon became evident that treachery was intended. Judas withdrew, assembled his forces, and fought another battle at Capharsamala, evidently near Jerusalem, since the defeated Syrians took refuge in the tower of David.

The priests in the temple tried to propitiate Nicanor, by showing him that they offered sacrifices, and prayed for the king's health; but he insulted and abused them, vowing that he would burn and lay waste the sanctuary, unless Maccabæus were delivered up to him; and he then went out, taking with him many unwilling Jews of the party of Alcimus, to attack Judas in his stronghold in the Benjamite hills.

Judas was at Adasa, where he was greatly comforted by a dream, in which Onias, the last good high priest, was praying for the whole body of the Jews, and Jeremiah the prophet, " with white hairs and exceedingly glorious," stood by him, and placed in the hand of Judas a sword of gold as the gift of God. Nicanor lay at Bethhoron; and there the battle took place, and proved the third great victory of the chosen people on that favoured spot. Thirty-five thousand enemies were slain, and among them "Nicanor lay dead in his harness." The pursuit drove the fugitives fairly out of the country, and the head and right hand of Nicanor were brought to the temple, and hung on the outer walls of the city.

This victory gave the Jews tranquillity for the time, but Judas felt that to be more than a brave outlaw he must be strengthened by some foreign alliance against a power of such disproportionate resources as was Syria. Egypt had fallen into helpless decay, and he therefore decided on having recourse to the great Roman republic, which had already put a bridle upon the Syrian power. The uprightness and discipline of the Roman seem to have waked a sympathising admiration in the mind of the great warrior-priest, and he sent an embassy to entreat the alliance of the Senate.

A favourable answer was returned. It was the Roman policy to depress and annoy the Syrians as much as possible, and the cause of a little subject state was exactly the handle they desired to take up. A letter was written on tables of brass and sent to Jerusalem ; but the brave hand it was intended for never received it. Alcimus, with his friend Bacchides, had come forth with another invading host ; and it would seem that the alliance with the Romans had been displeasing to some of the Jews, for Judas could only get together 3,000 men, and they at the sight of the 20,000 camped at Eleasa were so alarmed that only 600 remained by their leader.

Still he refused all solicitations to retreat, saying worthy last words for a hero, " God forbid that I should do this thing, and flee away from them ! If our time be come, let

us die manfully for our brethren, and let us not stain
our honour."

The battle lasted all day, but it was one in which numbers gave the advantage.   Judas fell before the end of the
day, and was buried in the sepulchre at Modin, while the
song of David rose up from the mountains, " How are
the mighty fallen ! "

He fell B.C. 162 ; but his country's cause was won.   His
brothers well kept up the spirit he had roused, and for
nearly a hundred years Judæa was a brave and independent state, revived out of her dust, and observant of
her Law as she had never been in her most splendid days.

CAIUS JULIUS CÆSAR.

B.C. 100—44.

THE verdict of our forefathers has placed among the three Worthies of classical antiquity one to whom that title is due rather from his rare abilities than from his moral character, which, in some respects, fell far short even of the heathen pitch of excellence; for, in truth, his endeavour was rather to be great than to be good. He had no real faith in the remnants of truth in the national religion, nor had he any standard of ideal excellence, like the earnest students and actors of philosophical systems. He was not the obedient self-sacrificing servant of his country's law and glory that others made themselves; still less was he a worshipper and would-be restorer of the past. His philosophy was the Epicurean, which chiefly took heed to present advantage and enjoyment; and though his wonderful genius and practical nature made him seek these often in a generous and beneficent manner, yet there was a want of elevation in his aims; and though his clear sense discerned what was the only practicable course for his countrymen, and forced them into it, his work was more one of personal ambition than of patriotism.

Nevertheless, with all his crimes, Caius Julius Cæsar was undoubtedly, in his own time, " the foremost man of all this world," and in the front rank of the great men of all time; and his powers and some of his qualities merit from us the careful attention that our ancestors claimed for him by numbering him with the Worthies.

He was born in a time when virtue was hard of attainment. Traditionary gleams of truth had nearly disappeared from both the Greek and Roman myths, when they had been mixed up together with importations from Egypt, Syria, and Phœnicia, and philosophy had nearly worn its clue threadbare in the labyrinthine mazes of speculation, so that all life and light were gone out of the inner man; even while the education, which had been first taken up by the Cornelian family, had been carried to the highest pitch, and scholarship, learning, and wit were in the utmost esteem. Moreover, the very conquests of Rome were changing her whole character, and making some difference in her constitution necessary, so that the rottenness of the state showed itself in horrible convulsions at the centre. All Italy, Greece, and Carthage had been subdued; Syria had no longer a king; Egypt had been scotched, and was nearly at the last gasp; and the surrounding nations were either abject allies existing on sufferance, or enemies fighting the last battles of independence. The old, stern, simple race of peasant kings had, as Cato the censor foresaw, departed for ever. A consul, after his year of office at Rome, instead of coming back to his farm, had five or three years of government in one or other of the provinces, where he was absolute for the time over the lives and property of the natives, and helped himself nearly as he chose, being secure that a barbarian would hardly be listened to at Rome if he complained of a Roman magistrate. The provinces were so many in number, that not only ex-consuls, but ex-prætors and ex-quæstors looked to them as their employment and reward at the end of the year of office, and came home with great wealth, and habits of solitary unquestioned authority, that made them evil companions to one another, and fierce, boastful tyrants to those beneath them in rank, while their wealth was used to the detriment of their family and the corruption of the plebeians.

All these great prizes lay in the gift of the Roman people ; *i.e.* those who held the franchise or power of election—the old patrician and plebeian races. The patricians, having been always a limited number of families, without any opening for promotion of others into their ranks, naturally became fewer in number, while the plebeians increased, since any man who obtained Roman citizenship was added to their ranks. Many of this order were very rich ; and as they were eligible for magistracies, they acquired seats in the Senate, and their older and better families were, to all intents and purposes, on equal terms with the patricians ; but it was the mass of idle poor who were the great difficulty. Having the disposal of such enormous prizes in their hands, they were naturally courted by all who desired to be elected, and were kept in good humour by supplies of provisions, and by perpetual shows. What would have been the use, they argued, of ruling the world, if they had not plenty of food and amusement ? So Sicily and Egypt were expected to keep them supplied with corn freely distributed, and every person who wanted to be elected to an office, every victorious general who came home for a triumph, contended who should display the most exciting entertainment, showing either strange wild beasts set to tear one another to pieces for the amusement of the people, or, still worse, slaves called gladiators, trained to fight with one another for the public diversion. Brutal, selfish, and turbulent such a state of things could not fail to make the people of the single city that held the government of the world in its hands ; for though there were many other citizens resident in the few favoured Italian cities or in the colonies, no votes for Roman magistrates could be given except at Rome itself. The best hope for Rome would have been to have diminished the number of plebeians who lived on little but their vote, by settling them upon Italian farms; and this had been attempted by Tiberius and Caius Sempronius Gracchus, the grandsons of the great Scipio Africanus, but they had both perished in the attempt to contend with the patricians and the wealthy plebeians. As another remedy, it was proposed to admit many more Italian cities to the franchise, which would have made the interests of Rome those of the whole country, and freed nations of kindred blood and like manners from the galling condition of provincials; and this point was the subject of the fierce struggle, fought out with all the reckless fury of patrician and plebeian jealousy, and with the bitter personal hatred of two rival generals, at the time when the greatest man of all Rome came into the world—a most disorganized, ferocious, and demoralized world. He was born at Rome on the 12th of July, B.C. 100—the month that bears his name—and was the son of one of the very oldest patrician families, whose nomen of Julius was said to be derived from Iulus, the son of Æneas of Troy, and thus, according to tradition, the grandson of the goddess Venus. The cognomen of the family, Cæsar, was by some explained to apply to their long hair (*cæsaries*); by others to the Punic name for an elephant, which a Julius of old was said to have killed. His prænomen of Caius had always been given to the eldest son of the family, and he was the only son of his parents, Caius Julius Cæsar and Aurelia, who had besides only two daughters, both called from their father, Julia.

The father could not have been a man of mark, since he never attained any rank beyond that of prætor; but this may have been on account of early death. The mother, Aurelia, was a woman of very distinguished abilities, highly educated, and of much resolution; and she is said to have done much for the instruction of her son, who was certainly not only the greatest scholar and general of his day, but likewise the most graceful, polite, and considerate of gentlemen.

His personal attractiveness was great. The worn, aquiline profile familiar to us was that of his later years; but though it has gained in power what it has lost in beauty, yet it is full of grandeur; and we can well believe that the deep, soft, yet piercing dark eyes, and smooth, white, marble-like skin, the black hair, and rounded outlines, rendered the countenance one of the most beautiful in all Rome. His figure was tall and slender, with a great air of dignity, and of easy gentleness and affability; and though his health had at first been frail, he had become strong and hardy as he grew up. He could ride with the reins dropped and his hands behind his back, and was excellent in all martial exercises. His voice was clear and trumpet-like, and his natural eloquence was cultivated to the utmost by the study of rhetoric—the art as needful to a republican statesman as the use of arms to a warrior; and he was further instructed in systems of philosophy by one Gnipho, a Gaul by birth, but who had studied at Alexandria, which rivalled Athens as the University of the ancient world, and had become deeply learned in Greek literature and science. For many years he kept school in the Julian house on the Palatine hill, where almost all the grandest old families of Rome had their hereditary abodes. Within these were handsome marble-lined buildings, arranged around a cloistered quadrangle called the peristyle; but outside they were encrusted with little cell-like houses of slaves, freedmen, clients, and shopkeepers, like the shell of a crab with corallines and parasites; and the larger such a following was, the wealthier and more formidable was the great man within. The philosopher Guipho profited by the shelter of this great household to keep his school for the Roman youth, and all that the young Cæsar there learnt was made the more interesting to him by his mother, Aurelia, who made his education her especial care.

By birth his family belonged to the exclusive patrician party ; but his father's sister, Julia, was married to the stout old plebeian general Caius Marius, the great champion of the extension of the franchise to the Italian cities, and the savage foe of Publius Cornelius Sulla, the equally able and more cruel if less rude defender of the patricians. In the year 86, that of Marius's success and bloody vengeance, Cæsar was but thirteen years old, and the only benefit he derived from the pre-eminence of his relative was the being made Priest of Jupiter, one of the dignities reserved for noble birth, and he was also betrothed to Cossutia, a rich heiress.

Just in the zenith of his power, on the sixteenth day of his seventh consulship, Marius died, and two years later the elder Julius Cæsar died suddenly at Pisa, and Caius Cæsar (as his contemporaries generally called him) being left to act for himself, broke off his engagement to Cossutia, and married Cornelia, the daughter of Lucius Cornelius Cinna, the chief friend and supporter of Marius, and who was consul for the fourth time. Scarcely, however, had the marriage taken place, before Sulla, after a grand course of victories over Mithridates, king of Pontus, was reported to be coming home, thirsting for revenge ; and Cinna, who intended to oppose him, was murdered by his own troops just before he embarked.

Sulla came home furious, and being eagerly welcomed by the patrician party, was made Dictator, and set himself to restore order by the most violent and bloody measures, which filled Rome with terror, and drove almost every one to submit to his pleasure. The young patricians who had married into the families of partisans of Marius were commanded to separate from their wives; and all obeyed in the most abject manner except Cæsar, whose wife had just borne him a daughter, Julia, his only child, and who, though only seventeen years old, showed himself resolute in not giving way to interference that no Roman law sanctioned.

As Dictator Sulla could do whatever he pleased: and he caused the contumacious youth to be deprived of his priesthood, deprived of his wife's dowry, and declared incapable of inheriting his father's property. The band of murderers whom Sulla employed to cut off all the enemies he could not condemn openly were known to be in search of him; and though he was very ill at the time, with one of those low fevers that have always been the curse of the Campagna di Roma, he was forced to wander about the country, never spending two nights in the same place.

At last the assassins actually came up with him, and he found himself in their clutches; but his persuasive tongue, and the promise of two talents, gained over their chief to let him go; and while he still lurked in the Sabine country, his uncle Aurelius, his other relations, and the Vestal Virgins, who had power to save the life of any criminal, interceded for him. It was represented that he was a mere lad, whose very obstinacy in his passion for his young wife showed him to have no aims beyond the amusements into which he had already thrown himself ardently, and that the costly rings that adorned his dainty hands, his long fringed toga, bound round the loins by a belt after the newest fashion, and his elegant custom of arranging his black locks with one finger, betokened him to be a mere fine gentleman, delicate in health and manners, and chiefly occupied with adorning his handsome person.

Sulla, the most far-sighted man of his time, yielded against his judgment. " Let it be as you will," he said, " but you have begged for the ruin of our cause. There is many a Marius in that young trifler."

He could not, however, endure to remain at Rome, and set off for Asia Minor, where hostilities were smouldering on with Mithridates, and where he served his apprenticeship in arms after the fashion of young patricians, who used to form a sort of volunteer staff, dining and consorting with the general in command. The prætor, Marcus Minucius Thermus, seems to have discerned his talents, and employed him in the siege of Mitylene, where he saved the life of a fellow-soldier, and was rewarded by the wreath of oak-leaves, a civic crown, as it was called, which commemorated the rescue of a Roman citizen. He was also employed in negotiations with Nicomedes, king of Bithynia, one of the fragmentary realms of Asia Minor, and managed them so well, that some years after this petty kingdom was bequeathed to Rome by the childless monarch.

He was serving in the fleet of Caius Servilius against the nest of pirates who harboured in the rocky nook of Cilicia, when tidings arrived of the death of Sulla, whereupon he instantly hurried back to Rome ; but though he impeached two of Sulla's officers before the Senate for their ill-treatment of provincials, and carried through his case, he found that matters were not ripe for an attack upon Sulla's system, and that his youthfulness—for he was but twenty-one—prevented him from acting as a leader, while a follower he neither could nor would be.

He therefore set forth for the island of Rhodes, where a great Greek rhetorician, named Molo, kept what was then the most celebrated school of eloquence, which was frequented by Romans, Greeks, provincial Gauls, and Spaniards, as the place where elegance in oratory, and aptness in illustration or argument, could best be practised by debates presided over by this able master. On his way thither, near the little isle then called Pharmacusa, the galley that conveyed him was boarded and captured by a crew of Cilician pirates, savage semi-Greeks and Syrians, who from their bays and gulfs infested the whole eastern Mediterranean. When they caught a Roman magistrate, they were wont to put him to death, to show their contempt and hatred for the city that was enslaving all the rest of the world ; and it was well for the tall, pale, elegant-looking gentleman whom they had seized, that he was too youthful to have borne any office. They however suspected the rank and wealth of their prey, and they promised him his release for a ransom of twenty talents. He coolly told them he was worth more, and that his price ought to be fifty ; and messengers were sent to raise the sum from the provinces of Asia Minor, while he remained in the pirate ship with only his physician and two slaves. To show that he had no intention of trying to swim off, he never loosed his belt or took off his sandals ; and meanwhile his easy ascendency mastered them all so entirely, that they might have been taken for guards around a prince, and were silent whenever he sent them word that he wished to sleep. He wrote verses and composed speeches to recite to them, and diverted himself with their rude criticisms ; and he joined in their sports and exercises, so as quite to gain their hearts, though he always told them that as soon as he was free he should come after them, and give them their deserts.

He kept his word. After thirty-eight days his ransom was brought ; he was released, and went straight to Miletus, where he hired ships and sailors, and led them himself to attack and capture his captors. He put them into the prison at Pergamus, and went himself to the proconsul of Asia, Junius Silanus, to give an account of his prisoners. He was told to sell them as slaves, but this would probably only have been giving them an opportunity of escaping and beginning their trade again, and the idea of making money by them seemed to him an offence. So he caused them all to be crucified, and it was regarded as a great stretch of mercy that he had them previously strangled.

He then went to Rhodes, and pursued his studies there, until his uncle, Aurelius Cotta, came out to take the government of Bithynia on the death of Nicomedes, under whom he served for some little time. On the sudden death of Aurelius, Cæsar was named in his stead *Pontifex Maximus*, or chief of the college of priests—the head of all the religious ceremonies of Rome. Probably, in the decline of the great patrician families, there were few persons qualified by birth for this office ; for it seems a strange one to have conferred on so young a man, who had done nothing memorable as yet, and was absent from Rome. He never was more than a mere political public minister as regarded worship, with little or no faith in the deities it professed to honour, and yet his having been Pontifex Maximus had important consequences which we still feel. He was thus obliged to return to Rome, and knowing that the Cilician pirates were on the watch for him, that they might revenge the death of their compeers, he crossed the Adriatic Sea in a little four-oared boat, accompanied only by two friends and ten slaves, that he might elude their notice. It was an anxious passage, and once, when a sail was seen in the distance, he sat with his hand clasped upon his sword, ready to sell his life dearly ; but it proved a false alarm, and these hair-breadth escapes contributed to a feeling that he bore a charmed life, protected by destiny.

He came back to Rome B.C. 74, twenty-five years of

age, and prepared to work himself forward, as any man of spirit could do in a republic, and as was especially easy to one of the aristocracy, and he already known to be attached to the cause of the lower orders, who always set an especial value on the partisanship of a man of noble birth.

The old constitution had been repaired and set in motion again by Sulla during his dictatorship, and it had the support of all the old conservative spirits, who looked loyally and regretfully back to the grand old days when Rome had been a temple, and her Senate a tribunal of peasant kings ; and shut their eyes to the fact, that without poverty it was impossible to maintain simplicity and· severity, and that the machinery that had been sufficient for the government of one city and a few adjacent provinces was incapable of working for a huge empire, besides being clogged at the very springs by the idle multitude at home. Factions were ever at work ; robbery and rapine reigned unchecked ; the provinces were mismanaged, the people oppressed, the rich shamelessly licentious, the poor starving ; but without a revolution no efficient remedy could be applied ; and the best of the men then living at Rome could only endeavour to set matters straight by their personal ascendency, or by appeals to old customs, without understanding the real needs of the times.

Three men stood foremost in the world into which Julius Cæsar now plunged. These were Marcus Porcius Cato, Marcus Tullius Cicero, and Cnæus Pompeius Magnus.

The first of these—whom if left to ourselves we should have chosen as the nearest approach to a Worthy of that period—was five years younger than Cæsar. He was the great grandson of the censor Cato, the enemy of Scipio, and had inherited much of his strong, stern integrity of nature, with something likewise of his severity, though with less captiousness and bitterness. Perhaps, however, our sympathies are more with him than with his ancestor, because the evils with which he fought were developed, and the elder Cato attacked the germ while it was yet apparently innocent, and showed· prejudice and hostility to a far more blameless man than was the foe of his descendant. The plain, self-denying habits of the censor were the model of the younger Cato, and the principles of the Stoic philosophy led him to the most resolute persistence in all that could tend to make the body only the servant of the soul. But though no one could fail to respect Cato, there were many who hated him as a perpetual rebuke both in word and example.

Marcus Tullius Cicero, who was born in 106, and thus was by six years the elder of Cæsar, is the Roman whose private life and character has become the most minutely known to us moderns, through his own ample correspondence. Belonging to the equestrian order, his wonderful talents as an orator and pleader had made him already renowned before he reached the legal age for holding office. He was a man of peace, essentially a scholar and a lawyer, and with all a lawyer's love for ancient precedent and dislike of change ; and he had, to a great degree, that intense sensitiveness and refinement which almost always accompanies great powers of eloquence. That sensitiveness made him vain, and anxious for applause, and though he could often take a grand, manly, and upright part, the unreserve with which he showed his alarms, vexations, and weaknesses, has made him, perhaps, to be less esteemed than he deserved. He had none of Cato's hard unbending character, but loved all kinds of refined enjoyment, and was one of the most elegant and cultivated of men ; and although as faithful as Cato could be in sacrificing himself and all he had to

the good of his country and to the maintenance of her
old constitution, what was proud satisfaction to the one
was acute misery to the other.

Neither Cato nor Cicero had any warlike turn, but the
third great man of Rome, born in the same year with
Cicero, but two months later, was great in arms after the
old Roman fashion, and his surname of Magnus was not
an inheritance, but had been bestowed by Sulla himself,
when at twenty-five years of age he had returned from
a great victory over the Numidians in Africa, while still
only a legate and having borne no public office, so that it
was with some difficulty that he obtained permission to
have a triumph. Pompey, as barbarous usage makes
English people call him, was a man of considerable
talent as a general, and thus had become the most
eminent man then in Rome, and was looked to as likely
to be the best defender of the old constitution; but he
was not as able a statesman as he was a soldier, and his
policy became wavering when he came in contact with
the perplexities that prevailed there. His demeanour,
too, had just that mixture of pride and vanity that is most
apt to give offence, and though his nature was high and
honourable, there was a selfishness in him that generally
made him fail under stress of trial. He was regarded as
the supporter of the old constitution at Rome, but as
being more on the plebeian side than on that of the patricians. The Emperor Napoleon gives a vivid picture of
the four great men of Rome, when he says that events
were like a torrent, inundating and bearing all things
away with it. Pompey thought he could command the
waves and direct them; Cicero at times let himself drift
with the current, at times fancied he was stemming the
flood; Cato stood resistless and dauntless, ready rather
to be swept away than voluntarily yield an inch; while
Cæsar endeavoured to dig a bed for the torrent. At the

time of Cæsar's return to Rome Pompey was absent, being engaged in quelling a formidable insurrection in Spain, where a Roman general of great ability had, in the universal disorganization, become very powerful; and the rebellion was not finally crushed till his assassination, which brought Pompey back to Rome a few months after Cæsar had arrived there.

The first step in the public service was given to Cæsar by making him a military tribune, thus giving him the command of 1,000 men; but he did not enter on any campaign, although there was a terrible war going on in the south of Italy with a multitude of runaway slaves and gladiators, who had their stronghold in the dormant crater of Mount Vesuvius, until they were at last put down by Marcus Licinius Crassus, who hanged 6,000 of them along the road-sides. Cato served in this war, but, when promotion was offered him, said he would not have it, for he had done nothing to deserve it.

Probably Cæsar saw nothing likely to gain credit could happen in this miserable war; so he remained at home, courting the favour of the people by such lavish gifts and splendid amusements, that he soon exhausted his means, borrowed of all his friends, was a universal debtor, and was regarded as one of the most wasteful spendthrifts in Rome. He made speeches in the Forum on every occasion, pleading the cause of any one who had a complaint against the patrician order, and making himself observed as the friend of the commonalty and opponent of exclusive privileges.

He was soon elected to the first of the magistracies that could be held—that of quæstor; and while he was in this office his young wife Cornelia died. The custom was that the corpse should be carried from home on a bier, preceded by musicians, wailing women, and liberated slaves in the cap of liberty, as well as by statues of the deceased and the family ancestors, and followed by the relations and friends of both sexes in mourning dresses, with dishevelled hair, lamenting aloud as they went to the family monument, outside which a pile was ready to consume the body with fire.

If the person was distinguished in any way, the procession halted in passing through the Forum, and one of the friends, ascending the rostrum, pronounced a speech to the people in his praise. This had hitherto never been done for any woman, except a few matrons of advanced age, and much respected ; and every one was amazed when Cornelia's ivory couch was set down, and her husband, ascending the rostrum, spoke an eager and mournful eulogy upon her merits. Remembering how, for the sake of this orphan daughter of Cinna, he had braved the wrath of Sulla, the impressible populace were greatly touched by the affection that insisted on paying her such unusual honours ; but there were others who murmured that Caius Cæsar could never lose a chance of bringing himself before the people.

A little later died Julia, his aunt, the widow of Marius. In Sulla's time an edict had been passed forbidding all honour to be done to the old demagogue, commanding that his bust and his image should never be shown. But at his wife's funeral his figure in wax appeared among the rest, and when Cæsar arose to make the oration, while he boasted of that descent from the goddess-born Æneas which his aunt shared with him, he also dwelt upon the exceeding bravery and skill of Caius Marius, and his love of the Roman people.

The next year he had to serve in Spain, under the propraetor, and worked so hard there, that those who had fancied him hitherto a mere idler thought he had been converted to diligence and public spirit by gazing on a bust of Alexander the Great at Gades ; but there is no

reason for this belief. Pleasure and action always alter-
nated in his life, and he never showed the love of self-
denial for its own sake. On his return from Spain he
married Pompeia, a cousin of Pompeius Magnus, and
on her mother's side the grand-daughter of Sulla, and
thus entered into an alliance with Pompey, promising to
give him his support in resisting patrician encroachments.

About this time Pompey was sent on a three years' mission to put down the pirates of Cilicia, and Cæsar continued to gain steps in promotion. He was made curator
of the principal Roman road, the Appian Way, and laid
out sums that he could ill afford in improving and orna-
menting it ; and when, two years later, he was elected to
the ædileship, in company with Marcus Calpurnius Bibulus,
who was very rich, he persuaded his colleague to launch
out into magnificence that had hitherto been never
attempted, though Cæsar's own debts were such, that he
confessed that he was worth 250,000,000 sesterces less
than nothing. The ædiles professed to have the care of
public buildings, and likewise of the sports and games,
and they thus had the opportunity of a grand display,
such as might lead captive the fancies of the crowd.

Porticoes were set up for the display of statues, ornaments, and curiosities, and all the public buildings were
splendidly decorated. At the feast of Cybele there were
the grandest fights of wild beasts that had ever taken
place, and Cæsar further professed to give a great show
of gladiators to do honour to his father's memory, displaying 320 of those unhappy slave-warriors in the arena,
with all their weapons covered with silver. Their number
was alarming to men who had lately had all their roads
endangered by a rebellion of the gladiators, and an edict
was enacted restricting their numbers. Cæsar contrived
that while Bibulus had far more than half the expense, he
himself had the lion's share of the credit, so that poor

Bibulus said, in jest, that the ædileship was like the Temple of the Twins, which was equally dedicated to Castor and Pollux, but was always called the Temple of Castor.

One morning all Rome was amazed by finding in front of the Capitol the statues and trophies of old Marius, freshly gilded, and bearing inscriptions that recalled his greatest services to the state. Every one knew who had restored them, and while the old soldiers absolutely wept for joy at seeing their beloved leader reinstated in his honours, the nobles impeached Cæsar for having transgressed the law. He defended the cause of his uncle and himself with his usual force, and though he did not convince the Senate, they were afraid, in the temper of the people, to censure him or to remove the statues, and the commonalty were delighted. After his year of office, he applied to be sent to Egypt, where it was said that the late king Ptolemy had made a will in favour of the Roman people. This splendid country would have amply paid all his debts, and enriched him for ever, and for that very reason the Senate did not choose to send him thither ; and, moreover, the will was doubtful ; so Egypt was left in peace and Cæsar remained at Rome, with the office of judge in cases of murder as the prætor's deputy.

In this position he condemned several of the murderers whom Sulla had employed, and continued his advance in popularity, and also in debt. The year 63 was a noted one in Rome as that of Cicero's consulship, and of the detection of the mischievous conspiracy of some wicked young nobles, of whom the chief was Lucius Sergius Catilina. They intended to bring about a revolution by murdering the consuls and senators, and setting fire to the city, and the plot was only just detected in time. Cicero impeached Catiline before the Senate, and made his grandest speeches against him. The wretched man fled, and put himself at the head of an army; but the partisans who had remained in Rome were tried before the Senate and sentenced to die ; but the consent of the people was likewise necessary, and they were in so factious a state that it was unadvisable to put the question to them. Cæsar made a speech, proposing that the criminals should be imprisoned for life, saying that a speedy death was too good for them, and, besides, exceeded the powers of the Senate. At this Cato was furious ; he accused Cæsar of having been in the plot : and, indeed, this was so much believed, that the Roman equites were ready to murder one whom they viewed as so treacherous and cautious an enemy ; but, in fact, Cæsar was far too wise a man to engage in such a plot with such confederates.

Full in the midst of the dispute a letter was brought to Cæsar, and Cato, supposing it to be from one of the con-spirators, insisted on having it read aloud to the Senate. Cæsar handed it over to him, and he saw in a moment that it was a love-letter from his own half-sister, Servilia, who, like many other of the Roman ladies of that shame-less period, paid a disgraceful court to the handsome, fascinating, and pleasure-loving Cæsar. Not a little stung, Cato handed it back, with the bitter words, " Take it, drunkard."

The Roman equites became so enraged that they broke in on the Senate, ready to massacre Cæsar as a concealed traitor, but Cicero and other senators threw themselves between, and he was rescued ; while Cicero, having gained the consent of the greater part of the Senate, caused the conspirators to be executed—an act for which he had afterwards to suffer severely, since it overpassed the limits of the law, and thus was a handle for his enemies.

It was almost the end of the year, and shortly after Cicero ended his consulship. Catiline was defeated and slain in battle. In 62 Cæsar, and his faithful Pollux,

Bibulus, entered upon their prætorship. The first thing Cæsar did was to attack Quintus Lutatius Catulus, the Prince of the Senate, and a man of good reputation, except that he had had the misfortune to be a personal friend of Catiline. He had been charged to superintend the rebuilding of the Temple of Jupiter in the Capitol, after a great fire, and Cæsar accused him of having been dishonest in the accounts, proposing that the honour of completing the work should be taken from him and given to Pompey.

There was a rush of all the nobles to vote in his defence, and it seems likely that Cæsar had only made the allegation to please the populace, who liked to see a great patrician attacked, as well as to pay a compliment to Pompey, who was on his way home.

It had been a campaign of wonderful success in the East. The Cilician pirates had been conquered, their ships annihilated, and themselves planted in an inland city, and the old King of Pontus, Mithridates, long the brave, cunning, and inveterate enemy of Rome, had been driven to extremity and suicide. Moreover, the race of Maccabee or Asmonean priests had, after assuming royalty, become degenerate and ambitious, Pompey had been called to settle their disputes, and, in support of the fugitive who had asked his protection, had taken Jerusalem by storm, and laid it under the Roman yoke of iron. He had even forced his way into the very Holy of Holies, and though he had done no material damage there, the pollution of his heathen presence was keenly felt ; and it was in truth a violation of the Roman rule of forbearance towards the religion of the vanquished. From that time it was noticed that the star of Pompey waned.

However, the proposal was to recall him and send him to destroy Catiline and his rebel army ; but this led to a hot and furious discussion, in which there was so much violence that the Senate suspended Cæsar from his office as prætor, and the story of his being in the plot revived. He went at once to Cicero, who declared that Cæsar was perfectly innocent, and had been the first to warn him of the danger ; whereupon he was honourably reinstated.

Soon after all the ladies of Rome, and the household of Cæsar in particular, were thrown into a state of violent excitement. One of the greatest rites of Rome, on which the fruitfulness of her soil and the number of her children was held to depend, was the festival of Cybele, the great Earth-Mother, commonly called the Bona Dea, or good goddess. All the womankind of Rome assembled on a certain night of December for the purpose, at the house of the Pontifex Maximus, where the Vestal Virgins conducted the sacrifice of a pig, and other observances took place which were called her Mysteries. No one of the male sex was allowed to come near the house, for his presence would have profaned the rites, and was supposed to draw down the anger of the goddess ; indeed, such a scandal was unknown in the annals of Rome.

What then was the horror of Aurelia, the dignified mother of Cæsar, when a female slave whispered in her ear that there was a man among them disguised as a lady ! No sooner had Aurelia heard it, than, hastily covering the goddess's altar lest the intruder's eye should fall on it, she caused the doors to be shut, and taking a torch in her hand, examined the countenance of every matron in the angry throng. The handsome face of Publius Clodius, a good-for-nothing young patrician whose garden-gate lay perilously near, was detected, and the ladies surrounded him in extreme wrath ; but there was a terrible suspicion in Aurelia's heart that this was not so much an insolent frolic as a concerted visit to her daughter-in-law, Pompeia, and lest he should publicly mention that name, she dismissed him from the house.

The ladies went home angry and dismayed, and every husband in Rome heard that night that the mysteries had been desecrated, the rites unperformed, the goddess offended. The whole population were in wrath and despair, the Vestal Virgins publicly declared that a great expiation was required, and, though philosophical students like Cicero observed scornfully that it would have been more reasonable in the goddess to blind the author of the sacrilege than to punish Rome, every one was eager for justice.

Cæsar himself had no reverence for the goddess, but as husband and master of the house he was deeply offended with his wife, who it seemed must have encouraged Clodius before, if she were not actually aware of his intention. He therefore dissolved the marriage, and returned her and her dowry to her family; but he did not choose to prosecute Clodius, as he was a member of the same party and a favourite of the mob, whom Cæsar never chose to offend.

However, it was an affair of all Rome, and Cicero, Cato, and other senators brought it about that Clodius should be tried; but his friends did not scruple to use monstrous arts of bribery upon a sort of jury chosen by lot, and he swore himself that he was absent from Rome on the night in question. Aurelia indeed bore the most positive testimony against him, and so did the slaves, whose truth was thought to be confirmed by torture; but Cæsar himself continued to declare he knew nothing about it, and, when he was asked why then he had divorced Pompeia, said, " Because Cæsar's wife must be above suspicion." After all, the prosecution failed, and the reckless intruder escaped chastisement.

So soon as the year of prætorship was over, before the arrival of Pompey, Cæsar went forth to take the proprætorship in the more distant half of Spain. The rich silver mines of Iberia were to serve as the means of acquitting his debts ; and what they must have been, in spite of Bibulus, is incalculable ; and he had to borrow still more largely in order to fit himself out for his office, and to raise the ten cohorts of soldiers which he added to the twenty he already expected to find there.

He did not get his instructions till April, 61, and then he made all speed to his province by land, taking with him a young African prince named Masintha, whom he had befriended in defiance of the Senate. In a rude cottage on the Alps, where he was halting, some of his officers asked him whether he expected to be as much beset with the entreaties of clients as at home, and his reply was remembered, " I had rather be first among these barbarians than second at Rome."

His province was the western one, the more untamed of the two, where fierce tribes lived in the mountains and tormented the sunny provinces of the Mediterranean coast, where all the luxury of Phœnicians, Greeks, and Romans had been flourishing ever since the days of Scipio. Far and deep into the mountains then did Cæsar hunt these independent tribes, pursuing them to the river Douro, which he crossed on rafts ; and then sending to Cadiz for ships, he sailed to what was probably Corunna, and thus pacified the country. Moreover, finding that those terrible usurers, the Roman publicans or collectors of the tribute, had contrived to get all the natives in the subject provinces into such complications of debt that despair often led to flight, revolt, and war, he set his clear brain and persuasive manner to put matters on a better footing, so that he won great gratitude and popularity ; and without gaining any character for rapacity, he contrived to collect an immense quantity of treasure, quite enough to pay his debts and to carry him through the election to the consulate for the year after his return.

He considered himself to have quite earned a triumph ;

and it would have been granted to him, but that he came back so late in the year that, as it was not permitted to a commander to come within the walls before his triumphal entry, he must have given up his canvass for the consul-ship if he had persisted in his demand. Therefore he laid aside the insignia of a general, and was soon in Rome, prevailing fast against the strong opposition of Cato and his friends.

Bibulus was again his colleague, but had now decidedly turned against him, and Cæsar entered into a union with Pompey and Lucius Licinius Crassus, surnamed Dives, or " the rich." Their object was to form a league to gain each their own ends. Pompey was offended by the Senate's having appeared desirous of making him render an account of his campaigns in Asia, and further desired the province of Spain ; Crassus wanted the government of Asia ; and Cæsar's aims reached far beyond what the other two understood. To draw the alliance closer Cæsar gave his own daughter Julia to Pompey, who offered him a daughter in return ; but instead of her he married Calpurnia, the daughter of Lucius Calpurnius Piso. He looked forward to another field of greater glory for the end of his consul-ship, for he had been promised the proconsulate of Gaul, the interior of which was still unsubdued ; but the jealousy of the Senate interfered, and threatened him instead with the mere supervision of the roads and forests.

He was resolved to secure the vote of the populace, and to obtain their goodwill he proposed a division of the state lands, one of those measures that the people loved and the patricians hated. The soldiers of Pompey would profit by it as well as his own, and the support of this powerful ally was thus secured ; and no one durst speak against it but Cato, who protested against all change.

This Cæsar declared was illegal, and he bade his lictors seize Cato and take him to prison. This was an outrage upon his dignity; many of the senators followed him to prison, one of them declaring that chains with Cato were better than freedom with Cæsar.

It was plain that Cæsar had made a false step, and he at once set Cato free, and dismissed the Senate for the day, adding, as he did so, that he had consulted them before the people that they might make any modification in the act that they chose, but that, since they set their faces against it altogether, he should appeal to the people.

When the people assembled in the Forum, he said that the law which would make the fortunes of so many would be passed in an instant, could they but gain the consent of his colleague ; but Bibulus, who had long grown weary of playing the part of Pollux, cried out, " Never during my year, though you should cry for it with one voice."

Then Cæsar consulted Pompey and Crassus, asking them whether they would support the act if it were opposed with violence. " Should any one draw his sword against it," said Pompey, " I would take my shield," thus implying that he would come armed to the Forum as if for battle. Sure of his support, Cæsar then ventured to defy the Senate by convoking the people in spite of Bibulus, who declared that he had observed Jupiter darting thunder, which was by the law a token that no business could be transacted. The Roman people were so much afraid that the Senate would hinder the assembly, or choke the Forum with their adherents, that they had taken up their station there long before dawn.

Both consuls appeared on the steps of the Temple of Castor and Pollux; but when Bibulus tried to speak against the act, his voice was drowned in clamour, he was pulled down the steps, his lictors bruised and wounded and their rods broken. Cato forced his way to the rostrum and tried to speak, but no one would hear him, and he was dragged down. The law was passed by the vote of the people, and the Senate felt that they could not but ratify it, though Cato refused to swear obedience to it ; and Bibulus never left his own house during the remainder of his term of office, but remained shut up there, only sending his officers to protest that he was observing the skies and taking omens, whenever any public affairs were transacted, by which means he hoped to render all his colleague's measures invalid and capable of being reversed.

So entirely was the power left to Cæsar that it was a jest among the Romans, that this was the consulship of Caius and Julius, and the superstition of the people connected his success with his possession of a wonderful horse, which had been bred in his own stables and had hoofs divided like the feet of a digitated animal, whence the augurs had predicted that its master would grasp the world. Like Bucephalus, it had been untameable till it felt the hand of a true "king of men" on it, and it allowed no one to mount it but Cæsar, who afterwards erected a statue of it in front of the Temple of Venus, his ancestress.

He used his power to enact a great many excellent rules, which were known as the Julian laws, and his ability and beneficence made themselves so much felt that his influence was unbounded, and he supported it by measures both worthy and unworthy. The villain Clodius being pledged to his party, he gave him every possible assistance in obtaining his election to the tribunate, which the wretch only wanted for the sake of being able to revenge himself on Cicero, by prosecuting him for the illegal execution of the companions of Catiline.

No sooner had the 1st of January, 58, passed, than Cæsar laid down the fasces of consul, and assumed those of proconsul of Gaul ; after which, being a military commander, he could not come within the gates for the ten years of his command; but while he was still close outside, Clodius showed his malice by proposing severe penalties against any one who had condemned a Roman citizen unheard. In hopes of obtaining Cæsar's assent, Clodius made the people meet outside the walls that he might give his vote ; but Cæsar only said that he had shown his opinion at the time, and that he disapproved of laws that looked backward and imposed penalties on deeds previous to their enactment. One element of greatness in Cæsar was, that he was much freer from petty personal enmity than any other man of his day : he really admired and respected Cicero, though they were always opposed to each other ; and he offered to make the orator his lieutenant, so as to withdraw him honourably from Rome till Clodius should be out of office ; but Cicero, who was never happy for a moment out of Italy, and thought himself able to resist his enemy, refused the offer, and had reason to repent it, for Clodius so far prevailed that he had to leave his beloved city as a fugitive, instead of as an officer on honourable service.

The other two triumvirs had obtained their desire : Crassus was proconsul of Asia, and Pompey of the enormous province including both Spain and Africa. Crassus left Rome, and shortly after perished in an expedition against the Parthians, while Pompey lingered in Italy, governing his province by his lieutenants, and trying to rule Rome by the influence he possessed over the senators, who clung to him as their only safeguard from Cæsar, the dangerous and dissipated adventurer whom they feared as likely to bring back the worst times of his favourite Marius.

Cæsar was one of those men who cannot undertake a service of any sort without so dealing with it as to make it grand and important, and he already knew that the province of Gaul offered such a field for distinguishing himself, and training up a devoted army, as did no other since the subjection of Mithridates. The southern portion of Gaul, called Provincia, or "the province," was indeed full of Roman colonies, and had been civilized up to the Italian pitch; and further north, the tribe of Ædui were the head of a confederation of clans, were in close alliance with Rome, and had learnt a good deal of civilization through the trade which their mineral wealth brought into their mountains ; but all beyond was an untried wilderness of fierce Kelts, chiefly known by their occasional forays upon the more cultivated regions. Of late the chief of the Æduan clan, whom the Romans called Divitiacus, had arrived at Rome, and, standing before the Senate, had made an harangue which, when interpreted, explained that a great German tribe and a king called Ariovistus had come across the Rhine, at the invitation of the Sequani, or dwellers on the Saone, and that the Ædui had been terrified into giving up their supremacy and making common cause against the Romans, but that he himself had not consented to break the league, and had fled from his country to lay the cause of his clan before their noble allies. Aid had been promised, but there was the delay occasioned by Cæsar's waiting to finish his year of the consulate, and then again by his waiting to collect troops, appoint officers, and make arrangements, while he entertained Divitiacus with great hospitality, and had much friendly intercourse with him, although neither could speak the language of the other.

Suddenly, however, there arrived tidings that another dreadful host of invaders, Helvetii by name, the wild Kelts of the Alps, were descending from their mountains, not for a temporary inroad, but bringing waggon-loads of their wives and children, intending to effect a permanent settlement in Gaul, and they would certainly fall on the cultivated lands of the allies of the Romans. They were actually on their way, intending to cross the Rhone at the bridge of Geneva.

From the moment of that intelligence till the work was done Cæsar ceased to be the ambitious Roman statesman, but became entirely the proconsul and general. He started instantly for the scene of action, aware that a nation with all their possessions must be slow in progress among wild mountains, while he, with only a few officers, relays of horses every few miles, and Roman roads all the way, could move with great speed; and, accordingly, in eight days' time he was at Geneva, ordering the bridge to be broken down, and leaving only a rushing torrent, too swift and wide for rafts or swimmers, between him and the Helvetii.

They were near at hand, and at once sent an embassy to Cæsar to entreat permission to cross the river, explaining that they had no designs against the province, but only wanted to make war upon the wild Kelts of the West. This was on the 28th of March, and Cæsar bade them return for an answer in a fortnight's time. He had found one legion in the province, and instantly set all the men to work to throw a rampart and ditch along the whole fifteen miles of the bank of the river from the point of the lake to the gorge of the Jura, and having thus strengthened the defences, he answered the Helvetian demand that no such thing had ever been granted by the Romans.

They made some attempts to force the passage, but, encumbered as they were, found it utterly impossible; so they gave up the attempt, and, turning to the north, obtained from Dumnorix, the brother of Divitiacus, permission to descend into Gaul through the Æduan lands.

The one legion under Cæsar's command was, of course, as nothing against a whole horde of barbarians; and, therefore, whilst the enemy were making their tardy way towards the north, he left his officer Labienus to guard the rampart of the Rhone whilst he himself dashed off into Northern Italy, or Cisalpine Gaul, which formed part of his government; and there he raised two legions, and summoned three more from their station, so that he brought back 30,000 men, through the shortest but most dangerous way, by the Cottian Alps, where he had to be on his guard against the natives. He hoped to be in time to prevent the Helvetians from passing the Saone, but he only came up when the greater number were across, and only a quarter part of them still remained on the further side. Upon these he fell, and cut them to pieces ; then setting his soldiers to build a bridge, he carried his army across in a single day in pursuit of the rest.

Dismayed at his swiftness, they again attempted to treat with him, and sent an old chief, who boasted of what the Gauls had once done to the Romans ; but Cæsar said that he was come to revenge the wrongs of his country- men and allies, and the only terms which he would offer were those of instant retreat from Gaul, and compensa- tion for the havoc they were making there.

The Æduans did not deserve the protection he was affording them, for they had first allowed the Helvetians to enter, and though they were now apparently fighting in Cæsar's army, they always took flight at every skirmish with the Helvetians, and took no pains to supply him with provisions. At last he found that the real traitor was Dumnorix, the brother of Divitiacus, and he caused him to be put down from his authority. Indeed, it was only the earnest intercession of Divitiacus that saved his brother's life.

Near Bibracte, the Æduan capital, a great battle was fought, which broke the whole force of the Helvetians, and forced them to sue for whatever terms Cæsar chose to grant. It was regarded as an act of mercy that he neither butchered them nor sold them as slaves, but merely sent them back to their old mountains, causing them to be supplied with provisions till they had had time to rebuild their huts and grow fresh corn.

This great achievement over, Cæsar had to deal with the Germans and Ariovistus, their proud chief, who almost anticipated the destiny of his people when he declared himself to be a conqueror like the Romans. " Let them keep to their province," he said, " and I will keep to mine." Moreover, another flood of Germans was preparing to follow him across the Rhine, and Cæsar felt that the battle must be fought before their junction. So he marched on in great haste as far as Besançon, but there found his army in great alarm and unwilling to advance. The young noblemen who had come to serve under him were disgusted with the hardships of Gaul ; and, besides, the Gauls told horrible stories of the ferocity and strength of the Germans, so that many were begging for leave of absence, and those who were steady enough to remain and face the worst were all making their wills and giving themselves up for lost.

Cæsar had to argue with officers and men in private, and in public he made them an address, shaming the panic-stricken by declaring that he knew he could trust the brave Tenth Legion, and that he had such confidence in his own destiny, that if all the others should fall away he would advance with them alone and feel secure of victory. His power of infusing courage was soon evident : there were no more murmurs, and he marched on to hold a conference in person with Ariovistus, upon a solitary hill rising from a plain where both armies were watching.

It was of no effect, and was broken up. The Germans remained still for some days, and Cæsar discovered that the cause of the delay was their expectation that the new moon would bring them luck. He therefore forestalled the moon, and by attacks on their camp forced them to come out in battle array, when he utterly defeated them, so that the whole host fled headlong to the Rhine ; and there was a terrible slaughter along the whole bank, Ariovistus himself only just escaping in a boat.

This victory had brought the country as far north as the Saone under friendly subjection to Rome, and Cæsar went as a victor back to Cisalpine Gaul for the winter ; but with the spring of 57 fresh cares awaited him, for the Belgic tribes, who inhabited the marshy country to the west, had formed a great confederacy against him. A tremendous battle was fought on the banks of the Sambre, in which their bravest tribe was nearly exterminated, their chief stronghold was taken, and then, after another winter spent beyond the Alps, he brought sailors from the Mediterranean, and built ships wherewith to hunt down and subdue the stout-hearted Gauls of Armorica ; so that by the end of B.C. 56 there was no people in the accessible portions of Gaul who had not been brought into subjection. But there were still dangers on the frontier, and tokens of an unbroken spirit among the Kelts themselves, which kept the proconsul fully occupied, and which he describes in his " Commentaries." These consist of the whole history of his Gallic war, minutely described by himself ; with the full account of his tactics, and of the motives of his marches and treaties ; with praise to his brave soldiers, and esteem for the skill and valour of his enemies ; but with all the indifference to real justice that might be expected from a Roman, and, with all his clearness of head, no perception that anything in the character of a barbarian Gaul could be interesting, save as it called out the powers of a Roman, and chiefly of Caius Julius Cæsar. It is, however, one of the best written and most valuable histories in existence.

When warfare could no longer be carried on, he always repaired to his Gallic province on the Italian side of the Alps, where he resided at Lucca, and thence kept up his influence over Rome, though as a general he could not enter it. Hosts of senators flocked to see and consult him, or pay their court to him, and for each of his victories he received the thanks of the Senate : and in the meantime he won over all hearts by his high-bred courtesy, such as appeared in trifles. It was told of him, that when at a banquet some asparagus was served up with sweet ointment instead of oil, he ate it without apparent disgust, and when his officers exclaimed, he rebuked them : " It is enough," he said, " not to eat what you dislike, but he who reflects upon another's want of breeding shows that he has it not himself." When forced by a storm on a journey to spend the night at a hovel by the road-side, he put the feeblest of the party into the one room, and himself lay outside under a shed.

During his winter absence the Teutons came over the Belgian border again, and the early part of 55 was spent in driving them back ; but Cæsar's curiosity had been excited by certain allies of the Armoricans, who were said to have come from an island beyond the waters that washed the coast of Gaul, and whose cliffs could dimly be seen from the Belgian heights. This was the Ultima Thule, the land of Frost and Fog, over which the Tyrian merchants had always thrown a veil of mystery, into which Cæsar was determined to penetrate, having already a notion that the natives were not very unlike the Gauls, with whom he had grown familiar in five years of alliance or of warfare : at any rate, the Gauls must not believe that there was any place whither the Romans could not advance, nor, what was even more important, must Rome suppose there was anything too hard for Cæsar.

So he embarked a legion and crossed the strait, to find the heights crowded with Britons, who followed his course along the beach, and bravely resisted his landing, so that the shore would scarcely have been gained but for the adventurous bravery of the standard-bearer, who leapt down among the natives, and thus forced his comrades to follow him, or disgrace themselves by the loss of their eagle.

A few days spent on the coast surrounded by hostile natives comprised the whole of this expedition; but it had really been for the purpose of reconnoitring, and the next year he set out once more, with three legions and 4,000 Gallic horse, landed, and fought his way as far as the Thames. Caswallon, the British chief in command, resisted bravely, but without avail; the Romans found a ford, crossed the Thames, and stormed the great enclosure of trunks of trees where the Britons had placed their families and cattle. Nothing was left for Caswallon to do but to acknowledge Roman supremacy, like his neighbours in Gaul, and give up some young chiefs as hostages for his submission, but really as visible proofs to the Romans that Cæsar had conquered in a land that was almost deemed fabulous. He also brought away a breastplate set with pearls from the river mussels of Britain.

On his return to Gaul he found all in confusion again, the Belgians up in arms, and Quintus Cicero, the brother of the great Marcus, in desperate danger, besieged with a single legion in his camp by a huge horde of savages. Cæsar's advance saved him, and the revolt was punished by the desolation of the country. It was at a critical moment in the march that Cæsar received tidings from Pompey of the death of Julia, his only child; and the manner in which he kept his grief from interfering with his efficiency was much admired by those around him.

The most notable effort of the Gauls to shake off the yoke that he was welding on their necks was made in 52, under the gallant young Arvernian chieftain whom Cæsar calls Vercingetorix, and who did all that sagacity and skill could do with a shifting, unmanageable, uncertain race, against one of the greatest geniuses in the world, with a perfectly disciplined army.

So formidable was the rising of Vercingetorix that Cæsar was forced to hurry back headlong from Italy, and to march into Auvergne over snow six feet deep. In spite of his rapidity, and of the burning and devastation with which he tried to strike terror into the Gauls, Cæsar had never been so hardly pressed, and in a battle on the borders of Provincia his sword was wrested from him to be suspended as a trophy in a temple of the Arverni. However, he succeeded in forcing the brave Gaul to shut himself up in a vast intrenched camp, at Alesia, where Cæsar blockaded him, and as the other Gauls outside had not constancy enough to bear reverses, no aid came, and the gallant chief gave himself up, for the safety of his people.

Cæsar sat cold, grave, unmoved, in his curule chair at the head of his troops, while the noble Kelt came forth on a beautiful horse, galloped round, wheeled about Cæsar's chair, then suddenly drawing his rein, leapt off and laid his arms and himself before the victor. No voice of mercy was spoken; only Vercingetorix was ordered to be guarded as a captive to honour the intended triumph.

That triumph was yet a long way off. Two years had still to be spent in taming the outlying tribes, and in so ordering Gaul that the old clan organization might be broken up and revolt become more difficult; and in this Cæsar's consummate ability showed itself. He never was severe without a reason for it, and knew how to make his favour and mercy thoroughly conciliating, and the ten years of his proconsulship secured a whole country to Rome, and gave her, instead of hordes of barbarous enemies, legions of intelligent and active soldiers.

But he was longing to assert his power in the arena where he now hoped to be first. Crassus had been killed in the East, and the Roman minds were divided between Cæsar and Pompey; moreover, the death of Julia had broken the tie that held her father and her husband together, and Pompey was manifesting a good deal of jealousy and dislike to Cæsar, and a desire to keep him as long as possible at a distance.

But this could no longer be done. Cæsar was actually in Italy, and though still not at Rome, was among Roman citizens, among whom he went about in the scarlet cloak of a general, attended by lictors with their fasces wreathed with laurel. Every city he passed through received him with rapture; the gates were clothed with boughs, victims were sacrificed, and men feasted in the market-place. He had almost as a right demanded the consulship of the year, without having as before to give up his triumph to come and ask for it.

Pompey, and with him all the conservative Romans, wanted to appoint a new proconsul, and thus deprive Cæsar of his army; but two of the tribunes, Marcus Antonius (more commonly known to us as Mark Antony) and Quintus Cassius, upheld Cæsar's interests. In right of the government of the provinces of Spain and Africa, Pompey too had an army at his disposal as proconsul, and the Senate was justly afraid that the two rivals, each at the head of their legions, would soon come to civil war. Some declared that the only safety of the republic lay in trusting to Pompey, others that Cæsar was its only hope. If " Cæsar remained in the north of Italy with his army, surely Pompey could not be spared with his force to counterbalance him," said one party, while others declared that the only condition on which Cæsar could be required to lay down his arms was that Pompey should be sent off to his province with all his troops. At last things came to a crisis. The Senate met outside the walls of Rome, that Pompey might be present, and agreed

to deprive Cæsar of his command, appoint a fresh proconsul of Gaul, and trust to Pompey to bear them through
with the consequences!

The tribunes protested, but were silenced. They declared that they were under coercion, and that the voice
of the law was silenced by terror; and they fled as if
for their lives to Cæsar's camp of one single legion, at
Ravenna, sending beforehand to call on him to save the
republic. Now was the turning-point! It was on the 15th
of January, 49, that Cæsar set out from Ravenna by a
branch of the great road called the Æmilian Way, which
led to the boundary between his own province of Cisalpine Gaul, where he still had the right to bear arms as
proconsul, and the home lands of the Roman republic, on
which it was not lawful for a home-coming army to enter,
save by the special leave and invitation of the Senate.

This boundary was washed by a little stream, called
the Rubicon, from the ruddy hue of the waters of the
peat-mosses whence it springs. It was a flood in the
winter, and was spanned by a bridge, and the crossing
of this bridge as an armed man, leading his troops, was,
as Cæsar well knew, the turning-point of his life.

He sent forward some of his troops in the morning, but
himself remained at Ravenna, where he was present at
some public ceremony, and afterwards entertained some
friends at dinner, only quitting them at sunset, as if to
return presently, but really mounting a car drawn by
mules, and driving along by-roads to overtake his
troops. The way was lost, it was quite dark, all the
torches of his attendants went out, and it was with
much difficulty that he found the troops he had sent
forward. The next morning he did what has become a
proverb for taking an irrevocable step in life—he crossed
the Rubicon; thus becoming a rebel against the formal
decree of the Senate.

He never mentions the actual crossing in his own Commentaries, but other historians have been so struck with the importance of the event, as to dress it up in graceful legend. Cæsar, it is said, stood hesitating. " Even now," he said, "we may return! If we cross the bridge, arms must decide our strife!"

Just then a beautiful youth appeared playing on a flute, so sweetly, that the soldiers and the shepherds who chanced to be in the camp gathered round him, until he suddenly snatched a trumpet, blew a wild and spirit-stirring blast, leapt into the river and crossed it ; then was seen no more.

" Onwards!" cried Cæsar, "where the gods point the way, and our foes invite us. The die is cast."

It was still early in the day when Ariminium was reached and secured, and there Antony and the other fugitive tribune were met. Cæsar waited there to collect the rest of his legions, eleven in number, and then marched on, to the horror and dismay of the Senate and consuls, who fancied that a reign of terror was coming, and fled in a body, without waiting to secure either the public treasure or their own property, but hurried southwards, sending out a summons to the faithful to rally for the defence of the Republic. On, however, came Cæsar, gathering strength at every step, and carefully making known that he was not coming as a cruel avenger like Sulla, but merely to assert his rights as a Roman citizen, slaying no one, and touching no man's property. All Italy grew enraged against those who had left them to their fate, and were retreating further and further to the southern extremity. In sixty days after he had passed the Rubicon, Cæsar had followed them down the whole length of Italy, even to Brundusium, and there finding the place not fit for defence, the consul, Cornelius Scipio, whose daughter Cornelia Pompey had married, took ship for Greece, and Pompey followed them in a few days, so that Cæsar was truly, as one of his lieutenants called him, master of Italy.

Cato, who was then governing Sicily, yielded it upon his summons, and joined the consuls. Cicero, who was living in retirement at his villa at Formiæ, was there visited by Cæsar, who did all he could to win him over to his side; but Cicero was staunch to his principles, and said, if he came to Rome at all, it must be to oppose Cæsar's measures, and the interview ended with cold politeness.

Cæsar went to Rome and convoked the Senate, making his two friends the tribunes preside in the absence of the consuls. All who were strongly opposed to him had fled or stayed away, and the rest were greatly won over by his unexpected clemency, as well as alienated from Pompey and the other party by their abandonment of their post ; and there was no one to oppose him when he seized the treasures that had been left behind, collected his legions, and prepared to destroy Pompey's army in Greece, where he was believed to be collecting a mass of barbarians with whom to return and revenge himself upon the Romans.

Cæsar marched by the coast road, and had a great battle at Ilerda with two of Pompey's lieutenants; an exceedingly well-contested and terrible battle it was, but the day was with Cæsar, and the defeat, together with want of provisions, forced the Pompeian army to lay down their arms. The victory was thought so important, that the anniversary was kept as a festival. After completing the subjection of Spain, he returned in time to receive the submission of Marseilles, which had been holding out for Pompey, and had been besieged for some months past; and he himself was appointed Dictator by his own party at Rome; and this gave him an unquestioned right to enter the city with his army, and to appear in the Forum.

The real nobleness of Cæsar was seen in the forbearance and placability which made his power so much less terrible to the vanquished than they expected. There were no proscriptions, no murders; but there were distributions of corn to make up for the withdrawal of the supply from Africa, which was Pompey's province, and the right of citizenship was extended to the Cisalpine province of Gaul. Still, however, Pompey and the senators who had fled with him were in full force at Thessalonica, and were gathering round them the petty princes of Asia Minor and Syria, who had become attached to Pompey during his Eastern wars, and were ready to fight in his cause, bringing large contingents with them, whom Pompey trained in the Roman manner of fighting.

It was high time to pursue them thither, when Cæsar with seven legions embarked at Brundusium in the autumn of 48, so suddenly, that his old colleague Bibulus, who was on the watch for him at Corfu, was entirely eluded, and he safely landed in Epirus. Still, however, he was delayed; for his legions were not complete in number, and the watch Bibulus kept deterred the rest of his troops from crossing. At last the waiting became so intolerable that he returned in person, Plutarch says, in the disguise of a slave, in a little twelve-oared vessel, in the face of a storm, to expedite matters. The tempest became violent, and the master of the vessel was terrified; but the unknown passenger rose up out of the bottom of the ship and consoled him with the confident words, "Fear not! You carry Cæsar and his fortunes!"

At last the rest of the army joined him, and he marched towards Dyrrachium, where Pompey lay with his army. Every one expected a battle, but it was long deferred, for Pompey was resolved not to fight till he had thoroughly trained his men. He therefore gave way before Cæsar, and let him form the siege of Dyrrachium, while he himself took up a position around a overhanging cliff called Petra, entrenching himself behind a rampart fifteen miles long, which enclosed a great quantity of cultivated ground. Cæsar in return cut him off from the place he had come to relieve and secured himself by a rampart seventeen miles long. And behind these earthworks the two greatest captains and finest armies then in existence lay watching one another, neither venturing on a move that would expose him to the other, and each hoping to weary the other out and take advantage of some unguarded movement. They had many skirmishes, but no battle; for though Cæsar's army was the superior in the proportion of genuine Roman legionaries, Pompey's was the most numerous and had many more light horse. However, famine was severely felt in the Cæsarean army; in the winter no bread could be obtained, and the soldiers were forced to dig up a kind of root which they boiled in milk, or bruised into flour and made loaves of. By way of defiance they threw these loaves into Pompey's camp, telling his outposts, "that as long as they had such fare, their siege should last;" and they, being higher up on the hills, were able to distress their enemies with thirst by stopping all the watercourses, so that the Pompeians were forced to sink wells in the sands on the sea-shore. In the daily skirmishes that took place, Cæsar's well-armed troops had the advantage, and on reckoning the numbers of the slain after several weeks of them it was found that they had only lost twenty men, while they had counted two thousand Pompeians slain.

At last, however, an attack was made upon a part of Cæsar's lines which were not yet completed, and where the men were at work without their arms; they and those nearest were put to flight, and were thus met by Cæsar, who, catching at one of the men to stop him, was struck at by the man in his panic, and was only saved by an attendant. He found it impossible to rally the men, and was forced to content himself with throwing up another rampart close to his camp, where he expected an immediate attack; and when the evening passed without it he said, " The victory would have been with our enemies if they had had a general who knew how to conquer;" and the night that ensued is said to have been the most anxious and melancholy of his life, for his position had become untenable, and he must retreat with the full expectation of being attacked at great disadvantage. Meantime there was the greatest exultation in the other camp from all but Cato, who, with the heart of a citizen, covered his face and burst into tears at the sight of the bodies of the thousand Roman citizens who had been killed. When he found that Pompey, still insecure of the quality of his troops, had decided against fighting, he thanked him ardently for thus saving bloodshed, while all the other captains murmured.

Cæsar then retreated, keeping a good guard, but unmolested, to Apollonia, where he found shelter for the many sick who had suffered from scanty fare, and finally took up his position near the town of Pharsalus, whither Pompey pursued him, with the senators, who had become so confident of victory, that they had sent to take houses at Rome fit for the state offices they expected soon to be bearing. Pompey himself was, however, much out of spirits, though their insistance forced him to fight—he being no doubt far better able than they to estimate the odds against them; and, on the other hand, Cæsar was almost equally depressed at the prospect of a hand-to-hand conflict with the flower of Rome, saying that, be the issue what it might, it could not fail to produce many evils.

All the omens were, however, in his favour, and he was one of those men who with little religious belief have a great confidence in such tokens of fortune. As he rode along the ranks, just before the battle joined, and called out to one of his centurions, "What cheer, Caius Crastinus?" the hearty answer came back, "We shall conquer nobly, Cæsar! This day will I deserve your praise, alive or dead." He was the first to rush upon the foe, one of the first to fall, and Cæsar took care that his corpse should receive distinguished honours.

The legionaries were pretty equally matched, and fought foot to foot; and Pompey put no faith in his Eastern allies, but kept them in the rear, where they did nothing but cramp and encumber his army. He relied more on his cavalry, a splendid band of brave young patricians, who he hoped would by a tremendous charge ride down the legionaries. But the staunch old soldiers held their solid ranks, and the order " Strike at their faces !" passed along; the stunning blow or thrust of the short sword laid many a gay youth low; and as the others fell back, they perhaps hardly deserved the sneer that they feared for their beauty. They broke and fled to the hills, and Cæsar's reserve marched up against the legionaries, who had been fighting all this time, and were prepared to sell their lives dearly and die where they stood. But their opponents, instead of striking, told them that Cæsar did not wish to kill Romans, only to be rid of that useless mass of barbarians in their rear; so the Pompeians, without any pity for their unfortunate allies, let them pass and make a dreadful slaughter of the poor wretches who had been brought from their homes by their lords' trust in Pompey.

That unhappy man had fled into his camp, and, after arranging to defend it, had shut himself up in his tent; but presently tidings were brought him that the enemy were thundering at the gates: " What ! into my camp too ?" he said ; and, hastily taking off his scarlet mantle and other insignia of a general, he mounted his horse, and galloped away through the gate in the rear, while Cæsar and his men poured into the camp, where they found tables spread and tents decked with ivy for a victorious feast. Cæsar was a good deal touched at the ruin he had made. "They would have it so," he said. " Caius Cæsar must have lost all and suffered death, had he not thrown himself on the protection of his soldiers." He would not let his troops enjoy the spoil till they had broken up all the remaining parties of the enemy, who had fled to the hills, and received the submission of those who saw that resistance had become hopeless, and that the Republic lay at his mercy.

Of these were Caius Cassius Longinus, an able officer, and Marcus Junius Brutus, one of the intensest devotees of the old iron age of the Commonwealth, and nephew and son-in-law to Cato. Cato himself, with Cicero and o'hers of the purest-minded of the senators, drew together in the island of Corfu, and waited, expecting to join Pompey in the great African province round Carthage, where he had two legions, and all the native princes were friendly to him. Instead of this, however, Pompey had, with his wife Cornelia and one of his sons, sailed for Egypt, where in the days of his greatness he had been appointed guardian of the young brother and sister king and queen, Ptolemy XII. and Cleopatra. He came in the midst of a civil war between them, and almost at the moment of his landing on the shore held by Ptolemy he was stabbed by order of the treacherous young king, his head was cut off, and his body left to the waves. It was cast ashore, and a faithful servant and an old Roman soldier making a pile with wood from an old fishing-boat, burnt it and placed the ashes in an urn.

Cæsar did not learn what had happened till he arrived on the coast of Egypt in pursuit, with 3,200 infantry and 800 cavalry, and one of the Egyptian courtiers came out in a boat to meet him, bringing him the signet-ring and the head of his rival. It was no small shock to Cæsar to find that the man whom he had wished to overcome in honourable conflict, who had once been his friend, and the husband of his beloved daughter, had been so miserably destroyed by these base barbarians ; and he turned away in horror and with tears in his eyes from the head, commanding that it should be consumed with sweet odours.

Cæsar was in pressing need of money, and therefore as consul demanded from young Ptolemy the sum—or part of it—which his father had promised the Romans, when nearly twenty years before they had made him king rather than entrust so rich a province to a citizen. Ptolemy's minister asked for time, and Cæsar landed, arrayed in all the splendours of a consul ; but this affronted the Alexandrians, who thought it a sign that he was come to take away their independence; and they made a riot in the streets, in which some of his men were killed. This, together with the smallness of his force, encouraged the Egyptian court to insult him, by serving his troops with musty wheat, and providing only earthenware dishes, instead of silver or gold, for his own table. He saw that if he let himself fall into contempt at this servile court the fate of Pompey might soon be his ; and he therefore boldly declared himself to be come with all the authority of Rome to decide between Ptolemy and Cleopatra and summoned them both to plead their claims before his tribunal. Ptolemy came ; but his party were so strong in Alexandria that Cleopatra could not venture in openly : whereupon she caused herself to be rolled up in a bale of carpet and carried into Cæsar's apartments. She was the most magnificently beautiful and captivating woman of her time, and full of wit and intellect, with the sweetest of voices ; and Cæsar was at once amused with her stratagem, enchanted with her beauty, and pleased by her confidence in him. He at once became her advocate, and insisted on her brother taking her back to share his throne.

Ptolemy was so much in his hands as to have no choice but outward submission ; but Cleopatra, with her overweening nature, was much hated both by her brother and the Alexandrians, and in the midst of the festival of reconciliation Cæsar's barber discovered a plot against his life. Moreover, a tremendous tumult broke out in the streets, Cæsar's soldiers were attacked, and his danger was so great, that the only chance he saw for safety was to make his way to the little island called Pharos, from the lighthouse on it, there defend himself till reinforcements should arrive from Rome, and to burn the Egyptian fleet to prevent their arrival from being obstructed. In this he succeeded ; he fought his way with his veterans through the streets, setting fire to the buildings near and the ships in the harbour, and safely reached Pharos, where he endured a sort of siege for many days, and once was so hard pressed that he was obliged to throw off his cloak and swim for his life among a shower of darts, which compelled him often to hide his head under water, though he kept the hand that held his papers safe above it all the time.

At last, however, he consented to an accommodation, and Ptolemy undertook to reign jointly with his sister but this had scarcely been arranged, when one of the allies for whom Cæsar had sent advanced upon Egypt, and Ptolemy marched out against him. In the battle that ensued the young king perished while trying to cross the Nile, and Egypt was at Cæsar's feet. He made

Cleopatra queen, with a much younger brother associated with her, and, having arranged matters at Alexandria, set forth for Asia Minor, where the king of Pontus was trying to make head against the Republic. Him Cæsar met and defeated at Zela; and the whole of Syria lay so completely at his disposal, that his despatch to the Senate ran in these three famous words, *Veni, vidi, vici,* "I came, I saw, I conquered." He collected huge sums of money from every part of the East, and then sailed back to Rome, but only to be freshly appointed Dictator, and to collect troops with whom to pursue the last remnants of the hostile force which he had beaten at Pharsalia.

These had, as has been already said, gathered together at Corfu, whence Scipio, their consul, had gone with the larger part of their army to Numidia, where Pompey's party had been successful. Cato and Cicero waited for further tidings, and when Pompey's wife and son brought the fatal tidings of his death, Cicero gave up the contest and sailed back to Italy; but Cato resolved to hold by the remains of his party, and be staunch to the old Republic to the last. So he sailed for Cyrene, but the city closed its gates against him; and he then proceeded along the coast until the storms of winter made it impossible to proceed by sea, and he was obliged to march for seven days along the desert, in exceeding distress from parching heat, drought, and the number of dangerous serpents. It was a wonderful instance of Roman patience and resolution that the whole army, defeated and dejected as they were, implicitly throughout their hardships obeyed this upright man of peace, whose only claim to their obedience was from his having borne the office of prætor, or judge, and who wept at bloodshed. He endured all the privations to the utmost, never mounting a horse through all the weary march; and indeed, in token of mourning, since the battle of Pharsalia he had never reclined on a couch at meals nor lain down in bed.

Thus in the spring of 47 he joined the body of his party at Utica, and there found Scipio, the late consul, and a force that altogether amounted to twelve legions, and a Numidian prince named Juba, who was apparently friendly. The Romans wanted Cato to take the command ; but he would not be put over the head of a man of consular rank, though he did all he could to prepare for Cæsar's attack, and was of opinion that it would be best to cross the sea, and try to raise Italy against Cæsar while he was still in the East.

He could not prevail, and in the last month of 47 Cæsar was in Africa, and landed with 3,000 foot and 150 horse near Adrumentum. One battle he fought without much success, though with great valour, before his reinforcements came up, and he remained training his men to meet the Numidians and to encounter their elephants, until the April of 46, when the decisive battle was fought near Thapsus, and a most frightful slaughter was made by Cæsar's ferocious Tenth Legion, from which Juba and Scipio barely escaped with their lives.

Cato was not in the battle, but was garrisoning Utica. When the tidings of the defeat arrived, he remained perfectly calm and resolute ; but as it became evident that there was no hope left for his cause, and that to attempt to hold out the city would only be to sacrifice so many lives, he advised all his friends to embark for Italy, and there make their peace with the conqueror. He waited till all were gone, and then, not enduring to bend to Cæsar, or to see the fall of Roman freedom, he slew himself with his own sword ; a death that high-souled heathen did not deem self-murder, but rather a courageous effort. The tidings were heard by Cæsar with the words, " Cato, I envy thee thy death, for thou hast envied me the saving of thy life." He spared Cato's son, and burnt all the papers he found, unread, not choosing to know the bitterness of his enemies against him.

Scipio and Juba both died by suicide ; and Cæsar had entirely subdued all opposition. No one, save Pompey's cousin, in Spain, dared to raise a hand against him, and he was the master of the Roman world. In expectation of his return, and in gratitude to the man who never slew a foe save on the battle-field, the Senate invented unprecedented honours for the triumph that had been due to him ever since the conquest of Gaul. There was to be a forty days' holiday ; he was to be Dictator for ten years, censor for three ; was to sit between the consuls in the Senate, and his figure in ivory would accompany those of the gods in processions ; his statue be engraven, " Cæsar, the Demigod." He asked for four triumphs : for his victories over the Gauls, the Egyptians, the Syrians, and the Numidians ; for the Spanish conquest was gone out of date, and the battle of Pharsalia had been with Roman citizens : but each of the others was celebrated on a different day, with an interval between.

His triumph was noted for his car being drawn by white horses, which were usually granted only to the gods, and had never been used by any general save Camillus. On the first day his chariot broke down, and, perhaps, this gave him an impression that a mortal might not assume divine honours, for he caused the word demigod to be erased from his statue. In the triumphs were led in chains the gallant Gaul, Vercingetorix, Arsinoë, the sister of Cleopatra, and the young son of Juba, with many other noble captives. All were spared save Vercingetorix, for whom, though the noblest of all, the Romans seem to have had no pity. Afterwards there were prodigious banquets, provided with the choicest wines, and the favourite dainties, among which were 6,000 lampreys. At one of these there were 22,000 tables, each table having three couches, on each of which, according to Roman fashion, three guests would recline, making a total of 198,000! He also entertained the people with shows of wild beasts and gladiators on a greater scale than ever before ; feeding their corrupt craving for idly looking on at the horrid scenes of bloodshed that he had too much taste to admire, and dazzling them by his magnificence. He even covered the circus with an awning made of silk, though this material was extremely costly, and hardly attainable even for dresses. He did a better work by erecting a new and beautiful forum, or market-place, with colonnades of marble pillars, arranged for all the purposes of public assembly, and which ever after bore his name as Forum Julii. This great work was, however, only just set in hand when he set off for Spain to put down the resistance that the two sons of Pompey were fruitlessly prolonging in the mountains, not out of zeal for the old Republic, but out of revenge for their father's death. The elder brother, Cnæus, was a ferocious and violent man, and the Spanish nature being always cruel, it was a terrible and savage war of butchery and retaliation, and it was well when it came to a crisis in the battle of Munda. The Pompeians fought well, and Cæsar was in so much danger, that he called out to ask his soldiers, "whether they meant to deliver him into the hands of boys?" and when by thus shaming them he had won the day, he said that he had often fought for victory, but never before for his life. Cnæus Pompeius was killed by the pursuers, but his brother Sextus escaped, and lived the life of an outlaw among the robber tribes upon the hills.

And now Cæsar had reached the summit of his glory, and had put down all opposition. He was all, and more than all, that a Roman citizen could become, and there was no one left to dispute his will. The enemies who had neither perished in battle nor by their own despair were left absolutely unmolested, and were, as he trusted, disarmed by his clemency; while those who had regarded him with dread as an unprincipled adventurer might, he had every reason to hope, have come to perceive that the whole constitution had become so rotten that his present authority was absolutely necessary for the reformations that must be carried out.

To these then he applied himself, and many of his regulations were wise and useful; but as they chiefly regarded Roman politics, it may be better not to dwell on them. Others showed the greatness of his mind—such as the endeavouring to obtain a perfect map of the Roman empire, and that reform of the calendar which we still profit by. This he carried out as Pontifex Maximus, since as chief priest of Rome he had authority to fix the recurring festival-days. He had studied astronomy during his stay in Egypt, and had grasped the right way of arranging the computation of time so as to allow for the odd hours that the earth takes above the 365 days of its course round the sun. All he did was the work of a great man, and for the good of the Romans, but still he felt that, though many were dazzled by his fame and many more courted him for his power, the best and noblest of the citizens viewed him with distrust and displeasure. His holding a triumph when he came back from Spain gave these Romans much displeasure, since a civil war was shame, not glory. Still he tried to conciliate all men, and there is a curious account in one of Cicero's letters of a friendly visit that Cæsar paid him at his villa, and the agreeable conversation, wit, and liveliness that seasoned the excellent dinner; but altogether, before the first year of Cæsar's undisputed power was over, he was weary of it and of the men around him, and was dreaming of the camp, where as general his will was law, and of the gorgeous East which he had barely seen, and where Alexander had triumphed.

Cleopatra with her Greek beauty and wit and voluptuous Eastern splendour had completely captivated him. She had followed him to Rome, and he longed to cast aside the quiet decorous Roman lady whom only as a citizen he could marry, and enjoy the intoxicating magnificence and luxury of the East with the Egyptian queen. Plans for marching upon Parthia in the very track of Alexander haunted his fancy, and he began to provide for the government of Rome in his absence, by appointing consuls and prætors for several years onwards ; but this was after all an insecure arrangement, and he began, it would seem, to listen to the whispers of his friends, especially the former tribune Mark Antony, who advised that he should endeavour to reign as a king.

This would enable him to rule by deputy in his absence, and to transmit his power to his great-nephew, who was now his nearest relation, and a youth of delicate health but of great promise. If Cæsar listened to the proposal, it was most secretly and cautiously ; but attempts were made by his friends to sound the temper of the people, who regarded that word *king* with a violent prejudice, though they would endure the exercise of far greater authority than that name necessarily implied.

A laurel wreath fastened to a diadem was by way of experiment placed on Cæsar's statue in the forum ; it was indignantly torn down by the tribunes, and the people applauded. Again, on the occasion of a procession through the streets, some voices hailed him as king, but no one took up the cry, and such angry glances were cast towards him that he was forced to exclaim, in a tone of reproof, " Not king, but Cæsar ! " while the tribunes seized those who had uttered the obnoxious words and threw them into prison. For this Cæsar rebuked them, saying that it was bringing suspicion on him to punish a foolish cry so severely as an offence against the state ; but when one of his own party declared that they ought to be put to death, he interfered on their behalf.

Still the attempt was renewed. The 15th of February, with its strange wild festival of the Lupercalia, came round. It had once been a shepherd's feast, in the old simple ages, and the rude peasant ceremonies still survived in the cultivated state of Rome, just as they had been carried on when the rough rustics of the Campagna really believed that the fruitfulness of their flocks could thus be obtained from the gods ; and, moreover, the popular mind connected the name with that of the she-wolf (*lupa*) which had nurtured Romulus and Remus. The place of celebration was the Lupercal grove, where the twins were said to have been found ; and Cæsar, as chief pontiff, sat in his golden chair to preside over the ceremonies, which to him as well as to most educated Romans were vain and ridiculous, and only kept up because the whole state system hinged on them and they kept the people occupied.

First, at the altar in the grove were sacrificed two goats and two dogs ; and Antony, who was one of the Lupercal priests, touched the brow of each of two young men with a sword dipped in the blood, while others washed the spot off with wool and milk, and the young men, according to the strange rite, burst out laughing. There was then a feast, after which the skins of the goats were cut into strips and wrapped round the bodies of the Luperci, who then, without any other clothing, took the remaining thongs of skin in their hands and rushed along the different streets, striking at whatever came in their way, as a sort of purification and

omen of good, so that all who were thus touched would
prove fruitful.

Such a half-savage rustic revel was in strange keeping
with the cultured city of Rome ; but Antony, while performing . his apparently mad dance, had a purpose in
view, and as he darted up to Cæsar with his thong of
goat's hide, he snatched from under the strip that girt
him the fillet of an Eastern king, and held it out to
Cæsar, calling it the gift of the Roman people. A few
hands were clapped ; but when Cæsar put the ensign oi
royalty away, there was a burst of applause, and again
he was forced to repeat, " I am no king ; the king of the
Romans is Jupiter ! " and he sent the diadem to be hung
up in the temple in the Capitol.

These experiments embittered the mind of the remnant
of the old party more than ever, and a plot began to be
formed against Cæsar. The chief conspirator was Caius
Cassius Longinus, an able officer, whom Cæsar had pro-
moted, but whom he always regarded with a certain
distrust and doubt. " I like not such lean, pale, eager
men," he said ; and Cassius, always brooding over the
wrongs of the republic, was assuredly one of the most
dangerous men in Rome. Marcus Junius Brutus was
the person to whom he first addressed himself. He
was the son of Cato's half-sister Servilia, the lady whose
love-letter to Cæsar had shamed her high-minded brother
in the Senate, and he had grown up with a fervent admiration for his uncle, and a great desire to imitate him,
and he was, moreover, the husband of Cato's brave
daughter Porcia. He had, however, like Cassius, held
office under Cæsar, and endured his rule with a sullen
acquiescence ; but when the hateful title of king appeared
likely to be revived, his indignation was such as to make
him ready to listen to the numerous whispers that called
on him to remember how his ancestor had been the prime

mover in the expulsion of the cruel kings of the house of Tarquin and the establishment of that grand republic which Cæsar was overthrowing. These were the foremost in the plot, and with them were joined fourteen more, of whom the most notable was Brutus's cousin, Decimus Junius Brutus Albinus, who had served under Cæsar in the civil war, had been treated as one of his most trusted friends, and had just received an appointment to the great province of Gaul, so that it seems almost impossible to imagine his motive for joining in the horrible conspiracy for murdering Cæsar at the meeting of the Senate on the Ides of March, the 15th, when it was expected that a proposal would be made to permit Cæsar to assume the dress and title of king, not in Rome, but in the Eastern provinces. Many may have known or guessed at the scheme—Porcia certainly did, and being hurt at her husband's not thinking her to be trusted with a secret, she pierced herself through with a dagger, and showed the wound to her husband some time after as a proof that she was able to hold her peace. Probably her father's stern upright faith would have denounced the project, and the conspirators durst not even mention it to Cicero; but Porcia fell into an agony of excitement and suspense, though she kept her counsel.

Others would fain have sent warnings to Cæsar without betraying from whom they came, and many such reached him, but he had steeled himself against them. His nature was fearless, and he had escaped untouched from a long course of perils, besides which he had always said that the only way to enjoy life was to banish all fear of death, and he persisted in walking about the city entirely unarmed and unguarded. He was heard to say, " I have lived long enough for nature and for fame ;" for he was past fifty and dreaded the approach of old age, and of power and success he had well-nigh had his fill. He had

found that they failed to secure him the cordial approba-
tion of any man whom he really esteemed, and that all
that he obtained was the adulation of the selfish and the
blind adherence of the multitude, whom he was forced to
gratify with alms and wild-beast shows. No wonder,
then, that he was really indifferent to life, and thought the
lengthening of it no boon worth perpetual alarm and
precaution. A soothsayer told him that the Ides of
March would be fatal to him, but he paid no attention.
And when on the previous night, at a supper at a friend's
house, some one started the question, "What was the
easiest death to die?" he answered, "The most unexpected."

However, in the night he was disturbed by the moaning
of his wife Calpurnia in her sleep, and when in the morning she told him of a dreadful dream, and conjured him not
to stir out of doors, he reluctantly yielded, and was just
sending to countermand the assembly of the Senate when
Decimus Brutus, who was the more afraid of delay because his cousin Marcus was on the point of betraying
himself by his nervous agitation, came in and laughed to
scorn the notion of putting off the Senate for a lady's
dream, so that Cæsar readily called back the bearers of
his letter and set out for the Senate.   On the way a letter
was handed to him with an entreaty that he would
instantly read it, but he kept it in his hand as he proceeded, and a slave was at that very moment warning
Calpurnia, having arrived just too late for him.   He saw
the soothsayer in the crowd and good-humouredly said,
"The Ides of March are come."

"Yes, Cæsar," was the answer, "but they are not past."

He left his litter, and walked up the steps of the Senate-
house, while one of the assassins engaged Mark Antony,
who was a man of great personal strength and warmly
attached to Cæsar, in conversation ; and one of the

conspirators named Cimber stepped forward to present a petition, the others thronging round as if to support him. On his refusal, Cimber caught hold of Cæsar's toga and pulled it over his arms—the concerted signal. Then Casca, another conspirator, drawing a small dagger from the case meant to hold the iron pen, plunged it into his victim's shoulder. Cæsar loosed his hand and snatched at the dagger, shouting, " What means this ? " And as the rest closed in, he struggled stoutly for his life in a manner that with one so dexterous and active might have given time for Antony and others to come to his help, had he not seen Decimus, whom he really loved, among the murderers. "Thou, too !" he said, and drew his toga over his face without further resistance as the deadly blows fell upon him on all sides, till, after staggering a few paces, he fell dead at the feet of Pompey's statue.

It was the 15th of March, B.C. 44, that Julius Cæsar fell, after having bridged the way between the Roman Republic and the Roman Empire. How Antony addressed the people over his bier, and stirred their hearts by the reading of his will ; how those "who struck the foremost man of all this world" stood appalled at their own acts, wavered and fell apart ; how Antony and young Octavius coalesced against them, and they perished by miserable deaths ; how Cicero shone out nobly in this time of distress, till he was slain through Antony's spite ; how Antony fell under the spells of Cleopatra, and finally was ruined by his infatuation for her ; and how Octavius triumphed over all enemies, founded the Empire, and reigned as the peaceful Augustus, it is not the part of this narrative to relate. It was in Augustus's time that light came into the world, and men ceased to live by the old revelation or by heathen guesses at truth. Henceforth the time of the Worthies of Judaism and Heathenesse was over. We have seen in Joshua the divinely led Israelite conqueror; in David the poet king, ever pious and devout, though sometimes erring; in Nehemiah the faithful restorer and reformer; in Judas Maccabæus the heroic champion of his faith and country. And, on the other hand, Hector shows the Greek's imaginary standard of patriotism in a falling cause; Aristides, and Dentatus, and Scipio simple-hearted dutifulness and devotion to the best faith they knew; Xenophon seems to put the Socratic teaching in action; Epaminondas tried to live up to the harmonies of Pythagoras; Alexander's best virtues had been learnt from Aristotle, and Cleomenes found strength for his reformation in the stern Stoic school; while the Hero whose claim to worthiness is most doubtful of all, and whose ambition brought him nothing but weariness and distrust, whose clemency could not win hearts, and whose beneficence was despised as mere self-seeking, whose work was more to destroy than to build up, was the only one among them all who was without real faith in aught that was unseen, and who entirely disbelieved in a future state.

THE END.

LONDON
R. CLAY SONS, AND, TAYLOR, PRINTERS:
BREAD STREET HILL

Works by the Author of

"THE HEIR OF REDCLYFFE."

THE CHAPLET OF PEARLS. Two vols.
Crown 8vo. 12s.

THE PRINCE AND THE PAGE. A Book for
the Young. Illustrated. 18mo. cloth gilt. 3s. 6d.

A BOOK OF GOLDEN DEEDS. 18mo. 4s. 6d.
Cheap Edition 1s.

HISTORY OF CHRISTIAN NAMES. Two vols.
Crown 8vo. 1l. 1s.

THE HEIR OF REDCLYFFE. Seventeenth
Edition. With Illustrations. Crown 8vo. 6s.

DYNEVOR TERRACE. Third Edition. Crown
8vo. 6s.

THE DAISY CHAIN. Ninth Edition. With
Illustrations. Crown 8vo. 6s.

THE TRIAL: More Links of the Daisy Chain.
Fourth Edition. With Illustrations. Crown 8vo. 6s.

MACMILLAN & CO. LONDON.

WORKS BY THE AUTHOR OF "THE HEIR OF REDCLYFFE" *continued.*

HEARTSEASE. Tenth Edition. With Illustrations. Crown 8vo. 6*s.*

HOPES AND FEARS. Third Edition. Crown 8vo. 6*s.*

THE YOUNG STEPMOTHER. Third Edition. Crown 8vo. 6*s.*

THE LANCES OF LYNWOOD. With Coloured Illustrations. Second Edition. Extra fcap. 8vo. 4*s.* 6*d.*

THE LITTLE DUKE. New Edition. 18mo. cloth. 3*s.* 6*d.*

CLEVER WOMAN OF THE FAMILY. Crown 8vo. 6*s.*

DANVERS PAPERS: An Invention. Crown 8vo. 4*s.* 6*d.*

DOVE IN THE EAGLE'S NEST. Two vols. Crown 8vo. 12*s.*

CAMEOS FROM ENGLISH HISTORY. From Rollo to Edward II. Extra fcap. 8vo. 5*s.*

MACMILLAN & CO. LONDON.

GOLDEN TREASURY SERIES.

Uniformly printed in 18mo. *with Vignette Titles by* Sir NOEL
PATON, T. WOOLNER, W. HOLMAN HUNT, J. E.
MILLAIS, ARTHUR HUGHES, &c. *Engraved on Steel by*
JEENS. *Bound in extra cloth,* 4s. 6d. *each volume; also in
morocco, plain and extra.*

THE GOLDEN TREASURY OF THE BEST
SONGS AND LYRICAL POEMS IN THE ENGLISH
LANGUAGE. Selected and arranged, with Notes, by
FRANCIS TURNER PALGRAVE.

THE CHILDREN'S GARLAND FROM THE
BEST POETS. Selected and arranged by COVENTRY
PATMORE.

THE BOOK OF PRAISE. From the best English
Hymn Writers. Selected and arranged by Sir ROUNDELL
PALMER. A New and Enlarged Edition.

MACMILLAN & CO. LONDON.

THE FAIRY BOOK.: THE BEST POPULAR FAIRY STORIES. Selected and rendered anew by the Author of "John Halifax, Gentleman."

THE BALLAD BOOK. A Selection of the choicest British Ballads. Edited by WILLIAM ALLINGHAM.

THE JEST BOOK. The choicest Anecdotes and Sayings. Selected and arranged by MARK LEMON.

BACON'S ESSAYS AND COLOURS OF GOOD AND EVIL. With Notes and Glossarial Index, by W. ALDIS WRIGHT, M.A.

*** Large paper copies, crown 8vo. 7s. 6d. ; or bound in half morocco 10s. 6d.

THE PILGRIM'S PROGRESS from this World to that which is to Come. By JOHN BUNYAN.

*** Large paper copies, crown 8vo. cloth, 7s. 6d. ; or bound in half morocco, 10s. 6d.

MACMILLAN & CO. LONDON.

THE SUNDAY BOOK OF POETRY FOR THE
YOUNG. Selected and arranged by C. F. ALEXANDER.

A BOOK OF GOLDEN DEEDS OF ALL
TIMES AND ALL COUNTRIES. Gathered and
Narrated anew by the Author of the " Heir of Redclyffe."

THE POETICAL WORKS OF ROBERT
BURNS. Edited, with Biographical Memoir, by ALEX-
ANDER SMITH. Two vols.

THE ADVENTURES OF ROBINSON CRUSOE.
Edited from the Original Editions by J. W. CLARK, M.A.

THE REPUBLIC OF PLATO. Translated into
English with Notes by J. LL. DAVIES, M.A. and D. J.
VAUGHAN, M.A.

MACMILLAN & CO. LONDON.

THE SONG BOOK. Words and Tunes from the best Poets and Musicians, selected and arranged by JOHN HULLAH.

LA LYRE FRANCAISE. Selected and arranged with Notes, by GUSTAVE MASSON.

TOM BROWN'S SCHOOL DAYS. By an OLD BOY.

A BOOK OF WORTHIES. Gathered from the old Histories and written anew by the author of the "Heir of Redclyffe."

MACMILLAN & CO. LONDON.